RED
MERCURY

RED
MERCURY

a novel by
Max Barclay

DOVE
BOOKS

ISBN 0-7871-0920-7

Printed in the United States of America

Dove Books
8955 Beverly Boulevard
West Hollywood, CA 90048

Distributed by Penguin USA

Cover design by Rick Penn-Kraus
Cover illustrations by Dean Kennedy
Text design and layout by Carolyn Wendt

First Printing: June 1996
10 9 8 7 6 5 4 3 2 1

To the Eleven

ACKNOWLEDGMENTS

In researching this book, I benefited from the generosity of many people and organizations.

In Atlanta, I am grateful for assistance, information, and interviews from the Atlanta Committee for the Olympic Games, the Atlanta Fire Department, *The Atlanta Journal-Constitution*, the Atlanta Police Department, Cable News Network, the Centers for Disease Control and Prevention, Coca-Cola USA, the DeKalb County Sheriff's office, the Federal Bureau of Investigation, Georgians Against Nuclear Energy, Hartsfield International Airport, the Neely Nuclear Research Center, Olympic Public Safety Operations, and the state of Georgia.

For his excellent daily coverage of Olympic security and his guidance, special thanks to Ron of *The Atlanta Journal-Constitution*.

In Washington, D.C., I appreciate the assistance of the Central Intelligence Agency, the Department of Energy, the Department of Defense, the Federal Bureau of Investigation, and the Nuclear Emergency Search Team (NEST).

In the U.S. armed forces, I salute the helpful people at the Army Aviation Center, Fort Rucker, Alabama; the 50th Space Wing, Falcon Air Force Base, Colorado; the 2nd Space Operations Squadron, Falcon Air Force Base; the 52nd Explosive Ordnance Disposal Group, Fort Gillem, Georgia; Aviation Plans and Policies, Marine Corps Headquarters, Washington, D.C.; and Marine Corps Air Station, Beaufort, South Carolina.

In Chicago, thanks to Borg-Warner Security Corporation. In Colorado Springs, hats off to USA Shooting. In Deerfield Beach, Florida, thanks to Sensormatic Electronics Corporation. In Indianapolis, thanks to USA Track and Field. In New Mexico, thanks to the Los Alamos National Laboratory. In New York City, thanks to NBC Sports. In Las Vegas, I am grateful to the Department of Energy's Nevada Operations Office. In Los Angeles, *todah LaConsulia Haisraelit*. And in Sunnyvale, California, I appreciate the assistance of Trimble Navigation Ltd.

The impetus for this book came from an article in *The New York Times* on March 21, 1995, about a tragic construction accident at Olympic Stadium in which ironworker Jack L. Walls was killed by a collapsing light tower. For background, history, and inspiration, a variety of published works were especially useful. For readers who might want more information, here is a sampling of sources: On Red Mercury: *International Defense Review* (June 1994), *Nucleonics Week* (July 1993), *The Independent* (April 1994), *Moscow News* (August 1993), and *Warsaw Voice* (January 1994). On loose nukes: *Avoiding Nuclear Anarchy* (July 1995) and *Bulletin of the Atomic Scientists* (November 1994). On nuclear terrorism: *Preventing Nuclear Terrorism* (1987). On radiation detection: *Science and Global Security* (Vol. 1, nos. 3 and 4, 1990). On nuclear weapons: *Denver Post* (May 1995), *U.S. Nuclear Weapons* (1988), *Nuclear Choices* (1991), and *Nuclear Arms Race* (1986).

On NEST: *Armed Forces Journal* (October 1995), *Washington Times* (October 1995), *The New York Times Magazine* (December 1980), *New West* (December 1979), and *Time* (January 1996). On terrorists: *Terrorism* (1994). On the Global Positioning System and the poor man's cruise missile: *International Security* (Summer 1995) and *Lawrence Livermore National Laboratory Director's Series on Proliferation* (June 1995). On sniping: *Sniper: The World of Combat Sniping* (1994). On the Harvey's Wagon Wheel Casino bombing: *Hard Evidence* (1995). On the National Security Agency: *The Puzzle Palace* (1982) and the *Baltimore Sun* (December 1995).

On the Olympics: *Olympics at 100* (1995), *The Complete Book of the Olympics* (1992), *The Olympics: A History of the Modern Games* (1992), and the *Official Olympic Souvenir Program* (1984). On Olympic security: *The Atlanta Journal-Constitution* and *Security Management* (July 1994). On the Munich massacre: *The Blood of Israel* (1975) and *Sports Illustrated* (July 1994).

On Turkmenistan: *Cadogan Guide: Central Asia—The Practical Handbook* (1995) and *The Central Asian Republics* (1994). On Vietnam: *Vietnam: A History* (1983) and *Death in the Jungle: Diary of a Navy SEAL* (1994). On Chelyabinsk-65: *The Economist* (December

1993), *Science* (February 1995), and *Nucleonics Week* (March 1995).
On Atlanta: *Insight Guide Atlanta* (1995) and *The Ultimate Atlanta Guidebook* (1994).

For incisive ideas, I thank Graham, Rich, and Owen at Harvard for loose nukes; Kristin for terrorist thinking; George for Olympic security; David for flying; Dr. Scott and Dr. Rosanne for medicine; Dr. Robert for math; Dr. Harriet for psyche; Scott for voices; Mahlon for NEST; Dr. George for nuclear research reactors; and Tim for GPS.

For help and encouragement at different stages and in different ways along the way, great thanks to Alan, Ann, Barry, Bernard, Carolyn, Chris, David, Dov, Erik, Gwyn, Harry, Horty, Jan, Jeffrey, Jon, Jonathan, Jessica, Karen, Lisa, Marie, Mary-Jane, Michael, Nat, Nicole, Nigel, Nina, Rocky, Ruth, Sue, and Wendy.

For extra effort with the final manuscript, big thanks to Doc, Scott, and Tim.

For helping to make it happen, thanks to Michael at Gendler, Codikow & Carroll; Joni, Deborah, and Dede at William Morris; Jordan and Elizabeth at Avnet/Kerner; Joan at CBS; Donald at SpyGaze; and Paul at Basic Books. Last but never least, to Phyllis at Avnet/Kerner, thanks for hammering.

At Dove Books, I owe much to Michael, who gave me the chance, and to Mary, Rick, Chris, Michele, and Wendy for all their help. I owe a particular debt to Beth for deftly guiding me from beginning to end with care and humor.

Very special thanks to Allison and Gary, in a league of their own, for pitching, volleying, and above all, showing the way.

Finally, to Mom (MSW) and Sis (MSHS)—much love. And to Dad—I can see you smiling.

AUTHOR'S NOTE

Red Mercury is a work of fiction grounded in reality and possibility.

Despite the sensitivity of the subject matter, I received extensive help and guidance from federal, state, and local officials involved directly in Olympic security. "Forewarned, forearmed," one lawman affirmed during an interview.

My aim was to describe names, places, events, and technologies as accurately as possible. For obvious reasons, however, I have deliberately disguised or altered certain facts and locations, as well as various security procedures and capabilities. For dramatic reasons, I have also fiddled with the actual schedule of sporting events at the Atlanta Games.

The main characters in the story are the offspring of imagination. Where real and recognizable persons play supporting roles, I intended only to entertain, and this desire applies also to the many companies and their excellent products mentioned throughout the book.

Security: a superstition.

—Helen Keller

It is easier to denature plutonium than to denature the evil spirit of man.

—Albert Einstein

Atlanta Committee for
the Olympic Games

July 1996

Dear Olympic Visitor:

Welcome to Atlanta and the Olympic Games. On behalf of more than 75,000 volunteers and staff, it is with great pride that we present the Games of the XXVI Olympiad, the largest peacetime gathering of nations in human history.

These are the Centennial Games, the biggest in history, with more countries, more athletes, more sports, more medals, and more tickets than ever before.

Australians, Cambodians, Estonians, South Africans, Trinidadians. World-class competitors from a record 197 countries.

These athletes consecrate their young lives to strike gold and to win a place in history.

And it is your opportunity to make history, too, to be a part of a once-in-a-lifetime Southern spectacle when the whole world gathers together for seventeen days and nights.

Atlanta has been getting ready to be your host for nearly eight years. And we're sure the Games will be an experience y'all will never, ever forget.

So welcome to Atlanta.

Let the Games and good times begin!

Donny Sanders
President and Chief Executive Officer
Atlanta Committee for the Olympic Games

The Olympic Ring
Atlanta, Georgia

GEORGIA TECH AQUA CENTER
- Diving
- Modern Pentathlon
- Swimming
- Synchronized Swimming
- Water Polo

ALEXANDER MEMORIAL COLISEUM
- Boxing

GEORGIA DOME
- Basketball
- Artistic Gymnastics

GEORGIA WORLD CONGRESS CENTER
- Fencing
- Handball
- Judo
- Modern Pentathlon
- Table Tennis
- Weightlifting
- Wrestling

OMNI COLISEUM
- Volleyball

MOREHOUSE COLLEGE
- Basketball

GEORGIA STATE UNIVERSITY
- Badminton

CLARK ATLANTA UNIVERSITY
- Hockey

ATLANTA FULTON COUNTY STADIUM
- Baseball

MORRIS BROWN COLLEGE
- Hockey

OLYMPIC STADIUM
- Opening & Closing Ceremonies
- Athletics

Olympic Village

Georgia Tech

IBC   Inforum

Olympic Center

ACOG Hdqrs.
MPC

Atlanta University Center

75 85

20

20

75
85

LEGEND

□ MARTA Station

PART I

READY

*He who does not expect the unexpected
cannot detect it.*

—Heraclitus

T he man peering through the zoom lens had not moved from the smoked window on Concourse C for most of the morning. You couldn't miss him—feet firmly rooted but his hands rotating in a compulsive sequence, readjusting his blue-and-gold baseball cap, checking his watch, fidgeting with the long lens.

From 75 feet away at a pay phone near the Delta check-in counter, Frank Torsella, a crew-cut Georgia Bureau of Investigation agent, whispered into a microphone embedded in the Olympic pin on his windbreaker.

"The gawker on Concourse C is still here," Torsella said. "We're gonna take a closer look."

"I've got you on CCTV," said a communications officer at the Olympic Aviation Specialized Management Center, one of six key security command posts set up across Atlanta for the Olympic Games. "Smile, you look pretty cute."

Torsella winked at the overhead camera. Dressed in T-shirts and shorts, he and his partner were a plainclothes ID team, one of several hundred deployed across Atlanta to identify early signs of trouble. First used successfully in the city during Freaknik '95, the rowdy annual spring gathering of college students, the teams from the GBI and the Atlanta Police Department had been specially trained for the Summer Games. They were the trip wires of the massive Olympic security operation, the active intelligence gatherers, the eyes and ears of law and order.

Pulling empty carry-on cases, courtesy of the GBI prop shop, Torsella and his partner sauntered up to the gawker.

"Excuse me, sir," Torsella said in a raspy drawl, "can you point us to the baggage area?"

Long Lens jumped, put down his camera, and slowly turned to face them.

"Pardon?" he said with an uneasy smile.

"Where's baggage?" Torsella asked again, studying the man's face, committing it to memory: late thirties, dirty blond, tanned, green eyes.

"Sorry," Long Lens said, "can't help ya. No idea where baggage is."

"Hey, that's some camera," Torsella said, trying to keep the conversation going so he could complete his assessment. "What're you shooting?"

"Just some pictures."

"Of what?" Torsella asked, looking out through the window pane toward Runway 8-Left.

"Like I said, just some pictures," Long Lens replied. "It's a free country, ain't it?"

Torsella laughed, but his eyes fixed more closely on the man. He was wearing an Emory University baseball cap and a thin gold wedding band, and he had small indentations on the bridge of his nose, no doubt from heavy eyeglasses.

Nothing unusual, Torsella reflected, except the man's nervous eyes.

Long Lens knew he had overreacted with the "free country" jab. These men did *not* smell like tourists. They were probably con artists looking for easy marks at the international terminal. Or maybe they were airport security.

"My folks are from Turkmenistan," he said, trying to cover his tracks. "Their Olympic team is about to land. First time ever at the Games. I'm getting a few snaps for the family scrapbook."

"Turk-*what*-istan?"

"Turkmenistan."

"Never heard of it."

"It's in Central Asia," Long Lens said. "Oil, gas, sand, and not much else."

"If it ain't got a Club Med, I'm not interested," Torsella said. "Thanks for your help. See ya around."

And the ID team turned away.

As they walked, the agents exchanged glances. Torsella spoke into his pin mike and looked up at the CCTV camera. "*Nada* on the gawker on Concourse C. Just a weirdo with a woody for Turkmenistan."

Long Lens waited until the two men had moved on. He had never been trained in the trade craft of an intelligence operative. Surveillance was not his forte, nor was counter-surveillance. He knew he would have to be more careful. He reached into a pocket and pulled out a bottle of Thorazine. He popped a few pills, waited five minutes, then headed down Concourse C to another window, where he resumed his watch.

The flight was very late, Long Lens thought, *but it would come.* It *had* to come.

He felt almost giddy with anticipation. He had spent more than a year orchestrating the special delivery of this one final ingredient, the last missing element in his revolutionary creation.

Fourteen hours earlier, his contact in Turkmenistan had watched the cargo as it was loaded onto a Boeing 757 in Ashkhabad, the desert capital of the former Soviet republic. After a send-off complete with marching bands, parading camels, and whirling dancers, the Turkmen Olympic team boarded the 757 and lifted off for the flight to Reykjavik and then on to Atlanta.

Unless something had gone wrong.

Through the heat shimmer at the end of the runway, Long Lens tracked each aircraft as it swooped in for a landing. Every fifty seconds, like clockwork, another plane touched down.

And then he spotted a two-engine jet painted dark green, with a white crescent and five stars on its tail. The plane was on final approach.

At last, he thought.

The 757 touched down on the 9,000-foot runway, quick puffs of smoke appearing, then disappearing, beneath its wheels. It turned off on Taxiway Dixie, rolled 2,000 feet, and then stopped near the old Eastern Airlines hangar south of Airport Loop Road. The Atlanta Committee for the Olympic Games, known locally as ACOG, had rented the forty-two-acre, seven-building Eastern facility from the city of Atlanta to help handle the crush of teams, officials, and journalists arriving for the Olympic festivities.

As the Turkmen national plane slowed to a stop, teams of cargo handlers rushed the aircraft with tugs and carts. Uniformed workers rolled a stair ramp festooned with Olympic banners to the nose of the aircraft. The door popped open and twenty-five athletes, clad in green Adidas track suits and squinting into the sunshine, stepped out into the heavy air. Long Lens scanned their faces. As the athletes felt the first blast of damp Georgia heat, their expressions betrayed their surprise. The temperature was stifling even by the standards of young men and women raised on the arid Kara Kum Desert near Afghanistan and Iran.

A blue-suited ACOG representative greeted the leader of the Turkmen delegation, presenting the visiting team with a wreath of olive leaves, a Centennial Olympic banner, and a framed declaration.

A band played the Turkmen national anthem. Then a hunched and bespectacled official from the International Olympic Committee delivered the standard welcoming speech to the Turkmen delegation and a handful of international reporters standing behind a gold rope. The athletes, stretching and yawning, were thoroughly bored by the formalities.

It was a welcoming ritual that had been repeated more than a hundred times in the previous month as Olympic delegations arrived from around the world. All told, 197 nations had been invited to the Atlanta Games, a far cry from the thirteen countries and 311 athletes involved in the first Modern Games in Athens in 1896.

One hundred summers later, more than 11,000 athletes were expected to compete for 1,879 medals. Each team landed at Hartsfield, was processed through the converted Eastern hangar, and was then dispatched to the Olympic Village.

Long Lens searched the airport apron for signs of the massive Olympic security presence. He counted half a dozen remote-controlled CCTV cameras panning back and forth from fixed rooftop positions. Two-member security teams in dark blue uniforms patrolled the tarmac on foot. The guards were contract employees of Borg-Warner Security Corporation, a national firm hired by ACOG for the Games. Long Lens was certain that somewhere, not far from the Eastern hangar, heavily armed Atlanta Police Department SWAT teams were on stand-by with their signature matte black trucks. And across Runway 8-Left, in an egg-white unmarked warehouse, Long Lens knew the Department of Defense had deployed special forces teams and heavy equipment just in case local, state, or federal law enforcement agencies needed to call in the cavalry.

Training his camera on the belly of the 757, Long Lens watched the Turkmen luggage and equipment cases as they were disgorged one by one down the conveyor belt. Many of the crates were enormous, and he guessed they were loaded with racks of free weights and barbells. Turkmenistan was home to the world's greatest power lifters. At the recent World Track and Field Championships, Turkmen weight lifters had won ten gold medals and twenty-five silver and bronze medals.

At last the pallets began their parade. His Canon EOS zoomed in on one loaded with track and field equipment.

"Yesssss!" he said. "There you are!"

He focused on a single green case—the size of a small filing cabinet—with Cyrillic markings on the side.

Through the zoom lens, the man followed the rectangular green case as it was loaded onto a forklift and moved through the 50-foot open doors of the old Eastern hangar where Customs and INS agents were waiting.

Lemuel Denson, a surly Customs inspector whose tan uniform was stained with perspiration, glanced at an intelligence report on Turkmenistan before beginning his inspection. The information on his clipboard was gleaned from the FBI, CIA, Pentagon, and State Department. According to the national intelligence community, Turkmenistan was judged to be a low risk/low threat country. Although it bordered Iran, the country had managed to avoid becoming embroiled in Teheran's state-sponsored terrorism. Denson knew the inspection would be quick and easy.

"Whatcha got in these cases?" Denson asked Yagmur Ovezov, a muscular forty-year-old Turkmen coach and equipment manager. Unshaven and pockmarked, Ovezov's face was as scraggly as a sisal rug. A petite Olympic translator, one of hundreds on loan from the United Nations in New York, interpreted the Customs agent's question.

"Sporting equipment," Ovezov said in a throaty accent.

Denson paid little attention to the response. The questions and answers were pointless. Smugglers and terrorists, after all, never fessed up to the truth. If they were sneaking something into the country, they weren't about to come clean.

Instead, U.S. Customs relied on four separate screening systems to ferret out contraband. In just one week of Olympic inspections, Denson had stopped diamond smugglers from Namibia, Thai nationals with boxes of six-inch lizards skewered on sticks, and a Vietnamese official packing a roasted pygmy loris monkey, an endangered species.

As Denson continued down his checklist of perfunctory questions, two drug-sniffing German shepherds scampered around the green case. The dogs were the first of four screens. Goliath, one of the FBI's top dogs from the Hazardous Devices School in Huntsville, Alabama, climbed up onto the box and sniffed the white crescent and stars painted on the lid. The dog grunted, jumped off the case, and moved on with its handler to other luggage.

Next, the case was moved through the $165,000 Egis 3000 made by Thermedics Detection of Woburn, Massachusetts. Like the FBI's German shepherds, the Egis "sniffed" for minuscule traces of explosives residue, and could detect less than a millionth of a gram of Semtex in a suitcase or under a terrorist's fingernail. Originally developed in the early 1980s in response to the deadly attacks on the Marine Corps barracks and the American Embassy in Beirut, the Egis was modified and put to work at U.S. and international airports after the 1988 downing of Pan Am flight 103. Egis's only shortcoming was that it sometimes mistook silk clothing for bombs. The nitrogen in silk confused the machine.

Without a beep, the Egis vetted the green Turkmen case.

The case was then hauled to the third screen, the CTX 5000, a $1 million explosives detector made by InVision Technologies of Foster City, California. Nothing could get past CTX, a 7,350-pound machine the size of a compact car. Using CAT-scanning tomography technology from the world of medicine, CTX sent a fan beam slicing through packages, baggage, and freight to analyze the density, shape, and chemical makeup of the contents. Advanced computer software then evaluated the cross-sectional images and assigned colors to different items. Explosives were red and detonators were blue-green. At top speed, CTX could evaluate a package in seven seconds, and an alarm would sound if it spotted plastic and fertilizer explosives, dynamite, or drugs.

Luanne Sipple, a twenty-nine-year-old Customs agent operating the CTX, examined the image on her screen. Moments earlier, equipment crates carrying javelins, hammers, and discuses had passed through the machine, so Sipple paid little attention to the six shapes in front of her now. She rotated the picture to double-check herself, then marked the CTX CLEAR box on the tag attached to the case.

Finally, the rectangular box was placed on Lemuel Denson's table for the fourth and final screen. Denson observed the case had no locks, so it was unlikely there was anything valuable inside.

"Open this baby up," Denson said.

"Yes. Open up," Ovezov responded. He flipped the latches, and the inspector glanced at the contents surrounded by foam. Denson poked his fingers into the spongy packing material, checked Ovezov's reaction, and then slammed the lid closed.

Denson made a few final notes on his clipboard, then wrapped two thick bands of tape around the case. The yellow strips were marked with a single word repeated every six inches in square black lettering: SANITIZED.

Olympic cargo workers hoisted the case into the luggage compartment of an ACOG passenger coach. All twenty-five members of the Turkmen team were already on board.

The trip to the Olympic Village, the most fortified city on earth, would take thirty minutes.

And on Concourse C, the man with the long lens vanished into the crowd.

The morning was cold and clear, and the sky over the Santa Fe National Forest was high-desert purple. A lone red-tailed hawk floated on a mountain updraft.

From the fifteen-foot-high observation tower, two men peered through binoculars at the teams lined up on opposite ends of the dirt field. A ten-man wedge charged forward from one side of the clearing, kicking up clouds of dust. Each attacker wore a yellow rain suit, rubber boots, and a Scott air pack. At the other end of the field another team formed a human chain, lined up along a thick gray hose connected to a 150-gallon tank on wheels.

"Fire when ready," Mack McFall shouted from the Test Area 17 tower.

A stream of black ooze shot from the high-pressure nozzle, splattering the yellow rushers. One by one, as each was hit with so-called sticky foam, the runners slowed to a crawl, then stopped moving altogether, like bees in molasses.

Mired in goo, the men were stuck.

"We call this our high-tech lasso," McFall said to his guest, dropping the Pocketscope binoculars from his eyes. "Those folks won't be moving again until someone cuts their rain suits off."

"Let's go have a closer look," he said, leaping down from the viewing tower. Lean and fit at forty years old, McFall hit the ground effortlessly, his legs taking the fifteen-foot drop like a single step.

"None of that cliff diving for me," Rear Admiral Chalmer Taylor said, eyeing McFall below. "I'll take the slow boat."

Sixty-five years old and overweight by as many pounds, the admiral worked his way slowly down the rickety wooden ladder. "Got to get out more from behind my desk," he mumbled.

The two men walked toward the tarred bodies.

"You may want to hold your nose," McFall suggested, brushing thick brown hair from his eyes. "We don't know what to do about the smell."

The noxious odor of burnt plastic wafted over the field.

"Tacky, nonhardening thermoplastic material," he said, dabbing at the glop on one of the immobilized men. "Slightly more dense than water. Expands thirty-five to fifty times after being sprayed."

"So what are you planning to do with it?" Taylor asked.

"It's ideal for crowd control. Our boys used an early version in Somalia during Operation Restore Hope. But we've been improving it to safeguard the nuclear stockpile. Spray this on someone trying to rip off one of our gadgets and they're not going to get very far."

Taylor nodded with approval. The Deputy Assistant Secretary of Energy for Military Application and Stockpile Support liked what he saw and thought it was well worth the budget battles back in the nation's capital. But the group's name—the Weapons of Mass Destruction Countermeasures Task Force—was more than a mouthful.

The best part of all this, Taylor thought, *is that Mack is back.* He was one of America's premier nuclear weapons designers, a small club of eighty men and women spread across the Department of Energy's three weapons labs. After graduating from the Naval Academy and a highly decorated stint with the Navy SEAL team, McFall had earned his Ph.D. at MIT and gone straight to work in the DOE's Weapons Program. For years, he had built smaller yet ever more powerful nuclear weapons. Then recently, he had been given his most challenging assignment: design and field the futuristic equipment and weaponry needed to stop nuclear terrorists.

Another ten men marched out into the clearing. A worker with what appeared to be an ordinary green garden hose sprayed the dirt around the human guinea pigs. Almost instantly, the men began to slip and slide. One after another, they fell to the ground. Each struggled to stand but could not find firm footing.

"That's slippery slime," McFall said. "It has major applications for asset immobilization. We really could have used it on the Highway of Death near Basra in the Gulf War. But we designed the slime to protect the stockpile. A bucket of this stuff on a runway or highway or hallway and the bad guys are going nowhere fast."

"What's it made of?" Taylor asked, watching the men slosh and squirm.

"Split-pea soup from the lab cafeteria," McFall said, his smile punching a dimple in one cheek.

Taylor slapped McFall on his shoulders. "Mack, it's good having you back on the hill. You know, for a while there, we thought we'd lost you to the Joint Special Operations Command."

"Hey, what can I say? JSOC needed a little help with their counter-prolif capabilities. Anyway, I got to spend some quality time on the obstacle course at Fort Bragg."

McFall checked his Timex. "Look, we'd better get you back to the lab for that meeting with the mucky-mucks," he said to Taylor. The two men headed for the dirt parking lot.

In the pine forest 150 yards away, shrouded by tree branches, a man crouched on one knee and followed McFall through a high-powered scope. A Heckler and Koch MP-5 submachine gun rested at his feet. The man murmured into a headset microphone: "Heads up. Omega is moving." Then he picked up his weapon and sprinted deeper into the woods.

McFall and Taylor approached a beat-up blue Ford Bronco.

"So level with me," McFall said. "Where do we stand? I'm supposed to drown you in sticky foam if you don't promise full funding for CP."

"Counter-proliferation is one our top priorities," Taylor answered.

"Come on, Mr. Inside-the-Beltway, give it to me in English," McFall said.

"CP is where the action is," Taylor said, lightening up. "That's why we brought you back here and wrote the blank check. But we're getting killed by congressional budget cutters. The idiots want to slash most of the CP budget and also take a chunk out of emergency operations. They're *even* going after the Nuclear Emergency Search Team. These guys just don't get it."

"How typical," McFall said, imagining his nuclear counter-terrorism program being gutted by penny-pinching political hacks. "Story of my life," he grumbled. "Shot at and missed but shit at and hit."

He opened the door to the Bronco. Crouched in the front seat, his golden retriever bounded out the door.

"Whoa, boy!"

The dog raced around the truck in a tight circle, picking up speed, then leaped back into the front. "Back seat, Nuke. Go on, scoot!"

McFall climbed into the car, opened the passenger door for Taylor, and then reached for the bottle of Advil.

"Still hurting from last night?" Taylor asked.

"A few too many at altitude," McFall answered. "My liver's still acclimating."

The night before, McFall and his colleagues in the Atomic City had celebrated the fifty-first birthday of the Bomb, an anniversary most of the planet would scarcely remember, let alone fête. To this insular gathering of weapons designers, however, July 16, 1945 was the most important date in the history of the world. At 5:29 A.M. in the Jornada del Muerto desert, the atomic age had arrived with a bang.

McFall and Taylor bounced down the dirt trail toward the main gate of Test Area 17. As if from nowhere, two black vans with mirrored windows pulled in front of and behind the Bronco.

McFall hit the brakes.

"Jesus," Taylor said. "Do you really need these muscleheads following you everywhere?"

"Hey, it wasn't my idea," McFall said. "Someone in Washington gave them to me as a present last year after we locked up Ramzi Al-Asifa and his Iranian gang."

"Was that when Ayatollah What's-His-Name put out the *fatwa* on you?"

"Yup," McFall said, nodding.

"Hey, it's a rare honor," Taylor said. "Not every guy has an Islamic death sentence hanging over his head."

"I guess it's an occupational hazard when you work for the Great Satan."

"Mack McFall, the Salman Rushdie of Los Alamos," Taylor said.

"Aw shucks," McFall said, "flattery'll get you everywhere."

A uniformed LANL security guard pulled open the razor-wire gate to Test Area 17. McFall waved and made a left turn onto State Road 4. The black vans followed closely.

They rode in silence through the Santa Fe National Forest, past the wide, grassy bowl of the Valles Caldera, where a volcano had erupted one million years ago. The blacktop twisted down the mountains toward Los Alamos. Ahead, across the valley and over the Sangre de Cristo range, the sun was streaming through the clouds.

"I hate bringing this up," Taylor said, breaking the silence, "but I wanted to say how sorry I am about Jenny."

"I really appreciate it," McFall said. "Your note meant a lot to me. I just haven't been up to dealing with all the flowers, letters, and calls."

"Take your time," Taylor said. "There's no rush. Trust me, it takes a few years."

McFall did not answer. In minutes, they were back on the rocky red fingers of the Pajarito Plateau, elevation 7,424 feet, making their way down the wide, empty streets of Los Alamos. McFall pulled into the circular driveway of the Administration Building off West Jemez Road. The two black vans waited on the street.

"Thanks for the show," Taylor said, getting out of the Bronco, "and go easy on yourself."

"Aye-aye, Admiral."

"One more thing," he added, taking a deep breath of mountain air. "You'd better work on the stink of that black goo before the EPA comes to take you away."

"Just keep the dough coming, and we'll have it smelling like lavender."

"Glad you're back, Mack."

"Me too, maybe," McFall said, shifting into gear.

He crossed the bridge spanning a steep canyon and turned right on Trinity Drive, past Fuller Lodge and the clapboard Los Alamos Ranch School, where the birthday party had been held the night before. Up ahead was the Hill Diner, his morning haunt. The black vans kept their distance.

Why did Taylor have to bring up Jenny? he thought, struggling to force the memories of his wife back into the closet in his mind.

As he parked in front of the diner, his car phone rang.

"This is McFall."

"Mack," a familiar but alarmingly unsteady voice said. "Please help. I'm in trouble."

"What's happening, Stan? Talk to me."

Stan Treadwell, veteran nuclear scientist and McFall's mentor and friend of more than twenty years, pleaded: "I need help. It's bad. Real bad. Please, Mack, please come fast."

I n the distance, a single point of light floated up and down, back
and forth, tracing easy arcs in the darkness. All the doors were
sealed and the red exit signs carefully taped over. If not for the
chill of the central air-conditioning system, the hovering dot far away
in the blackness might have been a lightning bug in the summer night.

There was silence, then a hiss barely louder than a whisper.

Suddenly, white muzzle flashes flickered like strobe lights, and
the eruptions of semiautomatic weapons ripped the stillness. Red
tracer rounds corkscrewed down the long room. There was the shrill
sound of destruction, wood ripping, metal shredding. Then, as precisely as it started, the gunfire stopped. The echoes trailed away, the
smell of burnt powder sooted the air, and the speck of light continued
to glide back and forth somewhere in the darkness.

Thirty seconds passed, the thick smoke cleared, and then again a
hiss.

More explosions, tracer flashes, wood shattering, metal tearing.

Then quiet, eerie quiet.

And the lights came up slowly on the Olympic Shooting Range.

In the viewing stands, 1,500 journalists squinted, adjusting to the
brightness of the halogen lamps overhead. On the rifle range, twelve
men in ghillie suits removed their night vision goggles. As eyes began
to focus on the targets 150 meters away, a wave of commotion rippled
through the press gallery.

At the far end of the shooting range, amid heaps of blasted targets, a woman stood alone in a blue tailored blazer and short flared
skirt. In her hand she held a cigarette, its orange-red tip still glowing.
She tossed the cigarette onto the concrete floor and crushed it under
the toe of a black pump.

Television news cameras zoomed in on the shattered targets, cut-out comic book caricatures of grimacing villains now riddled with bullet holes. Then they panned to the woman, who serenely slipped a pair of protective glasses into her pocket and began walking toward the reporters.

Tall, with flowing, brown hair, Kyle Preston stepped down the shooting range with the confidence and stride of a model on a fashion runway. In her thirty-nine years, however, no one had ever mistaken her for a cover girl. Up close, she was not a natural beauty. The line of her nose had been thrown off in the middle by the notch of a field hockey stick from her prep school days. Her cheeks were round and her chin fell back slightly from her mouth.

Still, Preston knew this carefully orchestrated photo opportunity, a catwalk in high heels through roiling smoke and demolished targets, would be a slam-dunk on television news programs around the world. "It's a no-brainer," one of her young press aides had observed on the ride over from the Olympic Joint Command Center. "Just don't trip! Three billion people will be watching."

Preston approached the microphone, paused, and smiled softly toward the rows of flashing cameras and whirring video recorders.

"Welcome, ladies and gentlemen," she declared, "to the opening day of the Games of the XXVI Olympiad. I want to thank you for coming to the Wolf Creek Shooting Complex. I trust it was worth the early wake-up calls."

The hard-living international press corps did not typically begin work until 10 A.M., and the ACOG press handlers had been well aware that a 9 A.M. photo op was a risky proposition. Still, they were certain that a little bang-bang in the morning would wake up the reporters and fill the news cycles all day. The press team had lifted the event right out of the Olympic playbook. Once before, in the run-up to the 1984 Summer Games in Los Angeles, the FBI had introduced its fifty-man Hostage Rescue Team with explosive fanfare.

HRT agents had jumped from helicopters, tossed live flash/bang grenades, and shot targets to smithereens in the Los Angeles demonstration. "If you come here we'll kill you," one bloodless FBI special agent had growled in a legendary on-camera interview. The news coverage had been extensive, and the security message delivered.

"First things first," the woman at the microphone said. "My name is Kyle Preston, and I am squad leader of the FBI's Olympic Counter-Terrorism Task Force."

Well-scrubbed ACOG press aides in blue blazers and khaki trousers scurried up and down the bleachers, handing out Preston's three-page biography. Her record was simple and straightforward: born and raised in Macon, Georgia, Emory BA in political science, Georgetown Ph.D. in international affairs, White House Fellowship, FBI special agent at the Summer Games in Los Angeles, Bureau liaison to the Games in Seoul and Barcelona, and most recently, deputy section chief of the FBI's Critical Incident Response Group headquartered in Quantico. Her honors and awards filled an entire page. And so did her list of articles and publications in international policy and law enforcement journals.

"It gives me great pleasure on this first day of the Games," Preston said, "to introduce you all to something brand new in 1996. Ladies and gentlemen, I want you to meet the Olympic Javelin Force."

Behind her, the men in Kevlar helmets and Aramid face masks stood up from their firing mats and fell into line. Each carried a state-of-the-art sniper weapons system. Four clutched modified Remington M-24 rifles with powerful AN/PVS-10 Night Sights. Another four held custom-made Barrett 82A1 semiautomatic rifles. The rest had newly developed SR-25 semiautomatic sniper team support rifles.

Preston took a few steps, as if inspecting the troops. "The Javelin Force is the Olympic team of U.S. law enforcement," she said. "Each one of these specialists trained for months and competed to win a place on this elite squad. More than ten thousand law enforcement officers fought it out for just twelve spots. And each one is the best of the best. They are the very finest from the FBI, DEA, ATF, Secret Service, Marshals, and thousands of police and sheriff's departments across the country."

"Why can't we see their faces?" shouted an AP photographer.

"The reason should be entirely obvious," Preston said dismissively.

She glanced back at the hooded Javelin Force leader, who took a step forward and handed her a piece of paper.

"In this demonstration of what we call blackout surgical shooting," she said, studying the slip, "the Javelin Force fired 500 rounds of ammunition in ninety seconds. According to official Olympic scorekeepers, 499 rounds hit seventy-five electronic targets at a distance of 150 meters."

"Hey," she said, turning to the snipers, "only 499 out of 500? I thought you said you never miss!"

The masked Javelin leader threw up his hands and bowed his head in mock embarrassment. There was laughter in the bleachers and Preston smiled, sweeping the bangs from her green eyes. It rarely took more than a few minutes before people were drawn in by her charisma. The surly international press corps was eating it up, unable to resist the images of a woman surrounded by masked men with guns.

It was the surefire television news formula: great character, great visuals, great story.

"So let the message go out," Preston proclaimed, wrapping up her presentation. "You don't want to be on the receiving end of *this* javelin. . . ."

"Ms. Preston?" a *Jerusalem Post* reporter barked, interrupting her carefully scripted sound bite. "Why are you introducing the Javelin Force on Day One of the Games?"

"Think about it," she replied coolly. "If we're ready to show you this demonstration, just imagine what surprises we have in store for anyone who tries to disrupt the Games."

"Is this a preemptive strike?" the reporter followed up.

"Call it what you will."

"Can you confirm or deny the FBI has received credible threats from terrorist groups operating in the Middle East?"

Preston's taut smile seemed to say, "you've got to be kidding."

"It is our policy *never* to discuss threats," she said and gave a discreet signal to her aides that the press conference was over.

Mack McFall drove as fast as he dared toward Tech Area 39, his five-acre fiefdom surrounded by DANGER: EXPLOSIVES signs, electrified fences, and ponderosa pines. It was less than ten minutes to the advanced weapons lab.

The Los Alamos National Laboratory was a sprawling complex that stretched across forty-three square miles and occupied 2,224 buildings. McFall's domain was hidden in a rocky canyon in the most remote and heavily guarded area of the lab.

The Bronco tipped as he accelerated out of a turn. Dislodged from his corner in the back, Nuke eyed him with reproach. The dog was not enjoying the ride.

Stan Treadwell's voice on the cellular phone had been out of control, terrified: *Please help. I'm in trouble. It's bad. Real bad. Please, Mack, please come fast.*

McFall couldn't fathom what had gone wrong on a lazy Friday morning. Most of the scientists had cleared out of town for a long July weekend. They had gone to Taos or Albuquerque. What could be so bad?

Stan Treadwell had been McFall's mentor, colleague, and friend for more than twenty years. They had met at the Academy in Annapolis. At the time, Treadwell was a forty-five-year-old Department of Energy recruiter for the weapons labs and was prospecting for bright young minds. Their first dinner at the Officers and Faculty Club had gone late into the night as they discovered their common backgrounds. Both were the sons of Naval officers, both had stroked the Navy Varsity crew, and both had a rare gift for atoms and subatomic particles.

Their greatest affinity, though, was that both men had lost their fathers when they were young. Over cigars and after-dinner drinks, the two discovered they were card-carrying members of the same miserable, nameless fraternity of men who had never really known their fathers and who spent their lives searching to fill the void.

Over the years Treadwell attempted to be McFall's mentor, guiding him through his early stages in the Navy with the SEALs. And eight years after their first dinner in Annapolis, McFall flew to New Mexico to work behind the fences with Treadwell on the country's most advanced nuclear weapons designs.

They had known each other for more than twenty years. Where had all that time gone, McFall wondered as he sped toward TA 39. What could have happened to his friend? Systematically, McFall considered the possibilities.

He prayed it wasn't the RM project.

Despite an almost unanimous consensus of nuclear weapons designers that it could not be done, McFall and Treadwell were attempting to create an elusive substance with unfathomable, almost mythical, explosive power. RM stood for Red Mercury, a cherry-red gel believed to be the key ingredient necessary to build a miniature pure fusion device. An RM weapon, no bigger than a football, would pack destructive power even greater than a traditional intercontinental ballistic missile.

McFall had stumbled onto Red Mercury entirely by accident while on a covert mission during the war in the Persian Gulf. He had been brought out of retirement to lead a special operations mission into Iraq to neutralize Saddam Hussein's secret nuclear development program.

He had gone in with the X-ray team, an elite special forces unit from Fort Bragg that he had helped create and train. The squad was made up of twelve operators with the technical expertise in nuclear physics to eliminate rogue actors or states developing or deploying atomic devices.

In Basra and Mosul, at least a half dozen shady weapons dealers were rumored to be selling RM 2020, a high-explosive compound. Although he could never get his hands on the goods during the mission to Iraq, McFall had known he was onto something when a few of these murky RM merchants turned up in the gutter with a bullet behind the ear.

On his return to the Joint Special Operations Command at Fort Bragg, McFall had begun to keep a file on Red Mercury. A cursory newspaper database search had turned up a number of obscure references from Jerusalem all the way to the Cape of Good Hope. Slowly, very slowly, he gathered a litany of shadowy accounts: security agents in Argentina, Germany, Singapore, and Switzerland claimed to have arrested RM smugglers; a Bulgarian journalist described his purchase of the gel in Sofia; and in Riga, police announced the seizure of a gang of Latvian traffickers with a twelve-kilogram shipment.

In the files of the International Atomic Energy Agency in Vienna, McFall came across one South African report from the early 1990s that was particularly vivid. The dismembered body of a man—Alan Kidger—had been found stuffed in the trunk of a BMW. His corpse was slathered with an oleaginous red substance containing mercury. Johannesburg police suspected that the victim had been smuggling Red Mercury to a Middle East buyer, possibly Iraq. Investigators speculated that Mossad agents killed the man as a warning to Israel's enemies. In July 1994, South African police had again questioned Interpol about three similar murders linked to Red Mercury.

Moscow and Washington, however, downplayed the existence of the substance. The Russians branded it bogus: during a visit to the Russian Academy of Sciences, McFall had been shown a collection of fake Red Mercury concoctions from around the world ranging from ordinary quicksilver dyed with red nail polish to strawberry jam sprinkled with powdered mercury. Officials had even handed over a classified Security Ministry report dismissing Red Mercury as a scam and concluding RM was underworld slang, "like the word *cabbage* for money."

Then in 1993, Admiral Chal Taylor had called from Washington and offered McFall a new job at Los Alamos. No more nuclear weapons design, Taylor had promised. After all, the lab wasn't building nuclear devices anymore. START II and the Nuclear Test Ban Treaty had put the bomb factories out of business.

Taylor said the DOE needed McFall's help building a high-tech counter-terrorism arsenal. "You're the only one who knows what we really need," Taylor said, "and we'll give you anything you want."

The offer had appealed to McFall's patriotism and his preoccupation with nuclear terrorism, and he had taken the position with alacrity. Once back behind the fence, he had mapped out an R&D plan and put together a team, including his old mentor Stan Treadwell, who had taken early retirement and moved to Key West.

The two friends had reveled at the prospect of working together again. In particular, they were fascinated by Red Mercury. Pure fusion was one of the last great challenges in nuclear weapons design. McFall and Treadwell knew they needed to be the first to make the RM breakthrough. Only by understanding RM's properties would they be able to devise the tools to thwart it if it fell into the wrong hands.

McFall barreled down the road in front of TA 39. The low-lying hodgepodge of dun-colored forties Quonset huts was deceptive. Behind the peeling paint and corrugated metal, scientists designed and developed the nation's most advanced weapons.

The lanky security officer on duty waved him right through the checkpoint. The lot was deserted except for Treadwell's brown Chevy. McFall parked his Bronco and hurried toward the side entrance of Bungalow A, where the RM experiments were conducted.

He shoved his magnetic ID card into the slot and slapped his hand on the palm reading access control unit. The doors opened, and Nuke raced into the building. His paws scratching the polished floor were the only sounds in the deserted corridor.

One hundred feet down Corridor Two, McFall could see shafts of bluish light streaming from the windows of the RM mixing lab. He ran down the hall and punched a six-digit code into the cipher lock.

The laboratory was empty. The equipment from the previous day's work was in a jumble in the corner. A lab notebook was open next to a rack of test tubes and beakers. The blue control panel of a gamma ray spectrometer glowed in the corner of the room, creating an eerie underwater sensation.

There was no sign of Treadwell.

Then McFall heard moaning.

In the corner of the lab, hunched over on the floor, Treadwell was shaking uncontrollably, his face dripping sweat, his eyes gripped with fear.

In his hands, a Geiger counter clicked relentlessly, like a frantic SOS signal in Morse code.

Lieutenant Colonel Vincent Fusco scanned the sports pages of *The Washington Post*. After nearly two weeks of round-the-clock duty helping gather and disseminate intelligence for U.S. troop movements in Bosnia, Fusco had a problem.

A big problem.

The DEFCON 4 crisis of the moment: his eight-year-old son, Huck, wasn't happy with his dad.

Since he had not won the Olympic lottery for any of the eleven million tickets to events in Atlanta, the forty-year-old Army colonel had promised his son they would catch some of the soccer qualifiers in the Washington area. But then Bosnia had flared up, and he had forgotten about the soccer. Fusco turned to the classified ad pages, searching for tickets to the Olympic soccer preliminaries over the weekend at RFK Stadium.

There was nothing in the paper, and the agencies were charging an arm and a leg. Fusco was out of options. He ran his hands through his closely cropped red hair and looked around the watch floor of the National Military Command Center, the very heart of the Pentagon. All these amazing machines controlling America's war-fighting capability wouldn't help him one bit when he got home.

Fusco checked the secure IBM computer screen on his desk. His office was located in a warren of blue-gray cubicles in the Russia, Eurasia, and Ukraine section of the NMCC, a world unto itself. One of the most secure installations in the United States, the NMCC was the main command and control center for U.S. military operations and intelligence worldwide. Located on two floors connected by gunmetal spiral staircases, the command center was actually an office building within an office building, hidden deep inside the Pentagon, with conference rooms, showers, sleeping areas, and a small mess.

Fusco's office was twenty-five feet from the Emergency Action Room, which during the Cold War had responsibility for coordinating any U.S. response to a nuclear launch from the former Soviet Union, or FSU. The EAR was a surprisingly small space, with racks of computer equipment and communications gear. On one wall, a 1950s-era marking board listed the entire U.S. chain of command and their whereabouts: home, office, and away.

If the EAR was the old nerve center created to respond to a Soviet nuclear first strike, then Fusco's Russia, Eurasia, and Ukraine desk was the new hot seat. Seven days a week, his job was to run the Pentagon's far-flung intelligence team monitoring so-called loose nukes.

The former Soviet Union's sprawling nuclear complex was home to 20,000 tactical nuclear weapons and 10,000 strategic nukes. All told, there were 200 tons of plutonium and 1,000 tons of highly enriched uranium, enough weapons-grade fissile material to make 100,000 critical masses. Detecting the theft of one nuclear bomb by a terrorist was the equivalent of noticing the deletion of a *single word* from the *collected* works of William Shakespeare.

It was in this context that Pentagon planners and intelligence officers such as Vince Fusco recognized that the historic preoccupation of U.S. defense policy-makers—two simultaneous major regional contingencies—was obsolete and misguided.

The greatest emerging threat to American security was loose nukes, the proliferation of nuclear weapons or fissile materials seeping out of the former Soviet Union's unwieldy nuclear complex.

And the threat of nuclear leakage was not just some fantasy dreamed up by presidential candidates, novelists, and screenwriters. Fusco knew this new scenario had been well documented in an authoritative Harvard University monograph, *Avoiding Nuclear Anarchy*, published in July 1995 by a team from the John F. Kennedy School of Government's Center for Science and International Affairs. "Absent a determined program of action as focused, serious, and vigorous as America's Cold War strategy," the study warned, "Americans have every reason to anticipate acts of nuclear terrorism against

American targets before this decade is out."

The report's statistics were sobering. In the early 1990s, for instance, German authorities alone investigated more than 700 attempted nuclear sales. In 1994, there were 100 nuclear smuggling incidents reported in the former Soviet Union. The year before, there were 11 attempted uranium thefts, 900 illegal entry attempts at nuclear installations, and 700 attempted document thefts.

Any one of those leaks, Fusco knew, could explode into the ultimate nightmare. Indeed, if the Oklahoma City bombers had used an easy-to-make nuclear device with forty-five kilograms of highly enriched uranium pilfered from the Russian stockpile, the blast would have been the equivalent of 20,000 tons of TNT. All of Oklahoma City—not just the Alfred P. Murrah Federal Building—would have been flattened.

At 10 A.M. on this Friday morning, however, Fusco was not worrying about loose nukes or atomic yields. He needed tickets to an Olympic soccer match.

Fusco barely noticed the Motorola STU-III ringing on his desk. When the secure telephone finally grabbed his attention, he glanced at his computer screen showing a map of the former Soviet Union. A flashing blue flag indicated the call was originating at the U.S. Embassy on *Novinskiy Bul'var* in Moscow.

"This is Fusco," he said.

"Zdrastviytye tavarisch," a defense intelligence agent greeted him.

"Greetings, comrade," Fusco replied. *"Kakaya syevodnya pagoda?"*

"Zharka i dushna," the agent said. "It's hot and humid."

"Same here," Fusco said. "So what have you got for me?"

"Vince, I think we should go secure on this."

Fusco reached for the key in the safe by his desk and inserted it in the STU-III to scramble the conversation.

"Okay, what's up?" Fusco asked.

"Something's definitely going down at Chelyabinsk-65," the agent said.

"Like what?" Fusco said, punching a few keys on his computer to pull up a map of Russia's nuclear archipelago and its ten secret cities.

Chelyabinsk-65, located 930 miles east of Moscow near the Ural Mountains, was the former Soviet Union's first nuclear weapons facility during the early days of the Cold War. Recently renamed Ozersk, the number 65 after Chelyabinsk stood for the secret city's zip code. And if only to stymie Western spies even more, the number had been changed in the mid-1980s: Chelyabinsk-65 was originally Chelyabinsk-40.

"*Federalnaya Sluzhba Bezopasnosti* troops, you know, the Federal Security Service, are crawling all over the place," the agent said.

"Good," Fusco said, "it's about time those ex-KGB-niks had something to do."

"It's a full mobilization, colonel. They've put tanks and armed troops around the perimeter of the city. They're sealing borders with Kazakhstan, Ukraine, and Poland. They've thrown up roadblocks all over the place, even on the unmapped roads. And their airports are locking down."

"What've they got going on at Mayak these days?" Fusco asked, pointing his cursor at the icon representing the plutonium reprocessing facility in the center of Chelyabinsk-65. *Mayak*, Fusco knew, was the Russian word for beacon.

"They're pumping out Mox," the officer said. "That's mixed oxide fuel. It's experimental. It combines oxides of uranium and plutonium."

"That's the stuff they use to power their reactors?"

"You got it."

"So what about the FSB mobilization? Any exercises scheduled?"

"I'm telling you, colonel, these aren't exercises. The Russkies have lost something, and they want it back real bad."

"Any contact with them yet?"

"No, but it's early."

"Recommendations?"

"May I speak openly, sir?"

"Please."

"Three words, sir. Seal the borders."

"Whose borders?" Fusco asked.

"The borders of the continental U.S. of A."

"What a wise guy," Fusco said. "You got any other useful advice for the commander-in-chief?"

"I'm serious, colonel. It wasn't all that bad when they had a big fence around this country with guard dogs snarling every few hundred yards. Sure, it was prison, and nobody ever got out of here alive. But no nukes *ever* got out of here either."

"I'll be sure to tell the secretary of defense you have a personal request. You want the Iron Curtain to go back up ASAP," Fusco said.

"It wouldn't take iron or steel," the agent said, "but a chain-link fence would be a big improvement on what they've got now."

"Noticed and noted. I'm signing off. Thank you, Moscow."

"Bye, colonel."

Fusco put the phone down, pulled the key from the STU-III slot, and tucked it back in his safe. Then he turned to his computer and punched a few keys.

The Top Secret Chelyabinsk-65 window popped up.

Fusco raced through screen after screen. This was hardly the first time the secret city had attracted the attention of the West. For years, Chelyabinsk was widely considered to be the most toxic place on the planet. Its radioactive lakes and rivers made New York's notorious Love Canal near Niagara Falls look absolutely inviting.

In the early 1950s, Chelyabinsk dumped more than 70 million cubic meters of radioactive waste into the Techa River. Villagers received radiation doses nearly 2,000 times the annual allowable exposures. Then in September 1957 a storage tank in nearby Kyshtym went up in flames when a nuclear waste-cooling mechanism broke. The explosion blew the three foot concrete lid off the tank, spewing twenty million curies of radioactivity into the atmosphere and exposing nearly half a million people in a 12,500-square-mile area. Naturally, the victims were not informed.

Over the years Chelyabinsk poured its radioactive waste into Lake Karachay, which evaporated in 1967. The wind from the Urals swept away more than one hundred million curies. That contamination made Chernobyl's twenty million curie release seem like a blast of fresh air.

Fusco clicked his cursor on the file describing a more recent emergency at Chelyabinsk. In early 1994, police seized several batches of weapons-grade nuclear material in Germany. Western nuclear experts said the material probably came from the Mayak nuclear facility.

Fusco switched screens and studied the city's estimated nuclear inventory. In an unmarked wooden warehouse, 35,000 plutonium pits were being stored in metal drums. The pits—ten to sixteen pounds each—were the fissile cores from dismantled Soviet nuclear weapons. Not far away in a red brick building, twenty-five metric tons of reprocessed plutonium shaped like hockey pucks were stored in 10,000 thermos-sized containers. The plutonium came from Russian nuclear reactors.

Fusco reviewed Chelyabinsk's security precautions.

The U.S. Department of Energy had provided equipment to Chelyabinsk-65, including metal and radiation portal detectors, two-person access controls, personnel identification equipment, and video cameras with motion-detector alarms to monitor the storage facilities.

Fusco could not help laughing over the recent discovery that FSB troops actually removed the high-tech surveillance cameras from the plutonium storage facility at night and locked them up in a vault with the weekly payroll. They were afraid the valuable security equipment would be stolen during the night.

Fusco concentrated on a detailed spy satellite picture of the wooden warehouse holding 35,000 plutonium pits. In daylight, the building was hardly secured. At the front gate, he could see a *Boyevaya Mashina Pekhoty*, or BMP armored personnel carrier, and a fifteen-man FSB squad. At night, an infrared picture showed the BMP and FSB team had left the site to go home.

Next, he examined a tourist snapshot of the wooden warehouse. It had been taken recently by a team of U.S. scientists who had visited the facility for a lab-to-lab exercise, a joint effort between the U.S. and Russian nuclear weapons facilities. The photo showed a lineup of white-coated scientists, all wearing big smiles. Behind them was a huge hole in the chain-link security fence. Workers had cut a space in the chicken wire so they could get to the cafeteria more easily.

Maybe the defense intelligence agent had been right, Fusco thought. Maybe the world was safer when the Iron Curtain was draped across Eastern Europe. Maybe all this freedom was sending the world spiraling out of control.

He typed a simple alert message into his computer and hit the E-mail button for it to be circulated to the intelligence, national security, and law enforcement communities. The sentence read:

(CLAS) CP ALERT. LEVEL 3. INCREASED SECURITY PRESENCE REPORTED AROUND CHELYABINSK-65. HUMINT WILL REPORT W/IN 12/24 HOURS. RCMND INCREASED VIGILANCE.

In seconds, the entire security apparatus of the U.S. government had been notified of the situation in the southern Urals. The CIA and National Security Agency were probably already on the case. Teams at the Department of State, Department of Justice, and FBI would mobilize for the alert. The INS and Customs would increase inspections. And the Department of Energy's Nuclear Emergency Search Team, NEST, would be put on standby at Nellis Air Force Base outside Las Vegas, Nevada.

It would be a long day, Fusco thought, looking at the red digital ZULU readout on the wall that indicated Greenwich Mean Time. Huck and the Olympic tickets would have to wait.

Buddy Crouse coiled up at the starting line in the three-point runner's stance.

"On your mark, get set, go!"

But when the gun sounded, Crouse did not break out into a sprint. Instead, he stood up straight and began to cheer as eight disabled athletes raced down the track in wheelchairs.

The event was part of a training session for the Paralympic Games. And Crouse, a U.S. Olympic decathlete from Montana, had stopped by to lend support.

"Go, Jimmy! Go!" Crouse shouted. "Yeah! Keep it up, Ted. Push!"

Crouse felt the inspiration of the moment as he watched these amazing paraplegic athletes giving it their all, gritty, determined, going for gold. They were a quarter of the way around the track when Crouse took off to catch up. Sleek and fast, he ran like a bobcat, gaining on the pack. But they were too fast.

"Way to go, T.J. Go, Freddie! You can do it. Yeee-hahhhh!"

The athletes rolled across the finish line, panting and drenched. The stifling heat definitely took its toll. Finishing in last place, Crouse was immediately surrounded by Paralympic athletes and coaches. They all wanted autographs and pictures with the long-haired co-captain of the U.S. Olympic team.

In the background, an NBC Sports camera crew videotaped Crouse's every move. It was the final shoot for a profile that would air on the final day of the decathlon.

"Are you going to win, Buddy?" a muscular man in a wheelchair asked.

"I'm gonna give it everything I've got," Crouse said.

"We know you're gonna win," a visually impaired woman said.

Crouse smiled and said, "From your mouth to God's ear."

K yle Preston hurried through the cavernous Joint Command Center, the humming central nervous system of Atlanta's Olympic security operations. Housed in the old Sears Roebuck & Co. southeastern administrative offices on Ponce de Leon Avenue, the Joint Command Center resembled NASA's Mission Control, only twice as large.

Preston crossed the "infield" where agents from fifty-five different law enforcement agencies from across the United States had set up watch posts.

"Just saw you on CNN," a young Coast Guard desk officer said as she passed by. "You looked great in the middle of all those targets."

"Thanks," Preston said, "it was a hoot."

One half of the JCC was brightly illuminated; the other half was in near darkness. The bright side was for the infield, offices, and meeting rooms, the dark side for security technicians and their toys.

Preston stopped at the Warning Desk, where the ID teams and other intelligence assets filed their reports.

"Any action?" she asked the desk officer.

"Yeah," he said, looking at notes on a clipboard. "We just got an urgent call from Georgia Power headquarters. The heat index hit 115 yesterday and the city broke a record for electricity consumption. Something like fifteen million kilowatts in one hour. They're worried about brownouts if this heat wave doesn't snap."

A combined measure of heat and humidity, the heat index was the South's equivalent of the North's wind-chill factor.

"All right, we're ready for that," Preston said. "But do one more thing for me. Give the Big Guy in the sky a call and tell him to cool it."

The desk officer laughed.

"Keep me posted," Preston said.

"Will do."

Preston crossed the line into the shadows of the dark side and made her way to the Sensor ID Room.

"Morning, Scott."

"Hey, Kyle," said Scott Worrell, a wiry thirty-three-year-old systems designer on loan from the National Security Agency outside Washington.

Kyle noticed his disheveled hair. "Out all night?" she asked.

"Looking for Ms. Right. Story of my life. How about you?"

"Stayed home. Watered the plants and caught up on homework. So how's the system this morning? Fixed those last few bugs?"

"Think so," Worrell replied.

"Give me the latest numbers."

"Hold on a sec," he said, typing "Run JCC Systems" on his keypad. On a rectangular monitor, the computer spit back:

```
13:17:22          JCC SYSTEMS
                  ALL OPERATIONAL
                  TEST RUN // 12 GIG
```

Next, Worrell typed "List Systems." The computer answered:

```
SENSOR I.D.    OPERATIONAL    3 GIG
VRS 2000       OPERATIONAL    3 GIG
SPEEDDOME      OPERATIONAL    2 GIG
```

Worrell entered a nine-digit password and then typed: "Number of badges?" The computer flashed:

```
BADGES              169,323            31 VENUES
```

"We're up to 169,323 official entries at thirty-one sites around the country," he said. "That includes venues in Savannah, Columbus, Athens, the Ocoee River in Tennessee, Birmingham, Miami, Orlando, and Washington, D.C."

"When will we break 175,000?"

"Probably in twenty-four hours. We've still got a few journalists arriving, and a few delegations haven't gotten here from the far side of the earth."

"How about a little fun?" she said mischievously. "Find Donny Sanders for me."

"Why would you ever want Donny at this hour?" he asked, punching the Olympic Committee president's name into the system.

The computer blinked:

```
13:18:05              BADGE: 2088815
DONNY SANDERS         ACOG PRESIDENT
LCTN: PRIVATE         WEST PACES FERRY ROAD
```

"Well, if that don't beat the quilt!" Preston said. "He must still be in his bathtub. Thanks, kiddo. See ya later."

Worrell watched her leave the room and then turned to the computer. He typed "Nicole Gardner."

The computer answered:

```
13:18:40              BADGE: 7608944
NICOLE GARDNER        ACOG HOSPITALITY
LCTN: GA DOME         WEST LOBBY
```

"Finders keepers," he whispered to himself. The night before, he had met Nicole Gardner at Atkins Park Restaurant and Bar. Supposedly the oldest continuously open bar in Atlanta, it was a favorite watering hole for ACOG staff and volunteers.

Nicole was in her late twenties, pretty and coy. When Worrell had dodged telling her what he did or where he worked—Olympic security staffers were barred from discussing work—she had retaliated and evaded him on her own job. They drank a pitcher of Red Brick beer and when they parted at midnight in the alley behind the bar, Worrell said he would try to track her down.

"Good luck," she said, "it's a big city."

"I have my ways," he replied.

Indeed, all it took to track down Nicole Gardner was the password to Sensor ID, the electronic system he had designed that kept tabs on *every* athlete, team official, Olympic staffer, and journalist at the Games. The system was simple and effective: access to Olympic venues was possible only with a special badge. Each had a tiny transponder embedded in it, enabling twenty-four-hour monitoring of the wearer's movements. Using radio frequency identification (RFID) technology, microwave antennas positioned at 450 sites around the Games received continuous signals from every transponder in every badge. Thus all athletes, officials, staffers, and journalists were instantly traceable at headquarters.

Sensor ID also automatically controlled electronic gates and doors at every Olympic venue, allowing or denying access. If an athlete tried to get into a dormitory where he or she had not officially been cleared to enter, the electronic system would prohibit passage. Sensor ID was particularly handy for thwarting all the pesky journalists who wanted to roam freely and snoop on the Olympic Committee or the different teams.

Worrell tapped another set of instructions on the keyboard. A second later Nicole Gardner's phone number, birth date, Social Security number, and home address blinked beneath her name on the screen.

Jotting her number on a piece of paper, he cleared his computer. Surrounded by his brainchild, the most advanced electronic security system in the world, Worrell was entirely pleased with himself.

No one could hide from Sensor ID.

Mack McFall paced back and forth at the nurses' station. On a black-and-white television monitor, he could see a grainy image of Stan Treadwell lying under an isolation bubble in the green decontamination chamber. His barrel chest rose and fell in short spasms. His brown hair was plastered back against his head and his eyes were fixed on the stucco ceiling tiles.

Eight hours earlier the Los Alamos County HAZMAT rescue team had triple-dosed him with Valium. But even with the tranquilizer coursing through his body, the horrible events in the RM lab were edging back into his blurry consciousness.

Treadwell could not remember the precise sequence. He had been mixing a fresh batch of mercury antimony oxide when something had gone wrong. The radiation klaxon had sounded; he had called McFall for help. He remembered the bitter taste of Zofran, the antiemetic pills the rescue team had forced down his throat. Two young EMTs in the ambulance, both wearing protective suits, had tried to reassure him.

When the ambulance pulled up to the Los Alamos Medical Center on West Road, the decon team was ready. Built in 1951 by the U.S. Army Corps of Engineers, the fifty-three-bed medical center had been designed for the peculiar medical requirements of the Atomic City. The embattled-looking beige concrete building, with its four-foot-thick walls, was strong enough to withstand a nuclear blast. Its emergency room was specially equipped to decontaminate Los Alamos scientists and technicians exposed to radiation.

The decon room was right next to the emergency bay on West Road. For a monthly fee, the lab rented the drab room from the hospital and equipped it with state-of-the-art radiation detection equipment, decon gear, and scrubbing solvents.

It had been years since the room had seen a hot case, but a specially trained emergency team was always on call. After the EMTs had deposited Treadwell on the cold stainless steel examining table, four nurses in red protective suits had scrubbed him. At first, they had used only water. But the radiation readings showed the beta particles had penetrated his face and hands. So they tried stronger solutions to abrade his skin and scrape away the radiation. First bicarbonate, then EDTA, and finally permanganate.

When the radiation meters stopped clicking, the nurses left Treadwell alone. There was really nothing more they could do, except pump him full of morphine.

For Treadwell's affliction, there was no cure.

In the pale blue hallway, McFall stopped pacing and sat down on a steel chair. His SkyPager vibrated on his hip. Amazed at the ability of the 900-megahertz signal to reach him even in the shielded hospital, he fingered the message button:

```
DOD LOOSE NUKES ALERT
LEVEL 4
STANDBY MOBILIZ
FONE HQ AYC 4 INSTRUX
```

He clicked the Save button to store the message. It was probably another Department of Defense loose nukes training run. They were always beeping him for emergency exercises. And they always had the worst timing in the world.

McFall made a mental note to call his buddy Vince Fusco at the Pentagon as soon as Treadwell had been moved to a more comfortable room on the second floor, and the radiation experts from the lab had done everything they could for him.

McFall walked the halls, struggling to shake the image of finding his friend and mentor in the RM mixing room, curled up in a ball, moaning, trembling, hyperventilating. Treadwell had suffered acute gamma radiation exposure, the equivalent of several hundred thousand chest X-rays at once. The gamma radiation had beamed right through him, ionizing his entire body.

Typically, gamma exposure was measured by the amount of energy absorbed from the radiation per gram of tissue. It was known as the radiation absorbed dose, or rad. If a healthy person were exposed to 200 rad, it caused severe radiation sickness. Four hundred rad meant a fifty-fifty chance of death within one month.

Treadwell had been exposed to 1,000 rad.

McFall did not need to be a nuclear health physicist to know Treadwell would die. One by one, each and every cell in Treadwell's body would expire. Acute radiation exposure meant slow, excruciating death. In one day, Treadwell's stomach lining would melt away and his vomit would turn to blood. In three to five days, every hair would fall from his head, his eyebrows would peel away, and his lashes would drop from his eyelids. Within a week, lesions would colonize his skin, uncontrollable bleeding would commence, and hallucinations would capture his mind.

It was one of the inherent risks of the nuclear weapons craft, a danger the community knew all too well. It had happened in Los Alamos many times before. McFall thought of another young scientist who had died in the lab a week after America's victory in World War II. The physics graduate student had lost his handle on a brick used to shield radiation in an experiment. A runaway chain reaction blasted him with neutrons and gamma radiation in a pulse that lasted 200 microseconds, and he died with his skin peeling off in chunks. His body was so radioactive he was buried in a lead-lined coffin.

McFall reluctantly returned to the decon chamber. An hour earlier he had tried to talk with Treadwell, but his mentor was in a drug-induced sleep, and McFall had retreated to the corridor. For that hour he had been searching for something to say. How on God's earth do you console the man who taught you everything you know?

Treadwell was awake, gazing blankly at the ceiling, his face pale, his eyes bloodshot, his body blurred by the plastic bubble.

McFall entered the room quietly. Before he said a word, Treadwell spoke, his stare fixed straight ahead.

"I know what you're thinking, Mack," he began in a hoarse whisper.

"It wasn't your fault."

McFall did not know what to say. The ache in his chest was almost asphyxiating. He felt like he was thirteen years old again, visiting his father at the VA Hospital in Sheridan, Wyoming. Cancer had ravaged his dad's lungs and gone to his brain.

Now it was Treadwell, poor Treadwell.

He never should have been doing the RM metallurgy alone. In fact, he never should have been brought back from retirement to join the WMD Countermeasures Task Force. McFall knew it was his own selfish fault.

Treadwell had been the original founder and director of the Department of Energy's Nuclear Emergency Search Team in the mid-1970s. He was the best nuclear hunter in the business, and legend had it he could track down a whisper in a wind. But at age sixty-six, he should have been left in happy retirement, romancing the lonely hearts in the Keys, learning the salsa and rumba, and painting with watercolors.

"I should have been there with you," McFall finally said softly.

"Wrong," Treadwell said. "I knew what I was doing, and I made a mistake. Damn stupid mistake."

"What happened?" McFall asked.

"I lost track of the measurements," Treadwell said. "I did the math wrong."

He paused, as if absorbing the fact that an arithmetic mistake had cost him his life.

"Now don't you give up on RM, Macky-boy," Treadwell continued. "It's too important. We're almost there. You've got to keep pushing."

"Don't worry, Stan, I promise."

"And when you're in Stockholm someday with King Carl Gustaf picking up your million bucks, don't forget you owe me half!"

"Don't you worry," McFall said. "You'll get every krona you deserve!"

It was so typical of Treadwell. He was going to die an awful death, but he was still dreaming, carrying the torch of science, pushing the edges of knowledge.

McFall sat next to the hospital gurney for an hour as his friend drifted in and out of sleep. "I'm with you, Stan," he would murmur when Treadwell's eyes flickered. Otherwise, the only sound was the blowing of the ventilators feeding the oxygen tent. Treadwell looked like an infant curled up on the hospital bed. He was all alone. No wife, no kids.

McFall was the only family the dying man had.

If Treadwell were lucky, it would all be over in two terrible weeks, maybe three.

Yagmur Ovezov headed down the stairs of the Sixth Street Apartments, a new red-brick dormitory not far from the Olympic Aquatic Center. The Turkmen team was housed on the third floor of the modern building, nestled in the green, hilly campus of the Georgia Institute of Technology.

Dressed in a track suit, Ovezov sped down the stairs three steps at a time. A black shoulder bag slung over one shoulder and a Russian-made Zenit camera over the other, he passed uniformed ACOG security guards standing watch on each landing. Biometric locks governed entry and exit to each floor. Overhead, CCTV cameras supplied backup surveillance.

"Hey, how ya doin'?" one of the guards said to Ovezov as he moved by.

"Hey," Ovezov said. "How ya doin'?" His English wasn't very good, but he was an excellent mimic.

"You have a nice day," the guard said.

"You have a nice day," Ovezov replied.

With the exception of a few well-publicized events like the Javelin Force demonstration, the Atlanta Olympic Committee had tried hard to keep its security efforts hidden from public view. It was a regrettable response to the 1972 Munich Games: parallel to the euphoric public relations campaign to promote the historic Olympic themes of international harmony and cooperation ran an equally intense and necessarily secret security operation.

After all, the Games were a sporting, not a security, event and the Olympic Village was a global community, not a cell block. Indeed, the

Olympics began in 776 B.C. as a peaceful tribute to the gods. The first "call to the Games" was intended to herald a "sacred truce" during which participants could put down their swords and spears and compete for nothing more than a wreath of olive leaves.

More than 2,000 years later, the motif of the "sacred truce" was still manifest. The Atlanta Games were intended to symbolize a brief cessation to more than thirty-five wars and conflicts being waged around the world. And in this cease-fire setting, it was not entirely coincidental that the background of the five-ringed Olympic flag was pure white.

Beneath the bunting and parades, however, the security presence was everywhere, on every street corner, at every venue. Above all, it was most noticeable around the Hemphill Avenue Apartments, where the thousand-member U.S. team and the smaller Israeli squad were quartered.

With the tacit permission of the U.S. government and the Atlanta Olympic Committee, the Israelis had brought their own small army with defensive weaponry and fortifications. It was all camouflaged—additional bomb blast barriers and motion detectors—but even an untrained eye could see the extra precautions. There were sturdy men in mirrored aviator sunglasses with objects bulging beneath their windbreakers. And there were women in identical sunglasses who whispered into their shirtsleeves.

When the Israelis said, "Never again," they really meant it.

Ovezov strolled across the lobby of the Sixth Street Apartments and through the front doors. Getting out of the dorm was not nearly as difficult as getting in. To his left, he passed a row of biometric hand geometry access control monitors, special machines that verified an athlete or official's identity by scanning his or her palm prints. There were also four airport-style magnetometers, or metal detectors. Twenty-five feet past the front doors, Ovezov stepped through the gates of a ten-foot chain-link fence surrounding the dorm.

Planned and fortified by the Pentagon's Office of Special Events at the Washington Navy Yard, the entire Olympic Village was encircled by two perimeter fences patrolled twenty-four hours a day and reinforced with concertina wire, motion detectors, and surveillance cameras. Within the village, additional fences had been erected around dormitories and sporting venues. All the so-called White Support—fences, cameras, motion detectors—was on loan from the Department of Defense. And so, too, was the Black Support, special forces teams and equipment stationed not far away at Hartsfield International Airport, Dobbins Air Reserve Station, and Fort MacPherson.

Ovezov walked east on Sixth, crossed Ferst Drive and headed for the International Festival Zone, the main gathering place in the Olympic Village. As he moved across the plaza, he casually repositioned the black shoulder bag. Though it weighed just over forty-eight pounds, he could make it look as light as forty-eight ounces. Ovezov was not much taller than five feet and was built like a Russian-made *Oka* refrigerator—square, squat, indestructible. That's what a person became after thirty-five years in the Soviet sports machine.

Ovezov was born strong. At a summer camp for young Communist patriots, he had once killed a Siberian brown bear with his own hands. The animal had wandered into the kitchen and mauled a cook. When it threatened some of the young campers, Ovezov had stood his ground, wrestled the bear, broken its neck, and become a legend across the Soviet Union.

He made a good career from his strength, winning international acclaim on the Soviet wrestling team. At the Mexico City Games in 1968, during the height of the Cold War, Ovezov had pinned a popular wrestler from the United States to win the gold medal. It was a propaganda triumph, and upon returning to Mother Russia, he was honored as a national Communist hero with parades, posters, and postage stamps.

For the next twenty-five years, he had earned good wages and was rewarded for his sporting victories with all the perks and privileges of the Soviet system. But now, with the unraveling of the Communist yoke, Yagmur Ovezov, "the Iron Hammer" and hero of the old guard, became an outcast. Soviet legends like Ovezov were expunged from the record books and discarded in real life.

After many humiliating rejections from sports federations throughout the fifteen ex-Soviet republics, Ovezov had been lucky to find a job
when Turkmenistan hired him to help train the team and manage
equipment. It was not a job description worthy of a gold medalist, an
Olympian known around the world for vanquishing his American opponents. But it was respectable, and Ovezov had bills to pay.

After all, $75 a month went a long way in Ashkhabad.

Heading north through the village, Ovezov recognized some of the
high-spirited bands of athletes. There was the American Dream Team
III, made up of professional basketball stars and rumored to be staying in a luxury hotel downtown. Hakeem Olajuwon, Shaquille O'Neal,
and David Robinson were all walking together, as tall as giants, their
heads almost in the trees.

Ovezov had lived in many smaller sports villages and was dazzled
by the Atlanta setup. The 333-acre Georgia Tech campus was actually
a small city with its own mayor, ZIP code, police force, and newspaper. Ten brand-new buildings housed 13,000 athletes, coaches, and
Olympic officials, and three pyramid-shaped pavilions were open
around the clock with entertainment, dancing, and presentations. Visible for miles, three huge, brightly colored helium balloons floated
over the village.

Best of all, Ovezov thought, were the four McDonald's restaurants
open twenty-four hours a day where the food was free for athletes
and coaches. McDonald's had not yet come to Turkmenistan, he
regretted. And in Moscow, the McDonald's lines were too long and
the prices too high.

Ovezov approached the Tenth Street gate at the northernmost
edge of the Tech campus. Teams of guards with concealed semiautomatic machine guns patrolled on the narrow path between the two
barbed-wire perimeter fences. Several white Atlanta police cars were
parked on the street.

As he passed through the gates, a security guard handed him a
blue flyer with a warning about security outside the village. The
Atlanta Olympic Committee could guarantee the safety of athletes
inside the village and at the sporting venues. But athletes were on

their own when they went beyond the fences.

In the United States, people were free to go wherever they wanted, Ovezov knew, but their security was not and could not be guaranteed by the state. He had spent his entire life living behind fences.

Fences meant safety, Ovezov believed. Where there was no barbed-wire, there was no security.

He passed through the village gates and checked his tourist map. His drop point was less than half a mile away. He walked east on Tenth Street toward midtown. The road was closed off to vehicles. On his right, he passed Alexander Memorial Coliseum. Then he crossed the bridge over the interstate. Traffic stretched in both directions as far as he could see.

Off to the right, Ovezov could see his destination, the Varsity, reputedly one of the largest drive-in restaurants in the world. He readjusted the black leather bag on his shoulder and checked behind him. There appeared to be no one following.

Ovezov had never made a drop before. It may have felt like the clandestine work of the Cold War, but it was certainly worth it. For four years he had earned enough to pay for vegetables, clothes, and occasionally some meat.

His special payment for this small delivery would cover the bills for years. And the contents in the shoulder bag seemed so ordinary, nothing more than sporting souvenirs from the Turkmen Olympic team.

The one lesson Ovezov had learned during his long career inside the Soviet athletic system was not to ask questions. He knew to follow orders, especially when he was being paid generously. So he did not speculate or ask about this task. He simply did what he was told. He had brought a case into the United States and was delivering its contents.

The parking lot of the Varsity was crowded, and there were long lines of customers at the counter, which stretched the entire length of the restaurant. It was an impressive sight, all red and yellow, one continuous ordering counter the length of a city block. Pressed against it were hungry tourists from around the world, Atlantans just getting off work, and a few athletes and Olympic officials who had skipped out of the village in search of a non-cafeteria meal.

When he finally reached the front of the line, Ovezov consulted a Russian-English phrasebook and ordered the special. He paid with American dollars and took his tray loaded with two chili dogs, onion rings, and a soft drink to the smoking rooms facing Williams Street.

Ovezov positioned himself next to the wall at the end of a long table. He put the black shoulder bag on the floor next to his feet. The room was filled with smoke.

On the television he saw a teenage girl racing with the Olympic torch on a country road. A map of the United States showed the 15,000-mile route that the flame had traveled in eighty-four days in the hands of 10,000 runners.

The picture changed to an airport runway. A blond, blue-eyed TV reporter was talking about President Bill Clinton. Then the picture showed the American president and his wife stepping off a plane and into a waiting limo. They were here to attend the lighting of the Olympic Flame, just after 8:30 P.M. *Then the Games would finally begin*, Ovezov thought.

He glanced at his watch.

A man in a baseball cap sat down directly across from him. He was carrying an order of chili-smothered french fries and a Coke. He was in his late thirties with green eyes and a sunburn. A camera with a long lens was slung around his red neck.

The man nodded to Ovezov and then reached under the table.

Ovezov did not hesitate. He nudged the black bag with his foot and then groped in front of him under the table until his hand encountered the thick envelope.

Without saying a word, Long Lens reached down, hauled up the forty-eight-pound bag, rose, and headed out the door.

Ovezov was breathing hard; the exchange had excited him. He checked his watch. He scanned the room one more time to see if anyone was looking his way. Then he got up and walked out onto Tenth Street.

His work was done. In the front pocket of his sweatpants, he could feel his reward, a satisfying wad of U.S. dollars.

"**J**ared, not now!"

Kyle Preston strained to kick her office door closed for some privacy. It was a two-step motion she had mastered by repetition, stretching the phone cord to its limit without pulling the instrument off the desk, and then hitting the door with a controlled kick.

"This is *not* a good time," she said as the click sounded and she returned to her desk for another vending machine dinner of Diet Dr Pepper and Corn Nuts. On her desk was a framed yellow bumper sticker from the naysayers who had not wanted Atlanta to host the Games. It read: ATLANTA '96. WE'VE BEEN BURNED ONCE.

Preston poured the soft drink into a Georgetown Hoyas mug and took a sip. "Of course I love you. I promise things will be different when the Games are over."

Preston listened, winced, and put the phone down. No one who had ever seen her blowing away targets in Hogan's Alley at Quantico would have believed it, but for a split second the seasoned FBI veteran felt like walking out the door and going home to hide under her down comforter. Working full-time on terrorism and Olympic security never rattled her nerves, but the daily ritual with her soon-to-be-fiancé always left her someplace she did not want to be.

Jared Peterson was a management consultant at McKinsey & Company in New York City. In most respects, he was perfect: tall, dark, handsome, well educated, and rich. And rarest of all, he was *not* afraid of commitment.

But still, at an emotional level, Preston knew something wasn't right. Jared didn't understand what she was going through. Calling her every day and asking if she still loved him wasn't being supportive. Faxing her every day with questions about their Christmas ski vacation five months away wasn't what she needed.

She had already told him everything he needed to know. The Olympics assignment was going to be her final job with the Bureau. When it was over, she was going to hand in her badge and gun, move to Manhattan's Upper East Side, and start a family.

What more could he ask for?

Preston forced herself to focus on the FBI's Olympic Threat Assessment Summary on her desk. The OTAS was a daily inventory of all the dangers in the world, madmen on the rampage, terrorists rearing to strike.

Internal Only   Page 1 of 5

OLYMPIC THREAT ASSESSMENT SUMMARY
JULY 19, 1996   DAY ZERO   RING: GREEN

THREAT	CRED	CAP	PRIO	TOT
Al-Fatah (Palestine)	+	4	3	7
AN (United States)	+	2	2	4
ANO (Libya)	+	4	4	8
ASALA (Armenia)	+	2	2	4
Chukaka-Ha (Japan)	0	2	2	4
Dev Sol (Turkey)	0	2	2	4
ETA (Spain)	+	3	3	6
FALN (Puerto Rico)	+	4	3	7
FARC (Colombia)	0	2	2	4
FLNC (France)	0	2	2	4
GRAPO (Spain)	0	2	2	4
Hamas (Palestine)	+	6	5	11
Hezbollah (Lebanon)	+	6	5	11
HRB (Croatia)	+	2	2	4

IRA (Ireland)	+	3	3	6
Islamic Jihad (Iran)	+	6	4	10
JRA (Japan)	+	3	2	5
NPA (Philippines)	–	2	2	4
PLF (Palestine)	–	4	3	7
PLOTE (Sri Lanka)	+	2	3	5
PDFLP (Palestine)	+	3	4	7
PFLP (Palestine)	+	3	4	7
RAF (Germany)	–	2	2	4
Shining Path (Peru)	0	2	2	4

Her eyes always ran down the far right column first: the bigger the number, the greater the threat. Other columns gave appraisals of the credibility of the threat, the capability of the group, and the recommended law enforcement priority. On this day the usual suspects—Hamas, Hezbollah, and Islamic Jihad—were at the top of the charts.

Preston looked forward to the OTAS each day as much as she had looked forward to lifting up rocks with her brother on the family farm in Macon. All sorts of scaly things slithered into the mud. The OTAS was like a daily roundup of all those slippery creatures.

While full Olympic security readiness had been in effect for just one month, the Intelligence Specialized Management Center had geared up more than a year ago. And the FBI Olympic squad, headed by Preston, had anticipated nearly a thousand different emergency scenarios.

The security challenge of the Olympics, Preston thought, was tantamount to holding the Superbowl, World Series, NBA championship, Stanley Cup Final, Indy 500, U.S. Open, and Kentucky Derby *every day* for seventeen consecutive days in one single city. And so, crisis control plans ran the gamut. On one end of the scale, the Olympic security team was prepared to help a small non-English-speaking child who had lost a mother. They were ready to break up fistfights between fans frustrated by long concession lines. They had even anticipated an invasion of Southeast Asian prostitutes who knew the profits from two weeks of tricks would be worth the jet airfare. On the other end of the scale, they were ready for multipronged terrorist attacks at different venues across Atlanta and the United States.

On her bookshelf, Preston had hundreds and hundreds of pages of protocols for handling every scenario. The FBI planners had conducted countless command post exercises—CPXs—and worked out procedures to respond to every imaginable incident. As part of the Department of Defense's Interagency Terrorism Response and Awareness Program, or ITRAP, the Bureau had joined other government agencies in two full-scale tabletop exercises in preparation for the Olympics. They were ready for poison in the Powerade coolers on the track and field sidelines at Centennial Stadium; toxins in the pool at the Georgia Tech Aquatic Center; sabotage at the Georgia Power substation at Memorial Drive and Hill Street supplying the Joint Command Center; kidnappings of European royalty at the Equestrian Park; and anthrax spores dispersed through the ventilation system at the Omni Coliseum.

And so far, on the first day of the Games, nothing had gone wrong. A loose nukes threat had been issued in Washington, but there was no connection to Atlanta.

At least not *yet.*

Confidence on Day One, Preston mused, was like believing in the bottom of the first inning that a pitcher was going to throw a no-hitter.

She had another fifteen minutes before the FBI's nightly Counter-Terrorism Task Force meeting. She finished the OTAS and turned to the *National Intelligence Daily*, the CIA's top secret world roundup and analysis for senior government policy-makers. The lead paragraph on the first page stopped her:

NEAR EAST/SOUTH ASIA:
NSA reports multiple communications between Jihad cells in Gaza, West Bank, and Lebanon. Additional contacts between Jihad and USA contacts. HUMINT reports in Israel, Lebanon, and Syria and USA corroborate. Pattern suggests likely operation or action. TS NOFORN

Irrefutable proof, she thought, that Palestine should *never* have been offered membership in the IOC after the Middle East peace agreement in 1993. From the early 1930s until Israel was created in 1948, Preston knew from her briefing books, Palestine had an Olympic Committee with Jewish and Arab members, but its team was never able to compete because of World War II and regional unrest. Then the peace agreement had been signed with PLO chief Yasser Arafat and Israeli Prime Minister Yitzhak Rabin shaking hands at the White House, and Palestine was invited to send a team of athletes to Atlanta.

The black phone on Preston's desk beeped, and her secretary said: "Scott Worrell wants you at VRS 2000. ASAP."

Preston headed out of her office into the infield. She looked across the room toward the VRS 2000 Center, where security technicians kept a watchful eye on the Olympic venues and strategic sites around Atlanta and the United States.

VRS 2000, the visual reality system, was the software program controlling the SpeedDome security cameras positioned all over Georgia. Their exact number was a secret, but anyone interested could count more than a thousand closed circuit television cameras in key positions. The system also tapped into existing CCTV surveillance systems in hotels, stores, and office buildings.

If something—anything—was going on at the Olympics, SpeedDome controllers with a press of a button could observe on a wall of monitors what was happening across Atlanta and at Olympic sites from coast to coast. In addition to surveying entrances and exits, they kept their eyes on athletes in bathrooms, cafeterias, and dormitories. And when they were bored, they flipped the channel to the locker rooms at the Georgia Tech Aquatic Center, where swimmers dried and dressed.

"What's up?" Preston said, arriving in the VRS Center. "Has Peeping Tom been having fun?"

"We've got a hostage barricade at the Centers for Disease Control and Prevention," Worrell said. "Details are sketchy. But check out monitors 25, 26, and 27."

Preston's eyes moved swiftly over the silent screens. On monitor

25, there was an exterior shot of buildings 5 and 7 at the CDC complex on Clifton Road just eight miles northeast of downtown. Some 300 lab workers and technicians, following emergency evacuation procedures, were gathering at the front exits.

On 26, there was a picture of a darkened CDC hallway lined on both sides with rows of industrial-size stainless steel freezers. At the far end of the corridor, CDC security officers had set up a command post.

On monitor 27, there was a close-up of a laboratory door plastered with flower-shaped Biohazard stickers. The door was marked BL-4 RESTRICTED AREA. Behind the door was one of only two Biohazard Level 4 labs in the country where scientists in astronautlike protective suits studied the deadliest diseases on the planet.

"Give me audio on 26," Preston instructed Worrell.

He punched a button and the directional microphone on the surveillance camera in a grimy hallway switched on. Worrell cranked the sound. The CDC security team was busy evaluating the situation.

"Latest head count in the parking lot has twelve unaccounted for," one of the officers said.

"Do we know what this guy wants?" another officer said.

"Negative."

Preston hit the intercom switch and asked her assistant to pull the Vital Point emergency file and protocols for the CDC. In the run up to the Games, the Georgia Emergency Management Agency had compiled a list of more than 500 Vital Points that were potential targets for terrorists.

Preston's assistant delivered the orange file. Preston thumbed through the pages. Olympic security officials considered the CDC to be a Vital Point because of the lethal, incurable viruses stored inside the forty-year-old walls of the yellow brick complex. In hundreds of freezers, CDC scientists kept samples of the world's most deadly pathogens like Ebola virus, Hantavirus, and Marburg virus. Also locked away in cold storage were frozen vials of the smallpox virus. The only other smallpox samples on earth were stored at the NPO Vector Institute of Molecular Biology at Koltsovo in Russia's remote Novosibirsk region.

Security at the CDC had been virtually nonexistent until Olympic planners began examining the facility. Some of the buildings were so decrepit that Atlanta safety inspectors had strongly recommended they be condemned.

What if terrorists tried to take over the CDC and threatened to release lethal viruses like the Crimean Congo virus, Rocky Mountain spotted fever, Brazilian meningitis, or worse still, smallpox? There was no cure for smallpox terrorism.

With that scenario in mind, law enforcement officials hardened security at the CDC complex and brought in extra cameras, motion detectors, and armed guards.

On Scott Worrell's VRS 2000 screen, a red icon shaped like a gun was flashing. Next to it was a readout:

```
18:14:32
HSTG/BRCD              HRT EN ROUTE
CDC BL-4 LAB           BUILDING 6W
1600 CLIFTON RD        CLIFTON CORRIDOR
```

Worrell searched the thick black operations notebook on his desk for the protocols for a CDC emergency. He punched instructions into his computer.

"What's the location of the hostage rescue team?" Preston asked.

"In the air en route," Worrell said.

"What's their ETA?"

Worrell hit a few more keys on his computer.

"Three minutes."

"And what about the TEU?"

"The TEU team is on its way from Fort MacPherson," Worrell said. "They've got the gear in case stuff spreads."

TEU was short for the Technical Escort Unit, an Army team that had been sent to Atlanta from the Chemical and Biological Defense Command at the Aberdeen Proving Ground in Maryland. The TEU was the Army's chemical and biological SWAT team. Its members had been vaccinated against most disease agents. The TEU had helped destroy Iraqi chemical munitions after the Gulf War and most recently in April 1995 had backed up the FBI in responding to a potential terrorist threat at Disneyland that was linked to the sarin gas attack in the Tokyo subway.

"All right, get the crisis command group together right away," Preston said to her assistant, who was standing at the door. "I want everyone in the conference room or on SVTS in five minutes."

"What about Donny Sanders?" her assistant asked, referring to the ACOG president. "Do you want him on the Secure Video Teleconference?"

"Only one nightmare at a time," she said.

With a swift kick of his black boot, the wooden door turned to kindling. Federal Security Service Captain Vasily Tarazov dropped to one knee, waited, and listened. There was not a sound inside apartment 2332. The thirty-four-year-old officer, with a face as hard and flat as an anvil, motioned to his six-man squad of stormtroopers to move in.

Tarazov's special forces team was part of the FSB's Special Technical Operations Service. The group's name, STOS, was vintage KGB: it revealed *nothing* about its true mission. STOS was an elite battalion of ex-KGB *Al'fa Spetznatz* operators that had been assembled to combat atomic smuggling after reports surfaced from Arzamas-16, another secret nuclear city, that infiltration attempts at the Federal Nuclear Research Center had more than doubled.

Apartment 2332 was located in Block 47W of the massive Soviet period concrete apartment buildings in the residential quadrant of Chelyabinsk-65. The one-bedroom flat belonged to Gennady Sobchak, a veteran chemical engineer at the Mayak reprocessing plant.

Sobchak had been away on vacation for more than a month. When the Chelyabinsk-65 security forces reported there had been a theft from the plutonium storage facility, his name had turned up on a short list of Mayak insiders with access to the plant who had left the closed city within a day or two of the theft of 21.7 kilos of fissile material.

Tarazov's team had already spent forty-eight hours straight searching Chelyabinsk apartments, and the predawn raid on 2332 was the last stop. The work had been exhilarating and exhausting. Although he had no solid leads, he enjoyed kicking down doors and ransacking apartments. Brash and ambitious, Tarazov longed for the days when the KGB was the law. In those glory days, the Soviet security system had worked with brutal efficiency. Extreme tactics produced extreme results. But the democratic changes of the past five years had crippled the beast. Tarazov's STOS battalion was a vestige of the old guard, still conniving to dominate a nation that had ceased to exist.

In tribute to that time of absolute power, Tarazov wore a silver pendant around his neck with the likeness of Lavrenti P. Beria, Joseph Stalin's murderous security boss and one of the principal architects of the Soviet A-bomb program. Head of the NKVD, the dreaded secret police and father of the Soviet obsession with nuclear secrecy, Beria had selected the sites of the closed nuclear cities in the 1940s.

Tarazov had been inspired by Beria's biography when he joined STOS, and it was in Beria's memory that he and his squad worked every day. Tarazov felt lucky to have an important job when all around him the once omnipotent Russian military was collapsing, and more than 200,000 officers were homeless.

As he entered the filthy apartment, he was reminded once more that the economic allure of nuclear smuggling was inevitable. "Poor people are inventive," the Russian proverb said. Workers in the Russian nuclear complex earned only 309,000 rubles a month, roughly $60. Wages were never paid on time. And living conditions were abysmal. The monolithic concrete-slab apartment buildings stretching three city blocks were crumbling. Small children believed the structures were being blown away piece by piece, little by little, by the biting winds that swept down from the Ural mountains.

Tarazov hit the light switch in Sobchak's apartment revealing a cramped room lit by a single dangling bulb. The tattered window shades were drawn. Shelves of dog-eared books and scientific journals lined the walls. In the center of the room, there was a small coffee table with a china teapot, creamer, sugar, and four cups.

It was evident from the rumpled clothes on the floor and dirty dishes in the sink that Sobchak wasn't much of a housekeeper. Or did the crusty stockpot full of potato soup on the stove signal that perhaps he had left in a hurry?

Within moments of entering the apartment, Tarazov noticed an unmistakable odor, a smell that brought him back to his childhood in

Lipetsky, 200 miles south of Moscow. There was no doubt about it! It was definitely the odor that had permeated his youth, that had swirled around his cinder-block home on Pirogovskaya Prospekt. It was the heavy and bitter smell of melting, burning metal from the Novolipetsky Iron and Steel Combine across the railroad tracks. It was the smell that had blackened the air on the playground at his grade school, had clung to his father's filthy clothes when he came home at night from the factory where nine million tons of pig iron and another nine million tons of steel were produced each year.

Tarazov's curiosity was aroused. It was an utterly ordinary apartment. Its tenant was supposedly on holiday in Moscow. Why was there the pungent odor of a metalworks?

On a bookshelf, Tarazov found a faded color picture of Gennady Sobchak with his arm around a white-haired woman. He studied the faces in the photo. Was this man a traitor? A smuggler? Was this his grandmother in Moscow whom he was visiting, as his leave papers indicated? How old was she, and what kind of life had she lived? And who had given her the delicate gold amulet she wore around her neck?

Tarazov's FSB troops methodically combed the room, inspecting the cupboards and drawers, pulling books from the shelves, upending furniture. A soldier photographed every inch of the apartment.

Tarazov opened a closet, and the smell of metal was even stronger. He pulled clothes from the floor and uncovered a butane tank and a small cauldron. He put on his leather gloves, dragged more clothing from the closet, and inspected the equipment. There were metal shavings and lead ingots on the floor. There were also rubber molds and packets of green sand.

It was immediately clear that Gennady Sobchak had been making castings and pouring metal in his apartment. But why? Tarazov knew that nuclear scientists did all sorts of peculiar things with their free time. But running a small foundry was unusual even by Chelyabinsk standards.

Tarazov studied the casting equipment carefully.

"Dmitri, come here and help me with this," he said to a member of his squad, grabbing two thick white candlesticks from the small dinner table.

"Yes, Captain."

"Take these candles and melt them," he said. "Then pour the wax into these molds, and let's see what we can make."

"*Davayte,*" the sergeant said, calling together the rest of the team. "Let's do it!"

It was not standard procedure. Tarazov knew he should take the evidence back to STOS headquarters for analysis. But this was an official Minatom emergency. And Tarazov could always say the ends justified the means.

Sergeant Dmitri Silayev knelt on the floor melting candles while Tarazov pulled out his radio to call his commanding officer.

"Soyuz Base, this is Hammer One," he said.

"Hammer One, Soyuz Base. *Kag dyela?* How are things? What's your status?"

"*Ochen kharasho.* It's going well. We may have found something, Soyuz Base. Tell Commander Yurchenko that apartment 2332 in block 47 does not appear normal."

"What have you got?"

"A small metal foundry in a closet. Metal shavings and lead ingots on the floor. Tenant is a chemical engineer at Mayak with access to the storage facility. It seems he left town in a hurry."

"I'll tell the commander."

"*Spasiba.* Hammer One, out."

"*Nichyevo.* Soyuz Base, out."

Tarazov stepped across the room.

"Dmitri, how is it coming?"

"One more minute, Captain."

The FSB trooper pulled a lump of white wax from the mold and studied the shape in his hands. Then he handed it to Tarazov. It was a sphere the size of a small melon. On one side it had raised Cyrillic lettering and a small design.

Tarazov looked closely, cradling the sphere in his gloved hand.

The longer he inspected the white shape, the more clear the image became. The pattern actually consisted of six small shapes: a crescent and five stars. The writing in Cyrillic was less decipherable, but Tarazov could make out two words: *Tiurkmenostan Respublikasy.*

Tarazov reached for his radio again.

"Soyuz Base, Hammer One," he said.

"Yes, Hammer One."

"Urgent. Repeat urgent. Please advise our good friends in Ashkhabad to be on the lookout for our missing objects."

"Did you say Ashkhabad, Hammer One?"

"Da," Tarazov said, staring out the window into the darkness before dawn. "What we're looking for is in Turkmenistan."

onny Sanders posed in front of the bathroom mirror, admiring himself. For a sixty-one-year-old, he looked pretty darn good. His chest was broad, his eyes dark blue, and his hair still thick as the front lawn. Dabbing a shaving brush on his jaw, the chairman of the Atlanta Olympic Committee practiced his speech for the Opening Ceremonies.

"Welcome, one and all . . ."

Sanders frowned into the mirror and guided the straight-edge blade along his neck. Then he started again loudly. "Welcome, nations of the world!"

He stopped, as if listening to the words echo across Centennial Stadium. It was going to be one helluva speech, the crowning moment of his messianic, at times maniacal, crusade to bring the Games to Atlanta. From the moment he discovered in a history book that he shared the same birthday with Baron Pierre de Coubertin, the five-foot three-inch founder of the Modern Games, Sanders was sure he had found his calling. Olympism was Sanders's born-again faith. Since February 1987 he had traveled to 104 countries, wined and dined ninety-five voting members of the International Olympic Committee, and raised every single penny of the $1.7 billion it was costing Atlanta to put on the Games.

"Ladies and gentlemen, welcome . . ."

Bellowing at the mirror with only a royal blue towel wrapped around his waist, Sanders was a sight to behold. But Ian Hobbes, the thirty-five-year-old chief spokesman for the Olympic Committee, had seen it all before. Resting on the toilet seat in the corner of the ornate bathroom, Hobbes held a printed copy of Sanders's speech in his lap, prompting his boss. It was a typical work session. Hobbes had left

ACOG headquarters at the Inforum building downtown and driven through nightmarish I-75 traffic out to Sanders's palace on West Paces Ferry Road not far from the governor's mansion, all to sit on a toilet seat and help his boss rehearse a speech.

Usually Sanders was in the pool or on the tennis court when Hobbes arrived, and the young man would then confer with him in the bathroom while he went through his ablutions. Lyndon Johnson did the same thing, Hobbes had read, dragging staffers into the john in the Oval Office for meetings. Fundamentally, they were not dissimilar, Donny Sanders and LBJ. Each was sure as hellfire that he was meant to rule.

Sanders's hubris was already well developed back in the 1950s at the University of Georgia in Athens, where he quarterbacked the Bulldogs and was a first team All-American. Forty years later, he congratulated himself that he could still throw a tight spiral, and he loved to loiter on the sidelines at Falcons games, giving pointers to quarterback Jeff George.

The word *charismatic* inevitably preceded *Sanders* in the reams of gushing profiles that had been printed about him and the Atlanta Olympics, and he relished this epithet and worked hard to live up to his billing.

"Ladies and gentlemen, athletes of the world, welcome to Atlanta . . ."

Even with shaving cream dripping from his face, the words flowed from his mouth with a certain authority. No doubt about it, he thought, eyeing himself in the steamy mirror, the Games of the XXVI Olympiad belonged to him, the one and only, the charismatic Donny Sanders.

"You boys done foolin' around in there?" Marybeth Sanders called from the canopy bed in the flowery master bedroom. Sucking on a peach, the former Miss Georgia and Miss America Runner-up was lounging. It was almost 7 P.M., and she was still in bed.

Now forty, Marybeth had spent years parlaying her looks and velvet-glove smarts to hold on as the belle-in-perpetuity of the Atlanta social circuit. Upon meeting Marybeth, more than a few leading journalists compared her to a seasoned Scarlett O'Hara.

"Come on, Donny, it's my turn in there!"

"Hold your horses, darlin'. We'll be right out."

Huddled in the corner of the bathroom, Hobbes felt his Sky-Pager vibrating in his pants pocket. On call twenty-four hours a day to give a sound bite, he had been tethered to the beeper for longer than he cared to remember. He admitted to himself, not without embarrassment, that the SkyPager had become his most intimate friend. It wasn't bad that the little square machine vibrated. It was the only fun he ever had.

The LED readout on the beeper flashed a familiar number. It was Kyle Preston's personal office line. "May I use the phone, Mrs. Sanders?" he asked, stepping from the bathroom into the bedroom.

Propped up by half a dozen pillows, Marybeth was ensconced on the lacy bed, a gilded tray across her lap. She was delicately licking her fingers, and Hobbes could not help noticing that her pink silk dressing gown was negligently wrapped around her. She winked at him playfully, pulled the robe tighter across her chest, and motioned to the princess phone on the bed stand.

Hobbes dialed the number for the thousandth time. Preston picked up immediately. They spoke for thirty seconds.

"Kyle, you've definitely *got* to tell him *now*," Hobbes whispered into the phone. "I think he can handle it. He'll behave himself. Marybeth's here."

Hobbes put the phone down and called out to his boss. "We've got an emergency at the Centers for Disease Control. Kyle Preston needs you right away."

Sanders was in his dressing room, fastening his gold cufflinks. The mention of an emergency did not seem to raise his pulse at all. He marched over to the bed, kissed his wife on the cheek, picked up the phone, and listened for a few moments. Then his face reddened. "I don't care what it takes," he said firmly, "just fix the goddamn problem!"

Sanders paused, running his fingers through his slicked-back hair. "No excuses! Fix it! Do whatever it takes. Just make it go away! And don't let a fucking soul know about it. I'm on the way!" Then he slammed the phone down.

Sanders stood next to the bed, dressed only in a shirt, boxer shorts, and knee socks. "What are you looking at?" he snarled at Hobbes, who was leaning against the bedroom door.

"Nothing, sir," he answered, amused at his boss's sudden self-awareness.

The Ford Explorer pulled into the Days Inn on Turner McCall Boulevard. As the vehicle came to a stop, the doors flew open, and the Hollister family—Herb, Noreen, and little Vicky—stepped out.

The drive from Wilton, Alabama, to Rome, Georgia, had taken just a few hours, but the Hollisters were as thrilled as if they had reached Rome, Italy. It was the beginning of their big splurge summer vacation—a two-week trip to the Olympics.

They had tickets to gymnastics, swimming, and the Opening and Closing ceremonies. And although it could have been the North Pole, they were content to have a place to stay, seventy-five miles from Atlanta.

The city's 56,000 hotel rooms weren't enough to handle the Olympic throngs. Herb Hollister, a stiff, clean-cut CPA, had lost out in the official lottery for hotel rooms within forty-five miles of the Olympic city and had set out to find a place in the boondocks, which turned out to be Rome, roughly an hour and a half away *without* traffic.

Herb stretched and studied the five-story hotel. "Not so bad," he said.

"Could be worse," Noreen said. "You could have rented that RV near Atlanta for $200 a day."

"Not worth it," he said.

"Look, daddy, there's a sign to the swimmin' pool!" Vicky said, pulling on his hand.

"Slow down, girl. No swimming now. It's time for dinner."

The Hollisters unloaded their bags from the back of the Explorer.

One hundred feet away, in the crowded parking lot of a strip mall, a man with an Emory baseball cap was watching through a long lens. Snapping a few telephoto pictures, he followed the Hollisters as they made their way into the hotel lobby. Then he put the camera down on the seat beside him and started his truck.

The Hollisters had arrived. Everything was finally in place. He pulled onto Turner McCall and headed for I-75 to Atlanta.

"This meeting will come to order."

Kyle Preston studied the six men seated around the table in the "Fish Bowl," the glass enclosed conference room in the center of the Olympic Joint Command Center.

In the kingdom of Olympic security, this was the equivalent of a G-7 summit meeting. The six men and one woman at the marble conference table represented more than 25,000 security forces from more than fifty-five different law enforcement agencies, including the FBI, Department of Defense, Bureau of Alcohol, Tobacco and Firearms, National Guard, Georgia Department of Public Safety, Atlanta Police Department, DeKalb County Sheriff's Department, Border Patrol, and the Immigration and Naturalization Service.

"Day Zero, gentlemen," Preston began. "You may already be aware that we have a Red Ring situation at the CDC." The passive faces woke up, and slumped spines stiffened. "Frosty, bring us up to date."

Debra "Frosty" Cornell, chief of the Atlanta Police Department, opened a green folder. Cornell operated under the delusion that her colleagues called her Frosty because she was so cool under pressure. In fact, she had earned the sobriquet when she freaked out during a prison riot in 1989, melted down like a snowman, fled her office, and surfaced several hours later muttering to herself as she directed traffic in a downtown parking lot.

"At just past six," Cornell said, "we received a hostage/barricade call from the Centers for Disease Control. Kyle issued a Red Ring alert. We've activated emergency plans. The FBI's Hostage Rescue Team is on the scene. The Javelin Force is backing up the HRT. The Army's

TEU is there with chemical and biological response equipment. Atlanta PD has sealed the perimeter."

"Sounds like the gang's all there, but who's driving the train on this one?" asked Dax "Beast" Carrick of the Georgia Bureau of Investigation. He was a burly plug-and-grind sort of a man whose head, neck, and shoulders formed a thick triangle. The nickname had come in his teens when he worked summers as a strong man on the state fair circuit. Now in his early fifties, he had spent his entire career with the GBI, inching his way up the ladder by sticking to a Latin credo framed on his office wall: *Captivos Nullos Capere.* In English: Take No Prisoners.

"The FBI is running the show on this one," Preston answered.

"Now there's a surprise!" Carrick said. "I should have guessed."

Every single day, Carrick fought it out with the FBI and other law enforcement agencies over every inch of turf. Like nations at an international summit, the fifty-five different law enforcement agencies, regardless of size, were considered equal, each with its own jurisdiction and agenda. Many of the individual organizations had little or no previous experience in interagency cooperation. The U.S. Department of Defense, for instance, had never worked with the seventy-five-person Chatham County Police Department. And the U.S. Immigration and Naturalization Service had no idea how things were done by the tiny Stone Mountain Park Police.

The reason for the confusion was that *no* single individual or agency was ultimately responsible for Olympic security. There was no dictatorial security czar with absolute authority.

Preston glanced at the spaghetti graph on the wall that charted the organizational structure of the Olympic security efforts. It was a jumble of overlapping jurisdictions and interagency rivalries.

If only the United States had a national police force, Preston thought. *And if only the FBI weren't just an investigative agency. It would make life so much simpler. Russia, South Korea, and Spain, with their national police agencies, had it so easy!*

At the Moscow Games in 1980, Preston had read that one out of every ten people in Lenin Stadium's 103,000 seats was a security officer. Overall, the Soviet Union assigned 230,000 state police to the Moscow

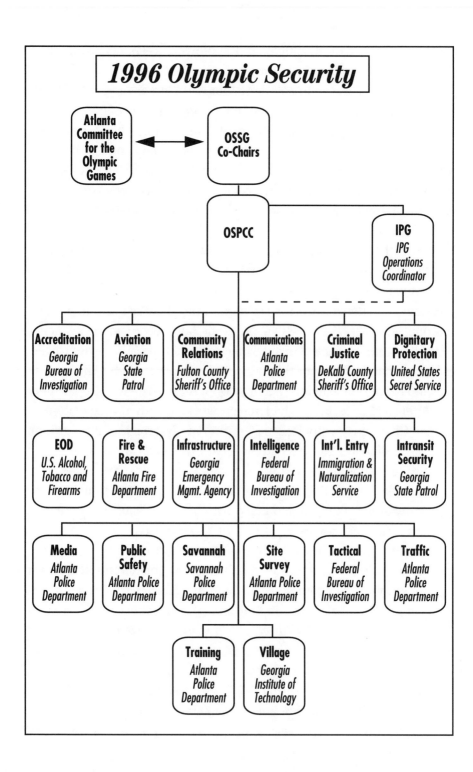

1996 Olympic Security

Games. South Korea had a national police force of 120,000 guarding the Seoul Games, plus armed forces of 620,000 on full alert. And Spain deployed 27,000 national police to protect the Barcelona Games, backed up by 5,000 city policemen and 5,000 army troops.

The fact that law enforcement in the United States was historically a local affair was the source of endless headaches and complications. When the 1984 Games were held in Los Angeles, the LAPD's 8,000 officers were in charge of security within the city limits. And in theory in Atlanta, the APD, with its 1,500 officers, was responsible for public safety.

The reality was that it never, ever worked that way. City police forces could barely keep the peace on a normal day, let alone manage the crush of millions of Olympic visitors. Inevitably, responsibility fell to the FBI. And despite endless negotiations, meetings, and memoranda of understanding, there was plenty of resentment.

"Folks, let's get all the dead cats on the table," Preston said. "If you've got a problem with the Bureau taking the lead on the CDC situation, speak now or forever put a clamp on it."

She glared at Carrick, who dodged the barb by changing the subject.

"Have we gotten a threat message yet from the CDC hostage taker?" he said.

"Negative," said Cornell.

Donny Sanders appeared at the glass door to the conference room and put his hand on the biometric access control panel. Noiselessly, the partition glided open and all heads turned. Sanders entered, paused for a moment as the soundproof door slid shut, and without any apology for his interruption, launched a barrage.

"What in God's good name is going on around here?" he shouted. "Y'all have the most expensive security system the world has ever seen! And you still let someone ruin our party? You people are hopeless. Y'all couldn't hit a bull's ass with a banjo."

No one said a word. Preston and Cornell exchanged glances. Each law enforcement official at the table had endured Sanders's tirades before and knew that like a summer squall, he would eventually blow himself out.

"Does anyone outside this room know about the CDC problem?" he asked angrily.

"Not yet," said Cornell. "And we're—"

"Well, if word gets out," Sanders interrupted, "the first thing they'll do is crucify me, and then there will be a goddam . . ."

Sanders did not bother finishing his sentence. It went without saying. Even a whisper that there was a crisis situation at the CDC involving deadly Level 4 hot viruses would whip up a media frenzy, then a stampede to get out of town.

Mass hysteria was the ultimate security nightmare. Controlling a crowd of 85,000 people at Centennial Stadium was tough enough on a good day. But there would be no way to manage three million panicked people trying to flee Atlanta, all at the same time.

"Donny," Preston said, "we're all over this like white on rice. Everyone understands we have to keep the lid on it. All of our special teams are on the scene: Javelin Force, HRT, and Explosive Ordnance Disposal. The Army's TEU is there to support in case of a biological release. Press handlers are there, too, in case cameras or pencils show up. The preset emergency plans are running smoothly."

She gambled and continued. "But let's not get worked up about this prematurely. We're not even sure this is a real hostage situation."

"Well, what the hell is it, Kyle?" Sanders exploded. "A reception for the team from Zaire? Get off your lazy asses."

For five seconds he paced back and forth along one of the glass walls, like a caged tiger. Then finally, veins bulging in his neck and forehead, he said, "Let me make something clear to y'all. No one is going to stop my Games. No one!" He jabbed the exit button and stormed out of the conference room.

Preston swore silently to herself. She concentrated on the agenda. She had a lot to manage and Sanders's theatrics were an unfortunate distraction. She flipped through her notes. She knew she had to keep the agenda moving. *The special teams would handle the situation at CDC, control the media, and let Sanders's games run their course*, she thought.

The glass doors closed behind Sanders. The men, their faces

registering various shades of incredulity and disgust, turned as one to her.

"Only sixteen more days of that crap," she said, "and then . . ."

She smiled and cut the air with her hand. Everyone at the table knew she had a black belt in karate. And the thought of destroying Donny Sanders was irresistibly delicious to her.

"The CDC situation is under control," she added. "Frosty and I will close it out when we're done here. Let's move on."

All eyes turned to the one page agenda that had been handed out at the beginning of the meeting. Number 2 on the list:

MUNICH MEMORIAL SERVICE:
Palestinian Olympic Committee refuses to participate in ceremony for 11 Israeli athletes murdered at 1972 Summer Games. Israeli PM, IOC President attending.

Time: Day Two; 7/21/96; 10:30 A.M.
Threat Level: One
Security Level: 100

"Simon," Preston said, turning to an intelligence officer on loan from the CIA's Counterterrorist Center, "what's the latest on the Palestinian situation?"

In his early forties, Simon Highet looked like a man who lived in the darkest recesses of Langley headquarters. His shiny skin was so translucent it appeared he had never been exposed to the light of day.

"Through sources in the DO," he began in a basso voice, "we have learned that certain Palestinians are planning reprisals if the Munich memorial service is not canceled."

"Reprisals?" Preston repeated.

"Yes, reprisals."

"Why wasn't this in the briefings?" Preston asked, searching the pages of the Olympic Threat Assessment Summary and the *National Intelligence Daily.*

"Very good reasons," he replied.

"Get the Javelin Force to the memorial service," Preston said, turning to Cornell. "And don't anyone think for a second about canceling it. That's out of the question."

"That's a bad idea," Highet said emphatically.

"It's not negotiable," Preston said. "The IOC has been planning this ceremony for years. It's the first official Olympic memorial service since the massacre twenty-four years ago."

"Then let the record show," Highet said, "that the Agency vigorously recommends postponing the service."

"Postponing it until what?" Cornell pressed.

"Until we locate Abu Azzam."

The five words hung in the air like tracer fire.

Abu Azzam was the last surviving member of Black September, the radical PLO splinter organization responsible for the Munich massacre. At least thirteen Black September terrorists linked to the Munich attack had been eliminated by Israeli hit squads over the years, but Azzam had always stayed a step ahead of the Mossad. The international intelligence community, not long on compliments, grudgingly respected Azzam. He was a cunning cat with ninety-nine lives.

"What do you mean, 'until we locate Azzam'?" Preston asked.

"We've lost track of him," Highet answered.

"Come on, Simon," Preston followed up. "That's spook speak. You people never lose track of anyone. Where is Azzam?"

"We don't exactly know."

Preston saw through Highet's deliberate choice of words.

"Okay, you don't know *exactly*. How about *inexactly*? How about within a thousand miles?"

"We think he's here," Highet whispered. "Here in the United States."

Lieutenant Colonel Vincent Fusco sat in his darkened office pondering his Moscow field operative's terse advice.

Three impossible words, a spook's idea of a joke: *seal the borders.*

Now, nine hours later, this jest had turned sour. The intelligence streaming in from Russia had forced the simmering situation in Bosnia to the back burner.

Chelyabinsk-65 was definitely heating up. An Air Force RC-135 Rivet Joint spy plane had intercepted high frequency transmissions from an elite FSB battalion in Chelyabinsk to STOS headquarters in Moscow. The HF transmission consisted of detailed photographs of a ransacked apartment. In addition, HUMINT in the closed nuclear city had gathered specific information about the unfolding crisis.

Fusco called up a file with a time marker showing it had just arrived in the National Military Command Center's computer system. He opened the "intelligence summary" document on his classified computer screen.

PAGE 1 OF 1

```
CLAS         CODE WORD (DIVING MANTA)
LC: MSCW     SRC: FSB


21.7 KILOGRAMS OF REPROCESSED PU-239 MISSING FROM
CHELYABINSK-65.
UNKNOWN TO MINATOM FOR FOUR WEEKS.
SHIPMENT BELIEVED TO MOVE THROUGH TURKMENISTAN.
FINAL DESTINATION U/K.
INTERNATIONAL BUYERS U/K.
```

Fusco rubbed his eyes. Was this a transmission error? By several orders of magnitude, twenty-plus kilograms of plutonium was the biggest leak of weapons-grade material *ever* from the former Soviet Union. It was easily enough fissile material to make five nuclear devices.

Fusco checked the torn page thumb-tacked to his bulletin board. He had ripped it from the Harvard loose nukes study. It listed six confirmed cases of nuclear smuggling from Russia.

Mid-1992: chemical engineer Leonid Smirnov steals 3.7 pounds of HEU from Luch Scientific Production Association in Podolsk, Russia.

November 1993: Russian Navy Captain Alexei Tikhomirov steals three pieces of reactor core containing 10 pounds of HEU from Sevmorput shipyard near Murmansk.

May 1994: German police find 5.6 grams of super-grade plutonium from Arzamas-16 in the garage of Adolf Jackle, an alleged counterfeiter in Tengen, Germany.

June 1994: Bavarian police capture 0.8 grams of HEU in sting operation in Landshut, Germany.

August 1994: German police sting operation yields one pound of near-weapons-grade plutonium at Munich airport. Material smuggled in suitcase on flight from Moscow.

December 1994: Authorities discover six pounds of HEU in two plastic-wrapped metal containers in the back seat of a car in Prague.

All together, Fusco calculated the material lifted in those six incidents did not add up to a fraction of the plutonium that was now missing from Chelyabinsk-65. *You bet the Russians were trying to seal their borders, were mobilizing MVD and FSB troops, and were locking down their airports.*

Fusco knew from experience that these efforts were too little, too late. They were shutting the proverbial barn door long after the horses had bolted for the fields. And the most alarming aspect of the preliminary field intelligence reports from Moscow was that there were no real leads.

Black-market informants who usually tipped American agents off to movements of materials had been silent for weeks. Could there be a connection to the FSB hunting for a nuclear chemist named Gennady Sobchak? When and if they found him, would he know anything and would he live long enough to tell?

The lieutenant colonel's mind wandered for a moment. What would the bullet item look like on his list on the wall when this case was resolved? Would the plutonium be found in Budapest or Teheran or Pyongyang? Would it be smuggled into Baltimore or Dallas or Minneapolis? Would there be a nuclear detonation?

Fusco snapped back to the wall-sized map in front of him. The plutonium could be going *anywhere* in the world. Rogue states from Libya to North Korea were known to have shopped for fissile materials and Russian nuclear expertise. Iran reportedly had dispatched "buying teams" to the FSU in search of materials and talent. And a plane of Russian nuclear experts was stopped by police shortly before jetting off to North Korea, where the scientists had been hired to work on Kim Jong II's secret atomic program.

And what—heaven forbid—if the plutonium was heading to America?

Fusco tried not to think about the question, for he knew that stopping it would be virtually impossible.

Again, his mind turned to the Harvard loose nukes study. In the continental United States there were 301 different legal ports of entry, and protecting them were 10,000 Customs inspectors, none of whom was trained or equipped to detect nuclear smuggling. There were loads of explosives and drug detection machines deployed at these entry points.

But there was not a single radiation detector.

Fusco laughed out loud. U.S. Customs would need thousands of radiation detectors to monitor the daily flow into the United States of more than one million visitors. And then there was freight: more than 3 billion pounds of cargo came every day by sea and 10.3 million pounds by air. At the seaport in San Pedro Bay, California, the nation's busiest harbor, 1.5 million containers entered the United States every year. Just 3 out of every 100 were ever opened and inspected.

Fusco couldn't resist punching some numbers into his calculator. The 47.8 pounds of missing Russian plutonium represented 0.0000015 percent of the total freight entering U.S. borders every single day.

In short, it would be almost impossible to stop the plutonium from entering the country. Indeed, one of Fusco's cynical friends in the counter-terrorism business was fond of saying if you really wanted to get fissile material into the United States, all you had to do was hide it in a bale of marijuana.

Item 3 in the intelligence summary document from Moscow drew Fusco's interest: "Shipment believed to move through Turkmenistan."

Fusco opened the CIA's World Book and scrolled to the selection on the former Soviet republic:

```
TURKMENISTAN              GOV TYPE: REPUBLIC
DIGRAPH: TX               POP: 4,075,315 (95 EST)
ADMIN DIV: 5 WELAYATLAR   GDP: $13.1B

INDEPENDENCE:  27 OCT 1991
ETHNIC:  TURKMEN  73.3%;  RUSSIAN  9.8%;  UZBEK  9%;
KAZAKH 2%; OTHER 5.9%
```

He switched screens and looked for recent economic and political developments. The material—page after page of detailed information about the country's defense forces—was mind-numbingly dull. Intelligence officers were not known for lively prose. Somewhere, there had to be a fact that would point in a direction. He was looking for a trail, any trail. His eyes were tired, and he wanted to go home. But he continued reading.

```
TURKMENISTAN  IS  LARGELY  A  DESERT  COUNTRY  WITH
NOMADIC  CATTLE  RAISING,  INTENSIVE  AGRICULTURE  IN
IRRIGATED OASES, AND HUGE GAS AND OIL RESOURCES. HALF
ITS  IRRIGATED  LAND  IS  PLANTED  IN  COTTON,  MAKING  IT
```

THE WORLD'S TENTH LARGEST PRODUCER. IT ALSO HAS THE
WORLD'S FIFTH LARGEST RESERVES OF NATURAL GAS AND
SIGNIFICANT OIL RESOURCES.

Enough about economics. What about the political scene? He switched screens and scrolled. The president of Turkmenistan, known locally as *Turkmenbashi*, was promoting a widespread cult of personality. Politics were the same the world over, he mused. Then Fusco saw a sentence that made his heart race.

FOR THE FIRST TIME IN THE HISTORY OF THE MODERN
OLYMPICS, TURKMENISTAN IS SENDING A TEAM TO THE
SUMMER GAMES IN ATLANTA. THE 25-MEMBER TURKMEN
TEAM FLEW NON-STOP TO THE UNITED STATES ON 19 JULY
1996. THE PRESIDENT'S PLANE CARRIED THE TEAM,
REFUELED IN ICELAND, AND LANDED IN ATLANTA.

Of course, Fusco thought, *the Olympics.* His son and the soccer match flooded his mind momentarily. *Not now*, he thought. Then he forced himself back to the plutonium.

"Damn," he muttered.

Could that be it? Could the plutonium already be in the United States?

Fusco dialed a number at Fort Meade, Maryland, where the National Security Agency spied on the world, eavesdropping on late night phone calls from sundry South American dictators to their mistresses; Russian Defense Ministry orders to tanks and troops in Grozny, Chechnya; and even Japanese *Yakuza* plots to push the Chinese Triads out of San Francisco.

If a sensitive conversation was taking place anywhere in the world—trade negotiations in Kuala Lumpur to pillow talk in Paris—the National Security Agency was probably listening. Nicknamed the Puzzle Palace, the NSA was so secretive that its 20,000 workers liked to come up with alternative explanations for the acronym. One popular option: NEVER SAY ANYTHING. Another: NO SUCH AGENCY.

"Hi, Eve, it's Vince. I need those pictures the Air Force sent over from its last Rivet Joint flight against Russia."

"No prob," said Eve Bigelow, a signals intelligence—SIGINT—officer, reaching for her GlidePoint touchpad. "I'll shoot them to you over INTELINK."

"Sorry about the quality of the images," Bigelow apologized. "They were degraded when we grabbed them from Russian air."

Fusco examined the shapes on his screen. His computer was wired straight to Bigelow's in Maryland.

"Can you go up two times on image number one?" he asked.

Bigelow moved the cursor arrow and double-clicked on the molds.

"Okay, now give me an oblique P.O.V. on image number two," Fusco said.

Bigelow manipulated the angle of the image, giving Fusco a different point of view of the white wax ball that had been cast from the rubber molds by the enterprising FSB officer.

"We've been running these shapes through our computers, trying to come up with a match," Bigelow said. "So far, we've come up with a list of 1,700 different objects that might fit."

"Like what?" Fusco asked.

"You name it," Bigelow said. "Industrial-sized ball bearings. Italian bocce balls. Antique cannonballs. Hell, even the proverbial prison ball and chain!"

"Can you pull up those little shapes on the ball?"

Bigelow clicked the "Zoom 10X" icon on her screen and Fusco's monitor was instantly filled with a new image.

A white crescent and five stars.

Fusco began to line up what he knew: four plutonium pits stolen from the warehouse, curious rubber molds in apartment 2332, a flight in mid-July from Ashkhabad to Atlanta.

It all started fitting together.

Fusco's mind was racing. "Thanks, Eve. I'm done."

"See ya, Vince. Have a good weekend."

"You, too, Eve."

Fusco knew this couldn't be pure coincidence. There were too many connections. Too much overlapped.

Fusco instantly reached for the STU-III on his desk. He paused before hitting the speed dial number for the National Security Council. *Had he lost his marbles? It was only a hunch, but it all fit together. But what if he was wrong? How humiliating! It certainly wouldn't look good on his record. But then again, what if he wasn't wrong?*

Fusco punched the speed dial button and asked to speak with the deputy director of the National Security Council's Coordinating Subgroup or CSG. It was the NSC's secret interagency team that handled terrorism incidents. He quickly briefed the skeptical deputy director on the situation and then dialed a 505 area code beeper number.

There was only one man in America ready for this job. And he was somewhere in the wilds of northern New Mexico.

Rebecca Deen opened the door to her apartment. At first, she only noticed the lights were off. It was cool and quiet. Then she smelled garlic and wine.

"Quinn, are you there? Quinn?"

There was no response. Deen put her briefcase and laptop computer down by the front door, dropped her gym bag, and pulled the ACOG Sensor ID badge from her neck. She threw the tag and her car keys into the Braves mug on the table in the entryway.

"Quinn, where are you?"

Again, no response.

Deen flipped on the hall lights and headed toward the living room. She paused at the mirror in the den and ran her hands through her short blond hair.

Twenty-nine years old, she thought, *going on forty-nine.*

She felt like a wreck. Her eyes ached from another sixteen-hour day at ACOG headquarters. Her neck was in spasm. She wasn't sure she was ready to face Quinn. And this was his last night in town. She wanted to make him happy, but she wasn't sure she had the energy. The first day of the Games had been grueling for the Olympic media relations team. And there were sixteen more to go.

Deen turned the corner and saw the lone candle flickering on the dining room table in the alcove next to the window. There were place settings for two and a long-stemmed red rose on one of the plates.

What a devil, she thought.

"Where are you?" she shouted. "Where's my man?"

Deen threw open the kitchen door.

"There you are!"

Quinn Lazare stood at the sink, listening to a Sony Walkman, slicing red peppers and tossing them onto a heap of salad. He was thirty-nine years old, with a long, thin face, dark eyes, and black hair that fell in a single swoop to his shoulders. He wore a black T-shirt, Nike running shorts, and thick white socks.

Lazare looked up and smiled. Deen could feel his eyes burn straight through her. "Welcome home," he said, pulling the earphones from his head.

"So what do you think you're doing?" she asked, twirling her hair with a finger.

"Just a little going-away present."

"But you're the one going away," she said.

"I just wanted to let you know how much I—"

Deen threw her arms around Lazare. Effortlessly, he lifted her off the ground, spun her around, and put his mouth against hers. He set her on the marble kitchen counter, pushing the salad bowl into the sink. They clung to each other for a long moment. Deen felt the life pour back into her body.

Then, suddenly, Lazare released her and spun around.

"Salmon's ready," he said, dropping to one knee and inspecting the broiler. "Time to eat."

"But what about—"

"Later," he said. "Dinner will be on the table in five minutes."

Deen sulked into the bedroom. She quickly undressed, threw her suit on the pile of clothes on the armchair, washed off her makeup, and put on a white terry-cloth robe. She made mental lists of all the things she hadn't finished at work that day. She would go into the office early tomorrow, unless Quinn kept her up all night.

"*A table*," Quinn called out in a mock French accent. And then with a twang, he added, "Come 'n get it."

The two sat in the shimmer of candlelight twenty-five stories above Atlanta. The view from the downtown apartment on Marietta Street faced south toward Atlanta-Fulton County Stadium, the 52,000-seat home of the Braves. Farther south was the Olympic Stadium.

"A toast to Atlanta, a phoenix risen from the ashes!" Lazare said.

"Hear, hear," Deen said.

They clinked glasses of Chablis.

"You know, I watched the Opening Ceremonies on TV," Lazare said. "It was amazing!"

"Yeah, Don Mischer's an incredible producer. He's been working on that show for more than a year."

"Pretty cool," Lazare said, "all that Centennial stuff and Southern flavor."

"What did you think of Donny's speech?" Deen asked.

"A big snore," Lazare said.

"But *he* thought it was great," Deen said, "and that's what matters."

"Did you get to meet President Clinton at ACOG?" Lazare asked.

"Unfortunately not. He breezed in and out of Donny's office and shook hands with a few folks. But we were all too busy foaming the runways for a disaster that almost happened."

"What kind of disaster?" he asked, his interest piqued.

Deen did not hear Lazare as she dug into her salad. "Mmmm," she said, licking her lips. "What did you put on this?"

"Just a little something."

"Boy, can you cook!" she said, giving him a look. "I'm not sure I'm ever gonna introduce you to my mama. She'll want you for herself."

"What kind of disaster?" Lazare asked again, ignoring Deen's teasing.

"I could tell you," she deadpanned, "but I'd have to kill you."

"Come on," he said. "What happened?"

"Since when are *you* so interested in the Games?" she asked. "I mean, you actually watched the Opening Ceremonies. And you actually asked what I did today. I thought you didn't want to hear any more about the Olympics."

"Fine, don't tell me," Lazare said, his expression darkening. He stared out the window, gazing at the gold dome of the State Capitol in the moonlight.

"Hey, don't pout," Deen said, trying to reel him back. "We just had a little hostage barricade situation at the CDC."

"Yikes," said Lazare, pretending. He could feel the tension leave him. He had stayed too long. He should have left weeks ago. But he wanted to soak it all in. He wanted to feel the city come alive for the Games. He wanted to experience the crowds and listen to the trumpets.

"How come there wasn't anything about the CDC on the news?" he asked.

"'Cuz I'm so frigging good at my job," she said. "That's what I do all day: spin the press. Just imagine how awful the story would have been! We might as well have kissed the Games good-bye."

She picked up a spoon and pretended it was a microphone. "Good evening, this is Rebecca Deen reporting live from Atlanta. On this, the first day of the 1996 Summer Games, a deranged man took twelve hostages in a Biohazard Level 4 lab at the Centers for Disease Control. The man threatened to release the deadly smallpox virus unless—"

Lazare laughed and said, "Stop, I get the picture."

"It sure wasn't easy keeping a lid on that one," she said. "We've got 15,000 reporters crawling all over this town looking for a scoop."

"So how did it end?"

"The FBI's Hostage Rescue Team took care of the situation with a little assist from the Olympic Javelin Force. The poor guy didn't see what hit him. Boy, our team is good."

"What do you mean?"

"Well, the bad guy turned out to be an angry lab worker carrying a hunting knife. You know, one of those Wild West specials? He was pissed off about CDC budget cuts or something like that. The Hostage Rescue Team and the Javelin Force were ready. They've spent a year rappelling up and down every building in Atlanta. They've crawled down every sewer line. Needless to say, Daniel Boone was no match for our boys and their toys."

"No match," Lazare said laconically, his eyes fixed on some point in the distance.

Deen studied the man across the table. Although they began sleeping together almost immediately after a chance meeting at Bytes Cafeteria in the Inforum lobby three months ago, she had to admit that she knew almost nothing about him. She had been taking a quick lunch break from her work on the sixth floor in ACOG's Purple Quadrant where the executive offices were located. When he had asked her out for a drink and then pursued her, she had been flattered because in the year that she had been working for the committee, he was the first man to show any interest.

She could never get him to say exactly what he did. Passing through town on business was how he described himself. And most of their conversation was banter. Often she felt he emotionally and mentally removed himself, just like this evening. He was gone, some-place else. Perhaps she could bring him back later when the lights were out.

They finished eating, and she cleared the table. Lazare sat quietly next to the window. "Where are you?" she said, collecting the silver-ware. "Earth to Quinn. Mission control calling Quinn."

"I'm sorry, girl, I'm just thinking about my trip."

She climbed onto his chair and put her arms around him.

"Come to me," she said, guiding his face to her neck.

Their three-month affair had been fast and furious. She was work-ing sixteen-hour days, and he traveled almost every week. There wasn't much time for a relationship. But there was time for what mattered.

Lazare carried Deen into the bedroom and turned off the lights. Two hours later, the bed was a shambles.

Staring up at the ceiling, Lazare listened as the young woman next to him drifted off to dreamland, her breathing slow and heavy. He lay at the edge of sleep, rousing himself twice to check the green num-bers on the clock radio. For some strange reason, like a broken record, his mind replayed a memory from childhood.

Mr. Faziano's eighth-grade astronomy class in Winston-Salem, North Carolina. Lazare was twelve, and it was his turn to present a report to the rest of the class. The ambitious topic: black holes, white dwarfs, and deep space. Almost immediately, Faziano, a mean little wretch known as Fazi the Nazi, began ridiculing Lazare and the topic.

"Which one are you, Lazare?" Faziano said. "A black hole or a white dwarf?"

Lazare's eyes welled up with tears. He was too young —and humiliated—to understand that his teacher, a failed physics Ph.D. candidate, resented his gift for science and his uncommon promise.

The rest of the class took the teacher's cruel cue and joined in, taunting Lazare, calling him names. "Lizard's a white dwarf! Lizard's a white dwarf!"

Young Lazare ran from the room.

Older Lazare felt the rage burning again.

At 5 A.M. he slid out from under the sheets, showered, and quickly stuffed his belongings into a duffel bag. He dressed in a black polo shirt and jeans and pulled his hair back in a ponytail.

He knelt next to Deen and caressed her on the cheek.

"Bye, baby."

"Please don't go," she said sleepily. "Do you have to leave me?"

"Got a plane to catch," he said, checking his watch. "Don't worry. I'll be back."

Then he headed for the front hall. He opened the coat closet and felt for a brown paper shopping bag on the dusty floor in the back. He opened the sack and pulled out a black leather shoulder bag. It was heavy, forty-eight pounds to be precise.

Then he turned, scooped up Deen's laptop computer and her ACOG Sensor ID badge, and headed out the door.

It had been a long night at the hospital. The thick clipboard of medical charts dangling from the end of Stan Treadwell's decontamination tent chronicled his deteriorating condition.

Crammed into a recliner next to Treadwell's bed, McFall was sleeping soundly. His beeper sat on an untouched food tray. McFall had been paged repeatedly through the night, but he had not heard the calls. He had switched his SkyPager to vibrate mode and then accidentally left it on the tray. Every sixty seconds, it shook the small bowl of Christmas-green Jell-O.

Dr. Gerome Pappas, one of Los Alamos Lab's resident radiologists and the world's foremost authority on gamma radiation, opened the door to the hospital room. McFall cracked open his eyes and recognized the doctor. They had worked together at the lab on a number of health physics projects aimed at developing antiradiation medicine to be taken by troops and civilians in the event of exposure. This kind of antiradiation research had been going on *without* significant success for fifty years. The pills and potions never worked. Nor for that matter did Russian antiradiation treatments like vodka and wine. Still, the quest continued.

"Hey, Mack," the doctor said.

"Morning, Doc." He checked his watch. "You're here early."

"I got here as soon as I could. Flew straight from a radiography conference in Kiev. How's Stan doing?"

"Don't know. I was hoping you'd tell me."

Pappas lifted the tent around Treadwell and conducted a short visual inspection of the sleeping patient. He pulled a reflex hammer from his coat pocket and tapped Treadwell's wrists and ankles. He leafed through the charts, made a few notes, and then pinned the oxygen tent flaps back into position.

"Our boy's lost consciousness," said the doctor, a slouching white-haired man in his sixties.

"How bad is it?" McFall asked.

"Level 10 or 11 on the Glasgow Coma Scale."

"Meaning?"

"The scale measures human alertness. The two of us are 15's, awake and alert. Treadwell is a 10 or an 11. He's in a light coma. His reflexes are attenuated."

"What's the bottom line?" McFall asked. He disliked the jargon of medicine and the way doctors hid behind their numbers and measurements. He knew there would be no good news, but why did doctors have to speak in mumbo jumbo?

"In healthy adults, it's possible to regain consciousness from level 5."

"Possible?"

"It's remote. Of course, his body is failing fast. The ionized cells are dying."

"So he'll keep slipping further and further."

"Unfortunately, yes."

A nurse waved from the station down the hall.

"Dr. McFall, we have a call for you."

McFall shook Pappas's hand and walked to the nursing station, an octagonal arrangement of desks and humming machines. He picked up the phone, expecting it to be Frank Handlin, the surly director of the Los Alamos National Lab.

"This is McFall."

"This is the National Military Command Center, sir. Sergeant Denny Hewitt."

"Yes, sergeant. What's up?"

"We've sent three urgent Skygram messages. Where have you been?"

"I'm a little busy right now," McFall replied, looking down the hall toward Treadwell's room. "I don't have time to—"

"We don't have time either," Hewitt interrupted. "Please hold the line for Colonel Fusco."

McFall was genuinely surprised. Why was Vince Fusco getting on the line? Normally, low-level dispatchers at the Department of Energy or the National Military Command Center gave the instructions.

If Vince Fusco was involved, it had to be serious.

Fusco came on the line. "Hey, buddy. I hear you've been hiding from us."

"Not really, Vince. I've just got my hands full."

"Well, don't fight us on this one. We've got an emerging situation at Chelyabinsk-65. This is no exercise. The problem is very real. I think you're going to need your flyaway pack."

"Where am I going? Russia?"

Fusco laughed uncomfortably. "I wish you were going overseas," he said. "But your ticket is first class to Atlanta."

"Georgia?" McFall asked incredulously.

"The only Atlanta I know."

"Jesus," McFall said. "Give me the headlines."

"DIA sources say something is missing in Russia. We have circumstantial evidence that it's heading our way."

"What do you mean 'circumstantial'?"

"I have a strong hunch," Fusco said, "that forty-eight pounds of plutonium have *already* been smuggled into the United States."

"How did it get in?" McFall asked.

"You won't believe me when I tell you," Fusco said.

"Try me."

"What weighs sixteen pounds and goes to the Olympics?"

"Vince Fusco, alias the Riddler?" McFall thought for a moment. The Olympic torch weighed less than sixteen pounds. So did the javelin, the hammer, and the discus.

"I'm guessing here," McFall said, "but how about a shot put?"

"Exactamundo!" Fusco said.

"You're shitting me."

"No shitting here. My hunch is the Pu-239 was hidden in shot puts brought in by the Olympic team from Turkmenistan."

"How did they do it?"

"It was pretty easy. Regulation balls are made of iron, brass, or steel. The plutonium pits stolen from Chelyabinsk were hollow spheres weighing roughly nine pounds each, maybe a bit more. We think a Russian scientist coated the pits with seven pounds of lead or steel cladding to shield the plutonium and make it undetectable."

"Jesus," McFall said. "There isn't a Customs agent or X-ray machine in the Lower 48 that could detect it."

"That's why we need you in Atlanta, Mack."

Reflexively, McFall weighed the assignment. Finding a few Turkmen shot puts couldn't be that hard. Security at the Olympics was tight as a noose. How far could you really go with a box of shot puts?

McFall stopped. He was kidding himself. The truth was that finding a few shot puts would *not* be easy. Security officials at the Games were on the alert for bad guys brandishing bazookas and rocket-propelled grenades, not radioactive athletic equipment.

"So who's already at the party?" McFall asked.

"A small NEST team was pre-staged last month in Atlanta. But a full mobilization has been authorized. The C-141 is already in the air from Nellis. You'll have all the equipment and support you need."

"How about X-ray?" McFall asked. "Are they flying from Fort Bragg?"

"They're on standby," Fusco said. "The president has been notified. The Coordinating Subgroup at the National Security Council is meeting right now at the White House. We're awaiting an Executive Order, then X-ray will deploy to Dobbins."

"Good," McFall said. "We'll need to be high-speed, low-drag, night-flight capable. So when do I fly?"

"We've got a Gulfstream landing at Los Alamos in thirty minutes to pick you up. You'll get another briefing en route. And you'll have the usual security escort while you're there."

"Thanks, Vince."

"Travel fast, Mack."

McFall put the phone down, turned to the supervising nurse, and wrote a telephone number on a prescription pad. "Beep me as soon as there's any news," he said and headed for the door.

He took a few steps, calculating how long it would take him to get home, grab his flyaway kit and then make it back to the airport: ten minutes down the hill to his home in White Rock, five minutes to get everything together, ten minutes to drive back up the hill to Los Alamos Airport, LAX as the locals called it. There was plenty of time.

He spun around and headed back to the decon room for one last look at Stan Treadwell. McFall did not know how long he would have to be in Atlanta. Given what Dr. Pappas had said, it would probably be the last time he would see his friend alive.

It was a sad irony that Treadwell, who had lived for nuclear emergencies, wouldn't be in the middle of this real threat. He had spent a lifetime preparing for these situations. There had been more than a hundred nuclear hoaxes over the past twenty-five years, and Treadwell had dispassionately seen each situation resolved. Calm and unflappable, he had a special sense about how a crisis would unfold.

Long ago, someone had even given him a silk turban like Johnny Carson's because in the nuclear terrorism world, Treadwell was a real-life Carnac the Magnificent. And he had luck, incredible luck. It was his Irish fairy, he used to say with a twinkle. A special spirit was watching over him.

Where was the Irish fairy when the gamma rays got him? McFall asked himself as he opened the door to the decon room. The curtains were still closed and the furniture and medical equipment were silhouettes in the darkness, backlit by two shafts of light leaking in from the window's edges.

McFall pulled the steel chair up to the side of the bed, sat down, and pressed his forehead against the plastic oxygen bubble. Treadwell's eyes were closed. The tent was like a barricade. The nurse had said he was no longer radioactive—the scrubbing had done its job—so McFall unpinned the flaps to move closer to his friend.

"Hey, partner," McFall whispered, "you there?"

There was silence.

"Can you hear me, Stanny boy?"

Again, nothing.

McFall took a very deep breath and let it out slowly, struggling not to cry. "Listen, I gotta leave you for a few days. Looks like we've finally got a real one to take care of in Atlanta. How about that?"

McFall paused and listened. He knew it was only wishful thinking that somehow, by reaching out with all his might, he could pull Stan back to consciousness. Treadwell was at level something-or-other on the Glasgow Scale. It wasn't good, and it wasn't going to get better.

Still, there was a chance that Treadwell could hear him.

"You hold on, Stan. You've got to hold on."

McFall knew it was hopeless. He had been to this movie before. Long ago, his father had slipped silently away in another hospital under another oxygen tent. One day he was throwing a football in the backyard, then he was sick in bed, then he went to the hospital. Soon came the coma, then death.

"You've gotta promise me you're gonna try to make it through," McFall said softly. "I know we're gonna need you in Atlanta."

Treadwell's breathing was raspy. A crop of gray stubble had sprouted on his cheeks and chin. McFall checked his watch. His internal clock was always right. It was time to roll.

"Wheels up," McFall said, shaking his head. "Sorry I gotta go."

He stood up and tucked the flaps of the oxygen tent back into place.

"Good-bye, old buddy. I guess I'll see you when I see you."

Trailed by two black vans, McFall pulled into the driveway of his two-story ranch house at 9606 Juniper Drive. Nuke jumped from the car and charged up the steps of the house, nestled against a rocky red cliff and looking across the valley all the way to Santa Fe. The name of the street always made McFall think of the old line: "Suburbia is where the developer bulldozes out the trees, then names the streets after them."

McFall opened the front door and headed straight for the phone. He could not deal with a national emergency in Atlanta until he got one personal problem under control. Teddy Kwong, his lab assistant, answered on the eighth ring—he had been sound asleep—and agreed, as always, to look after Nuke.

McFall took a thirty-second sink shower—wet hair, wash face and underarms—then pulled on khakis and a blue polo shirt. He surveyed the bedroom. What was he forgetting?

His eyes paused for a second on the picture frame sharing space on his nightstand with a flashlight and Mickey Mouse alarm clock. It was a vacation photo of Jenny, eyes afire, hair swept by the wind, sitting on a porch swing with tall grass and an ocean behind her.

McFall turned and went to the hall closet to get his prepacked travel bag with its toilet kit and week's supply of clothing. Heading out the door, he whistled good-bye to his golden retriever.

T
he two men in blue shorts, white shirts, and Delta baseball caps ambled across the tarmac and fell into line with a crew of baggage handlers. They were chewing bubble gum, and their clothes were caked with oil and dirt. For ten minutes, the pair helped unload luggage from the open belly of a Boeing 767 just in from Boston. The plane, *The Spirit of Delta*, had a deep-blue tail, stars, and the Olympic logo on its side.

As they worked, stacking bags on the conveyor belt, their eyes methodically scanned the tarmac.

On a normal day, Hartsfield International was the second busiest airport in the world, handling nearly 2,000 flights and more than 100,000 passengers. That kind of volume was routine. But on the first day of Olympic competition, bright and early in the morning, even Hartsfield was overwhelmed.

To cope with this "aerial sclerosis," as the air traffic controllers called it, Delta had staffed up, relocating out-of-town employees to pitch in temporarily, putting them up in makeshift housing at the sprawling gray Delta headquarters at the airport.

The two interlopers had taken full advantage of all the commotion. Ten minutes earlier, they had sliced through the chain-link perimeter fence on Terminal Parkway, made their way through the Delta complex past the landmark red-and-white FLY DELTA JETS billboard, and slipped onto the bustling apron under Concourse A. They were dressed in standard Delta summer uniforms and wore expertly forged ID tags around their necks. They had even smeared their clothes with grease and had rubbed their hands in dirt to blend in.

When they finished unloading the 767, the two men disappeared into the baggage processing area directly beneath the concourse.

Like toy trains, luggage tugs and carts criss-crossed the area. From the ceiling, two security cameras panned back and forth.

The two men checked the camera angles and went to work, quickly and methodically. During their scouting trip the week before, they had calculated the camera rotations were at least fourteen seconds out of synch, leaving one small area of the baggage room unmonitored fourteen seconds out of every minute. It was an unfortunate oversight on the part of Delta security. And it afforded enough time for the two men to get their job done.

Traditionally, terrorists planted bombs in suitcases that were loaded *onto* airplanes. But this was no typical operation. The focus of their work this time was luggage coming *off* of airplanes.

The men chose their targets deliberately: cases or bags with zippered exterior pockets and no locks. Hours of practice on Tumi overnight bags, Army surplus duffels, and American Tourister cases had paid off. The men moved in bursts of activity, timing their work with the sweep of the overhead CCTV cameras.

"How many more?" the taller, darker man said to the other, standing on a mound of suitcases.

"At least fifty."

"All right. We'd better hurry."

The man had his hand in the outer pocket of a Hartmann garment bag when he heard footsteps behind him. Then a Georgia drawl.

"Hey, you two, what the hell do you think—"

The Delta security guard did not see what hit him. There was only a *whoosh* and a stinging sensation in his neck.

One of the men shoved the air-powered dart gun back in his pocket and checked the security cameras. They were finishing their sweep of the far corners of the baggage area. The man pulled the flight-stabilized syringe from the fleshy part of the guard's neck. Death had been instantaneous: ricin, a poison more lethal than cobra venom, had acted immediately.

The two men dragged the guard behind a tug that was out of commission, calmly stuffed several dozen more suitcases, and then headed for the stairs to Concourse A. They paused in the stairwell to strip off their Delta outfits.

Moments later, as the doors opened onto the crowded Delta concourse, they were dressed as tourists in garish Hawaiian shirts and shorts. They walked along past the food court. Teams of Borg-Warner security guards and German shepherds patrolled back and forth.

The two men dropped down a steep escalator into Hartsfield's transportation grand canyon, where a talking train whisked them through an underground tunnel to the main terminal. The ride took three minutes, then the doors opened. "Welcome to Atlanta, home of the '96 Olympic Games," the grating robotic voice announced. On the wall, a big picture of Atlanta mayor Bill Campbell smiled down on them.

After another long escalator ride up, the men crossed the pink-and-white glass atrium of the central terminal with its eighty-two-foot-high arched ceiling. The two-story clock tower in the middle of the open space was playing "La Marseillaise," the French national anthem.

The men headed nonchalantly to the baggage claim area and the eight stainless steel Delta carousels. They joined crowds of Olympic visitors around carousel 7. The gathering looked like the lobby of the United Nations. Men, women, and children from around the world, dressed in their country's colors, spoke excitedly in a babel of languages.

The men waited, watching the first bags slide down the ramp and begin the slow spin around the oval. At last, a familiar duffel appeared on the carousel. Then a backpack, an overnight case, a big zippered bag.

The men exchanged triumphant glances.

Before the tourists could even hoist their bags onto push-carts, the two were gone, mission accomplished.

T wo undercover FBI agents sat nervously in the bleachers, their field glasses trained on the hulking Turkmen shot-putters who spun around in tight circles and then let steel balls fly. Each time one of the spheres landed, the agents involuntarily braced for a nuclear explosion.

"Jesus," agent 1 whispered. "Do they have to keep flinging those things?"

"Relax," agent 2 said unconvincingly. "Remember the briefing. Even if they're filled with plutonium, they're not going to explode."

"Do you believe everything they say in the briefings?"

"Hell no."

Across the stadium, another shot put arced through the air and landed silently.

Again, both agents felt their necks tense.

The Pentagon Loose Nukes alert about the Turkmen shot puts had arrived at the Bureau's Olympic Intelligence Center in the middle of the night. Agents had been roused from bed at their homes and hotels, and teams rushed to the Olympic Village.

But so far, the search had produced nothing but piles of stinking uniforms and dirty jockstraps.

Yagmur Ovezov lay in bed enjoying a Sheryl Crow CD on his new Sony Walkman. He loved American music and he relished going into the stores in the Atlanta Underground and buying what he wanted. It was not possible to have that pleasure in Turkmenistan because there was nothing to buy except carpets and camels.

Ovezov listened to Sheryl Crow's chorus: "All I wanna do is have some fun. I got a feeling I'm not the only one. Until the sun comes up over Santa Monica Boulevard."

The only words he recognized were *fun* and *boulevard*. He turned the volume up and began to think about the presents he would bring home to his family and friends. He had $10,000 stuffed in his shoe under the bed and he couldn't wait to go shopping after the main events were finished. He would bring home a fancy food processor for his wife, an Olympic Barbie doll for his daughter, and an American football, helmet, and pads for his son. Then he would save all the rest of the money for the future.

Through the window shades he could see it was another hot and hazy morning. The sun in Turkmenistan was different, not like here in Atlanta, soggy and wet, but dry and scalding like the desert. Would his athletes be able to perform in this oppressive weather? Would he be blamed for a dismal performance? Everyone always felt better blaming the trainers and coaches.

Ovezov checked the blue dial of his new Timex Indiglo watch, another gadget he had picked up downtown. He had set the watch's international time functions on Ashkhabad and Atlanta and loved flipping between time zones, imagining what his family was doing. It was late in the evening back home on Ulitsa Atabaeva, and his sons would be getting home from wrestling practice. His wife was folding laundry. Soon they would gather around the black-and-white television in their cramped little apartment to catch a glimpse of Papa in the United States.

He needed to get up. In twenty minutes he had to be downstairs in the basement training room for half an hour of meditation and stretching before breakfast in the cafeteria. Then the team would head to the stadium.

Sheryl Crow was luring him back to sleep. His imagination was enjoying a replay of the thrilling moment when he had felt the weight of a gold medal dangling from his neck. The prize was much heavier than it looked, and he could feel it, hard and cold, against his chest. The turgid Soviet anthem was playing, and flashbulbs were popping, and he felt his heart would burst. It was a sensation he would never know again, a feeling of accomplishment, triumph, real worth.

Would his athletes bring home gold? Would they know the exhilaration of standing atop the Olympic pedestal, and would they ever feel the heartbreak of abandonment by their homeland?

Ovezov turned the volume up, and let his thoughts wander. He did not hear the sounds at his door—first a few gentle taps, then voices in English, then louder knocks, and suddenly the door came crashing down. Masked men stormed into the room.

When he opened his eyes, he saw the barrels of four semiautomatic weapons pointed at his head. He counted eight intruders, too many for him to handle alone.

"Yoogmor Ozovoz," a voice said, badly mispronouncing his name. "You are under arrest."

He was surprised that the voice was that of a woman.

Kyle Preston pulled the Aramid hood from her head and stared at the bear-like man cowering under the sheets.

"Get out of bed! Stand up!" she said, jerking her head upward.

Ovezov did not understand her words, but her body language was clear. He clambered out of bed, clutching the sheets around his hairy frame.

"Mr. Ozevoov," she said, speaking slowly, "we're with the Federal Bureau of Investigation. My name is Kyle Preston."

"Menya zovut Yagmur Ovezov," he said, pronouncing each syllable distinctly. *"Ya nye panimayu Angliski."*

"He says his name is Yagmur Ovezov and he doesn't understand English," said one of the multilingual Javelin Force specialists.

"Fine," she said. "Then explain to Mr. Ovezov that in the United States, he has certain legal rights. And I have a responsibility to inform him of those rights."

Ovezov tried to pay attention, but his knees were trembling. Could this be about that delivery? Had he done something wrong? His first instinct was to complain that he could not understand the translator and demand to see the Turkmen officials accompanying his team.

Preston finished reading the Miranda rights, which were then translated into Russian, and motioned to him to sit down. She began asking questions.

He did not like sitting in front of this woman with only a sheet pulled around him. And all these other police—they made him nervous. Two were carefully searching the room, and two stood watch, one at the door, the other at the balcony. Ovezov did not know whether to deny everything or to help just a little. Either way, he wanted the protection of the Turkmen delegation. He would have to stall for time.

"Let's start from the beginning," Preston began. "Why don't you tell me about the green case you brought into this country?" She spoke to him directly even though he could not understand more than a word or two. The translator worked very slowly. How did they know about the green case? How had they pinpointed him? Ovezov hoped the astonishment did not show on his face.

"What green case?" he asked.

"Mr. Ovezov, I've reviewed security videotapes of the arrival of the Turkmen team, and I know you personally supervised all the athletic equipment. I also have various scanning images of the contents of that green case."

Ovezov rubbed his eyes and shook his head. The situation was getting stickier, and he needed time to think.

"Yes," he conceded, "I am responsible for the athletic equipment, but I don't know anything about the green case."

"Come on, Mr. Ovezov. Try to remember. A green case. Filled with shot puts. Where is it now?"

"I don't know," he said, wondering whether it would be a good plan to tell the police he had seen the case, but then deny any knowledge of what had become of its contents. He would act just as surprised as anyone that the shot puts were missing or stolen. The problem with that strategy was that these men would at any moment find a wad of U.S. currency in his running shoe under the bed.

"I don't believe you, Mr. Ovezov," Preston said, leaning closer to him. "I know where you have been since you arrived in the United States. And I know what you have been doing. So why don't you come clean? Tell me where the green case is!"

"I don't know," Ovezov said sullenly. He was getting hungry.

Preston pulled up a chair and sat as close to him as possible.

"According to our records, you left the village yesterday at 4:48 P.M. You were gone until 5:35 P.M."

Ovezov had the sinking feeling of being back in the old USSR, where the police were always watching. It was not supposed to be like this in the United States. Here, he had been told, there was unfettered freedom.

As a world-class wrestler, Ovezov knew when a match was over—when he was about to be pinned, when he lacked the strength to come from behind, when he would lose in the end on points. This game was definitely up. The authorities must know what he had done and where he had been. Now all he wanted to do was keep this matter quiet and not bring shame upon his family and his good name. *"Nilzya iz yaichnitzi snova sdelatz yaitzo,"* Ovezov said to Preston.

"That's a Russian saying," the translator explained. "It means you can't unscramble eggs."

"Well, tell him I'll throw him in the frying pan *with* the eggs if he doesn't cooperate."

The translator spoke and Ovezov's eyes widened.

The woman questioner reminded him of a wrestling adversary who never gave up, who attacked relentlessly, who barreled forward again and again. He did not want to answer any more questions until he spoke to Batyr Sardjeev, the leader of the Turkmen Olympic Committee.

Preston studied his expression. She thought she might be losing him, that he might be retreating. Soon he would demand to speak with the Turkmen Olympic officials, and then the diplomats would take over. Turkmenistan would stonewall. Ovezov would be flown back to his country.

"Mr. Ovezov, the American legal system looks kindly on individuals who help with law enforcement efforts. Do you understand me? We need to know where the shot puts in the green case have gone."

One of the Javelin Force specialists walked over to Ovezov and held up a Puma running shoe and a thick roll of green bills.

Ovezov realized it was all over. "I made a delivery to a restaurant," he said. "I don't know anything more."

"What restaurant?" Preston asked.

"The Varsity."

Preston thought it was a strange drop point, but it was unlikely that the frightened Turkmen coach would have made it up.

"How were you contacted?"

"By telephone."

"Who called you here?"

"I was not called here. I was given my instructions back home in Ashkhabad."

"What kind of instructions?"

"The day and date of the delivery. That is all."

"Who told you?"

"A man on the phone."

"Do you know his name or nationality?"

"No. I know nothing more."

"You'll have to come with us," Preston said. "Please get dressed."

Preston walked to the window overlooking the International Festival Zone. Hundreds of athletes in track suits were milling about the plaza. A marching band was playing for a small crowd. The Centennial Games were under way.

And her thoughts were filled with dread.

The fire alarm came straight to the 911 Center in Atlanta's City Hall East on Ponce de Leon Avenue. The center, brand new and filled with the best emergency command and control equipment in the country, was the outgrowth of Chuck Flagg's investigative series in *The Atlanta Journal-Constitution.*

Headlined "911: Every Second Counts," the exposé had revealed that emergency response times in Atlanta were often fatally sluggish. The mayor had been particularly embarrassed by the report since he liked to work on weekends, with plenty of reporters in tow, as a volunteer EMT.

In a partitioned workspace at the center of the room, four fire dispatchers heard the high-pitched alarm coming from the computer console. On a small screen, numbers flashed. Veteran supervisor Norma Ivy recognized the address as she tore the small tape printout from the front of the machine.

She pushed a button on the command console of the new 800-megahertz communications system designed to manage 150,000 emergency unit responses per year. Two low-pitched beeps, the first emergency broadcast of the day, sounded in every fire station in Atlanta.

"Engine 11, Truck 11," Ivy began. "Squad 4, Battalion 3, automatic alarm, 100 Marvin Gardens."

She checked the startled expressions on the faces of the other fire dispatchers as she repeated the command.

"Engine 11, Truck 11, Squad 4, Battalion 3. 100 Marvin Gardens. On the box."

Within ninety seconds, the steel doors of Fire Station 11 rattled open and two red trucks rolled onto North Avenue. First into the street was a Quality/Spartan 1,500 gpm pumper followed by an LTI/Spartan 100-foot ladder truck.

As they headed out on the call, the men and women of Station 11 knew this was no routine errand. Every Olympic site had been allotted a Monopoly board name by the FBI to throw off news hounds and fire freaks who monitored emergency scanners.

Marvin Gardens was the code name for the Georgia Tech Nuclear Research Reactor.

"We've got excitement at the Tech Reactor," Scott Worrell said, punching the keyboard of the VRS 2000 system. "Check out monitors 10, 11, and 12."

Kyle Preston had just returned to the Joint Command Center from the Yagmur Ovezov takedown in the village.

She scanned the bank of TV monitors. On monitor 10, U.S. Army troops climbed into bulky protective suits; on 11, nuclear scientists milled about in the parking lot next to the Georgia Tech Research Reactor; and on 13, two white-coated engineers in the reactor control room pushed buttons and spoke wordlessly.

"Give me audio on 13," Preston instructed Worrell.

He punched a button, and a microphone on the SpeedDome camera in the reactor control room switched on. The operators were speaking excitedly in a technical language that Worrell and Preston did not understand.

On the computer screen, a red icon shaped like a flame was flashing in the center of the Olympic Village.

```
08:35:23
FIRE ANNUNCIATOR
AFD EN ROUTE
G TECH NUCLEAR REACTOR        STORAGE ROOM
900 ATLANTIC AVENUE           OLYMPIC VILLAGE
```

Worrell searched the thick black operations notebook on his desk. He punched instructions into his computer. One floor beneath him in the data center, the IBM mainframe began to record the Sensor ID movements of every person in the village.

"I thought we didn't have any drills scheduled today," Preston said.

"I didn't think so either," Worrell replied.

He checked Olympic Security's daily schedule. There were no training exercises in the village. No emergency practice sessions on the books.

Preston's assistant brought her the Vital Points file on the Neely Nuclear Research Center. She flipped through the pages, refreshing her memory.

The five-megawatt Tech Research Reactor was the second most powerful of its kind in the country. Only the one at the University of Missouri was bigger. The Tech reactor first went on line in 1964 and was used for medical research and to teach the next generation of nuclear scientists.

Preston examined the blueprints of the reactor, located on Atlantic Avenue right next to the Olympic Village in the so-called research zone. She knew it really didn't matter whether the atom splitter was inside or outside the Olympic Village fence. It was like caring whether Chernobyl was inside or outside the Soviet Union. Barbed wire and Dobermans didn't make much difference when it came to radioactive fallout.

The Vital Points file on the Tech Reactor was as thick as the Atlanta Yellow Pages. For five years, the Olympic public safety team had agonized over the unnerving reality that university research reactors like the one at Georgia Tech were wildly underprotected when compared to the security at commercial power plant reactors. In a typical Georgia Power reactor, for instance, there would have been five separate security screens before one could get anywhere near the reactor core. And yet, these commercial reactors were fueled with low-grade uranium, essentially useless in the hands of bomb-makers.

At Georgia Tech, by contrast, the reactor employed highly enriched weapons-grade uranium-235, one of the most fissile materials on earth and a critical ingredient in an atomic bomb. And to get near the core, all one really needed was the key to the front door.

From Day One in Atlanta, Preston had wanted to close down the reactor and ship all the fissile material away. There was already a precedent for this extreme solution: for the Los Angeles Games in 1984, UCLA's 100-kilowatt Argonaut reactor had been decommissioned.

So in May 1996, after years of battles and a lawsuit filed by Georgians Against Nuclear Energy, five kilograms of weapons-grade HEU were removed from the Neely Nuclear Research Center and hauled off to Oak Ridge, Tennessee, for storage.

Unfortunately, in Preston's view, not all of the radioactive stockpile had been transferred from the reactor. In the spent fuel pool, 200,000 curies of cobalt-60 still remained. The maximum allowable exposure for radiation workers to cobalt-60 was *six millionths* of one curie per year.

In *theory*, Preston calculated, that was enough radioactive material to kill every man, woman, and child in the state of Georgia, with plenty left over.

She looked up at the SpeedDome CCTV images of the Neely Center and Atlantic Avenue. The fire trucks were arriving.

"Get Dr. C. K. Trivedi on the line," she said to her assistant standing at the door. "And alert the DOE's Office of Emergency Response."

A fire at the reactor, Preston thought. *Could be worse. Could be a bomb.*

Rome, 1960. One of the most famous moments in Olympic history. Or infamous.

Wim Essejas, an 800-meter runner, is the sole athlete representing Suriname, the tiny republic on the northeast coast of South America. Incredibly, Essejas misses the preliminary trials for his race. When officials go looking for him, they find the runner fast asleep in the Olympic Village. Essejas's main concern: "What are the folks back home going to say?"

Atlanta, 1996. After years dedicated to preparing for this golden sunrise at the Centennial Games, each athlete was wide awake. Everyone in the village could feel the excitement, the anticipation, the hope.

Buddy Crouse wandered around the Festival Zone, a Panasonic camcorder in his hand. A Montana cowboy with a broad smile and long hair to his shoulders, Crouse was twenty-nine, tall, and built like he could hunt bears with a switch. The U.S. captain enjoyed introducing himself to other athletes and soaking in the festive noise, the Olympic flags rippling on every building, the giant balloons in the sky.

A group of Americans sat near the fountain in the center of the plaza, discussing the number of teams representing the former Soviet Union.

"Just imagine," said one American volleyball player. "It's like the United States breaking up into fifty different countries, each with its own Olympic team."

"California would rule!" said a beach volleyball player from Santa Monica. The Atlanta Games were the first to have beach volleyball as a sport. Not surprisingly, every one of the players lived in Southern California.

"Yeah," said another athlete. "I just read in *Sports Illustrated* that in Barcelona, one third of the American medals were won by Californians."

"Let's write the California national anthem," said the beach volleyballer.

Buddy wandered closer to them and broke into song: *"I wish they all could be California girls. . . ."*

The group laughed. Someone slapped him on the shoulder. It was no wonder that Wheaties had already signed Crouse to sell cereal after the Games. If he won gold in Atlanta, Crouse would be a bigger commercial draw than sprinter Carl Lewis and skater Dan Jansen combined. He was every advertiser's dream: handsome, well spoken, and adored by the most important demographic group of all: women ages eighteen to thirty-four.

Crouse moved on, sauntering through the Olympic Village. It was like old Main Street back home in Billings, Montana, with a department store, bank, post office, camera shop, travel agency, hair salon, and newsstand.

"Hey there," Crouse said, greeting three lanky athletes from India. "My name's Buddy Crouse." He pronounced each syllable distinctly.

"Namastay, kya hal hay?" said one of the Indian athletes, who had a long mustache.

"What does that mean?" Crouse asked.

"How the bloody hell are you," the tall athlete answered in an impeccable British accent.

"Hey, you speak English!"

"Of course we do, old chap. Confused us with the natives?"

"No, it's just that—"

"No problem," the Indian said. "My name is Deebal Banerji. I play tennis for India."

"I'm Buddy Crouse, decathlon, USA. Sorry about the misunderstanding. Hey, would you mind saying hi to my grandparents back in Billings? They gave me this camera so I could show them my friends."

The Indian athletes stiffened up and waved into the camera. Crouse thanked them warmly, apologized again for his mistake, and stared behind them across the plaza.

He was watching a tall and graceful woman strolling alone through the arbor of trees. She had long, wavy brown hair and wore a blue-and-white track suit. Crouse did not recognize the team colors but he was determined to meet her. In a variation on the triple jump, he cut between a group of athletes, leaped over a small fountain, and pulled up beside her at an Olympic information kiosk.

"Smile, you're on 'Candid Camera,'" he said, slashing in front of the woman. She looked up at him, stunned, as if he were some crazed fanatic.

"Me American, who you?" he said with a big smile.

Her pulse pounded from the surprise.

"Leila Arens, Israel, shooting," she replied tersely.

"Nice to meet you. I was wondering whether you'd say hi to my grandparents back home in . . ."

Arens saw an opportunity to get a little revenge for his ambush.

"Of course," she agreed, then grabbed the camcorder from his hands and turned the machine on. Taking a few steps back, she began narrating her report.

"This is Jim McKay reporting for ABC," she said in a near-perfect imitation. "We have here Mr. Buddy Crouse, American athlete in the . . ."

"Decathlon," he answered, playing along.

"American athlete Buddy Crouse has high hopes for these Olympic Games. Mr. Crouse, what are your chances of getting the gold?"

Crouse grinned and tried to get the camera back, but she was quick and darted out of his reach. She dodged him as he lunged for her, then she broke into a run. Crouse raced after her across the plaza. He was gaining on her when she came to the perimeter fence on Ferst Drive, where several armed guards stood watch. Crouse caught up with her, panting.

"All force, no finesse," she said, looking him up and down.

"How'd you learn to do such a great impression of Jim McKay?" he asked, catching his breath.

"We *do* have television in Israel, you know."

This is going to take some effort, Crouse thought.

Suddenly Arens stopped playing. Her eyes turned angry and were fixated on eight athletes walking toward her on the sidewalk. Dressed in red, white, green, and black, it was the Palestinian team, the first ever to compete at the Games.

For the first time in Olympic history, athletes from *both* Israel and Palestine were living side by side in the Olympic Village. They were eating in the same cafeteria. They were cutting loose in the same recreation areas. And, most important, they were competing against each other.

As the Palestinian athletes passed Arens, each one gave her a long look. It was not out of admiration for her beauty or her skills with a .22 caliber rifle on the Olympic shooting range.

The Palestinians knew all about the young Israeli athlete and her dead father.

Arens felt her muscles tighten involuntarily. It was the most primal human instinct: fight or flight. Yes, there was peace in the Middle East between Jews and Palestinians, but for Arens, it was different. The scars from Building 31 in Munich had not healed. Now, seeing a group of eight Palestinians parading through another Olympic Village was too much to bear.

Without saying a word to her new American friend, Arens gave the camcorder back to Crouse and took off in a sprint, as if she had seen a ghost.

T he Gulfstream skimmed the flat sheet of clouds spreading to the horizon. The ride was smooth, and McFall rested in a leather seat, his legs propped up on a foot rest. Punching a button on the secure Motorola SECTEL cellular phone, he continued to leaf through a Pentagon briefing book marked "TOP SECRET/OPTIMIZE TALENT" as he waited for the crypto to synchronize.

"National Military Command Center, this is McFall," he said. "I need the latest from Atlanta. Patch me through to the Olympic Joint Command Center."

The pilot opened the cockpit door and pointed downward with his index finger. It was time for the descent into Atlanta.

"Dr. McFall," the operator said, "we've got the JCC on the line. Someone will be with you shortly."

There was a pause, then a familiar voice.

"JCC, this is Kyle Preston."

McFall's chest tightened, and he straightened up in his seat. "Kyle, is that you?"

There was a pause, and the phone buzzed with atmospheric interference. "Mack?" she said, her voice scarcely audible.

There was silence again, then McFall spoke. "God, it's been a long time."

He couldn't tell whether the sound on the other end of the line was intended to be a laugh or a snicker. In 1990, Preston and McFall had met at an FBI counter-terrorism conference at a government compound in the Virginia countryside. At first the sparks were purely cerebral. They sparred amicably at one early morning panel discussion on the threat posed by Pyongyang's nuclear program. At lunch later that day, the intellectual jousting eased into outright flirtation, and they spent the rest of the weekend together playing hooky from the conference proceedings.

"I'm surprised you can even remember," Preston said. Her tone was dry and dismissive.

"Come on, Kyle. I just—"

"Spare me the charm, Mack," she said. "In case you forgot, you couldn't hack it so you split. End of story. So cut the chitchat and stick to business, okay?"

McFall didn't say a word.

"Just tell me what you need," she said.

He thought for a moment. If that's what she wanted, he would play by her rules.

"The latest," he said. "What's the latest?"

"Haven't you been briefed?"

"Not entirely. That's why I'm calling."

"Fine," she said. "We've got forty-eight pounds of plutonium missing. It was smuggled into the Olympic Village right under our noses. And now it's gone. No suspects. Just a few mules, and they aren't talking. We think the plutonium is clad in lead, so we're not hopeful about picking the stuff up with any of your NEST detectors."

McFall ignored the jab.

"What's the threat situation?" McFall asked.

"Nothing surprising. Business as usual for the Olympics. Every political movement in the world is here to make a statement. Can't blame 'em. It's the biggest billboard in the world. Let's see, who've we heard from? Algerian communists. Aryan Nation zealots. Sikh separatists. Tamil Tigers. You name it. We've got a fire at the Georgia Tech Nuclear Research Reactor next to the Olympic Village. And we've got an Arab threat. One of the original Black September plotters from Munich seems to be making his way toward us. He entered the country via Canada and was last seen passing through Detroit."

"And don't tell me, Halley's Comet is going to hit Atlanta any second," McFall joked.

"Cute, Mack, cute. But cut the crap. When do you land?"

"Ten minutes."

"Report to *me* when NEST is up and running," she said and hung up.

McFall put the phone back in its case as the plane made its final approach for landing at Dobbins Air Reserve Station near Marietta. As the plane pointed down toward the runway and its spoilers grabbed the wind, McFall's thoughts returned to the first time he had headed out on a NEST mission.

It was December 1991. Two expressionless Department of Energy officials in virtually identical gray suits and rubber-soled shoes knocked on his office door at the lab. Would he come with them for a few weeks to work on a classified project that could save thousands, even millions, of lives? McFall almost laughed out loud at the notion of saving lives. It was the classic double-speak of nuclear weapons designers who would never think of their handiwork in terms of human carnage and destruction.

Their gadgets could vaporize entire cities in seconds, but the weapons designers spoke of life-saving work: nuclear weapons preserved the peace. He knew that theirs was a willful corruption, a mind game to preserve sanity.

McFall had read the DOE twins to mean they wanted him to develop a new weapon. He had cursorily checked his calendar, studied the lab schedule, and then apologized that he did not have time to spare.

Then one of the men threw a black folder on his desk.

"Take a look," the DOE official said. "We think you'll make time for this."

The black file had ROUND SQUARE printed in bold block letters on the cover. He opened it and read the first few lines:

THIS IS PAGE 1 OF 10 PAGES

OP:	ROUND SQUARE
CLASS:	CODEWORD (MAY POLE)
PRIORITY:	+++ URGENT +++
DATE:	12/16/91

SUMMARY: FOUR KILOGRAMS OF PLUTONIUM REPORTED MISSING FROM LOS ALAMOS NATIONAL LABORATORY. MULTI-PLE BREAKDOWNS IN INTERNAL CONTROLS IDENTIFIED. INTERPOL CHECKING.

CONTACT: MACK MCFALL, DIRECTOR, LANL ADVANCED WEAPONS DESIGN.

"Impossible," McFall said, looking up from the file. "This can't be true."

"If you don't believe us," one of the twins responded tersely, "maybe you'll believe a friend. May I use your phone?"

"Be my guest."

A few minutes later, Lab Director Frank Handlin arrived in McFall's office. His grim face confirmed the story.

"It's gone, Mack, four kilos. Vanished. It looks like an inside job. One of the techs in stockpile support is being interrogated."

"So who's got the stuff?" McFall asked.

"It's probably out of the country by now and on its way to God knows where," a twin answered.

"DOE wants you to get it back," Handlin said.

"Why me?" McFall asked.

"They stole your baby, all four kilos of your experimental pluto-nium mixture," Handlin answered. "You created it, you're the only one who knows its properties, and you're the only one who'll be able to find it."

In minutes, McFall was on his way to the tiny Los Alamos airport, one of the most frightening strips in the West. The 5,500-foot runway was slapped down on a slab of rock jutting out from the Jemez Moun-tains. Where the rock ended, the runway ended. Then came the sheer vertical drop, 750 feet to the floor of the valley.

"Hope no one's expecting you for dinner," a DOE twin had said as the Learjet lifted off over the red rocks and mesas. In less than an hour, they had touched down on Runway 2W at McCarran Interna-tional Airport in Las Vegas.

It was McFall's first flight into the secret world of NEST.

McFall snapped back from the journey in time as the DOD jet touched down on the runway at Dobbins. On three sides, the base was sur-rounded by thick green forest. Twelve F-16 ADF Falcons were parked in neat lines near camouflaged hangars, and two fighters were taxiing to the runway. There were rows of official state aircraft from around the world, flags emblazoned on their tails. McFall's jet taxied to the far edge of the base, where forklifts scurried around NEST's C-141 Starlifter cargo plane.

When the jet door popped open, Kris Aura, a thirty-seven-year-old NEST communications specialist, was waiting at the foot of the ramp. Two gray vans were also idling nearby on the tarmac.

"The team is on standby in the shed," she said, skipping the pleasantries.

"It's nice to see you, too, Kris," McFall joked.

"Sorry, Mack, I just thought you'd want to get straight to business."

"Straight to business?" he said, eyeing her shorts and sneakers. "Looks like you're all dressed for the office."

"Didn't have time to change. I was doing laps at the Y when the call came."

They headed across the asphalt toward an ivy-green hangar.

"Mack, where's your trusty sidekick?" Aura asked.

"Treadwell couldn't make the trip," McFall said. "He's got a med-ical problem."

"Sure hope it's nothing serious," she said.

McFall turned away, focusing on the pallets of equipment in shock-resistant flyaway packs that were being unloaded from the C-141 and put onto Army transport trucks. The gear ranged from state of the art to dime store ordinary. There were highly sensitive radia-tion detectors that could function from any vehicle, and there were detectors that could be hand-carried anywhere concealed in every-day items like leather briefcases, school knapsacks, construction-yard lunch pails, and trendy shoulder bags. And there were disguises aplenty—wigs, makeup, and racks full of costumes.

This was the stock-in-trade of the Nuclear Emergency Search

Team, created by Executive Order 11490 in 1975 with a mission to hunt down stolen or missing nuclear materials or weapons. NEST was the federal government's specially trained nuclear SWAT team, made up almost entirely of volunteers from the DOE's Defense Program and weapons labs. NEST operatives were assigned to identify nuclear terrorism threats, find improvised nuclear devices, disable them, or clean up the mess if one ever went off.

The team's very existence had been a secret for years and was the result of the federal government's near disaster controlling the Boston incident of 1974. On April 26 of that year, Boston Police Commissioner Robert di Grazia received a threat message. "We are taking this opportunity," the note said, "to inform you that a certain quantity of plutonium has fallen into our hands for reasons we don't feel we have to go into." The extortionists threatened to detonate a nuclear device twenty-five times more powerful than Little Boy at Hiroshima unless they were given $200,000 and four tickets to Rome, Italy.

An impromptu team of experts from various federal agencies was cobbled together to find and disable the bomb. Ironically, to keep the operation secret, Griffiss Air Force Base in Rome, New York, was selected as the assembly point. One of the teams, flying commercially, was diverted to another airport. Its luggage, packed with radiation detectors and other search equipment, was lost. The motley team soon found itself racing against the clock without proper tools. Searchers, for instance, did not have drills to install gamma and neutron detectors in rental vans.

"If they were counting on us to save the good folk of Boston," the mission's director recalled in a *New York Times Magazine* interview, "well, it was bye-bye Boston."

In the end, mercifully, the Boston threat proved to be a false alarm. A package of phony money left at the drop site was never picked up. Still, the U.S. law enforcement community was humbled, and President Gerald Ford ordered the creation of a permanent strike team to handle so-called suitcase nuclear threats and atomic emergencies.

By the winter of 1991, NEST had coped with more than 110

threats and hoaxes but never the real thing, a *genuine* nuclear incident. Then, a General Accounting Office audit of the Los Alamos radiological inventory discovered four kilograms of Pu-239 missing.

Within hours of the discovery, McFall was recruited into NEST. The frenzied three-week search for the stolen plutonium took him across the United States, Europe, and North Africa, culminating in a covert Delta Force raid on a French colonial prison-turned-weapons-lab in Fez, Morocco. With each new twist in the hunt, McFall had grown more horrified by the shadowy underworld of nuclear smuggling. In just weeks, he had stumbled across more than half a dozen international plots involving weapons-grade uranium and plutonium.

When he returned from the NEST odyssey, McFall grew impatient with his work. The Iron Curtain was collapsing. Democracy had triumphed over Communism. The future of the U.S. nuclear weapons program was in doubt. And McFall could not stop thinking about what he had seen in the nuclear netherland.

Unless thwarted, atomic smugglers would undermine America's hard-fought Cold War victory and destabilize the precarious global balance. But McFall knew the United States did not have the special military capability needed to hunt down and take out nuclear terrorists.

And so one morning McFall went to work early, cleared off his desk, and typed a one-sentence resignation letter. He reported for duty the next day at Fort Bragg to help the Joint Special Operations Command train its shooters to fight nuclear terrorists.

McFall made his way with Kris Aura to the corner of the hangar, where thirty NEST volunteers, who had been waiting on folding chairs, rose to greet him. Staff employees of the DOE's Weapons Program, they had all worked together most recently in October 1994 on Operation MIRAGE GOLD, a massive counter-terrorism exercise in New Orleans involving a search for three fake nuclear warheads hidden on ships in the harbor.

At an easel with butcher block paper, McFall began the NEST deployment briefing. "The facts are pretty sketchy at this point," he said, "but here's what we're looking for: three or four Pu-239 pits. They're probably hollow spherical shells about four inches in diameter and one inch thick. They've got nickel, aluminum, or steel plating or cladding."

McFall jotted a few key notes on the easel. "Here's the kicker," he said. "We believe the pits were smuggled into the United States disguised as track and field shot puts. Now, does anyone have a guess about what kind of signature those things are kicking off right now?"

The room was silent, for every NEST volunteer knew that Pu-239 in thick cladding would not give off much detectable radiation, if any.

But it was not exactly a surprise. It was one of the realities of the counter-terrorism community. If drug smugglers hid their shipments in lead-lined containers impervious to X-ray detection, why wouldn't nuclear terrorists?

"Here's what I want to do," McFall said. "Team 1 sets up the Tactical Operations Center right here. Team 2 implements standard ground-search protocols. I'm going with Team 3 in the 105-C to update the background map of metro Atlanta. Kris, when was the last time we did a base case mosaic?"

"Six weeks ago," Aura responded. "We've got a benchmark survey from June 4."

"Good. Then we'll be able to track changes."

McFall scanned the faces of the NEST volunteers. "Hey, folks," he said, "don't look so discouraged. The bad guys are going to have to take the Pu-239 out of the cladding at some point. And that's when we'll have our best shot."

He paused for a moment, massaging his forehead with his hand. "Now folks, as you can tell, this ain't no training run. It goes without saying, but if anyone wants out, please tell me now. I don't want folks with second thoughts heading into Atlanta."

Not a whisper could be heard. Nor was there a smile in sight. The men and women of NEST, volunteers all, were there for their country. There was not a chance any one of them would back out now.

"Turn that goddamn thing off," Dr. C. K. Trivedi shouted at the Georgia Tech security guard. Sonny Minchin dutifully switched off his black-and-white television. His hands were shaking, and his blue uniform was stained with sweat.

"Not the television, idiot! The siren. Turn off the siren!"

Minchin nodded and lumbered down the hall. He was followed by three firefighters wearing oxygen tanks. Minchin had no desire to go anywhere near the alarm controls in the back of the Georgia Tech Nuclear Research Reactor. That meant getting near the spent fuel room and fissile stockpile. Thanks, but no thanks.

Trivedi, the fifty-six-year-old, gray-bearded director of the Neely Nuclear Research Center, turned and headed for the second floor. The Atlanta Fire battalion chief followed him to the control room, which overlooked the reactor core and resembled a 1950s sci-fi movie set. The stainless steel instrumentation had not been changed in thirty years.

Flora Raynor, the senior reactor operator on duty, was sitting at the main control console, studying the dials and gauges. A thirty-six-year-old nuclear engineer with meticulously braided hair, Raynor had been asleep, actually snoring, when the fire annunciators first sounded.

"What have we got?" Trivedi asked, pulling on his long beard.

"Can't really tell," Raynor responded. "We've got an alarm in the storage room."

"How's the temperature in the core?"

"Cool as a cuke," she replied. "Scrammed the reactor as soon as the bells went off."

"How's the deuterium in the water?"

"Steady."

"Radiation?"

"Level."

"Have you reset the annunciator?"

"No," she replied.

"Give it a try," he said.

Raynor flipped a switch, deactivating the alarm. Three seconds later, the annunciator flashed again. From the warning console, it certainly appeared there was a fire in the storage room, next to the reactor core.

Trivedi studied the dials. Something was definitely not right about the alarm. His eyes fixed on the gauge measuring bromofreon in the automatic fire-extinguishing system. The pressure level had not changed.

"What've we got in the storage room?" he asked Flo Raynor.

"Plutonium, some tritium, cobalt, cesium, and some—"

Trivedi was already out the door, heading down the lime-green hallway on a hunch.

Hands shaking, C. K. Trivedi stared through the wire reinforced window of the storage room door.

He had been right. His surmise had been dead on.

There had been no fire in the reactor. Instead, on the steel wall at the far end of the small storage room, he could see a black canister with a flashing red light. The device had an LED monitor mounted on top.

The liquid energy display read 00:40:25, and it was counting down.

Trivedi reached for the building evacuation alarm next to the storage room door and, for the first time in his thirty years at the reactor center, forced the handle down as far as it would go.

Almost instantly, a computer-generated voice could be heard in every room of the building: "Evacuate immediately. Evacuate immediately."

The fire alarm had cleared almost everyone from the facility, but he had to be sure. Longtime staff like Flora Raynor in the control room usually ignored practice drills. Now she bolted upright as the overhead speaker barked the order to get out. It was the first time she had ever heard the evacuation command. In drills, the halting, computer-generated voice had always calmly announced: "This is a test. Please evacuate."

Raynor grabbed her bag and headed for the stairs. She almost collided with Trivedi, who was racing down the steps from the floor above.

"What's going on?" she shouted.

"There's an FO with a flashing red light in the storage room. Not sure what it is, but it could be—"

In atom-speak, FO meant foreign object. And before he finished his sentence, Raynor leaped down the last three steps and was out the door and into the parking lot.

T he Dodge Ram 1500 chugged down I-20 East in the slow lane. Quinn Lazare checked his speedometer. He was traveling sixty-three miles per hour, just below the posted speed limit.

Then he glanced at the rearview mirrors. He was watching for the metallic blue cruisers of the State Patrol, but there was not a cop in sight.

Georgia's highways and byways were swarming with law enforcement officers deployed to handle Olympic traffic and security. For the fine men and women of the State Patrol, the herds of visiting motorists presented both headaches and opportunities. Coping with the endless onslaught of vehicles meant long hours on the road with no time off. But with just a few weeks of effort, they could meet their ticket-writing quotas for the entire summer. No one shook a stick at that kind of providence.

Lazare looked out across the horizon—mile after mile of dust. He had made it most of the way across Georgia. Now he would stay on I-20 past Augusta into South Carolina, then from Columbia follow I-77 into North Carolina.

It was the long way. But it was safer.

The black leather bag was tucked under his seat, and he could not resist reaching down to check that it was secure. It was an irrational act, unbefitting his elaborately disciplined analysis and planning over the past twelve months.

For more than a year, he had anticipated every imaginable scenario. Drafting the plans was like designing a microelectronic circuit board. Every piece had a place, every wire a voltage, every question an answer.

With enough thought, even random variables no longer seemed random.

Now, suddenly, with his radioactive prize stowed beneath his seat, all those scenarios were no longer hypothetical. They were happening in real time.

The muscle in his right eye convulsed, and he breathed faster. Lazare was becoming physically aroused. The danger, the closeness to the precipice, thrilled him. *Cool down*, he told himself. *No time to lose control.*

Getting into the Tech Reactor had been a relative cinch. Flashing Rebecca Deen's ID cards to several sleepy Olympic sentries, he had breezed past two checkpoints, planted the crude device, and slipped away.

He flipped on the radio, half-hoping there would be a breathless announcer describing an unfolding emergency at the Georgia Tech Research Reactor. But he knew the FBI would do its damnedest to prevent a story of this magnitude from ever reaching the public. He found the all-news station, 640 AM, on the dial. A reporter was summarizing a small item in *Nature* on the accuracy of time-keeping devices used at the Olympics. The author of the article, an Indian physicist named Ramanand Jha, was being interviewed. "Olympic racers start running *after* they hear a pistol shot," Jha declared. "If the speed of sound is 1,100 feet per second and the starting line is at least 10 to 15 feet wide, all athletes do *not* hear the pistol shot at precisely the same moment."

Jha rushed to the conclusion of his argument. "An athlete in lane eight hears the shot two-hundredths of a second *later* than an athlete in lane one. Olympic races are often decided by time differences of a hundredth of a second, so how can anyone be sure the fastest runner gets the gold medal?"

Intriguing, Lazare thought. It posed a problem not unlike those he analyzed and conquered in his own line of work. Without any searching or warning, his brain brought up of one of Albert Einstein's well-known thoughts about relativity.

"Do not worry about your problems with math," Einstein once told an audience of college undergraduates. "I can assure you that mine are far greater."

Olympic timekeepers dealt in increments of one hundredth of a second. And the distances involved hundreds, even thousands of meters. Nuclear physicists, by contrast, dealt in nanoseconds, or billionths of a second. And the distances involved angstroms, one ten-billionth of a meter.

All problems are relative.

Lazare checked his rearview mirrors again and saw two men on motorcycles gaining on him fast. His pulse rose.

The men flashed their headlamps three times in a prearranged signal. He responded, pumping his brakes in three short bursts. Then he accelerated back to sixty-three miles per hour.

The winding two-lane blacktop led up the hill through the low rolling mountains of the Uwharrie National Forest in North Carolina. Lazare's truck moved slowly up the twisting road.

The ride had taken longer than expected. But ever since his brief encounter with two undercover security officers at Hartsfield International, he had been even more obsessive about covering his tracks.

Along the drive east, he stopped a half-dozen times, doubling back ten or fifteen miles, always checking to see if anyone was following. Lazare was not schooled in the trade-craft of evasion, but he had picked up a few tricks from television and the movies.

Short-leaf pine trees now lined both sides of the forest road. He had not seen another car in more than thirty minutes.

Lazare pulled to the shoulder and waited. The two men on motorcycles wheeled around the curve in the road and approached him. They had been following all the way across Georgia, dropping back and then catching up again, providing rear guard protection. It was not a well-choreographed dance, but it worked.

"All clear," one of the cyclists said as he pulled up next to Lazare's open window.

"See you in the Hole," Lazare said, pulling back onto the road.

The narrow road continued up through the hills. Lazare drove the ten miles, calculating how he could make up some of the lost time.

On the side of the road, Lazare passed two mountain bikers fixing a flat tire. Up ahead, he saw the turnoff and slowed down. He pulled onto the red clay shoulder and hopped down from the truck. The rusting iron gate had a weather-warped, hand-painted sign hanging from one post. It said OPAL CREEK.

Lazare spun the dial on the combination lock and pushed the gate open.

Then he whistled three times. The notes were short and soft.

From the forest, the response came back as gently: three whistles.

Lazare jumped back in the truck and drove into the woods. The curving dirt road led up the side of a hill. There were heavy boulders on both sides of the track. The thick forest canopy blocked most of the light. Lazare tried to keep his wheels in the wide grooves that had been hard-packed by logging and mining trucks moving in and out. Lazare breathed deeply. The raw smell of cut wood and diesel exhaust filled the air.

At the crest of the hill, the road emerged from the old growth forest and opened onto a sweeping vista of the Uwharrie, located on the eastern edge of the Piedmont and bordering the sandhill portion of North Carolina. The 50,000-acre National Forest was first known as Uharie, a word supposedly uttered by German settlers that meant "new home."

Lazare looked across several valleys and examined the dark swatches where trees had been clear-cut. They were like ugly brown stains on a green quilt. The Uwharrie had been heavily logged, and the scars of slashing and burning stretched to the horizon.

He turned right at a fork in the road and dropped down into a narrow dried-out riverbed slicing through a steep gorge. On both sides there were the remnants of abandoned mining shafts, holes buttressed by logs carved into the rock. Rusty trails of runoff from the shafts had dripped and dried on the sides of the gorge.

With the rocky walls mere inches from the truck on both sides, Lazare crept along the riverbed for half a mile before the path opened into a small valley. Pulling to a stop in a clearing where other cars and trucks were parked, Lazare got out and hoisted the leather bag over his shoulder. The wind whipped down the valley and bent the trees. Lazare surveyed the camp; not a soul stirred.

With its haphazard piles of logs, slag heaps, and heavy logging machinery, Opal Creek had the rugged look of any of the old mining or logging camps in the Uwharrie. Rows of dilapidated wood shacks stood partially hidden by pine trees, and a few tin chimneys spouted drifts of smoke. The well-used equipment lying around—buzz saws, drills, and sifters—gave the impression of a genuine operation to any Forest Service Ranger who happened by. The only tip-offs to the special project underground were the humming, camouflaged diesel generators near one of the mining shafts.

Lazare ducked into a dark tunnel cut into the rock. The smell of wet earth made his eyes water. He came to a thick metal door, which he kicked with his boot. A small window slid open, and Lazare could see an eyeball. "Let me in," Lazare said impatiently.

"Password," the eyeball said.

"It's *me*, you imbecile!"

"Password," the eyeball said again.

"Gone with the wind," Lazare said huffily.

The door creaked open. Eyeball stood on the other side, wearing green military fatigues and brandishing a Mossberg 500 shotgun.

Lazare passed by without saying a word and headed further into the dank shaft. A string of lightbulbs in little metal cages ran the length of the tunnel, glowing in the mist. He stopped at an iron ladder that descended farther into darkness. He shifted the weight of the black bag to his other shoulder, then clambered down the hole.

Moments later, he emerged in a vast cavern brilliantly illuminated with mercury vapor lights dangling from the ceiling. Rough concrete paved the floor. Two rows of makeshift laboratory benches stretched the length of the space. Piles of electronic equipment and a few pieces of heavy machinery lined the edges.

No doubt about it, the Hole did not look like a weapons factory. And it definitely did not look like a *nuclear* weapons factory. It was about as far from the sterile environs of Los Alamos or Sandia or Lawrence Livermore as one could imagine. No air conditioners. No stainless steel or linoleum. No sophisticated security or emergency equipment.

Jerry-rigged as it was, however, the Hole had what it needed.

Three men in green military fatigues looked up from their work as Lazare strode to the center of the room. "Gather 'round," he said.

Lazare stepped up on a small wood crate, flashed a self-satisfied smile, and began. "Friends, the first mission is a success." He paused and studied the expectant faces of his small, hand-picked team. "In this black bag," he said, reaching back with his left hand to pat it, "we have what we have been waiting for!"

Lazare allowed himself a moment of satisfaction as the men exchanged high fives.

"We're going to have plenty of time to celebrate," Lazare said. "Right now, we have a lot to do."

Self-consciously, the team settled down.

"Where do we stand, Shakes?" Lazare asked, turning to Gus Rybak, his deputy.

"We're . . . we're . . . we're ready to go," Rybak said. He was a short man with a square chest like a big sandbag. Long ago, his little sister had given him the nickname, Shakes, an affectionate, if blunt, recognition that he suffered from Tourette's syndrome, the neurological disorder marked by multiple motor and vocal tics.

He was certainly an unlikely terrorist, and Lazare had chosen him for this very reason. Rybak's periodic bouts of eye blinking, scratching, sniffing, whistling, and cursing were a perfect cover. His obscene gestures and outbursts of profanity were a distraction, diverting attention from the fact that he was up to no good.

For Rybak, the compulsions and wild excitements of Tourette's syndrome were compensated for by enhanced reflexes and agility of reaction and thought that were truly impressive and at times even diabolical.

"The assembly line is geared up," Rybak said, clawing at his chest. "The precision machining is done. And the chemicals are all measured and waiting to be mixed."

"Well, here's what you've been waiting for," Lazare said, reaching into the black bag. He pulled out one of the Turkmen shot puts and tossed it to Rybak, who caught it with both hands, cradling it like a newborn baby.

The sixteen-pound ball was slightly warm to the touch. Inside the cladding, the Pu-239 was decaying, creating heat that warmed the exterior. Rybak held the ball up to the light, feeling the warmth and power inside. He grinned, then grimaced, his face and neck flush red.

"Where are the action teams?" Lazare asked, interrupting Rybak's pleasure.

"Sapelo Team is in position," Rybak said. "The boats are ready, and they are awaiting the shipment. Sherman Team is on the ground, monitoring ground zero. And Mooney Team is tooling up."

"Good," Lazare said. He took the shot put from Rybak and rolled it back and forth between his hands.

"Okay, let's continue. What do Eyes and Ears know? Darren?"

Darren Dunn was the team's thirty-eight-year-old security specialist. A former Army intelligence officer, he was pale with hollow cheeks and had a two-fingered claw for a right hand. It had been mangled in an accidental bomb-making explosion in his basement. When surgeons reconstructed it with a rib and cartilage removed from his back, Dunn insisted they use a handgun as a mold so that he would still be able to defend himself.

"All clear," Dunn said. "There's been increased activity around the Olympic Village. Hard to tell if it's part of routine ramping up for the Games or whether there's been a threat or incident."

"What about outside the Village?" Lazare asked. He wanted to assess how good a monitoring job his team was doing.

"We've picked up something around the Centers for Disease Control," Dunn said. "Our sources don't have specifics, but there was a big deployment of special teams. Then it all went away very fast."

"Good work," Lazare said. The intelligence net was working well. His team knew about the CDC incident when 15,000 reporters from the international and national press did not have a clue.

"What about the Hole? Any snoopers?"

"No surveillance," Dunn said. "There've been a few hikers in the area, and a few small aircraft flying over. But nothing suspicious. We've got people on the mountain disguised as campers and loggers. We'll know if the law is coming."

Lazare could feel the excitement in the air, but his instincts warned him that something was not being said. He trusted this sixth sense, this radar. It had enabled him to survive for the past five years.

"Something's wrong," he said. "I can feel it. Shakes, I want a full report, now!"

It was not the first time that Rybak had experienced Lazare's instinctive assessment of the vibrations around him. He sometimes feared his boss had spies.

"We had a problem at the airport," Rybak said, scratching his chest vigorously, his voice uncertain.

"What kind of problem?"

"Everything went as planned with the baggage, but the team had to eliminate one of the airport guards."

"Why?" Lazare could feel his anger building. He had forbidden unnecessary killing.

"We don't have details. The team was behind you all the way home, so they should be here soon."

"This doesn't make me happy," Lazare said, stepping off of the crate and moving across the lab. With one arm, he smashed a row of glass beakers.

"This isn't the right answer, is it?" he screamed, turning and staring at his men. "Who gives the orders here? I do! And I said no unnecessary killing! And if you have to rough someone up or kill them, I want to be told right away."

Rybak's face twitched. He averted his eyes and the men were silent.

"I have given you more power than you could ever want! I have given you the ability to make nuclear weapons. And what do you do? You withhold information from me. And you don't execute your orders precisely. What kind of respect is that? Is that any way to show your appreciation?"

Again, there was silence.

"If I choose, there will be *no* nuclear devices made in this lab.

There will be no fun and games. There will be no final reckoning with the United States. There will be nothing! And you will all be nothing! Nothing!"

Lazare could feel himself losing control, losing *all* control, losing control the way he did when the DOE came to tell him his secret research project was being terminated, losing control the way he felt when he was let go from Los Alamos, losing control the way he felt when the FBI came after him for trying to sell some of his nuclear knowledge to interested parties in the Middle East.

He reached into a pocket and pulled out the bottle of Thorazine. He jammed two of the antipsychotic tranquilizers in his mouth, swallowed hard, and tried to catch his breath.

The men behind him were motionless, speechless.

When he dared speak, Lazare turned again and in a cool, controlled voice gave his orders.

"We're going to speed up the schedule. We can't take chances anymore. By now, they must be looking for the missing materials. And if a body turns up at Hartsfield, some lucky cop might make a connection between the events."

He paused, studying the young militia men before him. They had never been involved in a project like this. They had been hand-picked from more than 500 applicants. To preserve secrecy around the mission, they had never been told precisely what they would be doing. Just like the U.S. weapons labs, everything in the Hole was handled on a *need to know* basis. Lazare made sure all information was carefully compartmentalized. Everyone had a piece of the action, but no one knew the entire plan. That way, Lazare had complete control. And there was a lower risk of leaks.

"We have twenty-four hours to finish our work here. I want shifts going around the clock. The devices must be ready."

"Twenty-four hours seems a little—" Rybak began.

Lazare shot him a stare. "Do you have a problem with twenty-four hours?"

"No, it just seems like a rush."

"The fireworks will start early," Lazare said. "And that's final."

There was silence as the troops took in their leader's words.

"You can do it," he said passionately. "When I met you a year ago, some of you were still building militia bombs in your basements with ammonium nitrate and fuel oil. All you had was cow manure and gasoline!"

He looked at the men contemptuously. "I have given you power you never dreamed of, raw power you cannot even imagine, true power that transcends the universe. I have given you the power of the sun and the stars!"

He paused, breathing rapidly. "I have given you the power to achieve real parity with the U.S. government."

There was a glimmer of recognition in the eyes of the men, and Lazare pressed the point further.

"Do you even know the meaning of parity? Do you think you will ever be able to defend yourselves and your families against the government with your AR-15s? Do you think handguns will protect you from the black helicopter gunships of the United Nations? Do you think Molotov cocktails will stop M1-A1 tanks?"

Lazare knew he was hammering their hot buttons. This was red meat for these zealots. Of course, he did not believe a word of it, but his men were eating it up.

"Men, real parity with the government cannot be achieved with mail-order weapons and homemade bombs. We can *never* protect ourselves, our wives, and children with conventional weapons. We are outnumbered and outgunned."

Lazare raised his fist in the air for the coup de grace.

"But from this day forward, the balance of power will change!"

The words were scoring. Spirits were lifting. Lazare could feel the surging energy in the air.

"Friends, true parity can be achieved only with nuclear weapons. Yes, true parity can be won only with Red Mercury."

Lazare could feel the words spilling from his mouth. It was intoxicating, this feeling of real power. Now he was believing what he was saying.

"Yes, parity will be ours in only a matter of days. By the end of this week, the world will have to take notice. They will have no choice. They will have to listen to us. For we will own the ninth most powerful nuclear arsenal in the world!"

Officially, there were only five declared nuclear weapon states in the world: the United States, Britain, France, China, and the former Soviet Union. Unofficially, three other states—India, Israel, and Pakistan—were also known to have the bomb.

Each man ran the numbers through his head and knew Lazare was right. They had enough fissile material to make at least five nuclear devices, catapulting this ragtag underground minimilitia into the world's most rarefied club.

T he man trudged with exaggerated steps down the hallway, like an astronaut on the ramp to the space shuttle. Suited up in ninety-six pounds of full body armor, the 52nd Army EOD bomb disposal technician hoped he wouldn't melt before he reached the storage room of the Tech Nuclear Research Reactor.

It had to be a hundred degrees in the frag suit, and he only had a few more minutes before heat exhaustion would overwhelm him.

"Thirty feet," Staff Sergeant Milo Rosen said into the headset mike of his Aramid helmet.

"We see you," Preston said into the speakerphone on the JCC conference table. A wobbly black-and-white image from the video camera on Rosen's helmet filled the pull-down screen.

"Fifteen feet," Rosen said, moving toward the storage room door.

Thirty-three years old with red curly hair, Rosen had fiddled with all sorts of bombs since his teenage days making and selling July Fourth fireworks in Brooklyn. Now, he was a proud card-carrying member of FVA, Future Vapor of America, the informal professional association of explosive ordnance disposal technicians. His mother, Estelle, had not been entirely pleased with her son's career choice, but she was proud of the framed service awards he sent home every year.

Nothing scared Milo Rosen, not C4, not TNT, not PEMT; nothing, that is, except radiation. He had survived a stick of dynamite exploding right in his lap, and a parcel bomb had knocked him flat on his back and left him babbling like a baby for a week, but he had never come face-to-face with hot stuff. For EOD techs, radioactive materials were like kryptonite. Even if you survived the blast, the invisible particles would get you later.

And yet here he was, heading for the storage room in the Tech reactor. For this run, he was fully loaded. His bomb suit was made of Aramid fiber, a bullet-resistant material similar to Kevlar. Fire-resistant Nomex and other antistatic fibers protected the outer shell from bomb fragments. Kevlar protective shields were inserted into the inner lining of the suit.

Rosen approached the fuel room door and looked through the small glass window. With a Kodak throwaway camera, he took several pictures for his personal scrapbook. This was a definite first, a bomb in a nuclear reactor. Next, with a Nikon autofocus 35-200-mm zoom, he took crime scene pictures of the black cylindrical device on the far wall of the storage room. Looking through the viewfinder, he could see the LED counter.

"19:23 and still ticking," Rosen said.

"19:23," Preston repeated, checking her watch.

"Looks like a bangalore," he said. "The pipe is around eighteen inches long, probably packed with TNT or dynamite."

"Milo, how does the foundation look?"

"Storage room walls are made of thick steel. The entire building is encased in concrete. The device is probably too small to cause much damage."

"How can you tell?" Preston asked.

"It's just a guess. But from here, it looks like a firecracker in a parking garage. It'll make a lot of noise, but it won't destroy much."

Rosen set up a tripod next to the door, locked a Sony Hi-8 camera into the mount, and moved back down the hallway, unrolling video cable from a spindle.

"Stand by, Milo. We'll be right back," Preston said, hitting the intercom button for Scott Worrell in the VRS 2000 Room.

"Scott, I need an exterior shot of the Neely Nuclear Research Center."

The video image on the conference room screen split in half: Rosen's view of the reactor hallway appeared on one side; and on the other, there was an outdoor picture of the Neely Center as the remote-controlled camera panned down Atlantic Avenue, a quaint, tree-lined street that cut through the heart of the Tech campus.

"Thank God there are no TV trucks or reporters," Preston said.

"So far, so good," said Frosty Cornell of the APD. "Streets have been cordoned off. We've got guards dressed as Olympic hospitality staff at each of the corners blocking all traffic. And we've got press aides waiting in the van to deflect any inquiring minds who want to know. They've got generic press releases written months ago describing a 'false alarm' in the kitchen."

"Pretty clever," Preston said.

The image on the screen changed again. This time, U.S. Army Captain Henry Bultena appeared full face, staring into the camera.

"Building evacuated," Bultena reported, beads of sweat dripping from his brow.

"Captain, Kyle Preston here. How did this happen?"

"Don't know yet, ma'am. We're looking into it."

"Who had access to the building last night or this morning?"

"Still checking. At present, all personnel are accounted for."

"Thanks, Captain. Keep us posted."

The young Army captain vanished from the screen. Cornell hit a switch on the conference table console to speak to Milo Rosen.

"Milo, what do the X-rays show?"

Rosen had moved 100 feet down the hall, away from the storage room. He pulled the helmet from his head and flipped it around so the camera pointed toward him.

"Hi there," he said, looking into the lens. His boyish face, scarred by a two-inch skin graft on his right cheek, filled the screen. "We don't have X-rays yet. The shooter is on her way up."

"How long will it take?" Cornell asked.

"We'll scan the device and have it out of here in fifteen minutes," he said. "That'll leave plenty of time to run like hell if we're wrong. This is the Olympics, right? Most of the people around here can do four-minute miles!"

In a corner of the 52nd EOD's air-conditioned bomb truck parked outside the front door of the Neely Nuclear Research Center, a technician worked the instruments on the mobile X-ray processing machine. She was specially trained to develop film in sixty seconds, and this time she beat the clock. In just forty-five seconds, a dark image began to form on the acetate, like black thunder clouds in the afternoon sky.

Holding it up to the light box, the tech knew the X-ray would not be good news for the explosives team. She headed to the back door of the truck and pushed it open.

Rosen was sitting on the curb, gulping down Powerade. His bomb suit had been like a sauna, and he was sure he had lost a few pounds during his ten minutes in the reactor. Dehydration was far more dangerous than most of the gadgets he had encountered.

"It's ready," the tech said, handing the black-and-white plastic sheet to Rosen. He held it to the sunlight. Both the image of a cylinder and a small rectangle appeared matte white on a pitch-black background. A few wiry laces connected the cylinder to the box.

"Useless," Rosen said, handing it back to her. "The casing is made of lead. We'll have to go in blind."

He turned to his deputy. "Tell Andros we won't be needing him today."

Andros was the 52nd EOD's 700-pound remote-controlled robot who could maneuver on slopes as demanding as forty-five degrees, climb stairs, and clear obstacles up to two feet high. His mighty electronic arm extended five feet horizontally and nine feet above the ground. The claw at the end of his arm was ideal for grabbing things but was not adequate for more delicate manipulations. In this situation, where the radiological materials in the storage room were far more dangerous in an explosion than the bomb itself, there was no margin for error. Andros just didn't have the light touch.

Suited up again in full kit and towing what looked like a metal bucket on wheels, Rosen marched back to the storage room in the reactor.

The LED read 00:13:12.

Up close, Rosen saw that the gadget was quite straightforward— timer, connector, and explosive. In the movies, the daring technician snipped the green wire at the last possible second, the ticking clock stopped, and the credits rolled.

That scene always ruined the film's suspense for Rosen. Real life was much more complicated. Here, there was no way he could look inside this device to see how it was packed. The first thing he had to do was get it off the wall and into the netting inside the twenty-gallon containment vessel made of reinforced fiberglass.

On the street in front of the Neely Research Center, a bigger bomb container was ready. It was a four-wheeled trailer built to withstand the blast from a case of dynamite. The 52nd EOD and the Atlanta Police Department were on standby to move the device away from the Olympic Village and heavily populated downtown. They had mapped out the route to Maddox Park off Bankhead Avenue in West Atlanta. It was a big park with enough open space, if necessary, to detonate a bomb. An Atlanta PD squad car had already timed the route. It would take six minutes at sixty-five mph, and police officers had cleared a path through downtown.

Inside the building, Rosen muttered a quick prayer before putting his left gloved hand on the metal device. It was a simple invocation. *God watch over me.*

Then he tugged gently on the bomb, at the same time using a plastic wedge to lift the magnets away from the wall. He could feel his carotid artery pounding, and for a moment he felt dizzy. The LED kept counting. It was a good sign. If it had stopped, it probably would have meant the cylinder was packing a motion detector.

Not this time, Rosen thought. *Another day for the FVA.*

The device was heavier than he had guessed, and he put it carefully into the containment vessel. Then he spun around to give a vigorous thumbs-up signal to the EOD tech crouching 100 feet down the hall and watching him through binoculars.

Rosen headed for the elevator, pulling the containment vessel like a little Radio Flyer wagon. "I'm coming down," he said into his helmet microphone. "Seven minutes and counting."

Their eyes fixed to the video feed from Rosen's helmet-cam projected on the conference room screen, Preston and Cornell applauded and exchanged high fives.

With all the backslapping and self-congratulation, no one even noticed the frozen video image on the screen. Rosen had stopped dead in his tracks in the gloomy hallway of the reactor. The audio feed from his headset had been switched off in the Joint Command Center.

Only Milo Rosen of the FVA could hear the shrill beeping in the bomb containment vessel.

Donny Sanders was letting it all hang out. All of it, including every last expletive. He had blown a gasket when he got the message about the loose nukes *and* the situation at the Tech reactor. He had slipped out of the umpteenth Ritz-Carlton breakfast reception for the International Olympic Committee pooh-bahs and had headed straight for the Fish Bowl at the Joint Command Center.

On the wall above the conference table, a red digital chronometer flashed the local time. Next to it, the words THREAT LEVEL: BLACK RING appeared on a digital readout.

Conceived by French baron Pierre de Coubertin, the Olympic rings—blue, yellow, black, green, and red—symbolized the five equal, interdependent, and harmonious continents of the world. But in the JCC, they carried a more ominous meaning. Each one represented a different state of security readiness. Blue Ring signified the third highest level, like DEFCON 3 at the Pentagon. Red was the second highest.

"Black Ring!" Sanders was shouting. "Black frigging Ring! We haven't had one of these since Munich 1972. What the hell are we going to do? What about my Games?"

Sanders was definitely a maniac about the Olympics. In fact, behind his back, ACOG staffers called him King Donny. It was an ironic salute to the famed moment in 1912 when King Gustav V of Sweden told Jim Thorpe, the Olympic decathlon champion: "Sir, you are the greatest athlete in the world." To which Thorpe said: "Thanks, King."

There was little doubt that King Donny expected to be treated like an absolute monarch and, even more important, to be able to *act* like one. This narcissistic tirade was yet another reminder. He had stormed right into the Fish Bowl, ignoring the fact that Preston and Cornell were preoccupied with the bomb situation at the Tech reactor.

"Mother of Mary!" he was screaming. "There're fire trucks and police cars all over Atlantic Avenue. It looks like a traffic jam at a goddamn National Guard weekend exercise. And it's going to ruin everything!"

Appalled, Preston watched Sanders spin further and further out of control. Because he had been her father's college football pal, for two years she had silently suffered his patronizing lectures and chauvinistic slaps. But the dreaded moment would come when an actual emergency required that she take charge of the situation, the moment when Sanders—all 245 pounds of him—would have to be sacked.

"Donny, calm down," Preston said. "We're managing the reactor crisis right now. And we're following SOP protocols—"

"For chrissakes, Kyle," Sanders interrupted, "this isn't the Normandy invasion. I want everyone pulled out of there right now! Leave the EOD team inside, but yank everyone else out. Now!"

"No way," Preston said firmly.

"You and your General Schwarzkopf routine are pissing me off," Sanders said. "I've got a show to put on! Thousands of athletes and press are crawling all over Georgia Tech. And I don't want anyone stumbling on this."

"We've got it under control," Preston said. "We've got people—"

"Just do as I say, Kyle," he said, cutting her off again. "Pull the lights and sirens out right quick. We don't need a disturbance. Just let the Games go on."

Preston was fighting to stay in control. "Donny, I can't do that."

"Listen, girl, I've known you since you were knee high to a grasshopper in Macon. That was a long time before you ever became a big skirt with the FBI. So don't go telling me what you can and can't do."

Preston took a deep breath. "You're making this a lot rougher than it has to be, Donny. But face the facts: *these aren't your Games anymore.*"

It was simple and direct, perhaps a bit harsh, but to the point. Donny Sanders and ACOG were the proud hosts of the Summer Games. But with forty-eight pounds of plutonium on the loose in

Atlanta and a bomb ticking near the Olympic Village, Sanders was no longer in charge.

These aren't your Games anymore. Sanders replayed Preston's words in his head. His face twisted into a contorted expression. It was as if the words had fried the circuits in his head.

"What the hell do you mean by that?" Sanders yelled, standing up at the conference table. He still threw his gridiron frame around to score points.

"I mean this is a federal emergency, and we have experts to call the shots," Preston said, both fists on the marble countertop.

"Over my dead body, *girl*," Sanders said, stabbing the air desperately. He looked to the men around the table for backup, but their eyes were fixed on their laps.

"Back off, Donny," she fired back. "Nuclear terrorism is a federal crime under Title 18, United States Code Section 831 (a) (6). Even *threatening* to use an atomic device is a felony. So you can yell and scream all you want, but this is out of your league. *We're in charge here.*"

The words landed like a cluster bomb, but Sanders was still standing. "Well, if it isn't Miss Alexandra Haig! You're in charge here? I say bullshit. These are *my* Games and you're not going to take them away from me."

Preston studied Sanders's face. His vast cheeks were flushed, and he was beginning to sweat. She knew she had him just where she wanted him.

"Donny, let me see if I can explain this situation to you."

She paused, then continued slowly. In a strange way, Preston felt it was payback for all of Sanders's tirades. Sure, they went back a long way, all the way to Macon, where Sanders and his wife, Marybeth, had been friends with Preston's parents. But she had a job to do, and Sanders didn't understand.

"Here's the only way I can explain it," Preston said. "The Olympics are like a department store. And you're the chairman of that store. You have your own Borg-Warner security forces to catch shoplifters and thieves. But if someone threatens or commits a federal crime in your store, well, it's closing time, and the FBI takes over. You follow me?"

"Goddammit!" Sanders shouted. "You and your guns and badges. You cops don't know shit! You don't know who you're dealing with! There wouldn't be any Olympics without me. I *am* the Games!"

"Donny," Preston interrupted coldly. "You're going to have to take your hollering elsewhere."

The men's silence told her she had their support. The coup had been relatively bloodless. Now it was up to Sanders to decide how to fall on his sword. So Preston tried to make it a bit easier for him. "Donny, we're going to find who's behind the Tech reactor bombing. And we're going to recover the plutonium. And you'll have your Games back. Just let us do our jobs."

He stared at her with the rage of a bleeding bull ready to charge in one last act of defiance. Then he turned and stalked out of the arena.

The piercing, intermittent noise had started slowly, then accelerated.

For a moment, Staff Sergeant Milo Rosen thought of sprinting down the hall of the Tech reactor. But then he turned to face the containment vessel, putting his arms behind his back. It was standard procedure: if he survived the blast, he wanted to have his hands.

Peering into the bucket-shaped container, he saw the LED clock was still counting down. But the timer was in overdrive, ticking off ten digits per second.

00:05:50 . . . 00:05:40 . . . 00:05:30 . . .

Only fifty-three seconds left.

"Timer is accelerating," he said into his headset. "Fifty-three seconds remaining. No chance of getting the container out of here."

Down the hallway, the bomb tech with the binoculars headed for the stairs. Rosen knew every inch might make a difference and he pulled the container vessel farther away from the reactor core. Counting down to the last fifteen seconds, he pushed the vessel up against a wall and backpedaled as fast as he could.

"Fourteen seconds," he said. "Ten . . . five . . . brace . . ."

Rosen closed his eyes and thought of his mother.

The explosion ripped a fifteen-foot opening in the second floor ceiling of the Nuclear Research Center. The pressure wave slammed Rosen against a wall.

In the Joint Command Center, the live video feed showing the image from Rosen's helmet camera went black.

His ears were still ringing as he picked himself up. He brushed the shards of blast material from the front of his bomb suit. To make sure he was all there, he stomped his feet in the rubble, counted backward from ten, and then ticked off the 1969 World Champion New York Mets batting lineup.

Chunks of plaster continued to fall around him, and he looked up through the smoke and dust to the charred hole in the ceiling.

The EOD's containment vessel had done its job perfectly, directing most of the blast upward.

"All clear," Rosen said into his headset mike. "Smells like C4. Significant ceiling damage, no apparent structural effects. Repeat, all clear."

"Come home, boy," an EOD tech said cheerfully into his headset. "Your breakfast is getting cold."

As soon as he heard the "all clear" signal, C. K. Trivedi dashed into the Center, past the Army sentries and a handful of FBI agents. The bomb blast had been barely audible outside his Research Center, and he hoped the internal damage was also minor.

As he ran through the building, his Cambridge-educated mind raced. The fire alarms were blaring, but the high-pitched radiation klaxons were still silent. There had been no radioactive release.

The bullet had been dodged.

The elevator sped down the shaft to the Main Press Center located in the base of the Inforum and International Sports Plaza on Williams Street. Ian Hobbes, Olympic flack, primped and checked his blurry reflection in the chrome doors.

Showtime, he thought as the elevator slowed to a stop.

He had arrived at the Inforum just fifteen minutes earlier with Donny Sanders. In the mahogany-paneled conference room of Six Purple, the Olympic Committee's executive suite, they had held a tense meeting with senior staff. Sanders was still fuming over the exchange with Preston at the JCC.

There were three pressing issues for ACOG senior staff: how to keep a clamp on the Tech reactor explosion, how to quash the last traces of the CDC hostage barricade story, and how to manage the unfolding plutonium crisis. It wasn't even 11 A.M., but Sanders was already halfway through a Fonseca 10-10. The seven-inch Cuban cigars were especially popular with aficionados in Barcelona, where Sanders had discovered them at the 1992 Games.

While Sanders had updated the senior staff on the latest from the JCC, Hobbes had noticed the small, oak-framed quotation on his boss's coffee table. It was from Epictetus, the Greek philosopher. On a scorching day like today, words written 1,800 years ago were especially poignant:

> *There are enough irksome and*
> *troublesome things in life;*
> *aren't things just as bad at the Olympic festival?*
> *Aren't you scorched there by the fierce heat?*
> *Aren't you crushed in the crowd?*
> *Isn't it difficult to freshen yourself up?*
> *Doesn't the rain soak you to the skin?*
> *Aren't you bothered by the noise,*
> *the din, and other nuisances?*
> *But it seems to me that you are well able to*
> *bear and indeed gladly endure all this,*
> *when you think of the gripping*
> *spectacles that you will see.*

A gripping spectacle? Hobbes thought. *Except for a handful of people in Atlanta, no one had a clue!*

Routinely, Sanders prepped Hobbes for the morning briefing with the international press.

"Don't give the bastards a thing," the ACOG chief told his spokesman. "Remember how Kissinger used to open his press conferences: 'Does anyone have any questions for my answers?'"

"On hot topics, nothing if asked, right?"

"Right!" Sanders said, releasing a blue-gray cloud. "Stay on message. Offer nothing until you're asked. And when asked, *still* say nothing."

Hobbes stepped out of the elevator into the 183,000-square-foot exhibit hall where virtually every news outlet in the world had set up shop for the Olympics. The MPC was the biggest press center ever created, with two air-conditioned levels open twenty-four hours a day. It looked like the Ministry of Information in an Orwellian spoof. Haggard men and women raced in every direction. Reporters hammered away on laptop keypads. Many worked, ate, and slept in their cubbyholes. Television monitors and information screens flashed non-stop bulletins.

The MPC had everything a journalist could ever need, including a fully-stocked liquor store on the first floor. There was even a 20,000-square-foot state-of-the-art Kodak Photo Lab for news photographers and film couriers.

Hobbes passed the main cafeteria crowded with the *lumpen proletariat* of the press corps, reporters from small publications in the developing world. Not far away, haute cuisine restaurants catered to First World television journalists with expense accounts.

He nodded to a few familiar faces as he made his way toward the 1,000-seat auditorium where he would deliver the morning news. Depending on the story of the day, his face could be beamed to four billion people across the world from Calcutta's shanty towns to Rio's mansions. More than anything, he hoped they would tune in just down the street at CNN Center.

Calculating that he would get far more national television exposure speaking for the Olympic Committee than he would ever get covering hurricanes in Florida, Hobbes had given up a good job as a CNN general assignment correspondent to work for the Games. It had been a cunning career move, even if it meant having to handle Donny and the press animals.

Stepping to the podium, he looked out on the crowd of reporters. Many were still stuffing in the remnants of take-out breakfasts and reading the morning paper.

"Good morning, class," he said with a false smile. "I'm happy to report that all 197 nations have arrived and registered. The South African team—the first to compete at the Games in thirty-two years—has finally shown up. I can also report that 10,234 athletes are officially entered in competition. My staff will be handing out a fact sheet at the conclusion of this briefing."

Hobbes scanned the room. The Pencils—print reporters—were jotting notes. In the back of the auditorium, he could see a wall of tripods with dozens of cameras. The little red lights on the top of the Sony and Ikegami broadcast video recorders indicated the tapes were rolling.

"The president of the United States and the first lady are scheduled to depart from Dobbins this afternoon after attending several sporting events, including basketball and boxing preliminaries and some swimming. Not much else to tell you this morning, but I'd be glad to take any questions. Please stand and identify yourself before firing away."

"Nigel Fulford, *Daily Telegraph* of London. What arrangements have been made for pool coverage of the president's activities?"

"That's been taken care of," Hobbes said. "There will be a competition for slots. A 100-yard dash at the conclusion of this briefing . . ."

"Adrian Koffka, *Der Spiegel*. How many heads of state will be visiting Atlanta during the course of the Games?"

"Don't know the answer to that. I'd say at least forty, including President Clinton and the rest of the G-7. You can check with the Dignitary Protection Specialized Management Center at the DeKalb County Sheriff's office. Or, if you prefer, we'll get back to you."

"Beatrice Bournet, *Le Matin*. What sort of extra security precautions are you planning given the tensions in the Middle East?"

"Well, Mademoiselle Bournet," Hobbes began, admiring the pretty young French reporter. "Olympic security is the biggest and best in history. We've got 25,000 highly trained police officers and security guards stationed at Olympic venues across the United States."

Hobbes had given the same exact sound bite at least a thousand times. For this occasion, however, he added a few additional words for emphasis. "As far as *extra* security precautions are concerned, the Atlanta Olympic Committee has taken every imaginable step to make this the safest Olympiad in history. The word 'extra' implies there is more to be done. In Atlanta, the extra has *already* been done."

"Chuck Flagg, *Atlanta Journal-Constitution*."

The name kept public affairs officers in Atlanta lying awake at night, and Hobbes was no exception. A prize-winning local investigative reporter, Flagg was an intimidating combination of Southern folksiness and Northern relentlessness. Someday, his epitaph would probably read: DRANK HARD; WROTE HARDER.

At the *Journal-Constitution*, Flagg was a fish out of water, an ACLU card-carrying, antiestablishment liberal working for the city's old guard newspaper. His pugilism, verbal and actual, was notorious. For the duration of the Games, the entire staff had been given Olympic duties, and Flagg's summer assignment—soft news and features—had put him in an especially foul humor. He didn't even bother hiding his contempt for the commercialism of the Games, especially the official Olympic oven mitts, cufflinks, key chains, coasters, boxer shorts, barbecue sauces, and TV game shows like "Jeopardy" and "Wheel of Fortune." Flagg preferred toppling mayors at City Hall or exposing graft and corruption in state and county government.

"Hey, Hobbesey," Flagg began, "can you tell us what the hell has been going on at the Olympic Village? My sources at 911 tell me something happened there this morning. Something big."

"Chuck, we had a little false alarm up in the village," Hobbes said, without missing a beat. "A few fire trucks from station 11 were dispatched on a routine run to check it out. We also sent some backup just in case."

"False alarm?" Flagg asked incredulously.

"Yeah, false fire alarm. No flames, no harm, no foul. The trucks are already back in the station house."

Hobbes knew he was good at his job. He chose his words artfully, telling the truth, the partial truth, and nothing but the partial truth. It was indeed a false alarm. There had been no fire, no harm, and no foul.

Sure, there had been a bomb and an explosion at the Tech nuclear reactor, but you didn't ask that question, Chucky!

"Thank you all very much," Hobbes said, stepping out from behind the podium. "That's it for this morning. Y'all have fun out there today."

T he Messerschmitt-Boelkow-Blohm 105C helicopter hovered above the bustling city. McFall sat in the cabin area hunched over NEST's newest radiation detection equipment. He wore black headphones and made notes on a clipboard as he studied an amber monitor showing a grid map of downtown.

The chopper hung in the air next to the twenty-two-story Hyatt Regency on Peachtree Street. McFall loved the fact that thirty-four streets in the Atlanta area had the name *Peach* in them, even though the city was too far north for the fruit trees to grow.

He looked out the open cargo door, his sightline at the level of the Polaris Lounge, a revolving blue bubble floating on a small tower above the hotel.

For the past thirty minutes, the NEST helicopter had conducted a search of midtown Atlanta, sweeping back and forth, tracing a grid pattern as strict as a piece of graph paper. To take radiation readings, one helicopter skid bore a BO-105 Gamma pod, the other a BO-105 Neutron pod.

For more than thirty-five years, airborne radiation detectors had proven extremely effective in prospecting for uranium ore. There had been quantum improvements in the sensitivity of the equipment, but the idea was still the same. McFall and NEST were latter-day plutonium prospectors in a 131-square-mile city.

McFall thought the mission was like panning for gold in the Pacific Ocean.

The chopper headed downtown to the heart of the city to continue the grid search. It was not the first NEST survey in Atlanta. In fact, NEST had conducted three previous aerial searches to create benchmark maps useful in identifying potential problems and also as a baseline for a prospective nuclear emergency.

McFall studied the maps from the summer and fall of 1995 and from June 1996. They looked like standard AAA maps of Atlanta, but with dozens of small flags scattered around the city. Each red marker had a numeric code with a radiation reading—type and level—taken at the site.

He knew that the maps were no different from those of any other American city. Background radiation was emitted from diverse sources. In fact, natural radiation was everywhere. Freshly paved asphalt gave off radiation, and so did Vermont granite used in government office buildings. Camping lanterns discharged some radiation, and even bananas set off Geiger counters.

McFall's challenge was to determine if there had been any *meaningful* change in the background radiation picture since the last search in June. It was a possibility, however remote, that the stolen plutonium was giving off a faint signature that would be detected by NEST's ultrasensitive equipment. In theory, since all plutonium was radioactive, two different types of radiation could be detected a few yards or more from an improvised nuclear device: neutrons and gamma rays, or high-energy photons. Neutrons were created by spontaneous fission. High-energy gamma rays were generated from fissile material primarily as a result of radioactive decay.

"The physics really defeat us," McFall was saying to Kris Aura. "The farther you get from the radioactive source, the flux of neutrons and gamma rays declines inversely with the square of the distance."

"You lost me," Aura said. "I'm no Einstein."

"Okay, sorry. Let me try again. The further you get from the fissile material, the less radiation you can detect. It's a fixed ratio. So, the particle flux at three feet is nine times smaller than at one foot. At four feet, it is sixteen times smaller, and so on. At some distance— and in reality it's not very far—the radiation becomes undetectable. It just blends in with natural background levels."

The chopper circled the Westin Peachtree Plaza, a dark brown 723-foot glass tube. McFall could see tourists in the spinning Sun Dial Restaurant and Lounge on the seventy-second floor. The streets below were jammed with traffic. There were tens of thousands of pedestrians milling around, walking on streets that had been closed off for the Games. Atlanta looked like a giant street fair with hawkers on corners selling souvenirs and thick smoke billowing into the air from concession stands where food was being grilled.

McFall listened to his headset, which was hooked into the radiation-monitoring equipment. A computer-generated voice crackled when the gamma and neutron pods detected radiation levels above preset levels.

"Gamma Alarm Four . . . Gamma Alarm Four," the voice said softly, indicating the presence of low-level, trivial background radiation. McFall could see that the roof of the Westin had just been resurfaced with tar paper. It was probably throwing off some radiation, hence the false positive.

McFall felt like he was wasting precious time. There was not much chance they would find anything from the air. If the plutonium pits were clad in lead or iron, there wasn't much hope.

Then suddenly the pods came alive.

"Gamma Alarm One . . . Gamma Alarm One," the automated voice screeched in his ear.

Impossible! McFall thought. The machine had to be wrong.

He adjusted two dials on the machine and listened again. On the computer screen, two bright blips began flashing.

Jesus! Two gamma hits!

"Gamma Alarm One! Gamma Alarm One!" the voice said urgently.

McFall immediately radioed the NEST Command Center at Dobbins. "Birdcage, Canary One," he said.

"Go ahead, Canary One."

"We've got two big hits at the Westin Peachtree Plaza at 210 Peachtree Street. Roll on it. Standard tourist attire. Nothing special. The upper floors are hot."

"Roger that, Canary One. Westin Peachtree Plaza, wilco."

McFall could not believe his luck. Gamma hits were very rare, except near nuclear power plants, weapons facilities, or during NEST training exercises. Part of him wanted to believe this was the real thing, that he had found the plutonium. But years of experience warned him that this detection had been too easy.

He debated the possibilities. The average terrorist, if there was such a thing, was unlikely to know much about the properties of fissile materials. So, you really couldn't expect him to know how to hide nuclear materials from NEST's newest detection equipment. On the other hand, anyone sophisticated enough to smuggle plutonium into the United States would be capable of shielding the radioactive materials.

The helicopter continued the grid search up Peachtree Street, the carotid artery of Atlanta. The chopper swooped by more high rises, including the copper-colored NationsBank building and the modern Suntrust Plaza at One Peachtree Center.

McFall could feel his heart pounding. He had never before searched for the real thing in an American city. Training exercises always got the blood pumping, but this was entirely different. It was like free-falling from a low-flying Navy insertion plane on a moonless night over Vietnam. Would the chute *ever* open? Where would you hit ground? And when would the firefight begin? McFall had relished the exhilarating admixture of danger and uncertainty, vulnerability and aggression.

"Gamma Alarm One . . . Gamma Alarm One . . ." the voice said again, interrupting his thoughts. This time, the hits were coming from the Ritz-Carlton at 181 Peachtree Street.

Immediately McFall speculated the smugglers had divided the load of plutonium. But why would they hide it in two downtown hotels?

Again he radioed the Mobile Command Center. But before he could call in the news, the voice in his ear was speaking yet again.

"Gamma Alarm One . . . Gamma Alarm One . . ."

The helicopter was now above Planet Hollywood, the local branch of the worldwide celebrity-owned restaurant chain.

McFall could not believe the number of hits.

"Birdcage. Canary One," he radioed.

"Yes, Canary One."

"We've got more gamma hits downtown."

"Canary One, we will advise EOC in Washington."

"Birdcage, tell the folks at Forrestal I've *never* seen anything like this."

"Roger that."

The NEST chopper circled back and headed north toward downtown. McFall called in the coordinates of the latest hits.

And then again, the computerized voice intoned: "Gamma Alarm One . . . Gamma Alarm One."

Four hits in less than ten minutes, McFall counted. Atlanta was burning again.

T he countdown began in 1991.

When Atlanta was chosen as the host of the 1996 Games, security experts went right to work. For a team of about a dozen FBI agents and consultants from the Pentagon's Office of Special Events, the job was non-stop for five years. All told, the group ran up more than 100,000 hours preparing for the worst.

No doubt, it was a strange way to earn a living. The members of the security inner circle got up every day, kissed husbands, wives, partners, and children good-bye, drove into town, and then spent the entire day imagining how all hell could break loose.

There had been endless drills, tabletop exercises, and field training. The security team had worked through thousands of scenarios. They ate, breathed, and slept disaster. They traveled together to international sporting events around the globe from the Barcelona Summer Games to the World Cup in Los Angeles. They spent two weeks in Beit Horon, Israel, learning about Israeli counter-terrorist operations. They visited the FBI's National Academy in Quantico more weekends than they cared to remember. Even General H. Norman Schwarzkopf of Desert Storm fame was consulted on planning and logistics.

But of all the hours spent planning, one weekend stood out in Kyle Preston's mind as she evaluated the loose nukes crisis now unfolding in real time.

Spring 1995. Shenandoah Valley, Virginia. At the Federal Emergency Management Agency's heavily guarded Mount Weather Emergency

Assistance Center in Berryville, Virginia, the top Olympic security officials had worked through every imaginable possibility and then some:

> Planted one year in advance by a disgruntled construction worker, a sophisticated, improvised explosive device, or SIED, on a highly accurate, long-delay timer explodes beneath Centennial Park, wounding 2,500.

> A maniac with a homemade, shoulder-launched missile blows a ValuJet plane from the sky on its final approach to Hartsfield International, killing 250.

> A tornado touches down in Piedmont Park, sending 5,000 people fleeing in panic from an outdoor concert near the lake.

> A rush hour MARTA train derails on the North Line between Five Points and Peachtree Center, trapping 200 people in darkness.

> A low-flying Kamikaze pilot in an ultralight aircraft loaded with lethal VX nerve gas crashes into the Inforum building, setting the emerald-colored building on fire and poisoning most of downtown.

> A gasoline tanker truck flips over and explodes, triggering a twenty-car domino crash at "Spaghetti Junction"—the Tom Moreland Interchange at the north junction of I-85 and I-285.

And the list of nightmares went on and on. Even by the standards of professional law enforcement, the planning and preparations had been excruciating and exhaustive.

At Weather Mountain, the Olympic security team had battled through 159 different hypothetical emergency situations. FEMA trainers videotaped the sessions, analyzed critical decisions, and evaluated performance.

It had not been an enjoyable experience. In the early sessions,

FEMA officials had given the Olympic team failing grades, saying its blunders would have cost thousands and thousands of lives. Then, when the group was thoroughly disheartened, the trainers had sprung the final stumper of the session.

Loose nukes in Atlanta.

"A crude radiological device made from spent reactor fuel has been exploded in downtown Atlanta, creating a radioactive cloud one mile wide," an invisible FEMA official had announced over the loudspeakers in the conference room. The participants had come to refer to the disembodied voice as Satan, in tribute to the calamities he whipped up at will.

Satan continued: "More than three million people in downtown Atlanta will be exposed within 15 minutes."

There had been absolute silence around the 40-foot oak table as the stars of America's security agencies calculated their individual and collective strategies.

Kyle Preston had spoken first. The Bureau would coordinate with the Department of Energy to mobilize a Crisis Response Team from facilities at Savannah River, Georgia, and Oak Ridge, Tennessee. The Atmospheric Advisory Release Capability and the Radiation Emergency Assistance Center would be brought in. FEMA would implement emergency plans. NEST would be summoned.

Then Satan came on the loudspeakers again.

"A 35 m.p.h. southeasterly wind is blowing the radiological cloud toward Jacksonville, Florida. If the wind shifts, it could move southwest to New Orleans."

A longer and more uneasy silence followed.

Satan then emerged from the exercise control room next door. It had seemed almost too trivial to say that day, but he had gone ahead anyway and had summed up the final lesson for the group: "A nuclear incident has to be prevented on the front end."

Kyle Preston rose calmly from her seat and pulled a video screen from the ceiling of the Fish Bowl.

"Rule one," she said sternly to the Olympic security high command. "No press. Not a word about this situation to anyone. If you leak, you'll deal with me."

She let the thought sink in for a moment, then continued. "In sixty seconds, we'll have the DOE's Emergency Operations Center on the Secure Video Teleconference System. Admiral Taylor will brief us on Energy's appraisal of the situation."

She checked her watch and stalled for time.

"The good news is we're onto a few solid leads. NEST has turned up more than two dozen gamma hits. And we've got FBI teams all over Atlanta closing in."

From their glum faces, Preston could tell no one was particularly reassured by the update. The early stages of a crisis were always the worst—no hard information, no good theories, no sense of direction.

The screen behind her began to flash and an image formed of a sixty-five-year-old man with a flat nose and ruddy face. "Hello . . . hello . . . is anyone out there?" he called. Each time he leaned toward the camera, Admiral Taylor's round face appeared on the screen distorted, as in a fun-house mirror.

"We're here, Admiral. This is Kyle Preston with Olympic security. Go ahead."

"Good. Let me tell you what we're doing right now," he said. "If you haven't already heard, NEST is in the air. They've nailed down locations on the missing radioactive materials. That's a very encouraging sign. Mack McFall should be arriving at your headquarters any minute to brief you."

A few heads nodded at the table. It was the first sliver of good news all day. McFall had become something of a legend, a miracle worker, ever since he had retrieved four kilos of plutonium stolen from Los Alamos and smuggled to Morocco. He had also pulled off an astonishing capture of a nuclear-powered Soyuz satellite that had crashed in Canada in 1995. After the satellite's fiery reentry into the atmosphere, there had been a breathtaking race between a joint U.S.-Canadian government team and a gang of Middle Eastern mercenaries who wanted the radioactive contents of the satellite's reactor core. Dispatched by dogsled, snowplane, and icebreaker to the far reaches of the Yukon, McFall and his X-ray team got to the Soyuz wreckage first, set a trap, and helped put away the hired guns for a long, long time.

As if on cue, McFall appeared at the glass conference room door. In shirtsleeves, rumpled trousers, and black Ray-Bans, he looked more like a weekend golfer than a nuclear hunter.

Preston felt her nerves tense. She had not seen him in five years. He was still as handsome as ever. Forcing a smile, she straightened her jacket, walked over to shake his hand, then introduced him to the rest of the team. "Why don't you fill us in on the NEST grid search," she said. "We hear you've got good news."

"Good and bad," he said, slipping off the sunglasses.

A map of Atlanta flashed on a screen. It was dated 6/15/96 and showed twenty-four different small flags.

"This is how things looked exactly one month ago," he explained. He pointed to the little flags. Each, he explained, signified radiation. Several were in the Olympic Village at Georgia Tech, where a variety of nuclear research projects were conducted. Other flags indicated Georgia Power utilities in the area. And a few flags marked local hospitals where radioactive isotopes were used in medicine.

"I repeat," McFall said, "this is a picture of Atlanta four weeks ago. Now let me show you the city today."

The image changed and the map began to sprout dozens of red flags.

"What the hell!" Beast Carrick of the Georgia Bureau of Investigation exclaimed. "What in tarnation is going on?"

"Atlanta is lighting up like a Christmas tree," McFall said. "We've got gamma radiation emanating from more than fifty different sources."

"How's that possible?"

"I'm not exactly sure," McFall said.

"Pardon my ignorance," Frosty Cornell of the Atlanta Police Department interrupted, "but what exactly does this mean? How much damage are we talking about with forty-eight pounds of plutonium?"

"Good question," Admiral Taylor said over the SVTS. "We've mapped out two scenarios for you folks. Ms. Preston, are you ready?"

"Yes. Would you all please turn your attention to the wall map."

The group stood and looked out from the Fish Bowl toward the Olympic security wall map, glowing red, blue, and green in the darkness. Stretching half a city block and standing two stories high, the map was made of thirty glass panels lit from behind. It provided a detailed representation of every single street, building, and venue connected to the Games.

At the heart of the map was the so-called Olympic Ring, an imaginary circle with a radius of 1.5 miles centering on the Georgia World Congress Center on International Boulevard. The ring, a PR creation of the Atlanta Olympic Committee, was illustrated in incandescent blue and encompassed most of the important venues and sites, including the Stadium, the Family Hotel, the Village, and the Park.

As the group watched from the Fish Bowl, a yellow shape suddenly appeared. It was not a perfect circle. Instead, it was oblong and wavy, like a floppy Salvador Dali clock, spreading across the wall.

"Scenario number 1," Taylor said, "a radiation dispersal device. Just a few sticks of dynamite strapped to those missing plutonium pits would put enough radioactive particles in the air to leave Atlanta uninhabitable for years."

"What's the yellow amoeba?" Cornell asked.

"It's the plume from a dirty weapon," the admiral explained. "The Atmospheric Release Advisory Capability at Lawrence Livermore modeled this scenario, factoring for wind and terrain. That yellow balloon shape represents the radiation dispersal effect over the city center."

After a few moments, the yellow shape turned orange.

"Scenario number 2," Admiral Taylor continued. "An improvised nuclear device. For comparison purposes, recall that in August 1945, we dropped a plutonium-implosion bomb—MKIII Fat Man—on Nagasaki. Its yield was twenty-one kilotons. Between 40,000 and 70,000 people were killed, and at least that many were injured."

He paused.

"To put it bluntly, our situation is much worse. Fat Man used twelve pounds of plutonium. Today, we're facing 47.8 pounds of Pu-239."

McFall jumped in: "A rough rule of thumb in modern weapons

design is that you get 20 kilotons of nuclear yield from every kilogram of plutonium. So with 21.7 kilos of Pu-239, we're talking about a potential 434-kiloton yield. That's the equivalent of 434,000 *tons* of TNT."

"Might as well kiss Atlanta good-bye," Carrick said.

"Let's face it," Taylor said, "a surface burst with that much plutonium would make the fires General Sherman lit look like birthday candles. The orange shape on the wall map represents the immediate blast area."

In the center of the map, the orange shape glowed like the sun. It filled the entire Olympic ring.

The men and woman responsible for Olympic security took measure of their predicament, as a yellow wash spread slowly from the epicenter until it covered the entire wall.

The 1,000-seat auditorium was filled to capacity. Men and women sat quietly in their chairs. On the stage, 197 flags stood in tight rows. Front and center, the blue-and-white Israeli standard, with its Star of David, hung motionless. The lights in the Martin Luther King Memorial Auditorium dimmed as a white screen descended from the ceiling, eclipsing the rows of flags. The audience fell silent, and a grainy documentary replayed the nightmare.

Munich, September 5, 1972. The Games of the XX Olympiad. The proud German hosts call them the Games of Peace and Joy.

In the darkness of morning, eight men in track suits climb the six-foot-six-inch security fence encircling the Olympic Village, home to 10,000 athletes from 123 countries.

At 4:20 A.M., a security guard spots and ignores the group of men. Just another gang of carousing athletes sneaking in after hours. The intruders stop at the East German dormitory to pick up weapons. Then, donning ski masks and packing Soviet-made Kalashnikovs, they advance toward Building 31 on Connolly Strasse.

A few minutes before 5 A.M., a sleepy Israeli coach hears noise in the hallway, unlocks his door, sees gun-toting, hooded men, and yells to warn his teammates. The door is blown apart by gunfire and the coach is slain, the first victim of the Munich Massacre.

The terrorists invade. The athletes resist. A weightlifter grabs a knife in self-defense and is gunned down. A wrestler blocks a door and is overpowered. Two of the fifteen-member team manage to escape, dodging a shower of bullets.

In just minutes, Black September captures Building 31. Two Israelis are already dead; nine are hostages, bound and gagged. To leave no doubt about their ruthlessness, the Palestinians throw the body of Moshe Weinberg, the thirty-three-year-old wrestling coach, onto the street. They also drop flyers listing their demands from the windows: the hostages will be released in exchange for 256 Arabs in Israeli prisons. Lastly, they demand a jet to make their getaway.

The first deadline is set. The hours tick away as the world looks on in horror. The events are broadcast live around the world. Nine hundred million viewers in a hundred countries watch the crime unfold. One black-and-white image is indelibly imprinted on the collective global consciousness: a lone gunman in a black ski mask stands on a second floor balcony brandishing a submachine gun.

The clock is ticking. The fiery, long-haired terrorist leader Issa negotiates with German authorities, but the talks go nowhere. Israeli Prime Minister Golda Meir refuses to make any concessions. German Chancellor Willi Brandt runs out of options. Night falls and German officials arrange for the terrorists and their hostages to board two Bell-Iroquois UH-1D helicopters. Their destination: Furstenfeldbruck Air Base, fifteen miles away.

The choppers take flight and disappear into the night sky over the village. When they land at the Bavarian air base, three terrorists race across the tarmac to inspect the waiting Lufthansa 727. Giant floodlights illuminate the tarmac. As the terrorists return from their inspection, a German police sniper opens fire prematurely and wounds one masked man.

The battle erupts. A terrorist jumps from one of the UH-1D helicopters, turns and throws a grenade back into the passenger compartment. All four hostages die instantly in the explosion. Palestinians in the second copter shoot five more hostages in their seats.

When the smoke clears, all nine hostages are dead. Of the eight terrorists, five are killed, and three are captured. One German officer is slain.

The Games are suspended a total of thirty-four hours. Mark Spitz, the American swimmer of Jewish ancestry who set an

*Olympic record winning seven gold medals, quietly leaves the
Games for London because of fears for his security.*

*A memorial service is held at the Munich Stadium, built on the
site of the World War II airfield where Hitler and Britain's Neville
Chamberlain declared "peace in our time." The Munich Opera
House orchestra plays Beethoven's "Egmont Overture," and IOC
Chairman Avery Brundage announces: "The Games must go on."*

*Several subsequent inquiries reveal the German plan to stop the
terrorists never had a chance. Only five sharpshooters had been
deployed to eliminate eight terrorists. The ratio was dead wrong.
Moreover, the Bavarian marksmen were equipped with outdated G-3
rifles, and they did not have night-vision scopes for their midnight
mission.*

*The day after the massacre, coffins are loaded onto a plane at
Munich's Reim airport. At Building 31 in the Olympic Village, a
mother and child put a wreath at the site of the attack. A little girl,
dark-haired and freckled and looking prematurely old in a black
dress, stands next to a weeping woman, the widow of a slain coach.*

In the crowded auditorium, the silence was almost asphyxiating as the
documentary ended and the image of the grieving mother and daughter dressed in black froze on the screen. A spotlight searched the stage
and found two women standing behind a microphone, their features
remarkably unchanged despite the passing of twenty-four years.

The older woman was tall, with gray hair, high cheekbones, and
brown eyes. The younger woman appeared to be her daughter, with
dark skin and faint freckles.

"Mr. Prime Minister," the older woman said, addressing Prime
Minister Benjamin Netanyahu of Israel. "Mr. President," she said,
turning to Juan Antonio Samaranch, the head of the International
Olympic Committee. "Ladies and gentlemen, on behalf of the families
of the Munich Eleven, we thank you for joining us. My name is Miriam
Arens. Twenty-four years ago, my husband was murdered by Black
September. He was the Israeli shooting coach."

She paused, looked at her daughter, collected herself, and then returned to the 4 x 6 index cards in her trembling hands.

"It seems only yesterday that we lost the eleven in Munich and, with them, our dreams. In Germany after the murders, the Games were suspended for just thirty-four hours. A brief memorial service was held. Avery Brundage devoted just twenty-seven words to the memory of the dead. He called them 'our Israeli friends.' The words rang hollow and false. Since that day, there have been five Olympiads, but never an official tribute to the victims."

Tears welling in her eyes, she stopped, gathered herself together, and continued: "Although the pain will never go away, today we have the satisfaction of knowing that twenty-four years of denial and forgetting are over."

The woman stepped away from the microphone and her daughter, Leila, moved forward with the smooth step of an athlete. She wore a simple black linen dress and a cartwheel hat. "My name is Leila Arens," she began in a low, gentle voice. "My father died in Munich."

Buddy Crouse, sitting in the darkness of the auditorium, immediately understood why his new Israeli friend had invited him to the service. It was no wonder that her mood had turned black when the Palestinian team sauntered by in the village.

Suddenly, the rear doors of the auditorium flew open and a dozen men shouting obscenities stormed into the room. They were dressed in jeans and T-shirts, and they wore *kheffiyehs* around their heads.

"Jews out of Palestine!"

"Israel murders innocent children!"

Trained by years of war and terror, some Israelis in the audience dropped to the ground for cover. Others dashed forward toward exits at the front of the hall.

Leila Arens stood motionless on the stage, brown eyes searching the darkness of the auditorium.

Almost instantly, plainclothed Israeli security agents on the perimeter of the hall moved decisively to subdue the protesters with brutal, bone-crushing efficiency. The Arab demonstrators were silenced in seconds and dragged from the auditorium.

On stage, Leila Arens waited for the commotion to subside and members of the audience to return to their seats. Finally, there was silence, and she began again, addressing her remarks toward the area of the disturbance.

"The history of the people of Israel teaches a simple lesson," she said. "If you destroy our synagogue, we will build another sanctuary. If you burn our home, we will raise another roof. If you murder eleven, we will send eleven more. Each year in Israel, we hold a memorial ceremony to remember the eleven Israeli athletes. It is like so many days on the Jewish calendar. We pause once a year to remember, lest we ever forget."

Arens took a deep breath, then continued. "When we buried my father twenty-four years ago, I did not know about the Olympic Games or the Olympic movement. I did not know what it all meant. I was a little girl without a father. But when I was old enough to understand, I promised myself I would compete someday at the Games. They could murder one Arens, but there would come another. And although my father never saw me old enough to fire a rifle or compete in the sport he loved, I know he is always with me."

She brushed away a tear.

"Here, near the birthplace of Dr. Martin Luther King, Jr., and the American civil rights movement, we must rededicate ourselves to the Olympic dream of a world at peace. We must all find a way to live together. We must all respect each other, understand our differences, and celebrate our diversity."

She stared out into the crowd and thought for a moment that she could see her father's face in the brightness of the lights. Her voice broke, but she continued.

"Those were the Olympic ideals for which my father lived," she said, putting her arm around her mother, "and they are the dreams for which he died. I live for him, and for them, today."

Mickey Borba stepped out of the Barclay Hotel on Luckie Street and headed east toward Forsyth. The sidewalks were jammed with revelers heading to Centennial Park just a few blocks away.

The streets had been barricaded, and there were hordes of people moving in every direction. Borba hated all the commotion, and he was particularly annoyed with his choice of hotels. He planned to berate his secretary for booking him into the Barclay. It was smack-dab in the middle of the Games. And there was nowhere to hide from the mobs. Worst of all, there was no getting away from Izzy, the omnipresent Olympic mascot. He knew it was silly, but he hated the little blue creature with bulging eyes, lightning bolts for eyebrows, and red sneakers. Even the name annoyed him. The creature was born "Whatizit" but then became "Izzy." Over the past few months, Izzy had colonized the United States and the world. He was every-where. Borba thought that Matt Groening, the creator of "The Simpsons," had been right. Izzy was a "bad marriage of the Pillsbury Doughboy and the ugliest California raisin."

As he plunged into the crowds, Borba's scowl said it all. He was middle-aged, jowly, and looked like he was perpetually sneering. On this day, he was not where he wanted to be. He had never intended to be in Atlanta during the Games.

But business was business, and he would make the most of this trip.

He pushed through the waves of bodies with single-minded deter-mination. He was a man with a mission.

Mickey Borba, traveling salesman, wanted lunch.

At Forsyth, he crossed the street and stepped into the Eastern News-stand to pick up *USA Today* and *The Atlanta Journal-Constitution*'s free daily Olympic supplement. He tucked them into the Hartmann business bag on his shoulder and made his way to Poplar, where he ducked into the Tasty Town Grill, an old-style diner catty-corner to the imposing gray U.S. Court of Appeals building.

Borba slumped into one of the burgundy booths in the front room and studied the dog-eared menu. His eye fixed on "famous Italian spaghetti with tasty brown meat sauce and Parmesan cheese." There was a sign on the wall, probably unmoved since 1947: "Not just sauce, not just spaghetti, but an honorable concoction of celestial excellence! Try just once."

"Hey there," said Pete Makarios, the longtime proprietor of the Tasty. "Lunch is free if you can answer an Olympic trivia question." Decked out in a greasy apron with the symbols of all twenty-six Olympic sports, Makarios definitely had caught the fever.

"Go ahead, try me," Borba said.

"What did the *first* Olympic gold medalist do for a living?"

"Ancient or modern?" Borba said, stalling.

"Ancient."

Borba thought about the question—anything for a free lunch—and then promptly gave up.

"No clue," he replied.

"Come on," Makarios said. "Take a wild guess."

"Really, I don't know."

"The first winner was a cook," Makarios said proudly, adjusting his apron.

Borba ordered a tuna melt and a cup of coffee and then plowed into the newspaper. He had twenty minutes to eat lunch before he had to get across town. For an astronomical price, he had scrounged a ticket to the Olympic boxing preliminaries at Alexander Memorial Coliseum.

Buried in the sports pages, he did not notice six men enter the Tasty and position themselves at the front and rear doors. They were not especially discreet. Makarios, the proprietor, nervously asked one of the men if he wanted a seat at the counter. The man shook his head. Makarios retreated behind the grill and busied himself with a hamburger.

The men in suits fixed their eyes on the lone customer in the booth: Michael Vito Borba. Age forty-three. Paper products salesman from Baton Rouge, Louisiana. Married. Two children. No criminal record.

After a hand signal from the team leader, a woman entered the restaurant and approached Borba's booth. She looked like a business executive and carried a slim briefcase in one hand. As she cruised past Borba and headed to an empty stool at the far end of the counter she heard a gravelly, automated voice in her ear coming from a wireless receiver disguised as a hearing aid. The voice was being transmitted from the Samsonite case at her side: "Gamma Alarm One . . . Gamma Alarm One . . ."

The MACS Dual Modular radiation monitor inside the briefcase sounded especially frantic. Its ultrasensitive sodium iodide crystal detector was picking up gamma traces, and the woman carrying the case had never heard the computerized voice so agitated.

She had *never* been so close to the real thing before.

Mickey Borba and his Hartmann business case were hot.

The woman with the Samsonite took a seat at the counter, reached for a menu, and nodded to her teammates near the door. She could feel her heart racing.

Makarios approached her. "Hey there. Lunch is free if you can answer an Olympic trivia question."

"Try me," she said.

"What's the Olympic motto in Latin?"

"I don't speak Latin," the woman said. "How about a cup of coffee and a cherry cheese Danish?"

"Hey, it's your loss," Makarios said, reaching for the coffee pot and mumbling *"Citius, Altius, Fortius."*

Sondra Lavagetto, the woman at the counter, was an experienced health physicist from the Lawrence Livermore National Laboratory in California. Her specialty was plutonium. She had been trained at the DOE's Remote Sensing Lab in Nevada for this type of surveillance work. And she had flown all night to get to Atlanta to help NEST in the hunt. But in all of her training, Lavagetto never dreamed she would face the real thing. She never imagined she would end up within five feet of a suspected terrorist carrying Pu-239.

Borba finished the sports pages, checked his watch, and waved to a waitress for the check. In the next banquette, a family from Kenya was having a great time with the spaghetti special. At the counter, a Korean couple was experimenting with the lemon icebox pie.

The whole world had descended on Atlanta, Borba observed. Africans. Asians. South Americans. He knew it wasn't politically correct, but he wasn't sure he liked so many foreigners in *his* country.

Then he noticed the men staring at him. One. No, two. Wait, three. Three men in suits ogling him.

There were creeps everywhere, leering, staring.

He stood up to leave and reached for his case. Then he felt the cold barrel of a Sig/Sauer nine-millimeter pistol against his neck.

"Mr. Borba, please take a seat," a voice said calmly. "We're with the FBI."

Borba's legs began to shake.

"You are under arrest," an agent said. "You have the right to remain silent."

Borba's legs gave out, and he fell into the vinyl booth. Sure he had cheated a bit on his taxes; sure he had made a few stock trades on information overheard on airplanes and in hotel lounges. But Sweet Jesus, did he deserve the FBI with guns in his face?

Several agents closed in on the table, while others shooed customers out of the restaurant. Makarios frantically tried to collect their bills, but it was no use. He stood behind the counter, cursing silently.

Sondra Lavagetto saw an opportunity to get even with the Tasty Town's owner. She handed him a hundred dollar bill and said, "Keep the change if you can answer one trivia question."

"You're on," Makarios said.

"What was the mythical country that won all the gold medals in W. C. Fields's *Million Dollar Legs*?"

Makarios was stumped. The hundred dollar bill felt so good in his hands.

"I give up," he said.

"Klopstokia," Lavagetto said. "Sorry for causing any trouble. Keep twenty. And thanks for the Danish."

Kyle Preston and Mack McFall arrived at the Tasty Town just as Borba was being handcuffed. "What've we got?" Preston asked the FBI team leader.

"His name is Mickey Borba. Louisiana salesman. NEST ID'd his room at the Barclay Hotel down the street. He left the hotel and stopped here for lunch. The gamma radiation moved with him. He was alone, so we grabbed him."

"Nice work," she said. "Take him back to headquarters."

The agents lifted Borba from the seat and moved him out of the restaurant. A small crowd had gathered in front and was peering through the miniblinds. Borba was escorted through the onlookers to a black sedan, where he was helped into the back seat and driven away.

Inside the Tasty Town, McFall was busy talking with Lavagetto, who was still clutching her Samsonite. He opened the briefcase and was studying the MACS Dual Modular System readout. Preston came over to speak with him.

"Want to make a small bet on what's in the bag?" McFall asked.

"Cut it out, Mack," she said, all business.

"No, I'm serious," he said. "Guess what's in the bag. Loser buys dinner here. They say the spaghetti special is world famous."

Preston looked into McFall's eyes. How typical! He was always joking around, playing games, making bets. Worst of all, he was still toying with her. It was totally inappropriate here and now. She summoned her strength. She knew she could handle it, so she played along. "All right, you're on," she said.

"So what's your best guess?"

"I don't know. How about a shot put from Turkmenistan?"

"Could be."

"Or some plutonium from Chelyabinsk-65?"

"Maybe."

"Go ahead," McFall said. "It's your call. If you're right, I buy."

"I go with Pu-239."

"You're on."

McFall walked over to the Hartmann bag and put on a pair of lead-lined protective gloves. They were matte black with rubber-coated fingertips. He unzipped the front flap on the bag and poured the contents onto the Formica table. He sorted through a pile of sales catalogues, a Tylenol bottle, a Sharp electronic organizer, and a few spiral notebooks.

Just what he expected.

Nothing!

Then he took the case and shook it. No sixteen-pound shot put tumbled onto the table. Only a few paper clips and some Hertz rental car keys. He reached into the outer pockets and found more detritus from the life of a traveling salesman—a well-worn Official Airline Guide, a Seiko alarm clock, and a half-eaten roll of cherry-flavored Tums.

McFall's hands moved through the pockets.

Finally, he felt it.

There it is!

And he pulled it out. The size of a small envelope and made of gauze, it looked like a large tea bag. McFall held it in his gloved hands.

A sense of fear bordering on panic spread through him—the fear of a formidable adversary, the panic of an impossible challenge, the same rush of feelings of a young man fighting in a faraway place.

"What is it?" Preston asked, staring at the square-shaped packet in McFall's hands. "What is that thing?"

"It's proof positive the Olympics aren't just for amateurs any-more," he said, shaking his head.

PART II

AIM

We are in the paradoxical position of having a clearer understanding of the interior of the atom than we do of the interior of the mind of the terrorist.

—Jerrold M. Post

O f the fifteen former republics of the Soviet Union, Turkmenistan was without question the hottest and least hospitable. Most of the country resembled a moonscape, a vast expanse of sand and rock, dry and lifeless, traversed by the world's longest irrigation canal, which spanned 680 miles from the Amu Darya River across the Kara Kum desert, then on to the Caspian Sea.

Ashkhabad, the capital, sat at the base of the 10,000-foot Kopet Dagh Mountains on the border with Iran. Even though the city was well shaded by trees, it was said that at high noon in summer you could scramble eggs on the hood of a car in one minute and grill *shashlik*—a mutton skewer—in four or five.

Ashkhabad was certainly not a place Gennady Sobchak wanted to spend a month. But he had no choice. After driving across Kazakhstan and Uzbekistan with a stash of stolen nuclear materials and delivering them to the Turkmen Olympic coach, he had tried to disappear in the dusty capital. He had taken a cheap room in the Hotel Jubilienaya at the west end of Prospekt Svobody on Ulitsa Temiryasev. It was cheaper than the Hotel Ashkhabad in the center of town, considerably quieter, and he felt safer. The American Embassy had been temporarily located in the Jubilienaya until it had moved to its permanent home not far away.

The plan was for Sobchak to hide out until he was contacted. Then he would slip over the mountains into Iran. He would do a bit of lucrative freelance consulting on Teheran's nuclear program and then be spirited on to Prague, Budapest, or Berlin.

At long last, he would have money. He would no longer earn a measly subsistence wage in Chelyabinsk. He would no longer take home *less* each month than uneducated taxi drivers pulled in every week in St. Petersburg. He would no longer be officially instructed to plant and grow potatoes just in case Minatom, the Russian nuclear agency, could not meet its payroll. He would live in the West and would never have to go back to his dingy home in that decrepit concrete monolith.

Sobchak had passed his days and nights in Ashkhabad strolling around the quiet, shaded city, waiting to be contacted. The man on the phone from the United States promised everything had been arranged. And so he waited. And waited.

He dined most nights in the candlelit Restaurant Aini, where he ate *plov*, chunks of mutton and sliced yellow turnip on a pile of rice. In the afternoons, he strolled past the Muzei Istorii, the history museum on Ulitsa Shevchenko, to a quiet café where he enjoyed tea and ice cream. And late at night, he took vodka to the *pitseria* in the park near Hotel Ashkhabad and watched young men and women dancing under the stars.

On this July afternoon, he strolled down Ulitsa Engelsa and passed a Benetton, the only one in all of Central Asia. In front of the store, there were several tall and beautiful Turkmen women wearing long, iridescent silk dresses. Sobchak paused and watched the women. They were so attractive, and he felt so alone. Maybe with money, he would also have companionship. The two seemed to go hand in hand.

He headed for the Russian Bazaar on Ulitsa Zhitnikova and made his way through the crowded market. This was probably the best place in the world to buy Bukhara rugs. Sobchak headed west five blocks toward the Tikinsky Bazaar.

The city was serene, clean, and, unlike Chelyabinsk, without a single monumental Soviet-style block of apartments because of the danger of earthquakes. The city had repeatedly been flattened by temblors, most recently by the Big One of 1949, measuring 9.0 on the Richter scale and responsible for 110,000 deaths.

Sobchak took a taxi out of town to the market beyond the Kara Kum Canal on the edge of the desert. It was a wild and woolly place where camels, goats, silks, apricots, and surplus military equipment were for sale. Despite the stifling heat, the men wore huge, floppy, sheep wool hats. They were from the Turkmen tribe, the *Tekke*, renowned for raising horses, weaving carpets, and robbing desert silk caravans.

Sobchak sat in a shady corner of the market and had a cup of green tea. He nibbled on apricot kernels and daydreamed about his future in the West. In the corner of his eye, he saw a tall woman in purple silk gliding toward his table. She sat down next to him.

"Are you looking for a friend?" she whispered. She had dark skin and black eyes, and her hair was pinned up, framing her face with looping bangs.

"I don't know," said Sobchak, startled by her arrival.

"I think you *are* looking for a friend," she said again. "Why don't we take a trip over the mountains together?"

Oh lucky day, he thought. "Don't I need to pack my bag?" Sobchak asked, immediately focusing on practical matters.

"We've taken care of everything," she said.

Sobchak paid his bill and followed the woman to a Lada sedan. She opened the front door for him. They drove west out of town. To the right was the desert, a vast surface of sand and scrub. To the left was a craggy mountain range.

"Where are we going?" Sobchak asked the woman.

"To Old Nisa," she said.

"Why Old Nisa?"

"It is where your past meets your future," she said.

It was a cryptic response, but Sobchak was giddy with anticipation. The torpor of Ashkhabad was finally behind him, and he was on his way.

Old Nisa was the home of Parthian kings from the late third century B.C. to the early third century A.D. The desert fortress of Nisa, built in 150 B.C., was the capital of a Parthian empire that included Iraq, Syria, and Persia.

They pulled into a dirt parking lot at the edge of the archaeological site just as the sun was beginning to set in the west. The air was still hot, and the sky was a mixture of day and night, orange and blue.

The woman led Sobchak past a rickety guard gate into a field of ruined royal palaces, temples, and tombs. A pack of mangy stray dogs slunk along behind them as they passed by excavations of clay-walled rooms. They walked slowly up a hill toward the crumbled edifice of the Mithridatokert, the fortress of Mithridat, the first Parthian king.

It is a lifeless place, Sobchak thought, but then his eyes fell upon the sauntering woman leading the way, her silk dress shimmering in the twilight. For five minutes, they walked up the hill through rocks and rubble, past the remains of two Zoroastrian temples, until they arrived at a tin-roofed wood shack that had probably once served as a storage shed for archaeologists who excavated the site. Through cracks in the warped wood planks, Sobchak could see there was a light on inside.

"This is where you will spend the night before you leave us," the woman said as she opened the door.

Sobchak entered the room. Five men were sitting on the floor smoking pungent hand-rolled cigarettes. One man stood alone beneath a lightbulb on a wire.

Vasily Tarazov was in full FSB uniform, including his wide-brimmed hat. He put his hand on his Tokarev handgun. Sobchak froze in his tracks.

"*Dobriy vyecher, Doktor Sobchak,*" Tarazov said with a sneer. "Good evening. We've been waiting for you."

Sobchak's hands and knees shook.

"*U straha glaza vyeliki,*" Tarazov said. "Fear has big eyes."

The men on the floor laughed.

"Sit down," Tarazov ordered.

One of the thick men in uniform gestured toward a broken wicker chair under the bulb. Sobchak took a seat. He noticed a large reel-to-reel tape recorder on the floor.

"Let me be blunt, Dr. Sobchak," Tarazov began. "We've come a long way to speak with you. We're tired and want to get back to our families in Russia. So please cooperate with us. It's in your best interest."

"*Ya nye panimayu,*" Sobchak stammered. "I don't understand. What is this all about? What do you want?"

Tarazov struck Sobchak in the temple with a clenched fist. "Please, Dr. Sobchak. Do not waste our time. We know you took something from Chelyabinsk. We want it back. It's time for you to tell us everything."

Sobchak's nose trickled blood. There were tears in his eyes. "I don't know what you're talking about," he whispered.

"I think you *do* know what I'm talking about," Tarazov said. Then he reached into his pocket and pulled out a familiar gold amulet, dangling it in front of Sobchak's nose.

Colonel Vincent Fusco scrolled the screen on his computer at the National Military Command Center. The National Security Agency's eavesdroppers had intercepted another encrypted FSB high frequency transmission, this time from Turkmenistan to STOS headquarters in Moscow. Fusco noted that the field report came from the same enterprising FSB captain who had investigated the apartment in Chelyabinsk-65. He made a note to start a file on this FSB officer. He imagined he would be hearing more from him in the years ahead.

The document had been decrypted and transcribed by the National Security Agency:

```
FSB FIELD REPORT


TO:      STOS HQ
FR:      CAPT. V.I. TARAZOV
SBJCT:   DR. GENNADY SOBCHAK
DATE:    7.22.96


Q: WHAT IS YOUR NAME?
A: GENNADY IVANOVICH SOBCHAK.
Q: AGE?
A: 42.
Q: OCCUPATION?
A: I AM A NUCLEAR CHEMIST.
```

Q: Who is your employer?

A: I am employed by Minatom.

Q: Where do you work?

A: I cannot say.

Q: Answer the question. Where do you work?

A: I am forbidden from saying . . .

(screaming)

Q: I believe you were telling me where you are employed. Please continue.

A: I work at Chelyabinsk-65.

Q: How long have you worked there?

A: Four years.

Q: What do you do at Chelyabinsk-65?

A: I am a chemical engineer.

Q: What are your responsibilities?

A: I work with plutonium from dismantled nuclear warheads.

Q: Have you spent your entire career at Chelyabinsk?

A: No.

Q: What did you do before?

A: I cannot say.

(screaming)

Q: Tell me what you did before coming to Chelyabinsk.

A: I worked on a secret research project at Arzamas-16.

Q: What type of research?

A: I am forbidden to reveal . . .

(screaming)

Q: Again, what did you do at Arzamas-16?

A: I was senior scientist on Project Hermes. We were developing a new weapon.

Q: What type of weapon?

A: I cannot tell you . . .

(SCREAMING)

Q: YOU WERE TELLING ME ABOUT THE NEW WEAPON.

A: IT WAS A PURE FUSION WEAPON, BUT THE PROJECT WAS TERMINATED ABRUPTLY.

Q: WHY WAS IT TERMINATED?

A: I DO NOT KNOW.

Q: WHY DID YOU STEAL PLUTONIUM FROM CHELYABINSK?

A: I DO NOT KNOW WHAT YOU ARE . . .

(SCREAMING)

Q: TRY AGAIN: WHY DID YOU STEAL PLUTONIUM?

A: TO PAY MY BILLS AND DEBTS.

Q: WHO PAID YOU?

A: I DO NOT KNOW.

(SCREAMING)

Q: I REPEAT: WHO PAID YOU?

A: I DO NOT KNOW.

(SCREAMING)

Q: WHY DID YOU BETRAY MOTHER RUSSIA?

A: I HAD NO CHOICE. MOTHER RUSSIA BETRAYED ME.

(SCREAMING)

Q: DR. SOBCHAK, ARE YOU READY TO JOIN YOUR GRAND-MOTHER NOW?

A: I DON'T UNDERSTAND . . .

(SCREAMING)

TRANSLATOR'S NOTE: INTERVIEW TERMINATES ABRUPTLY.

K yle Preston stood in the doorway, one shoe on, the other in her hand. She had snapped a heel crossing the Joint Command Center.

"Will you check again with the lab on the body they found in the baggage area at Hartsfield?" she said to Curtis LaFalle, her surly deputy.

"What? Are you afraid you'll break a fingernail punching the phone keypad?"

The sarcasm, of course, did not merit a response. With a swift strike of her clenched right fist, Preston knocked the heel off the shoe in her other hand.

"Every girl should have a black belt," LaFalle scoffed.

"Give it a rest," she said. "I don't have time for your job envy crap."

Ever since the Olympic security activities had begun, Preston and LaFalle had been locked in a rivalry. Born and raised in Atlanta, LaFalle had wanted the top security job at his hometown Games. After sixteen months directing the field investigation of the Oklahoma bombing, LaFalle thought he deserved the Olympics as a reward. But the job had gone to Preston, who was plucked from the FBI's elite Incident Response Group. LaFalle had complained to friends that this was another example of the FBI's institutional racism. Black agents never got the top jobs. He had been relegated to the "menial" role of Preston's deputy.

"Call the lab and report to me in five minutes," Preston said. She turned to see McFall, a worried look on his face, standing at the NEST desk set up in the middle of the infield where two technicians with headsets were staring at computers. They were coordinating the movements of ten nuclear search teams across Atlanta using the Pentagon's Global Positioning System to track their locations.

McFall walked over to Preston. "Here's the latest," he said. "We've hunted down another six of those gamma hits."

"Any luck?" Preston asked.

"Nope," he said. "Just more of the same."

"And how were they dispersed?"

"Not sure, but I think the common link is that they all turned up in suitcases and bags that passed through Hartsfield in the past seventy-two hours."

"Hartsfield?" she said. "Maybe that explains the dead guard in luggage."

Preston checked her watch. It was time for the Emergency Response Team secure video teleconference. She and McFall headed across the Joint Command Center to the Fish Bowl, where the tele-conferencing equipment was set up. On the wall, there were six clearly labeled monitors that brought together groups of people in different government SVTS nodes around the country. Preston recognized it was an interagency working group meeting with representatives from the White House, the Pentagon, the CIA, the FBI, the DOE, Justice Department, State Department, and Lawrence Livermore National Laboratory.

Paul Attaway, National Security Council director for global affairs, called the meeting to order. A Washington lawyer with close ties to the president and first lady, Attaway had a reputation for being a mercilessly efficient straight-shooter.

"Atlanta, what have we got?"

Preston looked into the camera and gave the update. "We've got a hundred radioactive decoys dispersed across the city. More than a thousand FBI brick agents are pounding the pavement. They're working with NEST volunteers to track the decoys."

"The problem is that any one of these decoys could be the real thing," McFall added.

"That's right," Preston said. "It's killing us in terms of time and people."

"What do you know about the decoys?" Attaway asked.

"They're not very sophisticated, but they don't have to be," McFall replied. "Our scientists have done some preliminary spectrometry, and it's probably MUF—material unaccounted for—from any number of plutonium facilities around the country."

"Are the decoys deadly?" Attaway asked. "What's going to happen to all those people who were carrying them around?"

"It's a little-known fact, but plutonium and uranium can be handled safely even without shielding," McFall said. "Pu-239 is definitely radioactive, but the particles are unable to penetrate even the flimsiest materials, like paper or skin. But if you ingest even a microparticle of plutonium, you're as good as gone."

Judge Louis Freeh, the FBI director, signaled Attaway that he wanted to speak. He was seated at a horseshoe-shaped table with a wall-sized FBI badge looming behind him.

"I'm well aware of the problem we're facing," Freeh began. "I even testified to Congress two years ago about the extreme danger of loose nukes from Russia."

Freeh paused and looked at the people around his table and then looked at the camera. "But the bottom line is that we have *not* received a threat message. We haven't heard anything from anyone about this. Not a word."

"That's exactly right," said Preston. "We've gotten the usual threats this morning from a few reliable crazies, but nothing nuclear."

"Let's back up a step," Attaway said. "Let's ask a more basic question. Do we *think* this is real?"

"More to the point," said Freeh, "can and will terrorists go nuclear?"

This was an almost impossible question for security planners and counter-terrorism experts. And *everyone* had a different opinion.

"I think there's one thing we can agree on," McFall began. "They definitely have enough stuff to make a bomb. After all, you can create a nuclear explosion with as little as two pounds of plutonium or five pounds of HEU."

"That may be true," said Vince Fusco at the Pentagon. "But I'd say the probability of a nuclear strike by a rogue actor is *very* low." Fusco was seated at a long rectangular table, surrounded by aides in uniform.

"Why is that?" said Attaway.

"Terrorists have had ample opportunity to use WMDs before, but they haven't yet."

"That's right," said Dr. Elissa Arnold, a counter-terrorism specialist and highly regarded operative at the CIA. Matronly and flaxen-haired, Arnold looked more like Martha Stewart than Mata Hari. "Terrorists have had access to chemical and biological weapons of mass destruction for decades," she said in a Boston Brahmin accent. "And yet they haven't killed hundreds of thousands of people."

"And I don't think they will," Fusco said. "Imagine the outcry. It would destroy the very thing terrorist groups crave: recognition and respectability."

"Look, the bottom line is *nobody* knows the answer to this question," said Irving Stickle, a veteran terrorism expert at the State Department.

"Yeah," said Preston, looking straight into the SVTS camera. "All this theoretical mumbo jumbo doesn't help us much on the ground. We need hard leads. Like what's the latest on Aum Shinri Kyo in Tokyo. Their gas attack in the subway killed twelve people and injured thousands. They're not afraid of mass murder. And there's hard data that they were going after a nuclear capability."

"Hold on a second," Stickle at the State Department said. "Can we get back to terrorism theory? Sure, there are plenty of nutcases out there like that guy, you know, Shoko Something-or-Other, the leader of that Japanese cult. But that's really my point. The screwballs don't have the capability to pull this off."

"I agree," said Dr. Beryl Braikman, a psychiatrist and terrorism expert on loan to the NSC from the RAND Corporation. "The actual motivation to pull off an act of nuclear terrorism would require psychological disturbances that typically occur *only* in extremely sick people like sociopaths and paranoid schizophrenics."

"In other words, deeply messed-up people," someone muttered.

"On the other hand," Dr. Braikman continued frenetically, "carrying out an act of nuclear terrorism requires first-rate organizational *and* interpersonal skills. It would be an incredibly complex undertaking involving a clockwork team effort. So here's my point. Someone who suffers from acute psychopathology and would *want* to detonate a nuclear device would be fundamentally unable to get it together to design and build an atomic bomb."

"That is," said Attaway, "the analytical mind required to create an improvised nuclear device isn't consistent with the deranged mind required to detonate one."

"Exactly. The two are mutually exclusive," Dr. Braikman said. "Paranoid schizophrenics and sociopaths could definitely push the nuclear button, but they are probably incapable of designing, building, or stealing atomic weapons."

In the Fish Bowl in Atlanta, McFall and Preston looked at each other and shook their heads. *These people just don't get it.*

"So let's cut to the chase," Attaway continued. "Who do we think we're looking for here? One nutcase? A team of ten? Or twenty?"

"One thing's for sure," Dr. Arnold said. "Whoever it is must be a virgin, you know, never been dirty before. Otherwise we'd have heard something about it."

"Look, I've been designing nuclear weapons for a long time," McFall said, "and I think it's extremely unlikely any *one* person is behind this. There are just too many different areas of expertise involved. For instance, you need to know the physical, chemical, and metallurgical properties of the materials involved. You need to understand radiation effects. You need sophistication in high explosives and chemical propellants. And you've got to be familiar with hydrodynamics and electronic circuitry. And that's just the beginning of the list."

"It took more than 100,000 scientists and workers to build the first atomic bombs," the CIA's Arnold chimed in. "But the conventional wisdom is that today it would take a team of no more than four people to pull this off."

"Or as few as two," Stickle said. "All you really need is an explosives chemist and an electronics engineer."

Preston felt the steam building up inside of her. "Look, I don't want to be contrary here," she said, "but I'm gonna have to disagree with y'all on this. For starters, there's no such thing as a universal terrorist mind. With all due respect to Dr. Braikman, I don't buy into this psycho-logic. From what I know, all terrorists *do not* fit into a single, convenient DSM-IV psychiatric diagnostic category. Indeed, from my experience in the Bureau working alongside a bunch of obsessive-compulsive paranoids, most terrorists seem pretty darn normal."

There were a few smiles of recognition.

"And as far as building an improvised nuclear device—an IND—it really doesn't take much. For obvious reasons—and I mean no disrespect—the physicists *want* to make it sound difficult. It's their job. In fact, all you need is a strong lead pipe, some explosives, and some fissile material. The information has been around for years. Just check the public library. The basic reference article is in the 1973 *Encyclopedia Americana*. There's also that Theodore Taylor book, *The Curve of Binding Energy*. And what about the *Los Alamos Primer: First Lectures on How to Build an Atomic Bomb* from the University of California Press?"

"Why even bother going to the library?" someone added. "It's all on the Internet, for Pete's sake."

"What's your point?" Attaway said impatiently.

"My point is that the plutonium is already here in the United States," Preston replied. "And we're well past the point of wondering whether someone could do a lot of damage with it. That discussion is a waste of time. You can create a whole lot of mess with a dirty bomb using a very crude design. Or you can cause a lot more damage with a more sophisticated design. Either way, it's not that hard."

"All right," Attaway said. "Let's move on. What is our posture on informing the public? Do we need to issue an alert?"

He paused, concentrating intensely, and then continued. "And do we need to think about postponing or canceling the Games?"

The last question was almost unimaginable to most participants in the teleconference.

"That's out of the question," said Donny Sanders, who had been steaming in his seat for more than half an hour. "You can't *cancel* the Games. As far as I can tell, y'all are pole vaulting over mouse turds. There's been no threat message. Some plutonium is missing, so go find it. That's your job. Mine is to run these Games, and I'm going to go right ahead and do it like we planned."

"Well, with all due respect to the gentleman from Atlanta, I don't think the Games should continue," said the State Department's Stickle. "We can't guarantee the safety of the public, and we've got billions of people watching from around the world. It's not just the Olympics that are on the line; it's also America's reputation. We should call off the Games until we find the plutonium."

"Play this out," Sanders said. "You're going to call off the Games of the Century. You're going to pack up 20,000 athletes, coaches, and dignitaries and send them home? You're going to tell hundreds and hundreds of corporate sponsors they wasted their money? You're going to go to NBC and say we've got nothing for you to put on TV? Come on, people, you're out of your minds!"

Sanders paused, his face bright red, and then continued. "Just imagine the press conference! 'Ladies and gentlemen, we're postponing the Summer Games, but we can't tell you why because it might create mass hysteria.'"

"Okay, okay," Attaway said. "You're right, it's not an option. We can't go public with this."

"I'm probably in the minority on this," said Stickle. "But I think we have a responsibility to tell the public. People have the right to know."

"We don't even know what we're up against," Arnold shot back. "So we could be creating mass panic and we're not even sure the plutonium is here."

"So when do we go public?" Attaway asked. "As soon as there is a credible threat?"

"I don't know if we can *ever* go public with this kind of news," Arnold said.

"What?" Stickle responded. "Let people die in a fireball without knowing what hit them? Don't we owe them a chance? What if your family were in Atlanta? Would you want them around for the Games?"

There was a pause across the country as each participant on the teleconference thought of a wife, a husband, a child.

———————————————

NBC Sports Update. The crowd at Olympic Stadium is going crazy, screaming, clapping, waving. At the end of the runway, Sergei Bubka, the legendary Ukrainian pole vaulter, holds a 17-foot fiberglass pole in his hands.

This is his third and final attempt to clear 20-2 and break his own outdoor world record. Bubka is the only man on the planet to have vaulted 20 feet—and he's done it 10 times.

The blue-eyed athlete won gold at the Seoul Olympics in 1988, but embarrassed himself in Barcelona when he "no heighted," failing to clear any bar at all. In Spain, he twice knocked the bar down at 18-8 and on his last try tipped it at 18-10.

This time around, the 32-year-old athlete is determined to win gold. Silver will not do. Bronze will be a slap in the face.

One last chance. Bubka takes off down the track like a sprinter. The long six pound pole bobs up and down. He takes off, rising feet in the air. The pole bends, then launches him skyward.

Up, up, and away.

For a split second, he hangs two stories in the air, then he rolls over in a graceful motion, and falls back to earth.

The crowd roars. Bubka's wife Lilja and two sons Vitaly and Sergei Jr. scream.

Sergei Bubka, son of a Ukrainian farmer, sets his 36th world record and takes home the gold.

The little wooden sign on Erin Showalter's desk said it all: "Look up and say cheese for the satellite camera."

Showalter worked in a dark, quiet six-story office in a blighted neighborhood of Southeast Washington, formerly known in the intelligence community as Building 213. Surrounded by liquor stores and pawn shops, the corner of First and M was an unlikely home for the CIA's National Photographic Interpretation Center. Inside the windowless structure, photo interpreters—or squints as they were known before computers replaced magnifying glasses—analyzed data coming from America's spy satellites orbiting Earth.

At that very moment, a huge KH-12 Keyhole photo-electronic satellite was parked directly above Atlanta, peering down through the atmosphere and ozone, generating photos so detailed that Showalter could see things as small as a twelve-letter word on a piece of paper.

Tens of thousands of security forces and hundreds of CCTV cameras at the Summer Games were not enough for vigilant Olympic security planners. Thus the U.S. government stationed one of its most sensitive satellites in orbit above Atlanta for the Games. It had been done before without any notice or fanfare in Los Angeles, Seoul, and Barcelona.

An all-seeing eye in the sky, security officials said, was worth thousands on the ground. The spy satellites were able to do a job no earthbound mortal could accomplish. They recorded images every few seconds. The data were sent immediately to the country's most powerful computers, where they were processed and then dumped onto the computer screens at NPIC. In bad weather, there were also two giant Lacrosse radar-imaging space vehicles that could see through clouds and at night with resolutions approaching photography.

The job of digesting all the information from the satellites over the Olympics fell to Showalter, a thirty-five-year-old PI and reconnaissance specialist. It was the most tedious work possible for a satellite recon expert, and this particular assignment bored her out of her mind. It was called B&A—before and after—and it was time-consuming and dull.

Showalter enjoyed variety and action, like the time in August 1995 when she had helped India pinpoint the location of Kashmiri Muslim separatists holding four Western hostages in the Himalayan foothills. Or when she assisted environmentalists in Tanzania study Mount Kilimanjaro to see if the earth's rising carbon dioxide levels were killing its high forests. Or the time she aided emergency relief efforts after Hurricane Opal in Florida and the Northridge quake in Los Angeles.

The job of Olympic satellite surveillance was nothing like all that. The computers automatically flagged certain changes in the images, and then Showalter's monotonous job was to make a human evaluation. This same technology used at NPIC to spot changes on the ground at the Games was also being used to help detect breast cancer. The image-matching principle was identical: compare before and after pictures of the identical scene; superimpose digital images over each other; remove features that have *not* changed leaving only differences between the images.

On Showalter's computer screen, the software indicated a hit, a major change between consecutive images from the KH-12 over Atlanta. The flash piqued Showalter's curiosity. She punched the button to call up the file and studied the image on the screen.

Sure enough, there was something unusual going on in the unpopulated, heavily wooded outskirts of southwest Atlanta. As she magnified the image, she saw what looked like a barn. There were a few farm vehicles parked outside.

She switched screens. This time, she understood why the computer had flashed an alert. It had picked up traces of an intense thermal burst often associated with the manufacture of explosives.

Showalter typed an E-mail message to her boss. Then she picked up the phone to call the Olympic Joint Command Center.

As they moved through the woods and brush toward the barn, the men in black jumpsuits and body armor were drenched in sweat. An operation in broad daylight was tough enough, but the sweltering heat did not make the mission easier.

McFall had badgered the leader of the Olympic Javelin Force into letting him participate in this operation by warning him about the danger of finding an improvised nuclear munition ticking in the barn. Though he had the requisite training in special forces tradecraft, he promised the Javelin leader he would stay in the background. He just wanted to be there if they found the plutonium.

Before moving on the barn, the Javelin Force had meticulously analyzed the NPIC satellite photos and concluded the operation would be straightforward. They could see at least four sentries posted around the farm, two guarding the forest behind the main building, and two in the brush near the dirt road leading to the farm.

The specialists split up into three teams. One would take out the rear sentries, one would disable the front guards, and the third would close in on the barn. The entry would take place simultaneously from the front and rear doors of the barn.

Assigned to the main assault team that would take the barn, McFall watched for tripwires and booby traps as he crossed the woods. Though he had not been on a live mission in years, he'd repeatedly updated his training, and with the MP-5 in his hands, he felt confident. McFall's personal security force, not happy with his decision to go in on the mission, waited in the wings with the rest of the backup.

Systematically, the Javelin operators implemented phase one of the assault. With each success, the radio crackled in McFall's earpiece.

"Sentry one, out."

Then a pause.

"Sentry two, gone."

With the perimeter guards taken out, the Javelin Force closed in on the barn, a large building with a corrugated roof and red metal siding that dominated a small house alongside.

The Javelin team leader signaled his men. "On five," he murmured into a microphone, and instantly his teammates on every side of the barn began the count.

The tension, the anticipation, was extreme as the leader pulled the big barn door open a crack. Miraculously, the rusty hinges did not creak to alert the men hunched over three big tables supported by wooden saw-horses.

"Six men seated," the team leader whispered into his mike. For an instant, he wondered if the microphone could pick up the sounds of his pounding heart. "Two at a table. Looks like an assembly line. Weapons visible. Three G-11 assault rifles. A pile of RGD-5 antipersonnel grenades."

"On my count," he continued. "Three, two—"

Simultaneously, the front and back doors flew open. The team threw flash/bang grenades into the room.

"Freeze, police!" they shouted as they stormed in.

Several bewildered workers immediately threw their hands up in the air; others dove to the ground, scrambling for weapons.

There was the roar of gunfire.

McFall could feel his mind achieve its sharpest focus. Seeing clearly was his gift, his special edge. Most men lost perspective in combat, but McFall had always been able to cut through the fog of war. Over the years, McFall had dabbled in martial arts and Japanese swordsmanship. He had been taught in hand-to-hand combat to look upon the enemy as if he were a faraway mountain. Musashi, one of the legendary Japanese samurai, called this "a distanced view of close things."

As the men exchanged automatic weapons fire, the noise inside the sheet-metal structure was deafening. McFall's eyes swept the confusion. In the corner of the barn, he saw a worker had finished stuffing documents into a bag and was now squeezing out a trap door. Instinctively, he made a mental note: the man was five foot ten, with a medium build and black hair. He wore a red-and-black scarf over his face. McFall ran low along one of the tables, keeping his head below the whistling bullets, and headed out the hidden exit.

The man had a hundred-foot lead on McFall, who was wearing forty pounds of strike gear. The distance between the two began to grow, and McFall could feel his legs and chest aching. The man plunged into the woods. Recognizing he would not be able to keep up, McFall fired a few warning shots. The man zigzagged artfully. McFall knew immediately he was a well-trained professional, a soldier of some stripe. As the man ran between the trees in an unpredictable line, McFall automatically registered the classic E&E—escape and evasion—movements.

He panted into his mike: "Genie One, Javelin Twelve. In pursuit of a suspect. Dark skinned, five foot ten, medium build, black hair. Black pants and a white shirt. Small green backpack."

"Javelin Twelve, Genie One. Gotcha," said the female voice in his headset. "No worries."

Like a fox hunted by hounds, the man ran for his life.

For years, he had stayed one step ahead of Aleph and Beth, the two Israeli hit squads formed in 1972 by Mossad chief Zvi Zamir to avenge the deaths of the Munich Eleven.

All of the man's Black September brothers were dead, gunned down by Israeli agents across the globe. Their names flew through his mind as he sprinted through the trees. Abdem Wel Zwaiter was shot to death on the doorstep of his Rome apartment. An exploding telephone killed Mahmud Hamshari. Hussein Behir Abdul Kheir was shot in a Cyprus hotel room. And in the most daring stunt of all, an Israeli assassin disguised as a Palestinian woman knocked on the door of a Beirut home and gunned down Abu Yussef, Kamal Adwan, and Kamal Nasser.

The man running for his life knew he had a rare talent: he could always find a way to slip out of the noose.

But now in the heart of the United States, which he thought he had penetrated without detection, his hunters were much better than he had expected.

They would *never* stop pursuing him. They would *never* call off the dogs. There was truth to what the Israeli intelligence chief had told his hit squads: "Maybe God forgives, Israel never."

And so, once again, he was on the run. Yes, he was gaining ground. The noise behind him was getting farther and farther away. He turned several times and glimpsed only one commando chasing him. Up ahead, he could see a steep-sided gully. Maybe, just maybe, it would give him a way out. He jumped down into the ditch and spun around. His angry eyes were now at ground level, and he could see the lone man in pursuit wearing full assault gear and carrying a semi-automatic rifle.

An easy target.

He trained his Czech-made Skorpion VZ 61 machine pistol on the commando, looking for soft spots between the plates of heavy body armor. He flipped the switch to automatic, took a deep breath, and squeezed the trigger.

A burst of six rounds exploded from the muzzle.

McFall heard the reports only a moment before he felt the thud against his chest. In that instant, his feet kept moving. His brain was telling his legs to run, but his torso wanted to go in the opposite direction. The pain ripped across his ribs and down his arms. The heat burned through his spine. When he hit the ground, he lost consciousness immediately.

One hundred feet away, the ditch was empty.

Switching courses, the man headed north through the woods. There would be more pursuers, he knew, so he had to move like a sirocco. Up ahead, he could see a clearing and what looked like the highway. Just five hundred more feet and he would commandeer a car. Then he would have a hostage and make his getaway.

As he came out of the trees into the clearing, a UH-60A Black Hawk helicopter swooped down from the sky, rotors thumping, dirt and leaves flying.

The man's escape route was blocked.

"Stop! Police!" an amplified voice boomed from the helicopter. "Drop your weapons and put your hands up in the air!"

Two hooded Javelin specialists leaped from the hovering bird and trained their weapons on the man. He threw down his Skorpion and raised his hands. He was gasping for breath.

"Javelin Twelve, this is Genie One," one of the Javelin operators said into her headset mike. "Javelin Twelve, this is Genie One, do you read?"

There was no reply.

With one hand aiming her MP-5, Kyle Preston pulled off her Aramid mask and approached the man. She was taken aback when she pulled the red-and-black scarf from his face and looked into his piercing eyes. There was no mistaking who he was: Abu Azzam, the vicious Black September terrorist who had eluded the Israelis for twenty-four years.

But she could not stop to savor the moment.

"Cuff him and read him his rights," she yelled to her Javelin team-mates as she raced into the woods, looking for McFall. She ran through the trees, leaping over a dry gully, and saw him several yards away, flat on his back, legs crumpled.

Oh God, no, she thought. She sprinted toward him and dropped to her knees. The front of his jumpsuit was shredded. Carefully, she lifted his head, heavy and lifeless.

She put her ear against his mouth and prayed he would breathe.

"Come on, Mack! Come on!"

There were tears in her eyes. She heard nothing.

She pressed her forefinger into his neck to feel for his pulse.

Please, Mack! Please! Breathe! Come on!

Yes, there it is!

McFall's heart was beating, barely.

Rebecca Deen dropped *Sports Illustrated* and reached for the ringing telephone.

"Hi, honey, it's me."

"Dammit, Quinn, where the hell have you been for the past week?" Rebecca Deen said. She had been fuming for days.

"What'd I do?" Lazare asked playfully.

"Where's my computer?" she demanded, her voice intense and agitated.

"How would I know?"

"Well, it's gone, along with my ID card and badge. They were in the apartment by the door, where I always leave them. And they plain disappeared the morning you left."

Lazare was stretched out on a miserable Army surplus bunk bed jammed up against a cold, damp wall of the Hole. Twenty feet away in the next room, his team was working silently, assembling the improvised nuclear devices.

"Come on, love," he coaxed. "I don't even know how to turn on a computer! And what would I do with your ID cards? I'm not exactly blond, blue-eyed, and five feet five inches."

"That's for sure," Deen said, smiling at the thought of Lazare in drag.

"Are you positive you left 'em by the door? You've been so stressed lately. Maybe you forgot them someplace else."

"No, I definitely put them down in the entryway."

"Have you checked with building security?"

"What do you mean?"

"I don't know. It just seems you should tell someone." Lazare was on a fishing expedition. Had she reported the theft?

"That's no use," she said. "If I told ACOG I lost my tags, they'd probably kill me. Those badges are expensive. To get replacements, I told the accreditation office my dog ate the old ones."

"But you've got to tell them the truth," he said. "What if someone's using your ID cards to get into the Games?"

"They're probably having the time of their life. But what can I do?"

"Dunno," Lazare said.

"So," Deen asked, flipping her hair, "do you miss me?"

"All I ever do is think of you and go to meetings. Meetings, meetings, meetings. But enough about me. Tell me about you."

"Oh, just more of the same," she said, twirling an ACOG pen in her fingers. She pulled off her earring and looked up from her cubicle to see if anyone was listening. "It's getting pretty intense around here," she whispered. "Everyone's on the verge of losing it."

"What do you mean?" Lazare said with a smile.

"I mean Donny is storming around the Purple Quadrant screaming his head off. And Hobbes has the look of someone who has seen the devil. I mean *really* seen the devil."

"Well, what's going on? Is everything okay?"

"Everything's fine," she said. "It's just the Olympics, silly. But everyone is wigging out."

"Are you taking care of yourself?" he asked, feigning interest. His eyes were locked on three silent television screens resting on wood crates near his feet. "Hold on a second, dear," he said. "Room service just arrived."

Lazare hit the hold button on the telephone and grabbed the remote control from the concrete floor. He raised the volume on one of the TV monitors and listened to the CNN report. The story was coming from Atlanta and showed a picture of Saturday's edition of *The Atlanta Journal-Constitution.* A local investigative reporter named Flagg had broken a story about unusual police activity on a farm southwest of Atlanta. There were not many particulars, and local law enforcement was not talking. But unnamed sources confirmed that one lawman had been rushed by helicopter to Grady Memorial after being shot five times in the chest.

Lazare turned the volume down and picked up the phone.

"Sorry about that, honey, my dinner just arrived. Another night of rubber chicken and wilted lettuce."

"How awful," Deen said. "Why don't you come home so I can fix you something? You know there are still leftovers from that amazing dinner."

"I wish," he said. "I'll be home just as soon as we wind things up here."

"And when will that be?"

"Real soon," he said. "Say, what's this I heard about a shootout today in Atlanta? It's all over the radio and television."

There was a pause. Deen couldn't understand Lazare sometimes.

"Oh, that," she said, trying to remember the single page of talking points Ian Hobbes had circulated to the media relations staff. "There was a minor police raid on a drug factory. A guy from New Mexico or somewhere like that was shot."

"From New Mexico?"

"Yeah, some nuclear scientist."

"A nuclear scientist? Was he a good guy or a bad guy?"

Deen knew immediately that she had said too much. The reference to a scientist from New Mexico was definitely *not* in her talking points. The ACOG brass and the FBI had decided to handle the Abu Azzam story by enforcing a total blackout on all facts.

Donny Sanders had prevailed upon the feds. Some of the mucky-mucks in Washington had wanted to fly straight to Atlanta to announce the capture of one of the world's most dreaded terrorists. It was the sort of success that the federal crimefighters needed. In the wake of the World Trade Center bombing in February 1993 and the Oklahoma City explosion in April 1995, the news of Azzam's capture would make people feel more secure again.

Donny Sanders had called President Clinton personally to make his case. They were old hunting buddies and fellow Renaissance Weekend participants. Azzam's arrest, Sanders explained to Clinton, would make a lot of people feel good for a few fleeting moments, but then reality would sink in: one of the most murderous men in the world had made it all the way to DeKalb County, Georgia. It begged the question: who else was lurking in the shadows? The news would cast a pall over the Games. Sports, not security, should be celebrated, Sanders said. The successes of athletes, not lawmen, should be praised.

And so, Sanders had argued, the Azzam story should be quashed until the Olympic flame had been officially passed on to Sydney, Australia, where the 2000 Games would be held. Sanders could be an extremely persuasive man, and the president went along with his request.

On ACOG's executive floor in the Inforum building, word of the arrest of a world-renowned criminal had trickled out. Near the Xerox machine, Deen heard Ian Hobbes talking about one man who had been wounded during the assault. He was a nuclear physicist from New Mexico. Deen had not paid much attention to the conversation between Hobbes and Rex Stratford, the bombastic director of ACOG security.

Stratford, the swaggering former Seattle police chief who raised crocodiles on his farm outside of Atlanta, had bellowed that if he had been in charge of the Javelin Force raid, he wouldn't have allowed a pointy-headed scientist along for the ride.

"Rebecca, is he all right?" Lazare asked.

"Is who all right?" she countered.

"The guy who was shot."

"Look, forget I told you about this," she said.

"Forget you told me about *what*?" he joked. He knew that Deen had overstepped the boundaries and he wanted to let her off easy. He had everything he needed; his mind was in overdrive. A scientist from New Mexico? It could have been pure coincidence. But more likely, it had to have been a NEST raid.

How could it have happened so soon? Maybe one of the radiological decoys had been planted inadvertently in a suitcase that ended up in a drug factory. NEST had stumbled into a drug operation, and a scientist had been shot.

So NEST was already on the case! They were certainly moving faster than they used to when he worked at Los Alamos.

Lazare knew it was inevitable NEST would try to find him. He was titillated by the feeling. All those do-gooder scientists hunting for him with their puny detection equipment. All those blustering ACOG officials running around yelling the Games must go on. All of those hapless law enforcement officers criss-crossing Atlanta searching for clues.

It was exhilarating.

Lazare readjusted the pillow under his head. He was a hundred feet below Morrow Mountain, and he was holding all the cards. He knew their next moves, too. In fact, he could see all the way to the very *end* of the game.

When he was a boy in Winston-Salem, North Carolina, he had learned the rules of chess in fifteen minutes. Within days, he was thrashing adults. And within weeks, he was bored with the game. It was too limiting. There were only thirty-two pieces on the board and sixty-four squares. He was able to see the end of the game long before his opponents had even gotten going.

A brooding loner at the age of ten, Lazare wanted a greater challenge. And so he took up Go, the 4,000-year-old Japanese version of chess, which was played on a 361-square board. In chess, there were 20 legal opening moves. In Go, there were more than 300. And in Go, the total number of different board arrangements was estimated at 10^{800}. In chess, there were clear front lines. The game was analytical and logical. But what Lazare loved about Go was that there were no front lines. The action was everywhere, requiring analysis, logic, and most of all, *intuition.*

For years, Lazare's genius at game theory had been rewarded. His rare gift had been appreciated. His brilliance had been tapped for the betterment of humankind. But then suddenly, it was discarded.

"Quinn, are you there?"

Lazare had been carried away by his reverie and had forgotten that Deen was still on the line.

"I'm sorry, hon. It's been a long day. Maybe we should get off the phone."

"Hey, don't you have anything sweet to say to me?" she asked.

"I miss you," he said, but his mind was elsewhere.

"How much?" she asked.

"Lots."

"How much is lots?"

"I'll show you when I get home," he said. "Bye for now."

"Hey, give me a phone number where I can reach you."

Lazare heard the question but hung up the phone.

T he room was blurry and his chest ached.

McFall was twenty years old and in the hospital at the Nha Be Naval Base in Vietnam. He had been wounded in a SEAL Team 1 operation in the Rung Sat Special Zone on the northeastern edge of the Mekong Delta between Saigon and the South China Sea. McFall's mission in the endless mangrove swamp known as the Forest of Assassins had gone terribly wrong. Nearly everyone in his platoon had been mowed down.

It was his Achilles' heel: he had overintellectualized the mission. He had meticulously planned every last detail. As a midshipman at Annapolis, McFall had been inspired by J. F. C. Fuller's book, *The Decisive Battles of the Western World.* "Nelson did not fight in order to carry out a plan," Fuller had written of Lord Nelson. "Instead, he planned in order to carry out a fight."

McFall had memorized the line. He, too, planned in order to fight. But when the shots rang out in the ambush on the Soirap River, his plan turned out inadequate. He had seen and understood what was happening. It was clear that a massacre was afoot. But he had not trusted his intuition, and he had stuck to his hopeless plan. Many of his men had died, and he had been severely wounded, catching shrapnel in his neck and spine.

And after all that, when he returned to the United States, he had been honored for his bravery. In Casper, Wyoming, his hometown, they had put up his picture at City Hall and Natrona County High School. He was the local boy who made good.

McFall could still hear the nurse at the VA cooing in his ear. He was a hero. But he knew he did not deserve the medals. He did not merit the awards. The soldiers he led were dead. And all he had managed to do was make it out of there alive.

The nurse whispered in his ear. He could hear her. He shouted to stop.

"Leave me alone. Please! You've got to leave me alone."

He opened his eyes, and the wrong face was peering at him. He wasn't in the VA hospital. Kyle Preston stared down at him.

"Hey, it's okay," she said. "You're gonna be fine."

McFall just looked at her. His mind was working furiously. Where was he? What had happened?

"The doctor says the shock to your system was the biggest injury."

"What happened?"

"Five bullets bounced off your vest. The impact triggered a Vagal reaction. We almost couldn't find your pulse."

He tried to move his arms, but his ribs ached.

"Thank God," he said, his voice raspy. "And thank DuPont for inventing Kevlar."

"You've got two fractured ribs and some deep bruises," Preston said, pointing to the lightbox on the wall. There were several chest X-rays visible. Even an untrained eye could see the thin, jagged lines of the fractures.

McFall lifted his head from the pillow to look down at his chest. The welts and bruises were covered with bandages. Almost unconsciously, he ran through the checklist: arms, legs, fingers, toes. Everything was still attached. He was not even on an IV. McFall knew he was very lucky. He rubbed his temples and eyes, trying to shake the grogginess.

"You were calling out in your sleep for Jenny," Preston said. "And Molly."

He closed his eyes and took several breaths. His subconscious always brought him back to his wife and daughter. There was no escaping the pain.

"Mack, I'm sorry about what happened to Jenny," Preston continued. "I heard about it a couple of years ago. I just didn't know what to say to you after what we'd been through."

There was silence in the hospital room for a few minutes.

Then Preston said, "I'm sorry, Mack. I shouldn't have brought Jenny up. It's just that you seemed so upset in your sleep."

"No, that's okay," he assured her. "It's a miserable life without them. Jenny is a big, big hole that I try not to fall into. Molly's doing fine, though. I talk to her every Sunday night."

His wife, Jenny, had died two years ago. Their daughter, Molly, lived with her grandparents in Virginia.

McFall knew he had to bury those thoughts in the deep freeze of his mind. He forced himself to shift to the present, and the chase in the woods came into focus. "So what happened in the forest?" he said. "And who shot me?"

"You really hit the jackpot," Preston answered. "And you're gonna be getting all sorts of medals for running him down."

More medals. Just what McFall wanted. He caught five bullets in the chest, and someone was going to pin a ribbon on him. Why didn't more people get prizes for *dodging* bullets, for doing their jobs right, for *not* getting hurt?

"So who was he, and what did we get?"

"Abu Azzam."

She did not need to say another word.

It was incredible. Azzam had squirmed out of the most elaborate Mossad traps, and now the Olympic Javelin Force had just stumbled onto him. It strained credulity. But that was how law enforcement worked. Sometimes it was just luck. Dumb luck.

Of course, that kind of lightning had struck before. Carlos the Jackal, at one time the most notorious terrorist in the world, had been captured in Khartoum, Sudan, in August 1994 while under sedation at the doctor's office for—of all things—*liposuction*. A caller had phoned in a tip. The police raided the medical office, and Ilich Ramirez Sanchez, the chubby Jackal, had been nabbed.

"You know," McFall said with a chuckle, "if he'd gotten me in the forest and managed to escape, he'd be the one collecting the big prize."

"Right, the Ayatollah's *fatwa*?"

"The reward is six billion rials and a guaranteed place in heaven," McFall said. "Not bad for a day's work. So is Azzam talking?"

"Absolutely not."

"What did you get?"

"We got a lot of Semtex-H. Several hundred pounds of PETN. We also found plenty of weapons."

"What was their plan?"

"We're not sure, but we found a piece of microfiche in Azzam's belt buckle. Get ready for this: he had a complete set of blueprints to the Georgia State Capitol Building on Washington Street. We think they were going to drive a truck bomb right up to the front steps and blow the gold dome all the way back to Dahlonega where it came from."

"Why are you so surprised?" McFall asked. "In every suicide bomb factory in the Bekaa Valley they've got the blueprints to the major buildings in the United States, public and private. They've probably also got the construction documents for *every* Olympic venue. It's part of that freedom of information craze that swept the country in the 1970s. Everything's a public record. All you have to know is where to ask!"

"Well, Azzam definitely knew where to ask. The barn was filled with phony Olympic ID cards, bogus press credentials, and even a few official-looking Team USA track suits."

"Standard infiltration tools," McFall said.

"Yup," Preston agreed. "We also nabbed a few of Azzam's henchmen, including Nayif Boudia, the master truck bomber from Syrian-occupied Lebanon. He's the guy who runs the secret school that trains suicide bombers."

"So, scenario number one: a truck bomb near the State Capitol? Not bad, but how were they going to get anywhere near it? The surrounding roads are all sealed off for pedestrian traffic."

"Good question," Preston said. "But Azzam seems to have thought of that. We found forged Atlanta Police Department badges and some knock-off uniforms in the barn. And one van was painted white and blue to look like an APD vehicle."

"Jesus," McFall said. "So what about the plutonium? Any traces in the barn?"

"Nope," Preston said.

"Have you asked him about the plutonium?"

As soon as he asked the question, he wanted to withdraw it.

"Come on, Mack, if we ask him and he *isn't* involved, then he knows it's out there."

Preston didn't miss a thing.

"And that creates a whole new set of problems," she added. "So what's your gut? Is Azzam connected to the missing plutonium?"

"No gut," he said. "Just sore ribs."

G us Rybak strolled through the brightly lit White Star Discount on Albemarle Road and headed for the pharmacy in the back. On this stifling summer day, he wasn't surprised to be the only customer in the store.

"Afternoon, Gus!" said a round woman with a bleached white bee-hive and matching pharmacist's coat. She was sitting on a stool behind the counter, polishing the lenses of her pink eyeglasses. "Haven't seen you for a while," she said, her teeth big and yellow like a horse's. "You been busy?"

"Real busy," Rybak replied. "Hey, where is everyone?"

"Most folks are probably whoopin' it up at Lake Badin. There's a town picnic today."

"Oh, yeah," he said, pretending to know.

"You still driving rigs for Pilgrim?"

"Eighteen hours a day, coast to coast."

"How long're you back?"

"Just the weekend."

"So what can I do ya for?"

"Need a refill."

"Risperdal?"

"Yup."

"Working better than Haldol?"

"Yeah, I'm not stiff as a board," he said. "And my face feels better. No masked man anymore."

"Well, you look handsome as a crab," she said with a wink.

Rybak felt his forehead twitch, and he spun around so Beverly wouldn't see his face. A Tourette's attack was coming on. "I'm—I'm—I'm gonna go make a phone call. I'll be right back."

"Take your time," she said, turning to fill the prescription.

Rybak hurried out of the store, his arms flaying the air like a Navy semaphore signal man at warp speed. A flood of epithets burst from his mouth.

He crossed N.C. 24/27 and lurched to the pay phone next to the Quik Chek convenience store. He punched in a memorized number.

"Collect call," he told the operator, then a series of slurs poured from his mouth.

"Say what?" the operator said.

"Collect call," he tried again, and the phone began to ring.

"Hello?" a voice said.

"It's me," Rybak said, feeling the wave pass.

"What took you so long?"

"Lazare's been watching me like a hawk."

"What's the latest?"

"Everything's fine. He doesn't suspect a thing."

"How soon until—"

"Twenty-four hours max," Rybak interrupted. "Maybe less."

"Be careful."

"Don't worry, I will." Rybak said. "It's under control."

Vicky Hollister stood in front of the flashing sign and stared at the whizzing numbers. *4.73 trillion and growing 8,000 per second* . . .

"What's that, daddy?" she said.

"It's the number of drinks that Coca-Cola has served since a man named John Styth Pemberton started the company in 1886," Herb Hollister said, reading from the sign on the wall.

"How many is it?" Vicky asked.

"Almost five trillion," he said.

"What's a trillion, daddy?"

Herb Hollister looked to his wife, Noreen, for help. She shrugged.

"I think five trillion is five with twelve zeroes," he said.

"I'm thirsty," she said. "I want one!"

After parading through the three-story World of Coca-Cola

museum chronicling the history of the *real thing*, it was psychologi-
cally impossible *not* to be thirsty. The familiar jingle—*Coke is it!*—
playing softly from the hidden sound speakers penetrated deep into
the unconscious.

The Hollister family headed for the Spectacular Soda Fountain
room, where Vicky's eyes lit up. A glowing machine sprayed twenty-
foot arcs of liquid in measured bursts into little paper cups. Vicky
gulped Coke Classic, then Cherry Coke, gleeful that she could drink
as much as she wanted.

In the corner of the room, a man watched closely. He waited, timing his approach. Then he closed in. He circled the little girl, moved
close to her, tripped intentionally, and spilled a Coke on her dress.

Bulls-eye.

"Mom! Mom!" Vicky shouted.

"I'm so sorry!" the man said.

Vicky stared down at her sopping dress.

"Mom! My dress! That man spilled on me!"

"I'm really sorry," the man said. "Please forgive me."

Noreen smiled. The man was young and pleasant-looking and
seemed sorry.

"Don't worry. She'll be fine," Noreen said.

The man knelt down on one knee. "Hey, little cherry. I just bought
something at the souvenir store for my girl back home. Maybe you'd
like to have it. Do you want a present?" He was holding something
behind his back.

Vicky glanced at her mother. Noreen nodded her approval.

The man produced a Coca-Cola can from behind his back and
held it in his palm.

"Just flip this little switch here and watch what happens," he said.

The red-and-white battery-powered can began to wiggle, shimmy-
ing and shaking to the sounds in the room. Vicky's brown eyes
sparkled. "Wow!" she said, grabbing the dancing can.

"Say thank you to the nice man," Noreen said.

"Thank you," she mumbled.

"You're welcome, little cherry."

He nodded to Noreen, patted Vicky on the head, and moved on.

The first contact had been made with Vicky Hollister. The next would be *much* easier.

G rady Memorial Hospital regulations required that patients be taken to the exit in a wheelchair. So Preston pushed McFall down the lime-green corridors toward the front door. Two sturdy men in blue suits carrying bulging nylon briefcases trailed them at a distance of twenty feet.

After twenty-four hours in the hospital, McFall insisted he was strong enough to leave with Preston, who claimed she had dropped in to brief him on the latest security developments.

"The Games are over for the day," she began. "All the teams are in bed for the night."

"So what happened today?" McFall asked.

"Do you really want to know?" she said.

"Sure."

"Okay. Let's see. We had four defections from the Albanian team. A *Gone With the Wind* fanatic from Japan went looking for Tara and got taken on a very expensive taxi ride to Birmingham and back. A few athletes from Belarus were picked up for shoplifting. And we had a serious poison scare in the village's main cafeteria."

"Anyone hurt?"

"No, just a threat. But food and water are a huge headache. They're serving 1.2 million meals in the village over the next two weeks. I just checked the numbers. That's 240,000 pounds of beef, 150,000 pounds of poultry, 70,000 pounds of cheese, and 550,000 gallons of water."

"And it *all* has to be *sanitized*," McFall said.

"Exactly," Preston said. "Sanitized to eat and sanitized for security."

Preston paused and tossed her hair absently. "Let's see, what else? Oh, four suspicious packages were dismantled by EOD. Five hundred folks were treated for dehydration and heatstroke."

"Aren't there enough water buffalo on the streets?" McFall asked.

"The Army's bringing in another thirty big tankers to deploy so people can get a drink. That should do it."

"Aren't you forgetting something?" McFall said, cracking a smile.

"What?" Preston said, earnestly.

"What about the plutonium?"

"No threat messages yet. We've rounded up 101 decoys. NEST is in the air again doing another grid search, but it looks like we're clean for the time being."

"Any traces on the decoys?"

"The lab had trouble with the gauze. But they think it comes from a large commercial manufacturer of hospital supplies in Germany."

"They're good," he said.

"The nuclear smugglers?"

"No, the lab."

"I know. We've got agents en route to Bremen to visit the hospital supplies manufacturer."

"What about the plutonium in the decoys?"

"That's a little more tricky. We sent the materials to Los Alamos for analysis. And they haven't reached any final conclusions yet. Maybe you could help and put in a call."

McFall nodded. Suddenly, Stan Treadwell flashed in his mind. He had been so busy with the hunt for the plutonium and then with his own sorry state that he had not checked on his friend.

He reached for his beeper, which had been put in a plastic bag with his valuables. It had been turned off; they couldn't have reached him. He had no way of knowing what had happened. *Dammit*, he thought.

"Listen," he said to Preston. "I need to make a phone call. Can you give me a minute?"

"Of course," she said, wondering whom he needed to call so urgently.

And then she caught herself. Why did she care? Why did it matter whom he was calling? She pushed McFall toward a pay phone where he punched in numbers to check his answering machine in White Rock.

There was no message from the doctors or nurses about Treadwell.

McFall called Los Alamos information and dialed the number for the hospital. He held his breath. "This is Dr. McFall. May I have the latest on Stan Treadwell?"

"Please hold, Dr. McFall, while I check."

The wait was interminable.

Then the nurse was back on the phone, and McFall could hear her shuffling through the medical charts.

"Let's see. Stan Treadwell is, oh, I see . . ."

McFall's heart was pounding. *Finish the sentence, dammit. Finish the sentence.*

"Mr. Treadwell came out of his coma yesterday. He is sleeping at the moment."

McFall felt relief wash over him. "Will you give him a message, please?"

"Certainly."

"Please let him know that Mack called and that I'll be back in Los Alamos in time to walk him out of the hospital."

"But Dr. McFall, he's not in very good—"

"Nurse, just give him that message."

He put the phone down and turned around to look for Preston, who was sitting across the waiting room, legs crossed, foot wiggling impatiently. McFall smiled, and she stood up.

As she walked toward him, for a brief moment he felt something, a rumble of feeling somewhere deep inside. He had been numb for so long that he wasn't sure what the sensation was or what it meant. It may have been his medication. It may have been his fractured ribs.

Or it may have been Preston and the way she looked at him.

"Everything okay?" she asked.

"For the time being," he said.

"Well, let's get you out of here," she said. She pushed him toward the main entrance to Grady Memorial on Butler Street.

At the front door, McFall lifted himself out of the wheelchair and tried his legs. He was stiff, and his left side ached. It felt like *all* the football injuries of his youth rolled into one.

Preston opened the passenger door to her Saturn for him, and he settled gingerly into the seat. Two gray vans were waiting for them at the exit to the parking lot.

"So where to, boss?" she asked. "Where are you staying?"

"I'm at the Best Western across from the Inforum," he said.

"On Spring Street?"

"Yup."

The night was warm, and the air was thick and wet. They drove a few blocks in silence. McFall weighed the thoughts in his mind. He did not exactly know how to broach the subject. "Are you hungry?" he blurted out.

"Always," she said.

"So why don't we stop for dinner?"

Preston's automatic reflex overrode her thoughts.

"I'm really sorry," she said. "But I've got a lot of homework tonight."

How many times had she used that line in the last year? How many times had she buried herself in her work? What danger did this man pose? He had just been shot five times in the chest.

"Oh, come on," McFall persisted. "Just a quick bite. And then you'll have the rest of the night to study for the spelling bee."

She laughed.

"Remember," McFall went on. "You owe me dinner at the Tasty. We made a bet about the plutonium. And I think you were wrong."

"Wait a second," she said. "I won that bet."

"No, you didn't," McFall insisted.

They both laughed.

"How about some grease at the Varsity?" he asked.

"You've got to be kidding!"

"No, I'm *not* kidding. We want fast food, don't we?"

Preston nodded.

"Come on," McFall said, "where do *you* want to go?"

"I can think of a bunch of places. There's always Bone's for steak. And there's a great Thai place called Zab-E-Lee."

Then she had an idea. "I've got it!" she said. "Trust me. I know a really nice spot."

"Nothing fancy," McFall said, looking down at his rumpled shirt and chinos.

"Nothing fancy," she repeated, as she pulled into a Kroger supermarket.

"Give me five minutes, and I'll be right back."

Preston headed into the market, and McFall slowly got out of the car. He nodded to his security detail in the nearby vans, then took a few steps to stretch as much as he could with a thick Ace bandage around his chest. Dinner with Kyle Preston. McFall did not know what to think or where to file the feeling if he had one. She was an attractive and formidable woman. She was tough and decisive, athletic and energetic.

Just like Jenny. The thought hit him hard. They were similar, Jenny and Kyle. McFall's wife had been a high school principal in Santa Fe. They had met one June weekend at the flea market north of town past the Opera. McFall had felt a flicker then, and it grew into a flame. They were married six months later on Christmas Eve in St. Francis Cathedral near the plaza. He would never forget that night, a crisp and cold evening with all the twinkling luminarias decorating the streets and rooftops of Santa Fe.

Three years later, Jenny started coming down with inexplicable fevers at night. Doctors were baffled. Then one day, they found metastatic malignant melanoma in her lymph nodes. Apparently, it had all begun with a faint little mole on her calf. She died fifty-three days later. Fifty-three god-awful days. And when death came, McFall was away in Fez on a NEST raid.

McFall saw Preston coming out of the supermarket carrying a brown grocery bag. He hobbled over in a gallant attempt to help her, but she brushed him away with a smile.

They drove east, along Ponce de Leon Avenue, toward U.S. 78. They left Atlanta behind them and were suddenly moving through darkness.

They rode in silence.

McFall knew he should be worrying about the plutonium, and so did Preston. Yet here they were in the Saturn, heading east, through the humid night. And that fact, the informally agreed dereliction of duty, charged the humid air with electricity.

After fifteen miles of silence, Preston turned off the highway onto a dirt road. She pulled onto the shoulder and parked. Thirty seconds later, the two gray vans appeared.

"What do we do about them?" she asked.

"Pretend they're not here," he said.

"You were always such a romantic," she said, laughing. "Follow me. It's not far."

And the two headed into the night, through a stand of trees. McFall moved slowly, his chest aching. The moon poked through the clouds, and McFall could see the crest of a small mountain a quarter mile away.

They came into an open field. Preston looked around and sat down on the dewy grass.

She reached into the bag and pulled out a bottle of wine, two paper cups, a loaf of bread, three wedges of cheese, and some grapes.

"Dammit," she said, groping in the bag. "No forks and knives."

Mack smiled. "Where are we?" he asked.

"Stone Mountain," she said. "This is where I used to come and play when I was a little girl."

McFall imagined it for a moment. A little girl, like his Molly, playing in the field. It was dark. But the thought of Molly lit the field. Or was it the thought of Kyle?

"Stone Mountain is over there," she pointed.

In the distance, the shadow of the mountain cut a half-circle in the dark sky.

"It's the world's largest mass of exposed granite," she said, reciting what she had learned so many years ago from her mother, who loved geology. "I think they call it a monadnock. It's about 300 million years old and more than 800 feet tall."

"What are you, a park ranger?" McFall asked, tearing off a piece of bread.

"Every good Southerner has visited this shrine," she said. "It's our Mount Rushmore. The same sculptor, Gutzon Borglum, made the carvings of the Confederate leaders."

"Who's up there?"

"Robert E. Lee, Jefferson Davis, and Stonewall Jackson."

Suddenly, the mountain lit up, first blue, then red and green.

"It's the laser show," Preston said.

"I love 'em," McFall said, pulling the cork from a bottle of La Crema chardonnay. "I'll never forget the show at the pyramids in Giza."

"When were you there?"

McFall thought about whether he should be truthful or not.

"My honeymoon," he replied. "It was quite an adventure. Nile cruise, the works."

Preston felt herself recoil imperceptibly.

They sat quietly, watching the lights and colors on the mountain. McFall felt like a dolt for bringing up Jenny. He watched Preston close her eyes and revel in the night air lapping against her face.

"Where are you right now?" McFall asked.

"Right here," she said, opening her eyes.

"Thinking about what?"

"Really want to know?"

"Yeah."

"The Olympic Flame."

"What about it?"

"Whether it will keep burning for another hundred years."

"What do you mean?"

"I mean, sometimes I don't know what the point is anymore. I just don't know why we even bother with the Games anymore."

"Come on," McFall said. "You're joking, right?"

"Not really. We bring 197 countries together for two weeks every four years. We lock them up in the Olympic Village behind barbed wire and motion detectors. We separate Arabs and Jews, Bosnians and Serbs, South Koreans and North Koreans, Indians and Pakistanis. We monitor their every single move. We isolate them from the rest of the world but make it look like they're 'up close and personal.' And what do we call all that? The Olympic spirit. International peace and harmony. Competitive cooperation!"

"Whoa!" McFall said. "What kind of wine are we drinking?"

"I'm not foolin'," Preston said. "I'm serious. I'm just tired of the make-believe, the bullshit. Sometimes I feel like we're in Disneyland, you know, it's a small world after all! How many times do we have to hear about the Olympics as the Global Village? The truth is, it isn't about amateurism and cooperation anymore. It's about big-time corporate sponsorships and cutthroat competition. Just about everyone wants to make a buck, kill each other, or blow the whole thing up."

"So what are you saying? There shouldn't be any Olympics? That we shouldn't strive for the ideal?"

"That's so typical," she said, flashing him a look.

"What's so typical?"

"That's what we all have to say. It's the Olympic doxology: praise be to the Games! We all want a better world. Of course, we all believe in international cooperation and harmony. There is no alternative. But I'm making a different point. There are hidden costs to this pseudo-unity, not just in dollars and cents, but in human terms."

"Like what?"

"Come on, Mack, you should understand more than anyone. Just look at yourself! You've got government goons following you around the clock. You can't even go on a picnic without guys with big guns watching from the woods."

Simultaneously, they both looked around, wondering where the security teams were hiding.

"Don't you see what we're losing?" Preston said. "Don't you see that we're chained to our fears? We're slaves to security!"

"Better safe than dead," McFall retorted. "I mean, if it weren't for those guys in the bushes, I might not be here. And if it weren't for what we've done today, Atlanta would probably be in flames."

"You don't know that for sure," she said. "The threats so far have been pretty tame. They're playing with us, testing our capabilities. If it weren't for *all* the security at the Games, would it be enough of a challenge for the wackos and bad guys? And if it weren't for all the hoopla and hype, would the Games even be a target?"

"Come on, Kyle, you're dreaming."

"No, *you're* dreaming," she said. "You're dreaming the world is

different than it really is. I mean, don't you ever wonder why we even
bother with the Olympics in the first place? Why pretend that there's
a thing called peace when for a measly two weeks we can't even live
together unless there are counter-assault teams on every rooftop?
Think about it."

"I try not to think," he said.

"Why not?"

"My dad fought for this stuff, and I've been fighting for it all my
life. It's a reflex. I don't question it. I just do it. It's who I am."

"What do you mean, 'this stuff'? How can you *not* question it?"

"Soldiers aren't trained to ask questions. They storm castles. They
carry flags. They keep the peace. They live and die. And they don't
ask whether their ideals are worth fighting for."

"And dying for?"

"Absolutely," he said, although his expression had changed. "But
there's no point talking about ideals now."

Preston took a long sip from her glass. Then she moved forward
imperceptibly. Her lips were wet from the wine.

"What about Mr. Right in New York?" McFall asked.

"Like you said, no point thinking about ideals now," she murmured.

McFall leaned forward to kiss her. He felt the ache in his ribs but
soon forgot.

"What are you thinking?" McFall asked.

"Don't you know?" Preston answered.

"No, tell me."

"Never," she said with a sly smile, leaning her head back.

Chuck Flagg sat in the back of Manuel's Tavern and listened intently.

He stared at the mug of Sam Adams between his hands and concentrated his attention on the conversation in a wood-paneled booth fifteen feet away.

It was one of Flagg's favorite hobbies, his own lonely game of I Spy. In any public place—bars, cafeterias, even baseball games—he would try to tune in to other people's conversations. If he focused enough, he often was able to pick up nuggets of useful information.

Sometimes it was purely prurient—bosses screwing young associates—and other times it was newsworthy and wound up in the next day's *Atlanta Journal-Constitution*.

On this night, it wasn't easy filtering the extraneous noise from the raucous tavern. The air conditioning was on overdrive, creating a blanket of impenetrable white noise. And there was a jukebox blasting Hoagy Carmichael in the background. For an instant, Flagg thought that if he never heard "Georgia on My Mind" again, he would die a happy man.

Flagg concentrated on a table of young blond women across the room. He listened and began to pick up slivers of conversation. The debate was over the relative merits of indoor versus beach volleyball. Flagg's receiver picked up several clear words.

"Karch Kiraly" came floating through the air. Then "Kent Steffes." Flagg instantly recognized the names of the great American volleyball players.

Flagg scanned the room and searched for another wave band. A group of college-age men was engrossed in a debate about Olympic mountain biking. The sport was making its first appearance at the

Atlanta Games. Flagg detected that the table was divided about whether it deserved to become a permanent fixture.

Then Flagg heard four words from nowhere: "Georgia State Capitol Building."

They were clear and distinct. They came from a deep voice. And they rumbled over the din of the bar.

Flagg made a mental note. He dug into the boiled peanuts on the table and continued to scan. But he got nothing.

He leaned back a bit to reposition his invisible antennae. Then he shifted his body and looked up at the television monitors above the bar and pretended to be watching Olympic highlights. Near the TVs on the wall, a framed picture of FDR gazed down at him. And so did JFK. Manuel, the owner, was a Democrat with a capital D.

In his peripheral vision, Flagg could see a table of men hunched over their beers. All four were high-level officials of the Atlanta Olympic Committee's security operation. Flagg knew most of them from their long service with the Atlanta Police Department. Together, they had more than a hundred years on the force. When the Games had been given to Atlanta, they had taken early retirement and gone to work for big bucks at ACOG.

Flagg checked his watch. There was still another hour until the last deadline. Plenty of time to get a story. But what story?

He had been waiting for a big story, a scoop that would really sock it to the Olympics and their official sponsors. It had been days since he led the paper with a breaking story, with an article that set the town on fire, that had people talking at breakfast and all the way through lunch and dinner. He had gotten a little scoop about a drug raid at a farm outside of town. But that was nothing. He was sick of writing pieces that got buried in the back of the paper between the Doritos and WonderBra ads.

Flagg had just spent two excruciating days on the most imbecilic story of his career. It was called "The Two Georgias," a 2,000-word article on the Olympic team from the former Soviet republic of Georgia coming to the state of Georgia in the United States of America. The story was a one-liner. Once you knew the point, it was over.

"Shazzam."

The word glided across the room from the table of ACOG security officials, and it rode on the same deep, clear voice.

Then again, "Shazzam" and "Georgia State Capitol Building" in the same sentence. Then "high explosives."

Flagg wasn't sure about the last two words; then they came again: "high explosives."

Jesus, he thought. Maybe these were the seeds of the story he needed. Maybe this was news. Why were these Olympic security guys talking about the State Capitol and high explosives? And what about Shazzam?

He threw a few bucks on the table to cover his bill and went out to the parking lot. He decided to try Ian Hobbes first and see if he could pry any information from the Olympic flack. He punched Hobbes's number into his cellular phone and waited.

For the past month, cellular phone service in Atlanta had been completely disrupted by the Games. The city's airwaves were RF— radio frequency—dirty. With so much official wireless communication taking place, there were not enough radio frequencies for civilian cellular conversations, except late at night.

Flagg got Hobbes's voice mail. *Damn.* He left his number.

He thought for a moment and decided he'd get Josh Rattner, one of the eager summer interns at the office, to do some database research. Flagg dialed the paper's number.

Yes! The phone was ringing.

"Josh," Flagg said, "I've got a big assignment for you. We're gonna win a prize with this one. So gimme everything you've got."

"I'll try," Rattner said.

"I need a database search on a guy named Shazzam."

"Shazzam?" Rattner said. "How many have you guzzled tonight, Chuck?"

"Funny, Josh. No kidding, check the name Shazzam."

"And I'll also check Batman."

"Don't give me any lip, boy," Flagg said. "Just start typing. S-H-A-Z-Z-A-M. I also need the phone number for the superintendent at the

Georgia State Capitol Building. It may be somewhere on my desk in the pile of papers behind the phone. Or if it isn't, check with Libby. She may have it."

"Anything else?"

"That's it for now. Call or beep as soon as you have something."

"Bye."

Flagg put the phone down. It rang almost immediately.

"Flagg, this is Ian Hobbes. It's Saturday night. This had better be important."

"Hobbesey, thanks for calling back. Hope I'm not interrupting a date or something."

Hobbes did not like the sound of Flagg's voice. He had returned thousands of press calls for the Olympic Committee and he was tuned in to the different mannerisms of the reporters. Some were friendly before they bit you in the ass. Others were ornery as hell before they lobbed big fat softballs over the plate. Chuck Flagg? He was all sweetness before he lowered the ax.

"It's late, Chuck," Hobbes said, "and I know you're on deadline. How can I help?"

"Okay, here's the question. I've been diggin' pretty hard on a story about funny stuff at the State Capitol. Do you have any comment on what's been going on there?"

Hobbes did not hesitate. He was determined to call Flagg's bluff. "You tell me, Flagg. What's been going on there?"

Hobbes knew Flagg was on a fishing expedition. If he had anything solid, he would have cut straight to the point.

"Come on, Hobbesey. You know and I know that your security folks are all over that place."

"Chuck, of course they are. It's the Capitol Building! And with the brouhaha over the Georgia state flag and the stars and bars flying from the dome, we've taken extra precautions."

"Yeah, but—"

"But nothing. There's nothing goin' on at the State Capitol. Drive over to Washington Street and see for yourself."

Hobbes gloated for a moment. He remembered the old Hollywood line that sincerity was the key to success, and if you could fake it, you've got it made.

"Look," Flagg said, trying to squeeze everything he could out of what little he had, "my sources tell me y'all are wild and crazy about a shady character with two Zs in his name. You must know who I'm talking about. Does ACOG have any official comment?"

Hobbes paused for a moment. How could Flagg already know about Abu Azzam?

So he stonewalled. "I'm telling you, Flagg, I don't know what you're talking about."

"Come on, Hobbesey. Give it to me on deep background."

"Sorry, Chucky. I don't have anything to give you."

"You can go off the record, Hobbes. Come on, no one will know we spoke."

"Fine," Hobbes said. "Let's go off the record."

Flagg felt a flash of excitement.

"I'm waiting," he said.

"This is off the record, right?"

"Absolutely," Flagg said with anticipation.

"Then here goes. Fuck you for bothering me on a Saturday night with this crock of shit story!"

And the phone went dead.

"Screw you, too, Hobbes," Flagg muttered.

Then he had an idea. It was bold and audacious—or bodacious, as his friends would say. He would drive out to Donny Sanders's home in Buckhead and confront him. Showing up at Sanders's house in the middle of the night with a half-baked tip was a good way to get himself fired, but Sanders wasn't as smooth with reporters as Hobbes was. He might blow his stack and let something slip.

Flagg was in a gambling mood.

The phone rang.

"Chuck, it's Josh. I've got some stuff for you. There's not a lot in Nexis under the name Shazzam. But I played around with the spelling. It turns out there's a bunch on a guy named Azzam."

"Good thinking, kiddo. Who's Azzam?"

"A real bad dude. International terrorist. Backed by Syria. Home is Damascus. Supposedly the last surviving plotter of the Munich massacre in 1972."

Oh, baby! Flagg thought to himself. *Too good to be true!*

Rattner continued reading from the Nexis files. "Let's see. Over the years, Azzam has been the brains behind two dozen terrorist attacks. More than 150 deaths. Big bombs are his specialty. Very big bombs."

"Way to go," Flagg said. "What else does it say?"

"I've got a clip here from a British newspaper. Azzam gave an interview to a reporter last year and vowed 'to drown every last Israeli in the Mediterranean.' And he also called Yasser Arafat a 'Jew-coddling traitor.' Oh, and here's something good. The State Department's annual report, *Patterns of Global Terrorism*, describes Azzam as an 'extreme extremist.'"

Flagg could feel the adrenaline surging. He was on the trail of a hot story. Now he had to nail it down. He knew he had a scoop, an above-the-masthead, prize-winning scoop.

"Keep digging, Josh. Now put me through to Claude."

There was no way in a million years that it was *just* a coincidence that the ACOG security folks at Manuel's were whispering about Azzam, high explosives, and the State Capitol.

He had to get the *Journal's* managing editor Claude Guillory to hold the presses. It would take some more time to get two independent sources to confirm the story. Now, if only Donny Sanders would rise to the bait and bluster or blunder his way into confirming the story. All it would take was for Sanders to get a little crazy and lose control. Flagg was gambling that a reporter's knock at his front door on a Saturday night would probably nudge Sanders over the edge. Then, when he was ranting and raving, Flagg would set the trap: a few pointed questions, some enraged responses, and Sanders would have confirmed Abu Azzam's high-explosives threat to the State Capitol.

Ingenious, Flagg thought, *a page one scoop, right from the horse's mouth.*

The sky glowed orange and black, and the moon barely poked through the clouds.

Buddy Crouse pointed Leila Arens down the narrow stadium steps of Georgia Tech's Dodd Grant Field.

"Where're we going?" she asked.

"The fifty-yard line," he said.

The grass was thick and dewy under their feet, and he walked as close to her as he dared.

Dodd Grant Field, home of the Ramblin' Wreck football team, was closed for the day, lights out. It was used as a training ground for Olympic teams. Claiming he had left some valuables near the long-jump pit, Crouse had borrowed a security access card from a U.S. coach.

Crouse softly put his hand on Arens's back. She trembled slightly, and he could not tell if it was a welcome or a warning.

They reached the center of the dark, oval stadium. It was like standing in the bottom of a big soup tureen, pitch black all the way to the sharp edge of the rim, and above it, the reflection of Atlanta's lights glowed on the underside of the cloud cover. Outside the stadium the city was bustling, alive. Inside, it was still, silent.

"Why did we come here?" Arens asked, spinning around in a little circle, head back, arms outstretched.

"I thought all Jim McKay impersonators enjoyed football stadiums at night."

"Never seen an American football game before."

"Then where did you pick up that McKay impression?"

"From twenty-four years of watching all the ABC footage of Munich," she said.

Crouse didn't say a word, and the two stood in silence for a few minutes.

"Come on," Arens said finally, "tell me the truth. Why did we come here?"

"It's the only place I could think of to get you away from all the distractions."

"Distractions?" she said.

"Yeah, distractions."

"You mean the Palestinians?"

"I just wanted to be alone with you, to get away from the Olympic craziness."

Arens laughed, her eyes glimmering. "Where I'm from," she explained, "you get used to it 'cause you can never escape reality."

"I can't even imagine," Crouse said.

"It's not worth imagining," she replied.

Arens tried to do a cartwheel on the wet grass and failed. "So what's it like in Montana?" she said, laughing.

"It's different," Crouse said. "It's natural and raw. Someday I'll show you."

"Someday," Arens repeated.

Crouse reached out to push the curls from Arens's eyes. Reflexively, she caught his hand. For a moment, he was not sure if her sudden move was in self-defense.

Then she pulled softly on his arm and moved closer to him.

cFall flicked the remote control and surfed the SpectraVision channels. The Vicodin had numbed his body but had not knocked him out. He sat on the hotel bed with two mushy pillows propped behind his back.

His ribs be damned; he was disappointed that Preston had begged off staying for an encore. The dogs needed to be fed, she had insisted. That was a new one, he mused. Anyway, their intimacy had been somewhat limited by his fractured bones.

McFall paused for a moment on *The Amazing Colossal Man*, starring Glenn Langan. He knew the 1957 thriller scene by scene: Lt. Col. Glenn Manning puts his life on the line to save a stranger who stumbles onto a Nevada nuclear test site; a plutonium device explodes; Manning is fried to a crisp; his cells mutate and he grows sixty feet tall.

McFall had spent hundreds of sleepless nights in fleabag motels across the United States and the world. Over the years as a result, he had become something of a connoisseur of bad movies. Some people liked spaghetti westerns. McFall liked radiation horror flicks.

The Amazing Colossal Man, bald as a cue ball, marched across Las Vegas, ripping palm trees out of the ground and smashing neon casino signs to pieces. McFall's mind fast-forwarded to the end of the movie. All it would take to save—and shrink—the Colossal Man was an injection of an imaginary agent, sulfa hydrol.

If only it were that easy. For an instant, his thoughts turned to Stan Treadwell in Los Alamos. There was no miracle elixir for him.

Don't go there.

The Amazing Colossal Man tore the roof off the Sahara Casino.

To distract himself, McFall forced his mind to recite his list of radiation favorites. First and foremost, there was *The Incredible*

Shrinking Man, in which acute radiation exposure had the exact opposite effect. Then there was *The Beast from 20,000 Fathoms,* about a fishy creature whose Arctic hibernation was interrupted by a nuclear blast. There was *Godzilla,* the infamous monster driven crazy by atomic testing. Irradiated monster ants in *Them!* seized a city's sewers and wreaked havoc. And in a milder vein, *On the Beach* was about a group of people waiting for the fallout from a nuclear war that had destroyed all life on Earth. Now here would be the title for a picture on his own life: *Waiting for the Fallout.* Or maybe his story would be a remake of *Dr. Strangelove: Or How I Learned to Stop Worrying and Love the Bomb.*

The evening picnic with Kyle had definitely wound him up. The gentle kiss in the dark had overwhelmed him with old memories and new longings. And so had the careful tumble between the Best Western sheets.

After a long cold shower and wrapping the bandages around his chest again, he had tried to sleep. But he could not get Preston out of his mind.

He saw a grown woman, strong and beautiful. Then he imagined her as a little girl, running across the covered bridge at Stone Mountain. And then he saw Jenny, her long brown hair blowing in the wind. From these images, it was easy to begin ruminating about how overwhelmingly lonely he felt. Here he was again—in another hotel room on the third floor of yet another Best Western. He had spent the better part of the past ten years in rooms with fuzzy bedspreads, mildewy pillows, and bath towels as skimpy as napkins.

But why was he here alone? The hotel was not the reason for his isolation. If he faced facts, the loneliness was a function of his obsession with the atom. It had cost him everything beautiful in his life. Jenny was gone, and he had missed the moment to say good-bye. And Molly was growing up at her grandparents' because he was never home to look after her.

All in the name of holy national security . . . or his overweening ego.

McFall had always kept himself too busy to indulge in self-analysis, and tonight this break in the action had trapped him in something akin to self-flagellation. This was definitely not productive, he told himself. Get up and work out the connections and clues that the team had gathered on the plutonium theft.

So he turned on the light, crawled out of bed, pulled out his files, and began to study them. The top file was on Yagmur Ovezov, the Turkmen coach who had smuggled the plutonium shot puts into the village. He had been held for a few hours in a cell at the fortress-like maximum security U.S. Penitentiary in Atlanta, then was released into the custody of the Turkmen Olympic Committee. McFall examined the transcript of the initial FBI interview on the morning of his arrest.

PAGE 2 OF 11

FBI INTERVIEW CONTD.   7/23/95
SUSPECT: YAGMUR OVEZOV

Q: HOW WERE YOU CONTACTED INITIALLY?
A: I RECEIVED A CALL FROM A MAN IN RUSSIA.
Q: WHAT IS HIS NAME?
A: I DO NOT KNOW.
Q: WHAT DID HE SAY?
A: HE SAID HE WANTED TO SEND SOME CARGO DUTY-FREE
   TO THE UNITED STATES.
Q: CARGO? WHAT ABOUT THE SHOT PUTS?
A: HE SAID HE HAD PUT THE CARGO INSIDE THE SHOT
   PUTS FOR SECURITY REASONS.
Q: HOW MUCH WERE YOU PAID?
A: $5,000 U.S. UP FRONT. AND $10,000 ON DELIVERY.
Q: WHERE DID YOU DELIVER THE SHOT PUTS?
A: THE VARSITY RESTAURANT.
Q: DID YOU HAVE CONTACT WITH ANYONE THERE?
A: NOT EXACTLY.
Q: WHAT DO YOU MEAN?
A: A MAN MET ME TO PICK UP THE DELIVERY.
Q: WHAT DID HE LOOK LIKE?

A: I do not remember.

Q: Try hard.

A: I did not look at him closely.

Q: Please, Mr. Ovezov. You have committed a very
serious crime. You must cooperate with us.

A: He was wearing a hat with American writing on it.

Q: What did it say?

A: I do not read English.

Q: How old was he?

A: I'm not good at guessing these things.

Q: Please try.

A: Maybe 30. Or 40. I don't know.

Q: What about his face and eyes?

A: I don't remember.

Q: Come on, Mr. Ovezov. Think.

A: I did notice one thing. His skin was very red.
He had been out in the sun. It happens all the
time in Turkmenistan.

The transcript ran twelve pages, and the artist's sketch of the mystery man in the hat looked like any average white American male. Strange, McFall thought, how those drawings always looked the same. John Doe 1 and 2 in Oklahoma. The Unabomber with his sunglasses and pullover hood. They were all interchangeable, monochrome villains.

It was clear that Ovezov was only a mule, a beast of burden hauling a fissile load.

The next file concerned Gennady Sobchak, his apartment in Chelyabinsk-65, and his subsequent disappearance. McFall studied the intercepted transcript of Sobchak's inquisition. McFall thought it was interesting that the Russian scientist had worked at Arzamas-16, the Los Alamos of the former Soviet Union, and had been involved in a secret weapons project called Hermes. He made a mental note to check the database on that program.

One exchange from the Sobchak interrogation struck him with particular poignancy.

Q: Why did you betray Mother Russia?
A: I had no choice. Mother Russia betrayed me.
(SCREAMING)

McFall imagined the FSB electroshock wires running to Sobchak's tongue and scrotum. Or maybe the interrogators had just used a sock filled with sand. It really didn't matter. Sobchak was simply the insider, the man with the keys to the warehouse. He probably knew nothing, too.

I had no choice. Mother Russia betrayed me.

McFall remembered that Kim Philby, one of the most villainous traitors in the history of the Cold War, had answered a similar question with a phrase conveying an equally forsaken ideology: "To betray, you must first belong. I *never* belonged."

Did Sobchak belong? Could anyone *really* belong in the new Russia?

He flipped through pages and pages of transcripts, but there was nothing in them. There were plenty of leads, but no direction.

He tried to put his mind into the place where the samurai had taught him to go. Get loose. Give all the random variables some breathing space so they can come together in a pattern.

Have confidence. See the forest and the trees. A distant view of close things.

He thought of the framed Chinese calligraphy on the wall of his office in Los Alamos. It was from *I Ching, the Book of Changes,* and it showed the Chinese character for *chaos,* which meant "where brilliant dreams are born."

The chaos would coalesce.

Let it happen.

The sound of the phone startled him. He checked the clock radio. It was 4:50 A.M. Who the hell was calling? Had one of the NEST night teams found the plutonium? Or maybe something had happened to Molly. With annoyance and no little trepidation, he reached for the phone. "This is McFall."

"Sir," the voice said, "really sorry to bother you at this hour. This is Lieutenant Gene Barzilay in the Joint Command Center. We just got a call for you. Sounds urgent. The lady couldn't stay on the line. She said she'd call back in three minutes. Should we patch her through?"

"Sure," McFall said. "It's not like I'm doing anything else at this hour."

He switched off the TV as the Amazing Colossal Man was shot by bazookas and plummeted over the edge of Boulder Dam.

"Call me back when you've got the link," McFall said, hanging up. *Who could it be? Jenny's parents? Molly?*

He shuffled into the bathroom and splashed cold water on his face. He looked in the mirror. His ribs were wrapped with Ace bandages. His eyes were bloodshot and there were dark half-moons under them. His hair was standing straight up. He wouldn't need a dab of makeup to play an irradiated mutant.

The phone rang again, and McFall headed back into the bedroom. He eased himself gently onto the bed and with great effort shoved the pillows behind his back. Then he picked up the phone. "This is McFall."

"Hi," said a low, husky voice. "I'm glad I found you."

McFall searched his memory banks. The woman's voice did not register.

"Do you have a pen and paper?" she said.

"Yeah," McFall answered. "Who is this?"

"It really doesn't matter," the woman said. "I think I have some information you need."

An informant? McFall thought. *Maybe a break in the case.*

"You've been looking for something," the woman said. "And I think I can help you. Just take down the following numbers. Are you ready?"

Cryptic middle-of-the-night calls like this had previously sent McFall flying around the world. Black-market informants with a hot tip. He knew he would have only moments to assess the veracity of the voice.

"Who are you?" McFall asked again.

"I really don't have much time. Take down this information. It will help you see the light."

He didn't have a tape recorder, and the JCC operator who might have traced the call was off the line.

Dammit.

He needed time. He had to keep the informant talking. He grabbed a pen and a Best Western notepad from the nightstand.

"Okay," he said. "What have you got?"

"North 31 degrees, 23 minutes, 10 seconds and West 81 degrees, 16 minutes, 30 seconds," she said.

Automatically, McFall repeated the coordinates.

"6 A.M. Sunday," the woman continued.

"6 A.M. this morning?" McFall repeated.

"Yes, 6 A.M. sharp. And one more thing," she said. "Be very careful." Then the phone went dead.

Two hundred and fifty miles away, deep in the Uwharrie National Forest, Quinn Lazare flipped a switch marked SEXY LADY on the black box attached to his cellular telephone. Around him, his admiring team hooted with laughter.

In Atlanta, McFall stared at the numbers on his pad.

Instantly, an image of the navigation charts formed in his mind. Then latitude and longitude lines appeared on his mind map. His father had taught him how to visualize the charts as they sailed up and down the East Coast. They had spent their summers together poring over maps, navigating by the stars, quizzing each other about lats and longs.

In moments, McFall had vectored in on the coordinates. He had been there before; there was no doubt in his mind. The lat/long was just off the coast of Georgia, south of Savannah, in the barrier islands near Sapelo Sound.

T he White House Situation Room was an utterly unexceptional place. Low-ceilinged and cramped, the space hardly advertised that it was one of the world's most important crisis management centers. If anything, it looked like a smallish wood-paneled meeting room in a second-tier Wall Street law firm.

This particular predawn gathering in the Sit Room appeared even more ordinary than usual. The cushioned swivel chairs around the rectangular conference table were filled with senior government officials. Behind them, their deputies occupied the second-string seats against the walls.

When the urgent request to convene had come by phone from the Operations Center in the wee hours of the morning, no one had more than a few minutes to put himself or herself together. Some of these senior officials had slammed on hats and baseball caps to cover their unruly hair. Others, lacking time to fiddle with contact lenses, put on never-seen-in-public eyeglasses. Dress was strictly jeans or sweats, with one Department of Energy official comically overdressed in a rumpled ball gown.

Paul Attaway sat at the head of the maple table surrounded by representatives from the Pentagon, State Department, Department of Energy, and Department of Justice.

"Rise and shine, everyone," Attaway said, opening the folder in front of him. "Let's go."

Attaway liked the seat at the head of the conference table. It was the same chair a host of presidents had used in times of crisis going all the way back to the World Wars. And as he started the meeting, he wondered, looking at the sartorial hodgepodge around him, how many times the man sitting in that chair had been awakened in the middle of his REM sleep, dressed in the dark, and ended up with mis-matched socks.

Attaway rubbed his ankles together and continued. "Atlanta, what have we got?"

All eyes turned to the bank of television monitors at the far end of the room. On top of the monitors, two red digital clocks were glow-ing. One indicated Greenwich Mean Time and read: ZULU 10:20:08. The other was self-explanatory: COUNTDOWN 00:40:52.

Below the clocks was a screen with ATLANTA printed on a white card taped across the bottom. Kyle Preston sat at the JCC table with Mack McFall and the senior Olympic security team.

"We got an interesting tip thirty-five minutes ago from a mystery woman," McFall began. "The caller gave me precise geographic coor-dinates. She said 6 A.M. was the appointed hour. And she said, 'Be careful.'"

"So where are we talking about?" Attaway asked. He had not been briefed during the eight-minute ride to the White House from his townhouse on 32nd Street near Dumbarton Oaks in Georgetown.

"We're talking about Sapelo Island," Preston said. "If you take a look at the map on the screen, you'll see it's midway between Savan-nah and Brunswick. It's one of the barrier islands of McIntosh County, Georgia."

"Never heard of it," Attaway said. Others at the table shrugged.

"It's got a long history," Preston went on, glancing at some scrib-bled notes in front of her. "In 1802 a Scotsman named Thomas Spald-ing built a mansion, a sugar mill, and slave quarters on Sapelo. Over the years, it became a luxury resort."

"So what's the story today?" Attaway asked.

"Not a lot," Preston said. "The island is cut off from the mainland. It's only accessible by ferry from Meridian, a shrimping village along Route 99. This time of year, all you'd find are a few tourists and a whole lot of alligators, water moccasins, and white-tailed deer."

She turned the page of her notebook.

"The main activity is marine research. They've got thousands of acres of pristine marshland. It's all managed by the Georgia Department of Natural Resources and the National Oceanic and Atmospheric Administration."

"So have we taken a closer look at the place?" Attaway pressed.

"We've got a KH-12 overhead, but there's thick cloud cover. One of the Lacrosse infrared satellites is almost there. NPIC will flash the image as soon as they get it."

"All right, we'll wait. But what about the mysterious caller? Did you get a trace?" Attaway asked.

"No," Preston said. "We missed it. In fact, we didn't even get a recording of her voice."

"Shit. What did she sound like?"

McFall had already evaluated the tone, the word choice. It was no ordinary phone call. And the woman was no everyday informant. It was really off the wall to have a late-night tipster warning him to be careful. "She was clear and direct. She sounded nervous, but it did not seem real. My hunch is she's not an informant. My hunch is she's a principal."

"Why a principal?"

"Because I think this was the threat message we've been waiting for."

"It doesn't sound like a threat message to me," said Attaway. "It sounds like someone who wants to do the right thing."

"Quite frankly, it sounds like foreplay to me," said Dr. Samuel Haass, director of the Communicated Threat Program at the Lawrence Livermore Lab in California. The CTP was responsible for evaluating the credibility of nuclear terrorist threat messages.

"What exactly do you mean?" Attaway asked.

"Well, to mix my metaphors," Haass said, "it sounds like the wind-up for the big pitch. In other words, here's a little clue so you can watch closely what I'm going to do."

The square orange light on the STU-III telephone flashed in front of Attaway. He picked up the receiver and muttered a few words. "Yes, Mr. President. Absolutely, Mr. President."

Then he put the phone back on the receiver. "The president has been briefed by Tony and Sandy," Attaway said. "He wants recommendations in thirty minutes."

The intercom buzzed. "Paul, NPIC is on the line. The Lacrosse has sent pictures of Sapelo Island."

"Put them up on the screen."

All eyes turned to a single forty-eight inch monitor in the center of the rack of televisions. Slowly, an image of Sapelo Island formed on the screen.

Every five seconds, the image dissolved and was replaced by another image, significantly magnified. The tiny sliver looked as if it were getting closer and closer. Within thirty seconds, the image had focused on the south end of the island.

"That's the lighthouse," Preston said as the image zoomed in on a round brick shape. "It was built in 1820. During the Civil War, Confederate soldiers removed the Fresnel lens to stop Union soldiers from using it."

The progression continued, closer and closer, until there was an image of a rickety bench between the lighthouse and a small square building.

The coordinates appeared on the screen next to the bench: N 31° 23'10" W 81°16'30".

The satellite magnified the image again.

"What the hell?" Army General Ty Warren said under his breath.

"You've got to be kidding," Attaway said.

All eyes focused on a small box resting on the bench. The Lacrosse infrared satellite image was not crystal clear, but the shape and size of the object were unmistakable. Everyone recognized the little plastic handle.

"It's a fucking lunch box," Warren said.

The satellite continued to magnify the image until all that filled the screen was the picture of the lunch box. The image was snowy, but the words ATLANTA '96 were clearly readable. Nearby, a toy-sized flag flapped in the wind. The flag had a dark background and a vertical stripe on its hoist side. In the upper left corner there was a white crescent and five stars.

In Atlanta, Preston and McFall looked at each other and then back at the screen. McFall hit the mute button on the teleconferencing microphone.

"It's either a runaway baloney sandwich or a bomb in a box,"
McFall said.

"Come on, Mack."

"I'm serious. There's no way of knowing."

"What do you mean?"

"We have to get near it to know what's inside it."

She hit the mute button to rejoin the teleconference. Attaway was
still talking.

"So what's in the goddam lunch box?"

"It could be just about anything," said Dr. Arnold.

"I recognize that," Attaway said. "But what are we going to do?
Are we going to sit around here until 6 A.M. and wait and see what
happens then?"

"We've got thirty minutes."

"NEST," Attaway said, "what can you do?"

"If you can get us there, we can take a look at it," McFall answered.

Attaway turned to one of his deputies. "How long would that take?"

"We could have them there in twenty minutes," his aide replied.

"That would leave us about ten minutes to fiddle with the device
and no exit time," McFall said.

"What about the 52nd EOD?" Attaway asked.

"No time to get a bomb disposal team there from Fort Gillem,"
McFall explained. "There's just no way we're going to get anyone near
that lunch box in time to figure out what's in it. No way."

"Looks like our mystery lady timed this pretty well," said Preston.

"So what do we do?" Attaway asked.

"Can we evacuate?"

"Not a chance. There are at least a hundred residents on the island.
We don't have transportation nearby. There's not enough time."

"Help me, people," Attaway said, pounding the conference table.
"Think!" The china coffee cups rattled on the wood. "Come on, can
anyone guess what's in the box?"

The Operational Threat Assessment team leader from Lawrence
Livermore spoke up.

"Obviously, you need a crystal ball to tell what's in the lunch box,"

Dr. Samuel Haass said. "If we assume that it's got one or more of the plutonium pits from Turkmenistan—and that's a safe assumption—then there wouldn't be much room for anything else. If it's a nuclear device, then the physics package would have to be very, very small. That means it would be very sophisticated, probably an implosion-type device. On the other hand, it could just be a few sticks of dynamite tied to the plutonium pit, in which case we're talking about a dirty bomb."

"So what's the range of yield possibilities?" Attaway asked.

"Well, if it's a crude device, it'll kick up a lot of plutonium, but the yield won't be very big. The size of the explosion will be a function of the size of the box."

The group in the situation room nodded in recognition.

"Now, if it's a sophisticated nuclear design, you're talking about a yield measured in megatons. Even if it fizzles, the yield could still be in kilotons."

"I say we take it out," said General Warren.

"Take it out?" Attaway said.

"Yup, whack it good with a thousand pound laser-guided bomb."

"Hold your horses," Attaway said. "What about *Posse Comitatus*? The military is barred from law enforcement activities on U.S. soil."

"Yes and no," one of the NSC staff counsel said from the cheap seats. "Federal law forbids the military from arrests, searches, seizures, and other activities enforcing domestic laws. But there's a big exception when the offense involves nuclear weapons and materials. In those cases, the armed forces can provide technical and logistical assistance."

"That's just great," a young deputy assistant secretary of state muttered from the rear. "We have authority to drop a million dollar bomb on a $5.95 lunch box."

"Listen, boy," General Warren said, spinning around. "It's called a preemptive strike. Hit the box before it does even more damage."

"And what happens if there's only a pastrami sandwich and a Thermos inside?" Preston asked.

"Someone's gonna need a new lunch box," General Warren said.

"Hold on! Hold on!" Attaway said. "We're going from zero to the speed of heat pretty darn quick here. Aren't there any interim steps?"

There was silence around the table. In all the crisis management exercises that had been run in the White House Situation Room, the clock had never ticked so fast. The usual options were not feasible. There was no time for NEST to be deployed to make an inspection; no time for a Special Mission Unit, or SMU, to be dispatched to disable the device; no time for a FEMA alert and evacuation.

No time.

Everyone knew they were working off the back of the envelope, making it up as they went along.

"If this is in fact an IND," Preston said, "does anyone know what an air strike will do to the device? Will it set off a nuclear reaction?"

All eyes turned to the NEST team. McFall said: "There's a possibility of a nuclear detonation. But it's remote. The bomb would most likely destroy the physics package."

"And what about the radiation from the plutonium?" Warren asked.

"That's a problem. We can check with ARAC, the Atmospheric Release Advisory Capability, in Livermore. They can calculate the plume. But since it's on the water, you're talking about plenty of absorptive capacity. That's not the worst thing that could happen."

"So game this out," Attaway said. "#1. We strike the lunch box, a radioactive plume floats out over the ocean, and we're clear. #2. We strike the box, the device detonates, we flatten the island, and at least a hundred people die. #3. We wait until 6 A.M., the device detonates, the island is destroyed, and we have a major public relations nightmare on our hands. Or #4. We wait until 6 A.M., nothing happens, and it's all a hoax."

"I think the little waving flag from Turkmenistan tells us this isn't a hoax," said Dr. Haass.

"But we don't even know if the bad guys have the technical ability to design an improvised nuclear device," McFall said.

"And we're not sure we've received a threat message," Preston added.

Attaway glanced at the countdown clock on the wall. There wasn't any more time for this debate. "The president is going to have to make this decision," he declared. "One final question before I go up to the residence. What about the media?"

"That's a no-brainer," General Warren said. "We have to keep a tight lid on this. This is a military operation, and there is no point in scaring the public."

"Does everyone agree?" Attaway asked.

There were nods around the table and from the various teleconferencing centers.

In Atlanta, Preston was unconvinced by the entire course of the discussion. She didn't have a better idea about what to do, but she was not so certain there was a nuclear device in a box where a peanut-butter sandwich belonged.

She remained silent. There was no stopping this train.

"Tower, Bengal zero-four. Takeoff one."

"Roger, Bengal zero-four. Wind zero-six-zero at ten. Cleared for takeoff. Runway five."

Marine Corps Captain Brett Hyland took the runway in his F/A-18D Hornet and made one last mental double-check: flaps half, trim twelve, seats armed, canopy down.

Then he threw the throttles through the detent to the burners, eased off the brakes, and the fighter-bomber shot down the 12,000-foot runway at the Marine Corps Air Station in Beaufort.

Good light off, Hyland thought as the plane picked up speed. At 100 knots, the plane roared past the arresting gear, a stopping wire strung across the runway in case of emergency. At 150 knots, the plane lifted off the deck and into the soft morning air. Hyland eased back on the stick, checking the heads-up display velocity vector to maintain an attitude of four degrees nose up.

The F/A-18 was climbing at 300 knots while Hyland looked out on the darkness over South Carolina. At five o'clock low, he could see the twinkling lights of the town of Beaufort. The Broad River and marshlands were at three o'clock. He passed over Ladies Island and could make out the shape of Hilton Head Island at two o'clock.

Hyland smiled at the thin orange-and-blue strip of light on the horizon.

Day was breaking. It was a glorious time for a live fire-training run on the BT-11 bombing range off the coast of Cherry Point, North Carolina. In less than an hour, Hyland and his partner in the back seat would finish their mission and head home for coffee and scrambled eggs.

"Coast approach, this is Bengal zero-four," Hyland said. "We're feet wet. Request clearance into restricted space, whiskey one-thirty-four."

"Roger, Bengal zero-four. You're cleared as requested. Maintain 20,000. Squawk three-three-six-one."

"Roger. Three-three-six-one."

Hyland, an experienced pilot, was about to be sent over to Bosnia with the peacekeeping forces. This was his last training run before shipping out. He punched in the transponder code. Then he hit the intercom switch to talk to his "wizzo" in the back seat, weapons system officer Joe Plager.

"How's it going back there, Stinky?"

"Okay, Spanky."

Spanky and Stinky were call-signs given to Hyland and Plager years earlier when they first trained to fly with the Marines. The origins of call-sign Spanky were mysterious but related to a sprained right wrist Hyland suffered one lonely night in the barracks. To all who really knew him, call-sign Stinky was self-explanatory.

"Bengal zero-four, coast approach," the radio crackled. "We show you entering whiskey one-thirty-four. Squawk appropriate codes. Cleared to switch frequencies."

"Roger, cleared and switching."

Hyland switched to another UHF radio frequency.

"Navy targets, Bengal zero-four."

"Bengal zero-four, this is Navy targets. Good morning, sir."

"Good morning. Bengal zero-four is on station for a zero-six to zero-six-fifteen target time on BT-11 Navy barge LGB target."

"You're cleared to BT-11 laser-guided bomb target. Located at the prebriefed location."

"Roger."

"You're cleared onto the target. Report when complete. Current altimeter is two-niner-niner-seven."

"Two-niner-niner-seven, wilco."

Hyland flipped the ICS switch to talk with his partner.

"Stinky, go ahead and sanitize the area."

"Roger, Spanks."

Plager worked the controls of the Hughes APG-65 multimode radar. In one mode, he checked the air space forty miles around the Hornet. Then he switched to ground mode and looked for ships on the ocean surface.

"Spanky, all clear, sea and sky."

"All clear. Thanks."

Hyland was flying at 20,000 feet and 400 knots indicated airspeed. The target, a barge with reflective panels for the laser-guided munitions, was ten miles away, dead ahead at 12 o'clock.

It was time to make a low-altitude cold run over the barge just to make sure they were bombing the right target. Hyland rolled the plane over on its back and pulled the nose down, making a forty-five-degree dive on the target. The F/A-18 dropped 17,000 feet in fifteen seconds. Five miles from the barge, Hyland brought the throttle back to idle stops. He moved his hand to the left on the stick and rolled the plane again. He pulled back on the stick until the nose came down to forty degrees below the horizon. Then he stopped his pull and moved the stick back to level the wings.

Bengal zero-four was at 3,000 feet and flying 575 knots. Two miles away, Hyland could see the barge. He was about to go into a six-G pull-up to climb back to 18,000 feet and begin the bombing run when the radio hissed.

"Bengal zero-four, Navy targets."

"Targets, this is zero-four, go ahead."

"We have an emergency mission from CinC USACOM out of Norfolk. Are you ready to copy?"

"Whiskey Tango Foxtrot, over!" Hyland said in disbelief. In military aviation lingo, the expression meant *what the fuck?* This was supposed to be a routine training run, and now it was an emergency mission?

With his hand on the throttle, he flicked his thumb switch for the ICS intercom.

"Hey, Stinky. What the heck is this?"

"No clue," Plager answered.

"I've never heard of anything like this before."

"Spanky, let's authenticate."

"Good idea."

Hyland reached for the 3 x 5 card covered with columns of coded letters. Theoretically, anyone with a powerful UHF radio and familiarity with aviation jargon could try to give orders to military jets. The index card with authentication codes that changed daily was the way Marine Corps aviators distinguished the good guys from the bad guys.

"Navy targets, Bengal zero-four," Hyland said. "Authenticate Alpha Romeo."

There was silence for several seconds while Navy targets checked its authentication tables.

"Bengal zero-four. I authenticate Oscar."

Hyland checked his card. *Yes, Oscar was right.*

"Stinky, this looks real."

"Well, fuck me flying!" Plager answered.

"I'm gonna authenticate again." He flipped the radio. "Navy targets, Bengal zero-four. Authenticate X-ray Romeo."

There was another pause.

"Bengal zero-four. I authenticate Bravo."

Hyland was stunned. "This is the real thing, Stinky."

"Let's go, Spanky. Let's do it."

Hyland hit the radio switch again. "Navy targets, Bengal zero-four. Ready to copy. Switch to covered frequency prebriefed channel tango. If no joy, pogo tactical."

"Switching to channel tango."

There was a pause as Hyland dialed in the secure radio frequency, then the controller spoke again.

"Emergency mission from CinC USACOM. CinC USACOM has authorized emergency destruction of a probable terrorist WMD at the following location."

Hyland's throat went instantly dry. WMD stood unmistakably for *weapon of mass destruction.*

The orders continued: "Target is located at southern tip of Sapelo Island. Lat/Long is North 31 degrees, 23 minutes, 10 seconds, and West 81 degrees, 16 minutes, 30 seconds."

"Copy. North 31 degrees, 23 minutes, 10 seconds, and West 81 degrees, 16 minutes, 30 seconds."

"Bengal zero-four. Target is described as a lunch box—repeat, lunch box—on an outdoor bench approximately 100 feet north of the lighthouse."

"Copy. Lunch box 100 feet north of the lighthouse."

"Snap vector two-six-zero for ninety-five."

"Copy two-six-zero for ninety-five."

"Bengal zero-four. Attack and destroy target upon arrival."

"Roger."

"And one more thing, Bengal zero-four. Fly like hell. You have eleven minutes to complete your mission."

Fly like hell . . . eleven minutes . . . attack and destroy!

Hyland pulled the F/A-18's nose around, climbed to 20,000 feet, and headed to two-six-zero. In the back seat, Plager typed in the coordinates and began looking for the lighthouse on the ground-mode radar. Sapelo Island was eighty miles away. The trip would take less than eight minutes, leaving three minutes for the bombing run.

"Hey, Stinky," Hyland said, "call base and see if this is for real."

"Roger." Plager flipped his radio. "Base, this is Stinky in zero-four. Do you know what the hell is going—"

"Yo, Stinky, we got this call from the Group CO and he says whatever Navy targets tells you to do is for real. Be sure to authenticate."

"Already done that."

"Call us when you're RTB."

"Roger." He flipped the ICS switch. "Spanky, base says this is kosher."

"Roger," Hyland said.

In the back seat, Plager found Sapelo Island on the APG-65 radar.

"Spanky, I've got the lighthouse. Cursors are right on the target."

Twenty miles from Sapelo Island, Hyland dove to 500 feet. The drop took twenty-five seconds.

"I've got the island," Hyland said to Plager. "Nav is designating the target."

Hyland scanned the heads-up display, a see-through electronic

screen that displayed essential flight, radar, and attack/defense information without requiring him to look down at the dials and gauges in
the cockpit.

"Stinky, the TD box is right on the lighthouse," Hyland said.

"Roger, remember the real target is a lunch box on a bench 100
feet north."

"Oh, yeah," Hyland said.

At three miles out, Hyland could see the tower of the lighthouse.
At one mile, he could see the bench.

Roaring toward the island, Hyland calculated that he would have
around five seconds feet dry to make a visual inspection of the target.
He rolled the plane into a ninety-degree bank so that he was upside
down, looking straight through the canopy at white caps and rough
ocean below.

The island suddenly flashed beneath them, like a train roaring
past in the opposite direction.

Come on, baby, where are you? Hyland thought, searching for the
target.

Then he saw the lighthouse. And a bench. And, in a blur, a lunch
box. "Stinky, I got it," he said.

"Me too, Spanky."

"Oh shit, did you see that?"

"Holy crap."

There were two joggers on the beach. And three fishermen wad-
ing out into the water from a spit of sand.

Hyland flipped the switch on the radio. "Navy targets, Bengal
zero-four."

"Go ahead, Bengal zero-four."

"We just did a cold pass over the target. And we've got five civilians in the area."

"Bengal zero-four, say again."

"Five civilians in target area," Hyland said.

"Stand by, Bengal zero-four."

The controller was gone for what seemed like an eternity. They
would never order him to bomb a target with civilians around. No

way, no how.

Then Navy targets came back on the radio.

"Bengal zero-four, you are ordered to proceed. Attack and destroy."

"Ordered to proceed?"

How could he proceed? He had been ordered to strike a lunch box on a wooden bench with a thousand-pound laser-guided bomb. And there were civilians nearby. This didn't make any sense at all. It had to be some huge mistake or a cruel practical joke. And it was probably going to cost him his wings.

"Please repeat the orders," Hyland said.

"Repeat, Bengal zero-four. Proceed with your attack."

"Roger, proceeding."

Hyland rolled his wings level and eased back on the stick to a six-and-a-half G pull-up climbing to 20,000 feet. He took the plane into a big, wide wagon-wheel circle, counter-clockwise.

And then he got ready to bomb.

Plager reacquired the target with the FLIR, the forward looking infrared radar.

Hyland said, "TAMPS complete."

They approached the target from the five o'clock position and Hyland rolled the aircraft into a forty-five-degree dive.

The F/A-18 bombing run had begun.

Then he rolled back out.

"Wings level," he said.

"Laser's on," his partner said.

"Good track."

"Sixteen, fifteen, fourteen, thirteen. Stand by. Mark."

Hyland pressed the red pickle button on his stick: "One away. Off safe."

Hyland said a silent prayer: *God have mercy.*

The Hornet shuddered as the GBU-16 laser-guided bomb was released. The vibration came from two shells blowing the bomb away from the airplane.

Gently, Hyland pulled the nose up. In the back seat, Plager said: "Tracking. Tracking." Fiddling with little joysticks, he kept the laser energy painted on the bench so the bomb could find it. If the laser energy moved, the bomb would go stupid.

Eight seconds after the thump of separation, the bomb hit its target.

"Holy shit!" Plager exclaimed from the back seat. "Nailed it! Beauty!"

Hyland rolled the airplane and pulled it around so he could see his handiwork.

The roiling fireball was orange and red, like the sun peeking over the ocean.

I nstantaneously, the satellite image of the GBU-16 strike on Sapelo Island flashed on the large monitors in the White House Sit Room and the Olympic Joint Command Center.

At both locales, the tension was palpable.

In Atlanta, McFall scrutinized the explosion for the brightness of the flash and the shape of the burgeoning cloud of smoke and fire. It was discreet and limited, without a telltale mushroom cloud. He could feel the relief wash over him.

Even as they were examining the satellite images on the screen, an Aerial Measuring System team from Andrews Air Force Base in Maryland was approaching Sapelo Island. The team was part of FRMAC, the Federal Radiological Monitoring and Assessment Center. As soon as the order had been given to strike, the manager of DOE's Nevada Operations office had mobilized FRMAC, a cadre of highly trained and experienced scientists, technicians, and support personnel ready to respond to any radiological emergency in the nation.

The FRMAC Beechcraft King Air 200 had flown from Andrews Air Force Base straight to Georgia's barrier islands. The plane circled the explosion, taking radiation readings with aerial detectors and air samples with special filters and containers. The information was analyzed initially by the team of scientists on the plane, transmitted to the Remote Sensing Laboratory at Nellis Air Force Base located outside of Las Vegas for processing, and then forwarded to Lawrence Livermore for study.

All told, the collection and preliminary analysis had taken about twenty minutes. McFall already had the report in front of him. It was only a few lines.

```
LLNL PRELIM ANAL              7/28/96
GPD: ZOX-XOX101010      BLUE LIGHT


0 uCɪ/м2 Pu-239 > 1.0
0 uCɪ/м2 Pu-239 > 3.0
0 uCɪ/м2 Pu-239 > 10.0
0 uCɪ/м2 Pu-239 > 30.0
0 uCɪ/м2 Pu-239 > 100.0


0 uCɪ/м2 U-235 > 1.0
0 uCɪ/м2 U-235 > 3.0
0 uCɪ/м2 U-235 > 10.0
0 uCɪ/м2 U-235 > 30.0
0 uCɪ/м2 U-235 > 100.0


5  uCɪ/м2 D/T > 1.0
7  uCɪ/м2 D/T > 3.0
9  uCɪ/м2 D/T > 10.0
11 uCɪ/м2 D/T > 30.0
13 uCɪ/м2 D/T > 100.0
```

Oᴛʜᴇʀ ᴛʀᴀᴄᴇs ᴘʀᴇsᴇɴᴛ: ᴍᴇʀᴄᴜʀʏ ᴀɴᴛɪᴍᴏɴʏ ᴏxɪᴅᴇ.

McFall let the numbers sink in. He was completely taken aback. There was not a trace of plutonium from the explosion. All the readings were zero. But there was still a significant radioactive release. And there were ample signs of deuterium and tritium. And there were also traces of mercury antimony oxide.

McFall called Lawrence Livermore to speak with Dr. Marek Lukasiewicz, the Polish-born scientist who had run the analysis. "Luke, are you positive there was *no* plutonium present?"

"Absolutely," Lukasiewicz said.

"And what about the monitoring equipment? When was it last tested?"

"How the hell would I know?" the scientist said impatiently. "They just send us the data, and we interpret it."

"Sorry," McFall said. "It's just that it doesn't make any sense. What do you make of the mercury antimony oxide?"

"No idea. It's not from the GBU-16. It could be a high explosive. We're running it against other compounds in the databases."

"Thanks for your help," McFall said and put down the phone. He had a big knot in his stomach. He needed help. Reflexively, he wanted to call Stan Treadwell. He dialed the number of the Los Alamos hospital and braced himself again for more bad news.

Instead, the nurse patched him right through to Treadwell's room.

"Hey, big boy," Treadwell said, "how ya doin'?" His voice sounded woozy, and his words were slow.

"No better than you are," McFall said. "I need your help. I'm gonna fax you something. I've got some samples from an explosion off the coast of Georgia. There's deuterium and tritium all over the place, but no signs of HEU or plutonium. And there's also some mercury antimony oxide."

"Mack, are you thinking what I'm thinking?"

Separated by 1,410 miles, both men said the words simultaneously: "Pure fusion."

Then, an instant later: "Red Mercury."

"Un-fucking believable!" Treadwell said. "What do you know about the device?"

"Nothing," McFall said. "The Marines just blew it to Kingdom Come."

"And all you've got are the traces from the air samples?"

"Nothing else."

"No designs?"

"Nope."

"Well, you won't be able to do much with those samples."

"Could someone else have done it?" McFall asked.

"What do you mean?"

"I mean could someone have beaten us to the punch? Could someone have made Red Mercury?"

"It's possible. There were always rumors that the comrades at

Arzamas-16 were way ahead of us on RM. But no one—"

"That's it!" McFall interrupted.

"What?"

"That's it! The Russians! Sobchak worked on Project Hermes at Arzamas. I didn't make the connection before, but Hermes is the *other* name for the Roman god Mercury."

"Slow down," Treadwell said. "What are you motor-mouthing about?"

"It fits, Stan. They didn't smuggle plutonium in those shot puts. They smuggled Red Mercury!"

Donny Sanders looked out the window of his plush corner office in the Inforum building. Below him, stretching fifty acres across the southwest corner of downtown Atlanta, was his pride and joy, Centennial Olympic Park. Under the morning sun the skyscrapers cast long shadows over crowds of tourists and athletes strolling past the fountains in the park.

Sanders rolled the Fonseca in his mouth. He had sweated over the funding of every inch of the park and had even resorted to selling individual paving bricks for $35 each to thousands of enthusiasts who wanted to own a piece of the Centennial Games.

There it was, in the morning sunlight, a permanent jewel for Atlanta, a lasting monument to the Games after the nations of the world had gone home. Sanders's eyes passed over the many attractions in the park. There was the AT&T Global Village for the athletes and their families; an Olympic Superstore with official merchandise; and Southern Crossroads, a six-acre festival area celebrating American Dixie.

Day Nine of the Games had not even begun, but Sanders knew in his gut this would definitely be a six-cigar day. Or maybe seven.

He had invested everything in these Games. It had begun in February 1986, when he had awakened early one morning and gone to his law office before sunrise. With a blank yellow pad in front of him, he had made a list of things he could do to bring meaning to his life, work that would make a lasting difference for the city and the state he loved.

And like a bolt from the blue, the idea of bringing the Olympics to Atlanta had dawned on him. Now, ten years later, he was waiting for word from the FBI about whether the climax of his dream would have to be aborted.

Unbelievable!

Sanders felt out of control. It was a sensation he had not known in years, the momentary paralysis of dropping back to pass from his own ten-yard line and being blitzed by the Crimson Tide. Scrambling was futile. He could hear the grunting and feel the turf shaking as the Alabama linemen closed in. It was a moment of simultaneous exhilaration and terror—the moment when he saw the receiver down field and knew he could throw for a first down or when he braced for a bone-crushing collision as the defense tried to break his ribs and rip his head off.

That was how Sanders saw the world: it was a giant bowl game. He liked to throw long. He loved to run up the score. He craved the roar of the crowds. And he did not like being blitzed.

The phone on his desk buzzed.

"The Russians are on line two. It's Stanislav Burlatsky."

"What the hell does Burlatsky want at this hour?" Sanders barked.

"It sounds pretty urgent," his secretary said. Her voice was level despite the fact that she had been working virtually round the clock. "There was a lot of shouting in the background."

"All right," Sanders said, hitting the button for line two.

"Stan the man!" Sanders said, putting on his warmest voice. "Top of the mornin' to you, Stanislav. What's up, my friend? How are they treating you over at Russia House? Have you been in that fine swimming pool?"

Sanders was referring to the Greek revival mansion on Whitewater Trail that had been given, rent-free, to the Russian Olympic Committee for the duration of the Games. The elegant 2.8-acre private home was surrounded by the Chattahoochee River National Recreation Area and belonged to a prominent local stockbroker and close friend of Sanders.

Burlatsky, the cantankerous head of the Russian Olympic Committee, didn't have time for pleasantries. His raspy voice was imperious and accusatory. "Mr. Sanders, we have just spoken with Moscow, and we are calling to inform you the Russian team is leaving Atlanta. We are pulling out of the Games."

Sanders's heart literally skipped a beat. The cigar fell from his hand. *What the hell? Why was Russia pulling out of the Games?*

The intercom beeped and Sanders's secretary spoke again. "The Chinese are on line one. It's urgent."

Sanders covered the receiver of the phone. "Tell the Chinese to wait."

He took his hand off the phone and continued. "Stanislav, I don't understand. Did I hear you right? You're leaving Atlanta? There must be some misunderstanding!"

"Mr. Sanders, your country has made a mockery of Russia. We have no choice but to leave under protest. I believe that my government is calling President Clinton at this very moment. I will leave the international politics to them."

Sanders noted that Burlatsky was addressing him formally and in deliberate diplomatic parlance. They had worked together for nearly ten years. What was going on? He knew he had to scramble or call time out. "Stanislav, old buddy. Please, what's the problem? What can I do? Your team has been doing so well. Alexandr Popov just shattered the world record in the pool. You're racking up medals. Please?"

"Your country has humiliated Russia by conducting an above-ground nuclear test of some kind. Russian spy satellites have picked up evidence of a radiological explosion. And our government has ordered us to leave the United States immediately. Your nuclear test was in direct contravention of the Nuclear Test Ban Treaty."

Burlatsky sounded like he was reading from a carefully scripted text, probably a cable from the Russian Embassy in Washington.

Sanders could not believe his ears. Spy satellites, radiological something or other, nuclear testing?

Jesus H. Christ!

"Stanislav, I'm going to call my friend in the Oval Office right away. There must be some kind of mistake. Please don't do anything until I get back to you."

"Very well," Burlatsky said, "but Aeroflot is making immediate preparations for our departure."

They hung up.

"Kelly, who's on line one?" he shouted to his secretary.

"The Chinese."

Sanders picked up the phone again and Qian Li, the head of the PRC Olympic Committee, began shouting immediately.

The story was the same. A Chinese FSW-1 spy satellite had picked up evidence of an aboveground U.S. nuclear test off the coast of Georgia.

"China is leaving Atlanta immediately," said Qian Li. "Your country has committed a grave offense and it will not be tolerated by the People's Republic."

Sanders saw his Games unraveling, his dream destroyed. He closed his eyes for a moment, and he could hear the thunder of cleats as they tore up the gridiron turf. They were closing in on him.

He picked up the intercom and shouted for his secretary. She appeared almost instantly in his office. A tall, blond woman in her mid-fifties, she was wearing a fitted burgundy suit and carried a notepad. "Yes, sir?" she said, bracing for the onslaught.

"Get me the White House right away. I need the President immediately. And while you're at it, get Newt on the phone. Hurry!"

L azare's team heard within a few minutes of the explosion that the first strike had been a success. A spotter, watching from Meridian, a fishing village near Sapelo Island, witnessed the flash of white light across the water and heard the boom several seconds later, low and loud.

His call to the Hole had produced a kind of grim jubilation, and Lazare had broken out a bottle of Korbel champagne to celebrate this success and improve upon their spartan breakfast. The group hung around the small television, sipping champagne from Dixie cups, waiting for more news.

CNN had been reporting for several hours that there had been a radiological release off the Georgia coast. Meteorologists stood in front of maps and pointed out the prevailing winds. Several experts from the nuclear industry speculated that the radioactive cloud would be carried out to sea. The only question was whether the plume would dissipate by the time it hit land again in the Bahamas. No one seemed to have any answers.

Indulging himself with a little bubbly, Lazare paced back and forth, mulling over his next steps. He watched his men, who were jubilant that the first explosion came off perfectly.

But he could see ahead to the next several moves.

This celebration would not last. In a matter of minutes, maybe hours, the government would make its move. If the game were chess, they would desperately sacrifice a knight so they would have time to castle and defend their tottering king.

But Lazare was playing a different game, one on many fronts.

It was inevitable that his men would be disappointed and dismayed. They would be foiled. But even this was part of Lazare's plan.

"And now, a CNN Special Report," the announcer declared.

"Shhhh! Pay attention!" one of Lazare's men said. The conviviality disappeared, and all eyes focused on blue-eyed CNN anchorwoman Bobbie Battista.

"Good morning," she began, "and welcome to this CNN Special Report: Radiation in the Atlantic. In case you're just joining us, an explosion ripped the coast of Georgia early this morning. The location: tiny Sapelo Island. At present there is no reliable information about casualties, but there are unconfirmed reports that radiation has been detected in the area. Now live in a helicopter near the island, here is CNN's John Holliman."

The picture changed, and a fuzzy image appeared of a man, hair buffeted by the wind, crouched in the cramped cockpit of a helicopter. The noise of the rotors all but drowned out Holliman's voice. "Bobbie," he shouted, "we are circling one mile away from Georgia's tiny barrier islands. In a highly unusual move, the Pentagon has closed the airspace around the island. We can see a small flotilla of Navy and Coast Guard ships and other military planes in the area. Something big has definitely happened, but it is too soon to know much more."

In the Hole, someone shouted with sardonic glee: "You bet something big has happened!"

Battista returned to the screen. "Thanks, John. Now, with another live report, CNN's Lydia Vesper is on a small vessel approaching Sapelo Island. Lydia?"

Again, the picture changed and this time a young blond reporter wearing a blue L.L. Bean windbreaker was standing on a small motorboat. The vessel rocked violently in the rough sea, and the reporter looked distinctly unwell. "Bobbie, we are heading toward the island, which is about a mile away. We understand that the explosion took place on the south side of the island. Jim, if you could zoom in on the lighthouse. Now, you can see where the explosion is believed to have taken place near the—whoa! Jim, zoom out and get this shot!"

The camera pulled wide to reveal a 378-foot U.S. Coast Guard high-endurance cutter flashing blue lights and firing water cannons ahead of the CNN boat. In the background a klaxon was sounding, and then a deep voice was heard on loudspeakers.

"This is the United States Coast Guard. You are ordered to turn back immediately. Turn back now. You are entering restricted space. You have sixty seconds to cut your engines and turn around."

Lazare smiled. Millions of Americans were tuned into CNN. He grabbed the remote controller and flipped the channels. On NBC, Tim Russert of "Meet the Press" was chatting with James Carville and Mary Matalin about the presidential horserace. And on ABC's "This Week," Sam Donaldson and George Will were duking it out over U.S. policy in Bosnia. *Soon enough*, he thought, *all of the networks will be covering this story.*

Battista, back again on CNN, threw the story to the Pentagon, where a briefing was about to take place. Ashen-faced Defense Department spokesman Todd Somerville walked to the podium. He had a map behind him of the Georgia coast.

Lazare wondered for an instant if his predictions would be correct. Was this not a test of his mental prowess, of his gift for seeing the endgame? Could he intuit how this would all play out?

"Good afternoon," the Pentagon's spokesman said, shuffling his notes. He paused and looked around at the journalists in front of him. He wore thick bottle-glass lenses that magnified his eyes, giving away that he felt himself in uncertain, even enemy territory.

The men in the Hole were now silent. This was the moment of truth, the moment of glory, and Lazare knew, the moment of acute frustration that would actually propel the team forward.

"At roughly 5:59 this morning," Somerville began, "an explosion rocked the southern tip of Sapelo Island on the Georgia seaboard. As you all know, there have been conflicting news reports about the nature of the explosion."

Somerville turned to the charts behind him.

"I'm here to tell you what happened and to set the record straight. Let me start by saying there is no cause for alarm."

The men in the Hole grumbled in disbelief.

Gus Rybak turned to Lazare: "He's lying to the entire country, right? The man is lying to the United States of America!"

Lazare held a finger to his lips. Silence.

"On a routine training run this morning," Somerville said, "a Marine Corps F/A-18 Hornet accidentally dropped a 1,000-pound laser-guided bomb on Sapelo Island. There was a significant explosion because the bomb struck an underground oil cistern. I have preliminary information that five civilians were injured in the accident."

"Fuck. Shit. Liar!" Rybak shouted at the screen. His face convulsed, and he scratched his chest furiously.

"Cover-up!" screamed Darren Dunn, waving his claw.

Lazare could see it was time to intercede. He moved up front by the television.

"Silence. Silence, all of you. You're right! The fools are trying to control the damage. But just watch. They will not succeed."

Somerville pointed to a blown-up black-and-white picture on an easel. "This is a satellite photo of the scene," he explained. "You will see precisely where the GBU-16 struck. This is the crater. And these are the small brush fires that are now under control. The Marine Corps is interviewing the pilot of the F/A-18."

"What about the injured civilians?" an Associated Press reporter shouted. "Where are they, and how are they doing?"

"I don't have much on that," Somerville said, "but they've been evacuated to a nearby hospital."

"What about reports of radiation in the area?" the AP reporter followed up.

"I really can't say much on that," Somerville responded. "The specs of the GBU-16 are classified. Suffice it to say, there was *no* nuclear yield on Sapelo Island. There was no *nuclear* explosion involving fissile materials or a chain reaction. It is true, however, that some radioactive debris was released into the atmosphere. But it is important to understand that this was only a *conventional* explosion that incidentally scattered some radioactivity. And we are monitoring the situation."

"What about public health?" yelled a reporter from the *Washington Post.*

"Let me be very clear," Somerville said. "There is *no* danger to the public. The radiation amounts are trivial. I'm told by our experts that we're talking about levels lower than most people are exposed to by the X-ray machine at the dentist's office. There is no cause for alarm."

"How do you explain the accident?" barked a reporter from the *Wall Street Journal.*

"We are not happy about this," Somerville said. "In Vietnam, we used to call this a COMMFU. The first letters stood for Completely Monumental Military and I'll let you fill in the rest."

In a rage, Gus Rybak hit the mute button on the television.

"COMMFU? How about COMMFUC? Completely Monumental Military Fucking Conspiracy!" he shouted

"They're a bunch of scum-sucking liars!" Dunn said.

"Enough!" Lazare said. "Enough!" He paced back and forth, then spoke. "Remember, the government is now fighting on two fronts. On the surface, they have no choice but to control the damage. They have to reassure the public. They have to cover up the truth so that there won't be an international political uproar. But in reality, they know perfectly well what they're up against. And fear is spreading through the halls of power."

He rubbed his hands together furiously.

"Trust me," he said, "we have them right where we want them."

Lazare knew his men did not understand; nor did he expect that they would comprehend the *real* plan. What they would never fathom was that the ultimate danger to the United States was neither Pu-239 nor Red Mercury.

The mother of all menace was not fissile material but fear, the fear of chaos, the fear of a world spinning out of control, the fear of powerlessness in the face of tumultuous international change.

In June 1995, the Unabomber had proven this point when his threat to blow up a plane flying in or out of Los Angeles International Airport had all but shut down the entire nation. Lazare's plan made the Unabomber's ploy reek of amateurism. Indeed, he could not resist congratulating himself on the originality of his scheme: plutonium shot puts from Turkmenistan; radioactive decoys planted in tourist luggage; a pipe bomb at the Georgia Tech Reactor; an innocent looking lunch box. But Lazare's greatest satisfaction came from his intuitive confidence that it would be Olympic security officials, the nation's decision makers, and finally the American people themselves who would do most of the work for him.

FDR had been dead right at his first inaugural in 1933: "The only thing we have to fear is fear itself."

A cancerous fear would invade and defeat them, more than all the bombs in the world ever would. They would be forced to shut down the Games, and they would leave him alone forever.

"By now their search planes have taken readings from the blast site," Lazare told his team. "They will soon be aware that our device was no ordinary weapon."

He smiled. In fact, it did not really matter. It did not matter that the lunch box *did not* really contain a working Red Mercury device. All he needed were the ingredients: mercury antimony oxide, deuterium, and tritium. Then NEST and the U.S. government, with their worst fears and apocalyptic visions running wild, would do the rest.

"Attention!" the announcer said over the public address system. "Five, four, three, two, one. Start."

Eight women stood in a row on the firing line, rifles aimed at electronic targets fifty meters away. The sun was scorching and the smell of gunfire filled the air.

One by one, the women fired their small-bore .22-caliber rifles. Instantly, the results flashed on scoreboards and television monitors around the Wolf Creek Shooting Complex.

Leila Arens was standing at the far left in the position of the number 1 shooter. Like the others, she had fired seven of her final ten shots. As she lifted the German-made Anschütz 2007 rifle to her shoulder, she visualized shooting a perfect 10. She put her face against the walnut cheek piece that was covered with tennis grip to prevent slippage and expertly lined up her sights.

Despite the heat she was wearing a heavy blue-and-white shooting jacket by Kurt Thune of Finland. The body of the jacket was made of stiff canvas and the arms were suede. On her left hand she wore a Sauer shooting glove with black textured Top Grip on the palm and backs of the fingers.

The electronic target was so far away and so small that Arens could not actually see the rings around the 10.4-millimeter bull's-eye, a blackened spot roughly the size of a dime. From her position 164 feet away from the target, the ten ring—or bull's-eye—was no bigger than the *o* in the word *dot*.

Olympic shooters were barred from using optical aiming sights. Arens peered through the rear iris of the Anschütz. She shifted the twelve-pound rifle with her left arm, lining up the rear aperture with the front sight and the black dot of the bull's-eye. The red-ribbon wind flags on the range hung limp, and the air was hot and still. She and her coaches had studied the ballistic effects of Georgia heat, and she consciously executed this subtle compensation.

If she could hit the ten ring three more times, Arens knew she would take home the gold medal. She had a near-world-record score of 591 going into the finals. Ulrike Dassler, an unflappable German shooter and reigning world champion, trailed her by three points.

The gold was hers to lose, and she knew it.

Olympic shooting was a mental sport, not a physical contest. Holding the rifle, aiming, and pulling the trigger were technical feats that could be mastered by virtually anyone. The difference that separated world champions from weekend tin-can shooters was all in the head.

Arens had fired more than 100,000 shots in her life. Her first was at age six when she had used her father's rifle, the same one that he had brought with him to Munich and that had accompanied his casket home. Later, in the Israeli Defense Force, she had perfected her skills on a sniper team in the Golan Heights. And for the past two years, she had trained every day for the Olympics at the modern shooting range in Herzliya.

Now it all came down to three perfect shots. Three forty-grain bullets. Three squeezes of the trigger and she could end her competitive shooting career with satisfaction, knowing that with the gold medal around her neck, she had honored her father's memory.

Arens relaxed her mind and let routine take over. The first step was to lower her pulse. At the Olympic level, a single heartbeat could jostle the rifle, throwing a well-aimed shot off into the nine or eight ring.

Arens's exacting self-discipline had brought her to this day. Indeed, it was an article of faith for world-class shooters that if they observed a methodical system, they would nail the bull's-eye. They did not need actually to see the fine-lined rings of the target. They only needed to line up the shot on the black center dot. The rest was rote.

Gently she exhaled, then squeezed the three-ounce trigger past the first stage, until her finger met resistance.

The sights and target were in perfect alignment.

Arens broke the shot.

The rifle crackled, and the .22-caliber Federal bullet tore through the air and slammed into the Suis Ascor target. Instantly, the electronic box sensed where the shot had landed and sent a signal to the scoreboard. The shot and score flashed on television monitors around the shooting range.

Arens had nailed the ten ring. Another perfect shot.

In the stands, Buddy Crouse applauded enthusiastically. He was sitting with Arens's mother and the rest of the Israeli shooters' families. Crouse had the afternoon off, and Arens had invited him to watch her in the finals.

Crouse, unfamiliar with shooting as an Olympic sport, thumbed through the pages of the Wolf Creek program and studied the rules. The women's three-position, or 3 x 20 event, involved an athlete firing a total of sixty shots from the prone, standing, and kneeling positions. Competitors had two and one half hours to fire their sixty shots. A perfect score was 600. The top eight shooters then moved on to the final round. Shooters took ten shots from the standing position, one shot at a time, with seventy-five seconds allowed per shot.

Skimming the program, Crouse was surprised to learn that shooting was a traditional Olympic event going all the way back to the 1896 Games in Athens. In fact, Pierre de Coubertin had been a pistol marksman as a boy. In the nine-sport program at the first Modern Games there had been five shooting events, and the first gold medalist had been Pantelis Karasevdas of Greece in the free rifle event.

Old photos in the program gave proof that Olympic shooting had evolved over the years as different events had come and gone. At the Games in Paris in 1900, for instance, Leon de Lunden of Belgium won a gold medal for killing twenty-one birds in the live pigeon shooting event, but mercifully the sport never again appeared at the Games. Eight years later in London, Oscar Swahn took home a gold in the running deer shooting event, which also was later dropped from the program.

The crowd cheered. Ulrike Dassler, the German shooter, had scored another bull's-eye. Again, the pressure was on Leila Arens. Her mother covered her eyes. She could not bear to watch.

Arens was ready to shoot again.

Crack. The rifle recoiled, and the target flashed on the monitors. There was a hush in the crowd. Crouse heard the whispers. A man next to him from the U.S. shooting team said to a friend, "Woowee, did she yang that one."

Arens had landed the shot in the eight ring. From the expression on her face, it was clear this was a disaster. She appeared stricken. What had gone wrong? Why had her system failed her?

She looked over to her coach, then up toward her mother in the crowd. Then she turned back to the targets on the range.

In her heart she was speaking to her father, as she had done so many nights on sentry looking out over Syria. She summoned his strength. And she prayed for his steady hand to guide her.

But before Arens could shoot again, it was Ulrike Dassler's turn. She was tall and severe, with gun-metal gray eyes and crew-cut blond hair. In lighter moments in the locker room, some women shooters wondered whether Dassler's manliness was explained by a secret Y chromosome that even Olympic blood tests were unable to detect.

With one shot to go, Dassler's cold, methodical approach further unnerved Arens.

A bull's-eye for the German brought another cheer from the admiring crowd.

Next, Russian Tatyana Bragina fired and scored a perfect 10.

The scoreboards throughout the shooting complex showed that Arens was clinging to first place by one point.

Now it was her shot again. One more for the gold.

Mechanically, she went through the steps.

Relax! Thirty seconds, she thought to herself.

She peered through the sights at the little black box at the far end of the shooting range. She studied the heat shimmer. Was the wind picking up? She glanced at the red ribbons. Imperceptibly, almost unconsciously, she made minute adjustments in her stance and shaded the rifle to the right.

Her three rivals watched her intensely. Arens could almost feel Dassler's steely eyes boring into her back.

Twenty seconds.
Breath, exhale, sights.
Breath, exhale, hold.
Ready, aim . . .

Arens squeezed the trigger through the first stage. Then she fired and followed through.

There was a split-second of calm as the bullet ripped down the range. But the shot didn't feel right. In her mind, she imagined its point of impact.

And then, through her ear plugs, she could hear the crowd behind her.

But she did not want to look. She was afraid, alone. She didn't have to open her eyes to see what she instinctively knew: she had missed the shot, and the gold was gone.

C huck Flagg sat uncomfortably on the slippery leather couch. It was so slick, almost oily, that he feared he would slide right out of the seat onto the floor.

The seventh-floor editor-in-chief's office at *The Atlanta Journal-Constitution* was spacious, with modern furniture. Its big, wide windows looked out on Marietta Street in the center of downtown. Half a block east at Forsyth Street, Flagg could see the weathered 1891 statue of Henry Grady on horseback. Grady was the great Southern editor and journalist who coined the phrase "the New South." He was also the gadfly who tweaked Union General William T. Sherman—the man who burned Atlanta to the ground—for being "a little careless with fire."

Grady would not be proud, Flagg thought, *of what was happening at his newspaper today.* Nor would the other famous alumnus of the *Journal-Constitution,* Margaret "Peggy" Mitchell, who paid her bills by day as a reporter and spent her nights laboring over a certain novel called *Gone With the Wind.*

Flagg was exhausted. He had been up all night, speeding back and forth across town, trying to piece together an 850-word article about Abu Azzam and the State Capitol. At 1:15 A.M. he had filed the story, slugged TERROR, and had gone home to wait for questions from the night editor.

He was surprised when the phone had remained silent, and at 4 A.M., cursing to himself, he had jumped into his Mazda 626 and driven to the paper's headquarters. At night, the massive concrete building, with its vertical slit windows, looked something like a medieval prison. At the loading area, he stopped one of the delivery trucks on its way out and snatched a newspaper.

It made Flagg shudder to remember the burning sensation he

felt as he scanned the front page. His story was nowhere to be found on A1.

He ripped through the rest of the pages. *Nothing!*

Then he tore through the Special Olympic Supplement. Again nothing.

The story had been killed, and no one had even bothered to let him know.

Flagg was livid. Deliberately knocking over piles of newspapers and magazines, he stormed across the darkened eighth-floor news room toward his desk in what he called the "interns and outcasts" corner.

He threw himself down at his ATEX computer and the words burst forth.

GODDAMN YOU, CLAUDE!

GODDAMN YOU FOR SPIKING MY STORY WITHOUT TELLING ME.

GODDAMN YOU FOR NOT HAVING THE COMMON DECENCY TO CALL ME AND TELL ME YOUR CHICKEN-SHIT DECISION.

GODDAMN YOU!

IF YOU WOULD BOTHER TO PULL YOUR HEAD OUT OF YOUR ASS, YOU'D SEE WHAT'S GOING ON HERE. YOU HAVE THE SINGLE BIGGEST STORY IN YEARS RIGHT IN YOUR BACKYARD.

I HANDED IT TO YOU ON A SILVER PLATTER.

AND YOU SPIKED IT.

WELL, I QUIT.

I DON'T WANT TO HAVE ANYTHING TO DO WITH THIS SICK PLACE.

I'M TAKING MY STORY WHERE THEY KNOW NEWS WHEN THEY SEE IT.

GOOD-BYE,

CAF

Flagg scrolled through the letter. Too wordy. He could say it better and faster. With a few quick keystrokes, he blocked the text and deleted it all. Then he began typing again.

CLAUDE,

AS OF 4 A.M., I DON'T WORK FOR YOU ANYMORE.

I QUIT.

YOU KNOW WHY. I KNOW WHY. AND THE READERS OF THE AJC HAVE THE RIGHT TO KNOW WHY.

SO FUCK YOU AND YOUR SISSY BOW-TIES.

CHUCK.

Flagg hit the print command, tore the letter off the laser printer, and retraced his march through the news room and down the stairs to the editor's seventh-floor suite. With a thumbtack, he stuck his resignation on the office door. He knew he was no Martin Luther posting his 95 Theses on the door of Castle Church in Wittenberg. But he was making a statement, a statement that the *Journal-Constitution* would not soon forget.

Then he had gone home to St. Charles Avenue in Virginia Highlands, northeast of the city, and crashed in the recliner in the living room with a bottle of sipping whiskey by his elbow. The easy chair and Jack Daniel's were much better company than his wife snoring upstairs in the bedroom.

Twelve hours later, at 4 P.M., the call came. Claude Guillory wanted him in his office right away. At first Flagg said no way. He wasn't going anywhere near that "suck-egg mule of a newspaper." He had borrowed the insult from fossilized Republican Senator Jesse Helms of North Carolina, who had once used that phrase to attack *The News and Observer* of Raleigh, a progressive, yellow-dog Democrat newspaper where Flagg had gotten his start as a cub reporter.

But Penny Parmenter, Guillory's secretary, urged him to come down to the office. "Get your sorry ass here right away," she said.

Flagg threw on some jeans and a T-shirt and headed into down-town. When he arrived in Guillory's suite, there was an icy chill in the air. Penny, usually flirtatious, did not even look Flagg in the eyes.

Flagg was standing at the window, looking at the green, oxidized statue of Henry Grady, when Guillory arrived and shut the door, shaking his head in disapproval.

They eyed each other.

"Chuck, what the fuck is this letter about?" His words erupted in machine-gun fire. He picked up the resignation letter from his desk.

"Claude, what's the point of this meeting?" Flagg shot back. "If you've got something to say, then say it. Otherwise, I've got things to do."

"You arrogant son of a bitch," Guillory said, walking to the window. He fumbled for a cigarette. "The story you filed last night didn't have legs, and you know it."

"Bullshit," Flagg said. "It had two good legs. And that's never been a problem before at this newspaper."

Guillory had never been to Flagg's taste. The editor, now in his mid-fifties with an oval face and tortoise-shell glasses, was a good old boy, a company guy with Cox newspapers his entire career, a "lifer" as he liked to say. It had been six years since he arrived to restore order at the *Journal* after the previous editor, an old-style muckraker, had resigned in a dispute with the Cox CEO over corporate budget pressure on the news-gathering operation.

Known to enjoy the perks of his position, Guillory took full advantage of his membership at the elegant Capital City Club at the corner of Peachtree Street and Harris, where he sipped cocktails with Roberto Goizueta, the chairman of Coca-Cola, and hung out with the top executives of Delta, Georgia Pacific, UPS, and CNN. He made a fraction of what these men earned, but he was just as powerful. After all, everyone knew the saying: there was no point in getting in an argument with someone who buys ink by the barrel.

Guillory changed his mind about the cigarette and sat down in one of the leather chairs. He held onto the armrests as if he were about to take off. "Who are the anonymous sources quoted in the story?" he asked.

Strange question, Flagg thought. Guillory had never asked about sources before. Now, all of a sudden, he was interested.

"Can't tell you," Flagg said.

"What the hell does that mean?"

"What don't you understand? I *can't* tell you. I promised I would not reveal their identities."

"Well, if you can't tell me, then I can't run the story."

"What do you mean, you can't run it? Anonymous sources have never stopped you before from rushing to print."

"This is different," Guillory said, looking away.

This is different? Flagg pondered what could possibly be different about this story.

Guillory continued, "I know you don't give a rat's ass about the Olympics, but I do. And in good conscience, I cannot run this story. That's my decision."

"What does this have to do with conscience or the Olympics?"

"Chuck, that's my decision. And it's final."

"And what about your responsibility to your readers?" Flagg pressed. "Don't they have a right to know?"

"Know what?"

"Know about Abu Azzam and the threat to the State Capitol?"

"Come on, Chuck. The story isn't there."

"I've got two independent sources," Flagg said. "It *is* there."

"Well, our readers don't need to know about it right now," Guillory said. "There will be plenty of time later."

Flagg was beginning to understand. Guillory's decision had nothing to do with the accuracy of the story. It had to do with Atlanta and the Games.

Flagg decided to flush Guillory out of hiding. "So what does Donny say about this story?"

Guillory's eyes shifted uneasily for a moment. "I spoke with Donny this morning. He told me about your trespassing last night."

"Trespassing?"

"Did you really have to climb his fence?"

"I didn't climb any fence. That's a bunch of bullshit."

Flagg was beginning to see it really didn't matter. The *Journal* was never going to publish his story about Azzam and the State Capitol. The cozy relationships nourished at the Capital City Club would never let it happen. There was too much at stake. Atlanta had spent more than eight years fighting for the Games. And a story like his might undo all the wooing and negotiating, all the planning, all the Olympic spirit. And all the money.

Still, news was news. If a world-renowned terrorist had planned to strike the State Capitol and had been foiled by law enforcement, the public had a right to know. It was Journalism 101.

But the Atlanta Games weren't Journalism 101. They were Business & Boosterism 101. And Flagg's scoop would have the same commercial effect as cyanide in Tylenol or benzene in Perrier.

"I'm sorry, Chuck, but the decision is final," Guillory was saying. "When you've got harder information, maybe we'll reconsider. But as of today, the story is spiked."

His *ex-boss* was wrong.

There wasn't a doubt in Flagg's mind that the story was still alive and all too well. If he had to, he would leak it to the national newspapers or even to the TV networks. They would definitely have the intestinal fortitude to go with the Abu Azzam story.

Even with Guillory staring at him, Flagg felt a sense of growing excitement. For some reason, he remembered H. G. Wells' line about tabloid newspapers: "They were not so much published as carried screaming into the streets."

The Abu Azzam story, Flagg knew, would go screaming into the streets. It would just take a few more phone calls.

A few hundred yards from I-85 near Decatur, the FBI's Atlanta Division occupied the fourth floor of a sleek, cube-shaped building hidden in a tranquil industrial park lined with neat rows of trees, well-groomed lawns, and walking paths. The smooth, mirrored exterior of the building doubled the surrounding images of verdure and blue sky.

The interior, however, presented an entirely different picture.

The FBI's Atlanta field office, one of nine division headquarters in the United States, directed the Bureau's operations in the southeastern United States. More than a thousand additional agents had been called in from around the country to staff the Bureau's Olympic Security Task Force, temporarily installed on the second floor.

Now, all told, the FBI's presence in Atlanta amounted to 1 or 2 percent of the entire Olympic security apparatus; in the event of a crisis, however, the Bureau would bear 95 percent or more of the responsibility. Assignments ran the gamut, from command and control to explosive ordnance disposal, from aviation management to special teams. By FBI standards of bloodless restraint, the Olympic Planning Center was hopping. Spread out across the entire second floor and visible over waist-high blue partitions, the teams of agents gave the appearance of ants on a hill.

At the far end of the space, in an area with several folding tables arranged in a horseshoe, McFall sat at NEST's workstation, staring at the latest set of radiological survey maps of the Sapelo Island blast site. Directly across from him, Preston glumly thumbed through a copy of the *Olympic Public Safety Master Plan*, a thousand-page document dated August 1994.

They were waiting for three nuclear weapons designers from Los Alamos, Sandia, and Lawrence Livermore.

When they were at last ushered across the room, Preston was not entirely sure they looked like they had been worth the wait. Wearing shorts and dingy T-shirts, two of the scientists could have passed for scruffy Berkeley graduate students. The third, bedecked in Henry Kissinger glasses, a wide-collared beige shirt, and a plastic pocket protector, appeared to have been dispatched by Hollywood central casting.

"Stan, are you with us?" McFall said, looking at the videophone on the table.

"Yup, like it or not," Treadwell said from his hospital bed in Los Alamos. Hooked up to an IV and looking miserable, he was propped up with files on his lap.

"Good. So who wants to take a stab at what we're up against?" McFall continued.

"I'll start," said Pocket Protector, opening a file folder. "The easiest way to begin is by establishing what it *isn't*. It's definitely *not* a gun-type design like Little Boy at Hiroshima. The reason is physics: you just can't make a gun-type device with plutonium. It's made *only* with HEU."

"So at the very least," McFall said, "we're talking about an implosion device, like Fat Man at Nagasaki."

"Exactly," Pocket Protector confirmed. "Here's what it looks like. The plutonium pit is surrounded by a tamper encased in high explosives. When the high explosives are detonated, the plutonium pit implodes, forming a supercritical mass and beginning a chain reaction."

"It's a safe bet that we're dealing with a pro or team of experts because the implosion design is much harder to pull off," said the long-haired scientist in biking shorts. "I mean, the implosion has got to be perfectly symmetrical. That means the high explosives have to detonate simultaneously all around the plutonium pit. And that's not a job for amateurs or weekend repairmen."

"So where does Red Mercury fit in?" McFall asked. It was a rhetorical question, but he always sought fresh opinions from good minds.

The pony-tailed scientist in khaki shorts leaned forward. "One possibility is that the Red Mercury acts as a super explosive. It detonates evenly and uniformly around the pit and creates the chain reaction."

"And why is that such a big deal?" Preston asked, trying to get to the bottom line.

"Because a super explosive that detonates evenly and uniformly would mean a smaller weapon with a bigger yield," Treadwell explained. "It would be a significant breakthrough. The yield-to-weight ratio would be unprecedented."

"But there's another option," McFall said ominously. "It's a variation on the first. It would be *truly* revolutionary. Red Mercury could be the key to a miniature pure-fusion neutron bomb."

He paused as the words sank in. Treadwell was smiling knowingly.

"The idea was laid out pretty well in an article by Dr. Frank Barnaby in *International Defense Review* in June 1994," McFall said. "Basically, Red Mercury would allow weapons designers to create pure-fusion weapons that did not need fissile materials like plutonium or uranium."

"No uranium or plutonium?" Preston asked.

"Red Mercury is a very efficient explosive," McFall said. "It's what we call a ballotechnic. Subjected to high-pressure shock compression, ballotechnics generate large amounts of energy, which in turn could produce pure fusion."

"And why wouldn't there be any need for uranium or plutonium?" Preston asked.

Treadwell answered, "Because a Red Mercury device would use deuterium and tritium, two heavy-hydrogen isotopes. Thirty-five cubic feet of deuterium, completely fused, would throw off ten megatons of energy. And a quart of fused liquid deuterium would have the explosive power of nearly forty kilotons of TNT."

McFall watched as Preston and the three scientists digested the information.

"Here are the real problems," Treadwell said. "First, RM is undetectable by traditional means."

"Great," Preston said. "Geiger counters can't pick it up."

"Nothing we have right now can spot it," Treadwell said. "And the second problem—and this one's the biggie—is that Red Mercury would probably mean the end of the nuclear balance in the world. RM would prove a total disaster for controlling the proliferation of weapons of mass destruction because they're so cheap and easy to produce. And deuterium and tritium are *not* controlled by international safeguards under the Non-Proliferation Treaty."

"So what does this mean to Joe Q. Terrorist?" Preston asked.

"It means massive nuclear yields in tiny packages," Pocket Protector said, his expression quite earnest.

Biking Shorts added: "In rough terms, it would mean doubling the yield of a weapon while cutting its weight 99 percent."

McFall stood up and walked over to a white marking board. He drew two circles. One was small, the other large.

"The laws of physics govern nuclear weapons design," he said. "Things can only be so small. And yields can only be so big. The yield-to-weight ratios are well known. They're in every nuclear engineering text. Red Mercury would change all that *forever.* We've spent the last forty years designing smaller and smaller weapons with bigger and bigger yields. Miniaturization has been the last great challenge of the design world." He pointed to the large circle. "This circle is where we are today. This is what modern physics allowed us to do until now."

Then he pointed to the smaller circle. "With Red Mercury, boom! Bigger bang, smaller bomb."

"So why hasn't anyone created this Red Mercury yet?" Preston asked.

"Great question, no answer," McFall said.

"It's like alchemy," Pocket Protector said. "Creating Red Mercury would be like turning sand into gold. It would involve quantum leaps in knowledge and understanding, and no one is even close yet."

"How can you be so sure?" McFall asked.

"Well, who's been working on it?" Preston asked.

"We know the Soviets were the first into the RM game," Treadwell said. "In the 1960s, they began playing around with it in the cyclotron at the Dubna nuclear research center."

"Did they perfect it?"

"Not yet," McFall said. "Or they haven't told us if they have."

"Are there any other players?"

"I don't think so," McFall answered. "There have been hundreds of reports about RM showing up all over the globe. But whenever the cops seize something, it's never the real thing."

"What about the United States?" Preston asked. "What RM research have we done?"

There was a perceptible hesitation to answer. Preston guessed that McFall and Treadwell knew much more than they were willing to say. Or did they?

McFall took the lead. "We really haven't done a lot of RM work," he said. "There've been rumors about a U.S. Red Mercury program going back fifteen or twenty years. But that's all, just a bunch of rumors."

"Yeah, I've heard about some RM research at Los Alamos, but I've never seen anything hard," said one of the scientists.

"So what specifically has been done?" Preston asked. "Do you folks know anything real about this substance?"

That was a direct question, and McFall did not want to lie to Preston. "We've done a few investigations. Stan has run through some of the chemistry. Jump in, Stan, will you?"

"We've fooled around enough with RM variants in the lab to understand a little about what we're facing," Treadwell said. "But we aren't there yet. We haven't made it or even come close."

"So what about this device on Sapelo Island?" she asked. "Could it be an RM bomb?"

"No way," said Biking Shorts. "That's impossible."

"I wouldn't be so sure," Treadwell countered.

"Me neither," McFall said.

"So how are we going to find the next device if RM is undetectable?" Preston said.

"You're hard at work on that, right, Stan?" McFall said, half laughing, half pleading.

"Oh, yeah," Treadwell said, glancing around the hospital room at all the medical equipment. "I'm running the numbers between morphine shots and enemas."

"Any breaks?" McFall asked.

"A few," he said with a faint twinkle. "I may have something for you in a day or two."

"Keep pushing, old buddy," McFall said.

NBC Sports Update. Atlanta is a long way from Addis Ababa, Ethiopia. But long distance runner Haile Gebrsellassie doesn't seem to notice. He's already grabbed one gold medal in the Men's 10,000 meters. And he's well ahead of the pack in the Men's 5,000 meters at Olympic Stadium.

The 23-year-old Ethiopian is the latest long-distance phenomenon to emerge from East Africa, a trend that began in 1960 at the Rome Games when Abebe Bikila, running barefoot, won the marathon. Four years later at the Tokyo Games, Bikila won the 26.2 mile race again, but this time in shoes.

Born and raised 100 miles southeast of Addis Ababa, Gebrsellassie worked in the corn and wheat fields as a boy. Today, as the five-foot three-inch runner crosses the finish line to win his second gold medal, you can still see how it all began. Gebrsellassie races with his left arm bent slightly, this imperfect form a remnant from the days when he ran six miles to school—across the hills of Africa—with books under his arm.

Putting down the instruments on the makeshift lab bench, Lazare pulled off his safety goggles. He wiped the perspiration from his forehead and checked his watch. It was early afternoon, and he had been working nonstop since late morning. The improvised nuclear device, almost ready for final assembly, would take at least another eight hours of intense team effort.

And then the team would move into action, and the 1996 Summer Games would really begin.

His men now had specific countdown assignments. One was finishing up the electronics of the delivery system. Another was putting the final touches on some of the camouflage materials.

Lazare pulled a handkerchief from his green military fatigues and mopped his face. The Hole was chilly and damp, certainly not an ideal site for a nuclear weapons factory, but he felt like he was burning up. He inspected the digital thermometer. It was sixty-three degrees. He put the back of his hand to his forehead. Did he have a fever? The backs of his eyes throbbed. Was it the pressure of the work? Was it the cumulative effect of so much concentration? Were his head and his body rebelling against the unrelenting schedule of the past year?

Or was it just the flu?

Lazare had not been feeling well for weeks. The recurring symptoms were always the same. Low-grade fever. Aching eyes. Dry mouth. Sore throat. Upset stomach.

Each time the syndrome struck, he would make another excuse. Just another few weeks and then it would all be over. Hold it together, boy, and you'll have all the time in the world to rest and recuperate. A few more days and you'll never taste another god-awful Army surplus MRE—meal ready-to-eat.

Lazare looked over at his deputy Gus Rybak, who was hard at work on the wiring of the navigation system. "Hey, Shakes, I'm gonna take a quick break," Lazare said.

"Still not feelin' well?" Rybak asked.

"My head is killing me," Lazare replied. "I'm gonna lie down for a few minutes."

"Take it easy on yourself," Rybak said. "We've got everything under control here."

Lazare walked across the main work area and through the small steel door into the bunk room. There were three double-deckers in a row, all neatly made. Except for the rocky granite walls and the bare bulbs hanging from wires, the space could have been a military barracks.

He sat down on the lower bunk of the far corner bed and pulled off his shoes. Was his fever rising? He reached under the bed for his Dopp kit, opened a Bayer bottle, pulled out two aspirin, and gulped them down. Then he lay on the bed. Wedged into the mattress springs above him was a crumpled map of the so-called Olympic Ring in Atlanta, the 1.5 mile radius of peace and harmony surrounding the main Olympic venues.

Lazare studied the graphics. For the last year, he had gone to sleep at night with his eyes tracing and retracing the Olympic Ring logo. As his preoccupation with his goal began to overwhelm any other thought, the Atlanta ring metamorphosed into a different kind of circle: a nuclear destruction radius. This discovery delighted Lazare. He knew nuclear weapons designers drew circles to measure the impact of their fearsome weapons.

He loved the gruesome irony. The equation was so elegant:

Olympic Ring = Primary Nuclear Destruction Radius

He scratched his head and ran his hand through his long black hair. When he lowered his hand he could see ten strands were caught between his fingers. Was he going bald, too? What was all this—the nausea, the fever, the headaches, and now the hair loss?

Instinctively, he reached into his shirt pocket and pulled out the thermoluminescent Dosi-Lite radiation dosimeter that he wore whenever he handled fissile materials. As always, he had checked the personal radiation meter at the beginning of the day in the lab. And he had checked it again in midafternoon. It had been a routine repeated every day for months.

He held the dosimeter up to the light and peered through one end. It was like a miniature kaleidoscope. At the far end of the scope was a tiny radiation scale. Typically, the black line of the gauge registered less than fifty millirems.

Jesus!

Lazare could not believe his eyes. The black line had pegged at its maximum level. The dosimeter indicated he had been exposed to at least 200 millirems, not an insignificant amount of radiation. But where was it coming from?

He bolted upright in bed. It couldn't be the lab. The Geiger counters and wall-mounted detectors would have sounded. So where? Dammit, where?

As calmly as he could, he returned to the lab and grabbed a portable pancake-handle Geiger counter. Then he walked back into the bunk room.

The detector clicked randomly, indicating routine background radiation from the surrounding rock. He moved around the room. Nothing.

Then he approached his bunk.

The Geiger counter began to click faster.

By the time he reached his bed, the counter was almost rattling.

Lazare was stupefied. The Geiger needle was pegging next to his bunk bed.

Impossible.

He ran the counter over the mattress. Near his pillow, the detector made a buzzing sound because the clicks were so intensely bunched.

Lazare was bewildered. *What the hell?*

He tore the pillow from its case and ripped it apart with his hands, feathers flying everywhere. There was nothing inside.

The Geiger counter continued buzzing.

He ripped the sheets from the bed and pulled off the mattress cover. He examined it carefully. Near the top of the mattress, he saw four tiny stitches, like a surgical scar.

Lazare pulled the knife from his belt and stabbed at the mattress, ripping it open. The knife made contact with something metal. Was it a spring? Or the bed frame? Lazare dug through the mattress padding. And then he saw the small, gray clump of metal. It was instantly recognizable and equally horrifying.

For a moment he thought he was going to pass out. Then he carved the nugget of Cobalt-60 from the bed. It was hot to the touch—highly radioactive. He flung it across the room.

He felt rage growing inside him. *How could he have been so stupid? How could he not have guessed?*

Lazare sat down on the ripped-up bed. He switched off the groaning Geiger counter and put his head in his hands. He squeezed his head harder and harder. He felt like he was going to explode.

My God, it makes sense—the nausea, the headaches, the hair loss.

Someone was trying to kill him. Slowly. Very slowly. Someone wanted him dead.

But who?

There were only four choices. Four men worked in the Hole and shared the bunk room. He ran through the names rapid-fire, considered each personality, and zeroed in on Rybak.

It had to be Shakes. He had an outsized opinion of himself and constantly challenged Lazare's ideas and authority.

Just ten minutes earlier Rybak had pretended to be so concerned about Lazare's health: *"Take it easy on yourself. We've got everything under control here."*

Of course, Lazare thought. The oldest trick in the book. A paint-by-the-numbers military coup. A brash lieutenant kills off the general once the battle plan is set.

Lazare tried to regain his composure. He wanted to run out into the lab and kill. Kill! Yes, kill Rybak and his treacherous co-conspirators. This vivid image maddened him, and he squeezed his head even harder between his hands. His brains felt as if they were beginning to boil.

Kill them before they kill you. But wait! It would be pointless to upend everything before the job is done.

Revenge!

At once, the fury in his mind drained away. And he was left with the gnawing question of whether the radiation under his pillow would kill him, and if so, how fast.

What a perverse irony: death by radiation was a cruel, sickening fate.

Dead or alive, he would have his revenge. The plan formed in his mind almost instantly. He would exploit Rybak's weakness. But Lazare would have to wait a few days, hold his fire, and control his rage.

But the payback would be sweet, so very beautiful.

The old Arab proverb was right, Lazare thought. *Revenge is a dish best served cold.*

Three athletes, medals gleaming around their necks, stood triumphant on the Olympic pedestal before 10,000 avid spectators as the opening chords of the German national anthem filled the indoor arena of the Wolf Creek Shooting Complex.

Ulrike Dassler, the gold medalist in the women's 3 x 20 small-bore rifle competition, wiped tears from her eyes and sang the first words of "Deutschland Lied": *Einigkeit und recht und freiheit für das Deutsche Vaterland.*

Dassler held a bouquet of red roses in her arms. She looked down to her right and left at the Israeli and Romanian silver and bronze medalists.

With a faint nod, Leila Arens acknowledged Dassler's glance. In all their competitive encounters, she had never before seen the German shooter cry. This expression of emotion was almost as startling as the final outcome of the event.

Gazing up at the Star of David on the blue-and-white flag above her, Arens winced recalling the agonizing outcome of the shooting finals. Gone was the gold medal. Vanished was the hope of realizing her father's Olympic dream. Erased was the determination, the resolve, to triumph over the darkness in her life.

In that split second, her interior life was irrevocably changed. She would forever be required to live a lie of humble gratitude for winning the silver medal, covering her bitter disappointment from this moment on, enduring endless interviews with admiring Israeli reporters.

To the Israeli public Arens's achievement was still a novelty, a minor miracle. In the 2,000-year history of the Olympics, old and new, only two other Israelis had ever won medals: in Barcelona in 1992, when Yael Arad won silver and Oren Smagda captured a bronze in judo.

Standing motionless under the bright lights as the German anthem played, her smile a veiled grimace, Arens was not sure whether the emotions ripping her apart inside were shame or self-pity, anger or humiliation.

Was it her fault that she had bungled the final shot? Or was it God's wrath? Was she destined to fail? Was this some punishment? All of the confusion of her childhood came rushing back: the mind-numbing bafflement when her father failed to come home from Munich, the shattering loneliness, and her mother's deepening depression and alienation.

While Arens was apprehensive that this pain was her own private curse and could never be expunged, she had taken small steps over the years to ease the stranglehold of Munich, to release some of the demons. She had learned not to fear every Arab after her mother, with much effort, had convinced her that only deranged extremists were responsible for her father's death. She had trained herself to wake up at night, aborting her dreams to prevent nightmares from devouring her sleep. And she had come to think of her father's cemetery plot on Mount Carmel as a refuge of comfort and peace, not a bottomless pit of bitterness and pain.

But around every corner, with every new day, there was some fresh variation on the dark theme. What might her life have been like if her father had not been murdered in Munich? And the others: there had been so many casualties in Munich, so many lives disturbed forever. What might those gifted young people have accomplished had they lived?

Arens recalled the plight of one of the few Israeli survivors of the Munich massacre, an athlete who had escaped the terrorists. Upon returning to Israel, the man spent hours with a psychiatrist working through his guilt; but nonetheless, after a psychological evaluation, the Israeli Defense Force concluded he was unfit for service. He kicked around the Mediterranean, drinking and trying to forget what had happened. He was last seen driving a telephone repair truck.

The crowds were cheering, their bodies moving in rhythmic waves. Leila's mother was on her feet, fists in the air. Israelis, outnumbering

Germans in the bleachers, were chanting her name. "Lei-la! Lei-la! Lei-la!"

Arens reached into herself for strength. She threw her arms up as if to embrace her fans. Leaping down from the pedestal, she ran to her family and friends in the bleachers.

Her mother's arms enveloped her, and they wept.

"Aba haya kol kach ga'ay bach," her mother cried. "Papa would be so proud of you." The embrace of mother and daughter was raw and powerful.

Her mother released her, and the exuberant members of the Israeli shooting team surrounded her, chanting her name, hugging and kissing her, and finally hoisting her on their shoulders. Up above the heads of the crowd, with all eyes toasting her, she suddenly wondered how she looked. Could they tell she was crying inside? Could they see through to her unhappiness?

At last she was allowed to stand on her own feet. And immediately, a journalist thrust his microphone in front of her. Fans jumped in the air and waved the Israeli flag.

"How does it feel, Leila? A silver medal for Israel's darling?"

"It is the happiest moment of my life," she said, jaw clenched. For all her enthusiasm and smiles, she was unmoved inside. Not even with all of Israel watching on television, with the whole world acknowledging her skill, did she feel a part of this moment.

Leila Arens was alone.

"And what do you have to say to the people of Israel?"

"I couldn't have done it without your support," she said. "Thank you! Thank you!"

The reporter tried one last question: "Can you tell us about your American friend? There are reports you and an American decathlete are—"

They were engulfed in a swarm of bodies, and Arens let herself be swept away by the crowd. Fifty feet away she saw Buddy Crouse carrying a bouquet of flowers, fighting his way toward her. His smile seemed to say to her, *I understand.* He seemed to grasp her soul of sadness, her essence.

A young man from Montana and a young woman from Herzliya.

When he finally reached Arens, he lifted her in the air. He was strong, his chest hard, and his arms squeezed the breath out of her. She gasped for air as he spun her around.

"Mazel tov," he whispered in her ear.

She laughed.

"You're incredible," he said, twirling her around. "Just amazing!"

"Have you had too much to drink?" she teased.

"No, I'm sotally tober," he joked.

Twirling in the air in a powerful man's arms. It was a dizzying feeling she had known long ago when she was a sunny little girl. Arens closed her eyes. The smile on her lips felt real, at long last.

PART III

FIRE

Kill one man and you are a murderer.
Kill millions and you are a conqueror.
Kill all and you are a god.

—Jean Rostand

"I think I know who you're looking for."

Vincent Fusco's words floated from the speakerphone like hallelujahs from a choir.

"Way to go, Vinny!" Preston said. She was sitting on the edge of her desk, legs crossed, office door closed. McFall, bending a paper clip, sat across from her on the sofa.

"Go ahead, Vince, sock it to us," McFall said.

An hour earlier, Fusco had left the National Military Command Center at the Pentagon and traveled across Washington to the Department of Energy's massive Forrestal Building on Independence Avenue. He had gone to see a friend in the Weapons Program, picked up some classified files, and then gone straight to the underground DOE Emergency Operations Center in room GA-282 of the basement.

Now on the desk in front of him lay a secret CODEWORD file marked: RM EYES ONLY. Fusco was sitting alone in an ice-cold SCIF, a Secure Compartmented Information Facility, a specially guarded room for highly classified intelligence work.

"This is some very top secret shit," Fusco began. "There are probably ten people in the entire country who—"

"Spare us, Vince," McFall interrupted, snapping the paper clip in two.

"A little stressed out, Macky boy?" Vince asked.

Preston motioned to McFall to cool it.

"Sorry," McFall said. "We just haven't been getting any breaks."

"Well, your luck has changed," Fusco said, opening the file.

"Here goes. Page one. I'm summarizing now. Beginning in 1970, the United States embarked on an ultra-secret research project. It was called Red Mercury. A team of five elite scientists gathered at Los Alamos. They were given a secret lab away from the main plant. And they were told not to talk about their work. Never, ever."

"A full-fledged Red Mercury program within DOE?" McFall asked incredulously. "I don't buy it."

"And it's been going on for nearly twenty-five years?" Preston added.

"Not exactly," Fusco said, turning the pages in the file. "RM was America's most secret weapons development program since the Manhattan Project. The security and secrecy around RM made the concertina wire around the B-2 Stealth Bomber look like Christmas wrapping. I'm talking about the blackest program we *ever* had."

McFall began taking notes on a yellow legal pad. He was astonished. The DOE had conducted RM research for years, and yet, discounting the occasional wild rumor, he had heard nothing about it. It didn't add up.

Fusco flipped another page.

"In November 1989, when the Berlin Wall came down, U.S. arms control negotiators sat down with their Russian counterparts in Geneva and began to talk about the next forty years. They confirmed what we had known all along: the Russians had *also* been doing RM research since the late sixties. But the big surprise was that American and Russian scientists were at the exact same point in their research. Both sides were on the verge of a major breakthrough, one step away from a giant leap forward to miniature pure-fusion weapons."

"They were on the verge of unlocking the secret?" McFall asked.

"Exactly. And so both sides had to face a vexing question: what do we do with this awful knowledge? What do we do with the fact that once again—nearly fifty years after Hiroshima and Nagasaki—we were about to launch a new arms race? And this time, the technology could never be reined in. Inevitably, it would leak out."

"So what happened?"

"They reached an unusual agreement. I would call it a nineties interpretation of MAD: *mutually assured destruction.*"

"I don't follow," Preston said.

"Not the Cold War theory of MAD. It was the New World Order theory, a brand-new idea. Mutually assured destruction meant both sides agreed to destroy their respective RM programs."

"Destroy them? No way," McFall said.

"Yes way," Fusco retorted. "With an unprecedented level of secrecy, the United States sent a team of experts to Chelyabinsk-65 and Arzamas-16 to monitor the destruction of the Russian RM program. And the Russians sent a team to the United States."

McFall was writing furiously. His hunch about Gennady Sobchak and Project Hermes must have been right. No wonder the Russians had been trying to keep a lid on what had *really* been stolen from Chelyabinsk-65. The FSB intelligence reports from Captain Tarazov were deliberate disinformation. They claimed the missing material was Pu-239, but it *must* have been RM or some new variant.

"So the United States set about destroying its own RM program," Fusco was saying. "It closed down the secret RM lab at Los Alamos; it seized and incinerated the experiment notebooks; and it gave fat severance packages to the scientists."

"But," Preston said, "I know there's a 'but' coming."

"But not everyone seems to have been happy with the arrangement. One nuclear scientist in particular did not want to go away quietly."

"What was his name?" McFall asked.

"His name *is* Lazare," Fusco replied. "Quinn Lazare."

McFall scanned his mental files, but there was no match. "Who is Lazare?" he asked.

"He was an extraordinary nuclear chemist. Educated at the University of North Carolina, Chapel Hill. Recruited by the DOE Weapons Program right after completing his Ph.D. Spent a few years kicking around the labs until they realized he was *different.*"

"Different how?"

"I don't know how to put this any other way, but his DOE employment reviews say he was just smarter than everyone else. He could see things no one else could see."

"What the hell does that mean?" McFall said.

"It means the guy was a loner, an eccentric. He was living and thinking at the outer edges of physics, and the Weapons Program decided to harness some of that for its most secret program. He spent his entire career, fifteen long years, on RM. But that's not all. You're going to love this. From time to time, various DOE big shots called him in to give secret game theory advice on NEST strategy and tactics."

"No way," McFall said. "If he was involved with NEST, I definitely would have met him."

"Wrong," Fusco said. "This guy was an invisible consultant. His real name never appeared in government message traffic, and he had his own classified secret compartment, just like our spies in the Kremlin. Your boss's boss might have called him for help with a NEST problem. But you never would have been allowed to talk to him directly."

McFall was dumbfounded. His circuits were overloading from too many new inputs. A secret, long-term RM project at Los Alamos? And a mysterious NEST strategic consultant lurking in the shadows?

"So why didn't this guy Lazare want to go along with the RM self-destruct plan?" Preston asked.

"Because he had spent his entire professional life working on Red Mercury, and he didn't want it to be erased. The guy had given up everything for his work. He had nothing—no wife, family, friends. From all accounts, the guy was a recluse and kind of weird."

"What happened to him?"

"He sent a few menacing notes to the DOE. And then he disappeared."

"What do you mean, disappeared?"

"Vanished."

"People don't just vanish," Preston said.

"The guy didn't leave a forwarding address," Fusco said, "and no one's been able to find him."

"Has anyone looked?" McFall asked.

"Oh, sure. A lot of people have been hunting for him, and no one's managed to track him down. He tried to sell some secrets to Libya, he went into hiding, and he took a lot of knowledge with him, if you know what I mean. To tell you the truth, given what he can do, we were hoping he was dead."

Preston and McFall exchanged glances.

Fusco studied the grainy black-and-white surveillance photographs clipped to the back of the DOE folder.

"Lazare's definitely your man," Fusco said. "He's got the motive, the method, and the madness."

"Can you send us photos and files?" Preston asked.

"No problem," Fusco said.

"And anything else you've got on him."

"You betcha."

"Thanks, Vince. You're a prince," Preston said.

"Bye, Kyle. See ya, Mack."

McFall did not answer. His thoughts had turned to a memorable line from Joseph Conrad's *The Secret Agent:* "The terrorist and the policeman both come from the same basket."

The prospect of hunting Lazare, an ex-member of the U.S. nuclear family and former NEST insider, filled him with foreboding. No doubt, Lazare knew NEST's capabilities. He could elude their tricks and traps. And he would exploit their vulnerabilities.

On the battlefield in his mind, McFall recognized the grim reality: the enemy had a decided advantage.

A man with binoculars tracked the single-engine prop plane as it dropped out of the stratus clouds and buzzed the tree tops of the Uwharrie National Forest. He reached for his walkie-talkie. "Scope One to Brains. She's on her way in," the scout radioed. "Half a mile out and ready to land."

"Brains, Scope One. Roger that," Lazare said, pulling out his long-lens camera to watch for the Mooney 201 as it appeared over the ridge. He counted backward in his mind: "Ten . . . nine . . . eight . . . seven . . ."

Bingo!

There it was, a white single-engine plane with green stripes and 777PC on its tail. The plane's wings dipped back and forth. Lazare followed it down the slope of the hill and into the little valley. The flaps were down and the plane was slowing. He could see there were two men in the front of the aircraft.

He checked his watch. The plane was right on time.

The four-seater touched down in a swirl of dust on the 950-foot makeshift dirt strip and rolled to a stop. The pilot switched off the Lycoming engine.

The door above the wing popped open. Gus Rybak jumped out first, followed by the pilot, a middle-aged man with a big gut. He was wearing a golf shirt, jeans, and a baseball cap that said PILOTS DO IT WITH MORE THRUST. The man stretched and fished a cigarette from his pocket. He flicked a match against his jeans zipper and cupped his hands to light it.

Lazare watched the two men through his long lens. He waited for the signal. Rybak seemed to be enjoying himself. He had a big, friendly smile. He slapped the pilot on the back and laughed.

What's so funny? Lazare wondered. *What is Shakes up to now?*

It was impossible to trust Rybak with anything now that he knew his lieutenant was trying to eliminate him. The simpering fool! Lazare had calculated the pros and cons of sending Rybak on the critical errand of getting the plane and concluded the risks were acceptable. Lazare knew he would have to watch Rybak every minute. The double-cross was inevitable. The question was, when?

Lazare watched the ruddy-faced pilot and the traitor chat for a few more minutes. Then, Rybak nonchalantly touched the bill of his Yellow Jackets baseball cap, raising and lowering it twice. It was the signal.

All clear.

Lazare also saw Rybak reach for his chest and scratch it vigorously. What a giveaway, that Tourette's disorder, Lazare laughed to himself.

Lazare started up the Dodge truck and reached for the walkie-talkie: "Brains to Scope One, anything?"

"Nothing here, Brains."

"Scope Two?"

"Zippo on that."

"I'm going to the plane," Lazare said. "If you see anything move, I want to know immediately. Got that?"

"Got it," Scope One said. He was posted high on the ridge, looking down on the winding Forest Service Road 576 that ran through the Uwharrie and came within a few miles of the dirt clearing.

"Copy," said Scope Two. He was posted on another ridge with a good view of the airstrip and the little valley where the Hole was hidden.

Lazare pulled the truck out of its hiding place at the far end of the dirt clearing and drove toward the plane. He stopped near the six-foot two-inch propeller. Rybak waved. He looked as if he was in the middle of telling a joke. Both men laughed as Lazare got out of the truck.

"Hey there," Rybak said cheerfully. "How ya doing, Mitch? Good to see ya."

"You, too, Bart," Lazare said, using the scripted names.

"Let me introduce you to Dick Peet, pilot extraordinaire."

"Good to meet you, Dick. I'm Mitch Adler."

"Pleasure's mine," Peet said, flicking his cigarette.

"How was the flight in?" Lazare asked.

"A little bumpy coming down through the clouds," Rybak said, "but nothing this old Mooney can't handle."

"Well, good," Lazare said. "You boys ready to go to work?"

"You bet," Rybak said.

Lazare pulled a Ruger P94L from his vest. Dick Peet's eyes bulged when he saw the nine-millimeter handgun with a built-in integral laser.

"Surprise!" Lazare said, raising the gun and pointing the red dot of the laser at Rybak's forehead.

Rybak froze. Panic spread across his face, the unmistakable look of exposure, guilt, and fear. He grabbed his chest, scratching frantically.

Lazare grinned. Then he turned and aimed the laser sight at Peet's heart. Without hesitating, he squeezed off three rounds. Peet stumbled backward and crashed into the fuselage of the plane. Then he collapsed onto the ground.

"Jesus!" Rybak screamed at Lazare. "Fucking-A! You scared the shit out of me!"

"Sorry, Shakes," Lazare said icily. "I just lost my concentration for a second. Come on, let's go."

Rybak's face was contorted. He looked down at the dead pilot. His golf shirt was splattered with blood and his legs were buckled beneath him.

Lazare moved back to the truck, pulled the tarpaulin off of the flatbed, and loosened the ropes holding a small matte-black box the size of a microwave oven. He and Rybak carefully lifted the box from the truck, carried it to the plane, and loaded it into the cramped passenger cabin.

While Lazare strapped the black box into one of the back seats, Rybak went to the front seat of the truck to fetch a black briefcase. He carried it to the plane, put it in the cabin, and then pulled himself into the pilot's seat. Then he opened the case, took out a Toshiba laptop computer, and turned it on. After plugging a cable into the instrument panel, he began to download data from the computer into the plane's King KLN-90A Global Positioning System.

In the back seat, Lazare punched a ten-digit numeric code into the control panel on the black box, and a small green light began to flash. He repeated the code. The green light stopped blinking, and a red light switched on.

"I'm ready," Lazare said to Rybak. "How about you?"

"Just another few minutes," Rybak said. "I'm downloading the lat/longs into the GPS. Then we'll start her up."

The Toshiba flashed a message that the data dump was complete. The Mooney 201 was ready to go, except for one last bit of business.

"Now boarding, Flight 007 for Atlanta," Lazare said with a grin. He jerked his head toward the pilot lying in the dirt below, and the two men jumped out of the aircraft. Peet's bloodied body was much heavier than it looked, and it was hard work heaving him up into the cockpit, maneuvering him into the pilot's seat, and strapping him in.

Lazare then climbed into the co-pilot's seat and buckled up.

"Good luck," Rybak said.

"Thanks," Lazare said, asking himself what the double-crosser really meant. Lazare turned the key to start the 200-horsepower engine. He pushed the mixture forward and reduced the throttle to idle. The propeller began to spin. Then he flipped on his radios and taxied to the far end of the dirt clearing. He checked his fuel flow, oil pressure, and oil temperature readings. Everything was in the green. He revved the engine, checking the propeller-feathering mechanism and the magnetos.

He had practiced all summer for this flight—takeoffs, landings, fair weather and foul. He advanced the throttle with his left hand to twenty-nine inches of manifold pressure and 2,700 rpm. The Mooney bounced forward and rolled down the bumpy dirt strip, picking up speed. Lazare exerted back pressure on the yoke to avoid the ruts in the strip.

At sixty-five knots, the plane hit a jarring bump and lifted into the air too soon.

"Christ," he said aloud. This wasn't a picnic. His heart was pounding, and he was holding his breath. To avoid stalling, Lazare remembered to ease the nose over to accelerate in ground effect.

The plane gently dropped back down to the dirt strip and continued to pick up speed.

At eighty knots, he was heading straight for the row of loblolly pines lining the clearing. Lazare yanked the yoke back. The plane rose and grazed the treetops.

The plane climbed 1,000 feet per minute into the gray-blue sky.

Lazare dialed in 134.75 on his radio.

"Charlotte Approach, Mooney triple-seven poppa charlie, over."

"Mooney triple-seven poppa charlie, go ahead."

"Charlotte, we're sixty miles northeast of Charlotte climbing out of twelve hundred feet. Want to open up our IFR flight plan to Peachtree-De Kalb."

"Roger, Mooney triple-seven poppa charlie. Squawk four-three-six-four and maintain VFR. Charlotte altimeter three-zero-zero-three. Stand by for clearance."

"Roger."

Lazare dialed in the barometric pressure setting into the altimeter and pulled the throttle back to 25-squared—twenty-five inches of manifold pressure and 2,500 rpm.

"Mooney triple-seven poppa charlie. You are cleared to the Peachtree-De Kalb Airport via direct Charlotte, Victor-five-four Spartanburg, Victor-two-six-six to Electric City, Victor-three-one-one to the Corce intersection, then Victor-triple-two to the Womac intersection, then direct. Maintain eight thousand. We have you in radar contact at twenty-three-hundred."

"Roger. Mooney triple-seven poppa charlie is cleared to the Peachtree-De Kalb Airport." He repeated the VOR route of flight, then said, "We're out of thirty-five hundred for eight thousand. Over."

Lazare inspected the KLN-90A GPS to make sure the flight plan from Charlotte corresponded with the program Rybak had loaded in on the ground. Everything checked out. "Not a bad day for flying, Dicky boy?" Lazare said to the bloody pilot, who was slumped over the controls.

He howled, glanced back at the cargo behind him, and headed for 8,000 feet.

"Mooney triple-seven poppa charlie, please contact Charlotte approach on one-two-zero-point-zero-five," the comm radio blared.

Although watching the plane's flight controls, Lazare had been lost in a recurring memory, a disturbing one from his childhood. He was a small boy, five or six, on the Monsanto Inner Space ride at Disneyland. It was a journey inside the atom. The little tram whisked him into the darkness. His mother, who reeked of hair spray, sat next to him. Protons and neutrons flashed on the walls. A man with a deep voice described the interior of a molecule.

Young Lazare tried to get out of the moving ride to touch the glowing nucleus. His mother grabbed him by the collar and hauled him back into the tram. She hit him and yelled that she would never take him to Disneyland again.

Wouldn't Mama be surprised by what her little boy was doing now? Lazare thought.

The radio came to life, interrupting his daydream.

"Mooney triple-seven poppa charlie, over."

"Sorry, Charlotte approach, triple-seven poppa charlie, go ahead."

"Mooney triple-seven poppa charlie, please contact Charlotte approach on one-two-zero-point-zero-five."

"Roger," Lazare said, dialing in the new comm frequency.

"Charlotte approach, Mooney triple-seven poppa charlie. Level eight thousand."

"Roger, Mooney triple-seven poppa charlie. Charlotte altimeter setting is three-zero-zero-three."

"Roger that."

Lazare checked the instrument panel. The plane was 226 nautical miles from its destination. His indicated airspeed was 155 knots.

At full throttle, the plane was an hour away from ground zero.

The skies were clear, and he was approaching the first drop site on the North Carolina–South Carolina border near Kings Mountain National Military Park.

It was time to contact the ground team.

He dialed in another frequency, then said: "Enola Gay, Dream

Catcher."

"Dream Catcher, Enola Gay, go ahead."

"Are you ready?" he asked.

"Yes sirree, we're ready."

"Any attention?"

"Negatory on that. All clear."

Lazare hit the buttons to engage the King KFC-150 autopilot/flight director in nav mode. The system was slaved to the KLN-90A GPS. Lazare took his hands off the yoke, and the plane began to fly itself. He looked back at the black box strapped into the passenger seat. The control panel was still blinking red. Then he turned to poor Peet, hunched over in the pilot's seat, a pool of blood on the floor around his feet.

"Thank you for choosing to fly, I mean die, with us today," he said in his best flight attendant imitation. "And we hope you have a pleasant stay wherever your final destination may be."

After unbuckling the seat harness and reaching back to tighten the straps on the small shoulder pack he was wearing, Lazare pushed the safety button on the door and unlatched it. The door ajar alarm sounded, and the light flashed on the annunciator panel.

"Bombs away," Lazare said, straining to push the door open against 155 knots of wind. Opening the door in midflight was one part of the plan he had not been able to practice. It was much harder than he had imagined.

Dammit! Goddammit!

He took a deep breath and wedged his leg into the crack between the door and the air frame. With all his strength, he squeezed himself little by little out onto the wing. The plane banked lightly from the weight, and the wind blasted his face.

He paused for a moment to savor the exhilarating, burning sensation. Then he leaped up and out.

———————————

Tim Bartosh saw the blinking amber blip on his screen. It was marked 777PC and was heading southwest at 8,000 feet. The twenty-eight-year-old air traffic controller in Greenville, South Carolina, smiled when he recognized the tail markings. The plane belonged to Dick Peet, one of the most popular flight instructors and commercial pilots in the Southeast.

Bartosh punched a few buttons on his air traffic control screen and checked the flight plan.

What had old Peety been up to?

The Mooney 201 was flying what looked like a commercial run. The plane had taken off in Augusta, Georgia, headed north past Charlotte, picked up some cargo at a little private strip, and was flying on to Peachtree-De Kalb Airport.

Bartosh looked forward to handling the Mooney 201 because Peet was always good for a joke or two.

It was a slow day in Greenville, so he picked up the phone to call the Charlotte tower and get the latest flight information on Peet's plane.

Charlotte approach readily handed over the frequency—120.05—and responsibility for the plane. It was one less aircraft to monitor.

Bartosh punched in the numbers on his radio.

"Mooney triple-seven poppa charlie. This is Greenville approach. How ya doin', Dick?"

He waited, but there was no response.

"Mooney triple-seven poppa charlie. Contact Greenville approach on zero-three-five-point-five."

Again, silence.

"Triple-seven poppa charlie. Do you read me, Dick? It's Tim Bartosh at Greenville approach."

"Triple-seven poppa charlie, over."

Still nothing. Bartosh was beginning to wonder. It wasn't like Dick Peet to ignore air traffic control. Maybe he had the volume on his comm radio turned down low. Or maybe he had accidentally jarred the settings on the radio.

He tried again: "Triple-seven poppa charlie, over."

What was going on up there? Bartosh tried another tack. "All aircraft on one-two-zero-point-five. Change to my frequency one-two-four-point-seven." That cleared Peet's assigned frequency. Now there would be no interruptions or crossed signals.

He continued. "Mooney, if you hear my transmission, key your mike five times."

He turned the volume up on his panel, but all he heard was the hiss of static.

Bartosh felt a wave of anxiety as he considered the other possibilities. Dick Peet was seriously overweight and a chain smoker to boot. A heart attack at 8,000 feet? It wasn't out of the question.

As a last resort Bartosh flipped the radio to 121.5, the national emergency frequency. "Triple-seven poppa charlie. Do you read me, Dick? Come on, boy. What's going on out there?"

Again, there was no response.

"Mooney triple-seven poppa charlie," Bartosh repeated slowly and clearly, "it appears we've lost radio contact. Please squawk seven-seven-zero-zero. Request you land at the next available VFR destination. Flow control in effect in the Atlanta area."

———————————

From the Greenville tower, Bartosh phoned air traffic control in Atlanta.

The call was immediately patched through to Elias Scharffs, the on-duty desk officer at the Olympic Aviation Specialized Management Center, located in the FAA's Southern regional office northwest of Hartsfield's Runway 8-Left.

The ASMC coordinated all air traffic in and out of the restricted flight zone around Atlanta, and from the moment the FBI had declared a Black Ring situation, the center was in its highest state of alert. The staffers were already stretched to the limit. Earlier in the day there had been a tense incident involving a motorized hang-glider pulling a protest banner about cruelty to animals. The glider had flown so low and so slowly—less than thirty-five miles an hour—that it had not been detected by Atlanta Center radar.

This experience could not help but scramble the confidence of Olympic officials who in 1993 had begun formulating control procedures for the onslaught of aircraft expected during the Games. The main work had been undertaken by the Olympic Aviation Advisory Team, a group of airport managers from around the Southeastern

region, officials from the state and federal Departments of Transportation, and the Federal Aviation Administration.

Drawing on the successful 1984 Los Angeles air traffic control plan,
the group recommended severely restricting airspace in and around
the Olympic Ring, except for NBC helicopters and blimps. And so, at a
cost of $10 million, the Federal Aviation Administration implemented
the plan to protect the sky over Atlanta. Above downtown, for
instance, the FAA barred planes from flying below 3,000 feet within
three miles of the Georgia Dome and one mile of the Olympic Village.

Outside the Ring, the management of air traffic was a controller's
nightmare. There were hundreds of commercial airliners from
around the world, thousands of private jets bringing in fat cats for the
festivities, and myriad civilian pilots who just wanted to fly by. These
arrivals could be expected to have filed a flight plan, but there were
also the thrill-seeking parachutists who wanted to jump unan-
nounced into Olympic Stadium.

"Look," said Tim Bartosh, "I just wanted to give you early warning
that a Mooney is heading straight for Atlanta with no radio contact."

"Who's the pilot?" said Elias Scharffs. He had a cheek full of Red
Man chewing tobacco and a pewter spitting cup in his hand.

"The pilot is a guy named Dick Peet. He's a real pro and that's why
it doesn't make any sense. He knows the rules. He knows you're on
tactical alert in your airspace. And he knows if he's got a radio problem, he's supposed to land at the nearest available airport. If the
weather was real lousy, it would be one thing. But the sky is clear all
the way from here to Asheville. So he has no excuse. Something is
definitely going on."

"Thanks for the heads-up," Scharffs said, letting fly a black stream
of tobacco juice.

"Let me know if I can help," Bartosh said. "Peet's a good man."

"Will do," Scharffs said. "Gotta go." He dialed up the frequency—
120.05—and tried to radio the wayward Mooney.

"Mooney seven-seven-seven poppa charlie," Scharffs said,
"Atlanta Center. Come back."

There was no response.

"Mooney triple-seven poppa charlie. You are approaching Atlanta Class B airspace and the Mode C Veil. You do not have proper clearance. The airspace is restricted. Aircraft not in radio contact are prevented from proceeding into the area. Remain clear of Atlanta Class B airspace. Repeat. Remain clear of Atlanta Class B airspace. Acknowledge."

Scharffs imagined his radio message evaporating into the ether.

"Mooney seven-seven-seven poppa charlie. I repeat, you are approaching Class B airspace without proper radio callup. I say again: you do not have clearance to enter the restricted zone. You have two dozen aircraft at twelve o'clock."

Scharffs paused and flipped the pages of his Olympic aviation emergency protocols manual. Then he continued. "You are ordered by the FAA to turn one hundred eighty degrees and fly away from Atlanta. Fly away, triple-seven poppa charlie."

Come on, poppa charlie! Scharffs thought.

The blinking green blip on the radar screen kept its course, heading straight for Atlanta.

"Goddammit," Scharffs said to himself as he pulled off his headset. He studied the screen: the plane was traveling at 155 knots. At its current air speed, it was roughly fifty-five minutes away from downtown.

He punched up the Atlanta Center frequency.

"Attention all aircraft," Scharffs said. "Emergency air traffic operations are now in effect. Please stand by for emergency instructions. Repeat. Please stand by."

L azare had come down just where he had planned—in a grassy field in Kings Mountain National Military Park. The parachute landing was not by the book, but he broke no bones, and he took a measure of pride in that accomplishment.

Swaying in the parachute harness, he had fretted that the descent was excruciatingly slow. He had been sick to his stomach for two days, and all the motion, vertical and horizontal, left him even more uncomfortable. The brown South Carolina countryside was unexceptional. He could see Blacksburg and Gastonia in the distance. He wondered how many people were watching him come down.

Over the past year he had taken two dozen skydiving lessons at a school on the park's border, and he filched a sky-blue chute from the supply room to use today. Something about falling from the sky was exhilarating, but he did not like the vulnerability of being out in the open and exposed.

Darren Dunn had picked him up, and they were now heading south on I-85, across South Carolina, toward the Georgia border.

Lazare kept looking up into the sky from the Dodge truck, imagining where the Mooney would be. He checked his watch. The plane was already inside the Georgia line, and Olympic security was probably pulling its hair out. Lazare gave them about fifteen more minutes to figure out how to stop the plane. Or maybe they wouldn't be able to stop the plane. And then what?

Lazare imagined the fireball on the horizon.

At a distance of fifty miles, a one-megaton explosion would be brighter than the sun at high noon. And at 15,000,000 degrees Celsius, it would be as hot as the interior of the sun.

For some reason, Lazare thought of General William T. Sherman's famous cable to General Ulysses S. Grant in September 1864: "I can make this march, and make Georgia howl."

Make Georgia howl! Lazare loved it.

"How far to Hartwell?" he asked.

"Another hour and a half, maybe," Dunn said.

"Keep your eye on the speedometer," Lazare said. "Don't go a mile over the limit, you hear?"

"Yessir," Dunn said, his two-fingered talon wrapped around the steering wheel.

"Now let me sleep."

McFall's Buick Skylark came to a screeching stop in front of the pale blue building at Dobbins Air Reserve Station. Three military police with M-16s were standing guard in front of the giant metal doors.

He flashed his base pass and slipped into the Special Mission Unit hangar. Under blazing halogen lamps, two black AH-60 DAP assault-transport helicopters waited at the ready.

In the background, Tom Lehrer's song "What's Next" was playing on a boom box. It was the unofficial anthem of the X-ray Force. McFall smiled as he heard the lyric about staying "serene and calm when Alabama gets the bomb."

Serene and calm. It was exactly how McFall felt with the X-rays, his hand-picked special forces team selected from the SEALs and Rangers and trained during the year he had worked for the Joint Special Operations Command at Fort Bragg near Fayetteville, North Carolina.

He walked over to the makeshift ready-room and greeted Captain Jack F. X. Mannion, team leader of the X-ray Force.

"Hey, Doc, good to see ya," Mannion said.

"Good to see you too, F. X.," McFall answered.

"Your boys ready to roll?"

"You betcha."

"Then let's get outta here."

"Army six-six-five, you're cleared for takeoff."

"Roger that, Dobbins tower," Army Warrant Officer Mike Gendler said. "Army six-six-five cleared for takeoff."

The AH-60 DAP helicopter lifted gently off the tarmac at Dobbins and surged forward toward the northeast. It cleared a big red-and-white-checked water tower and soared over the giant Lockheed manufacturing plant.

The aircraft's orders had come straight from JSOC at Fort Bragg at the request of the Olympic Joint Command Center. Its mission: intercept the Mooney 201 and make a visual inspection. Its call sign—Army six-six-five—was deliberately innocuous.

The DAP was a flying weapons system designed to put fighting men and burning steel on target. DAP stood for Direct Action Penetrator. It was actually a converted Black Hawk assault transport helicopter belonging to the 160th Special Operations Aviation Regiment at Fort Campbell, Kentucky.

Designed to carry eleven fully equipped special forces operators plus a crew of three, the DAP had been specially modified for X-ray antinuclear operations. The large cabin was equipped with radiation surveillance equipment, and the skids were outfitted with gamma and neutron detectors.

The helicopter was also heavily armed, packing a 30-millimeter cannon, two 7.62-millimeter miniguns that fired 4,000 rounds per minute, and four Stinger missiles.

"Dobbins tower, Army six-six-five," Gendler said as he pushed the collective control forward with his left arm to give the DAP's rotor system more pitch. "Clear of your control zone to the northeast."

"Roger, Army six-six-five. Contact Atlanta approach on two-five-four-point-two-five."

"Thank you, Dobbins. Contacting Atlanta approach on two-five-four-point-two-five."

Gendler dialed in the new radio frequency.

"Atlanta approach. Army six-six-five is with you at one thousand and climbing."

"Roger, Army six-six-five. Squawk zero-three-two-one."

"Atlanta approach, Army six-six-five. Squawking zero-three-two-one."

Gendler punched in the transponder code and nudged the collective control forward, increasing power. Then he pushed forward on the cyclic to lower the nose and gain airspeed.

"Army six-six-five," the air traffic controller said. "Radar contact. Turn right heading zero-four-five. Climb and maintain 10,000 feet."

"Roger, Atlanta approach," Gendler said, easing the cyclic to the right to bank the DAP. "Army six-six-five is turning right to heading zero-four-five. Climbing through fifteen hundred to ten thousand."

Gendler nodded to his co-pilot and then looked back to the jumpseat where McFall was sitting. It was only a gut instinct, but McFall had felt instantly uneasy when he heard that a Mooney 201 without radio contact was flying straight for Atlanta. He had decided to go along for the ride. After being dropped by Abu Azzam in the woods, it was like getting back in the saddle.

As the DAP crossed over Peachtree-De Kalb Airport, McFall could see the Tom Moreland Interchange. From the air, Spaghetti Junction looked like a concrete amusement park ride with twelve ramps and fourteen bridges.

"Army six-six-five. Your unknown is 175 miles at twelve o'clock."

"Army six-six-five, Roger," Gendler said.

McFall wondered what they would find out there in the haze. It was probably just a pilot without a radio or a flyer who had fallen ill. If the pilot was conscious, the DAP would scare the bejesus out of the guy. Although he'd definitely need a new pair of underwear, he would have a story for the rest of his life: how a special forces helicopter almost shot him out of the sky.

The DAP powered across the bleak Georgia countryside. The crew was silent.

"Army six-six-five," the radio crackled. "Your bogey is at twelve o'clock, fifteen miles, angels eight."

"Roger that, Army six-six-five. Tally. Target's at twelve o'clock, fifteen miles, eight thousand feet."

McFall squinted and saw the little plane. He pulled out his binoculars, but the glare from the sun blinded him.

The DAP was flying at 185 knots. The Mooney was coming in the opposite direction at 155 knots. Head on, it would take less than two and a half minutes to close the fifteen miles separating them.

Gendler steered the DAP into a racetrack holding position at 10,000 feet. When the Mooney got a little closer, to gain airspeed he would dive on the single-engine plane.

He needed to time the intercept just right.

"Atlanta approach, Army six-six-five, descending to 8,000 feet for the intercept," he said into his headset.

"Roger, good luck."

The DAP dropped down behind the Mooney and kept pace. The two aircraft were 200 feet apart. Gendler was careful to keep several rotor discs of space between them.

McFall scanned the front of the plane. The door was open, flapping in the wind. He knew instantly that was a bad sign. "Let's move in," he said.

Gendler nudged the cyclic to the right, and the helicopter inched closer to the Mooney. McFall had a clear view of the cockpit and the pilot. His head was down. He was slumped over.

"The pilot's in trouble," he said into the intercom. "Move up a bit so I have a better angle."

The DAP moved ahead of the plane. McFall now had a clear view of the pilot's seat. Peering through the binoculars, he saw nothing but red.

His stomach tightened.

"There's blood all over the place. Can you get in closer?"

There was a light chop and both aircraft bounced. Gendler was careful not to draw too close. McFall moved the binoculars back through the cabin. A blinking light caught his eye, and he saw the black box strapped into the rear passenger seat.

"Holy shit," McFall said. "It's a drone with some sort of device."

Now the only question was whether there was any connection between the plane, the black box, and the nuclear threat.

It was a terrifying hypothesis.

"Let's get even closer. I want to turn on the gamma and neutron pods and see what we've got."

Again, Gendler tapped the cyclic and the DAP moved in closer, less than 100 feet away from the plane. McFall climbed back to the work space. He flipped the switches to turn on the radiation detection pods on the helicopter skids.

McFall adjusted the sensors. He wasn't looking for plutonium anymore. He was looking for Red Mercury. Stan Treadwell had figured out a way to pick up traces of mercury antimony oxide. The detectors had been jerry-rigged for the new task, and he wasn't sure if they would work.

He waited, watching the screen.

"There it is!"

The green grid lit up. No doubt about it: there was Red Mercury on board the Mooney 201.

McFall did not need any more data. He returned to the cockpit and got on the secure UHF radio.

"Dobbins, Army six-six-five. Emergency One. Emergency One. Patch us through to the Olympic Joint Command Center. Get Kyle Preston. Urgent."

"Army six-six-five, Dobbins. Emergency One. Patching you through to Kyle Preston at the Olympic Joint Command Center. Stand by."

McFall looked out into the haze. He could see the Atlanta skyline in the distance. Two skyscrapers—the 1,050-foot C&S Plaza and the 880-foot One Peachtree Center—were poking up through the dust and smog.

"Army six-six-five. The patch is live. Go ahead, Ms. Preston."

"Mack, where are you?" Preston said, out of breath from the sprint across the Joint Command Center to her office.

"Eight thousand feet and eighty-five miles away," he said. "We've got trouble. The Mooney 201 is a flying car bomb. And it's heading straight for Atlanta."

In that split second, Buddy Crouse had known it was all over.

On the second day of the decathlon in the sixth event—the 110-meter high hurdles—he had brushed the last obstacle and landed off balance on his lead leg.

Now he was flat on his back in the USA track and field trainer's room. His left knee was propped up, wrapped in ice bags. His hands were clenched behind his head, and his eyes were fixed in furious beads on the small television mounted on the wall. Why the hell did NBC keep replaying the goddamn tape of him banging the tenth hurdle with his trail leg? Why did they have to show the freeze-frame of his foot touching down on the track? Why did they keep running the slow-motion video of him tumbling to the ground, getting up, and hobbling in last place across the finish line? Why did they keep zooming in on him, hunched over, head in hands, circled by coaches and teammates?

And there was that old Olympian Dwight Stones on TV with his Telestrator. How could *he* explain the injury when Crouse didn't even know how bad it was himself?

The anger consumed him. And the humiliation. The rankings flashed on the TV screen. Now, Eduard Hämäläinen of Belarus was in first place overall, and it would take a miracle to catch him.

Live on NBC, track and field analyst Craig Masbach was outside the American locker room, just twenty-five feet away. *Thank God for Carl Lewis*, Crouse thought. The eight-time Olympic gold medalist was brushing off Masbach's questions.

"Buddy will be back!" King Carl exclaimed. "He's a fighter!"

"Damn straight!" Crouse shouted back at the screen.

In the NBC studio, Bob Costas continued the *postmortem* coverage. "Everyone says this kid from Montana is as strong as a horse," Costas declared. "But the odds aren't looking good that he'll be able to catch the pack and win a medal."

Fuck, Crouse thought. *Strong as a horse? They put down horses with bum legs like his.*

"For a closer look at decathlete Buddy Crouse," Costas said, "let's go to Jim Lampley with an NBC Olympic Profile."

This was supposed to be a victory lap story, a feature to be broadcast *after* he won the gold. Hell. NBC couldn't waste their money. They were going with the story now, while the world was taking bets on whether he would be able to make it back to the competition.

It took a year to put the ten-minute profile in the can. NBC Sports producer Bucky Brenner and a camera crew had followed him everywhere—to church in Billings, at family supper on Sunday nights, at training sessions in Colorado, and even on a horseback camping trip with his sisters in the Tetons. And they had interviewed everyone he ever knew: father, mother, grandparents, coaches, teachers, friends, even the local gas station attendant.

He didn't want to see it now, here.

This is your life, Buddy Crouse!

The door opened and Dr. Sean Alpert strode in. "Hey there, Buddy."

"Hey, Doc."

Sean Alpert was a lean, chiseled sports doctor who looked like he was on loan from the cast of "ER." In fact, Team USA had borrowed him for the Games from the famous Kerlan-Jobe Orthopaedic Clinic in Los Angeles. Now in his late thirties, Alpert had starred on the UCLA volleyball and soccer teams. In 1980, his Olympic dreams had been dashed by the U.S. boycott of the Moscow Games, and not long after, he opted for medical school instead of training and waiting four more years for Los Angeles.

"How's the leg?" Alpert said.

"Not great."

"I just looked at the videotape," Alpert said, unwrapping the ice packs. "How did it feel when you hit the last hurdle?"

"A sharp pain in the middle of my knee. There was a pop, then burning."

His knee was clearly swollen. "Does this hurt?" Alpert said, pressing on the medial joint line on the inside of the knee.

Crouse winced: "Yeah. Bigtime."

"What about this?" Alpert pulled Crouse's leg through a series of maneuvers.

"Hey, Doc, you're killing me!"

"Sorry," Alpert said. "Give me ten more seconds."

Flexing Crouse's knee thirty degrees, Alpert performed the Lachman test and made a note on the chart. "Clear translation with no endpoint."

"How bad is it?" Crouse asked.

"Not sure yet. I need to take a look at the MRI," Alpert said. He opened the envelope, removed the images, and put them on the light box. His suspicions were confirmed. The medial collateral ligament was torn off the femur, and the anterior cruciate ligament was completely gone. Crouse's knee was scrambled. It would take surgery and months of rehabilitation to get him back into competition.

"It doesn't look good, Buddy," Alpert said finally.

"Is it my ACL?" Crouse said.

"It's your ACL *and* MCL," Alpert said.

"Fuck me!" Crouse said. "It can't be!" He sat up on the table. "I gotta get back out there. Can't you do something? Please!"

"You've got four more events to go, Buddy," Alpert said. "Count 'em: discus, pole vault, javelin, and the 1,500 meters. I could give you Indocin and Lorcet for the inflammation and pain, but your knee won't make it. The ligaments are gone."

Alpert waited a few moments, watching Crouse's eyes fill with tears. "I'm sorry, Buddy. I really am."

The SVTS videoconference was to the point and on the fly. The participants were pulled suddenly out of meetings and, in one case, from a shower at the White House gym. They were joined electronically from discrete offices and agencies across Washington, from as far away as Livermore in California, and even from an AH-60 DAP flying at 8,000 feet over reddish Georgia farmland.

Paul Attaway of the National Security Council attempted to chair the discussion.

"Mack," he began, "if you can hear me, please give us the latest."

McFall was patched into the White House Sit Room on a secure videophone in the back of the DAP.

"We're looking at a poor man's cruise missile," McFall said. "It was only a matter of time before someone tried something like this. It's been all over the international security literature for a few years."

"So what are our options?" Attaway asked.

"Violent disablement is the only way to go," said General Warren of the Joint Chiefs. "We gotta take that thing out of the sky before it gets anywhere near Atlanta."

Warren was still running victory laps over his recommendation to order the F/A-18 strike on Sapelo Island. "One blast from the DAP," he insisted, "will solve the problem now and forever. This isn't a hard call. In the Gulf War we found out Iraq had developed three radio-controlled MiG-21 drones equipped for chemical weapons dispersal. We didn't mess around. We took them out."

McFall was dismayed. *The folks at Fort Fumble are still fucking clueless.*

He pushed the transmit button on the radio.

"This is McFall again," he interrupted. His voice was tense, and he was shouting over the rotor noise. "Blasting the Mooney out of the sky sounds good if you say it fast enough. But how about a reality check? The fallout from a nuclear explosion at 8,000 feet would irradiate most of northeast Georgia for years. And you'd see birth defects for generations."

"I'm not so sure about that," said Dr. Felix Diedrich with the Technical Threat Assessment Team at Lawrence Livermore. "The explosion would probably vaporize the device and the Red Mercury together. There wouldn't be much of a radiation effect."

"Probably, but what if you're wrong?" McFall asked. "Do you want to take that kind of risk? Think about it. The fallout would be with us for a long time. Here's one way to look at it. The half-life of Pu-239 is 24,000 years. So if someone had sprinkled plutonium on the first Olympic Games in 776 B.C., it would still have 90 percent of its radioactive properties today."

"Well, we took a chance on Sapelo Island," Attaway said. "I mean, we attacked the nuclear lunch box. And the fallout was negligible. Why not strike the plane?"

"A coastal island in the Atlantic gulfstream is different from the airspace over Georgia," McFall explained. "For Sapelo, we had Livermore plume models showing that even a large radioactive release would drift out over the Atlantic and dissipate. It's a whole different ball game here."

"I would agree with that assessment," said Dr. Diedrich. "I'm not sure about the radioactive scatter effects of striking the plane, but there is no doubt that the risks are much greater over land."

"All right," said Attaway. "The president is going to want an options list and a recommendation from us. So what have we got?"

"Option One," General Warren said. "Strike with a Stinger or the DAP's machine gun."

"Don't you people get it?" McFall shot in. "That's not an option. In case you're wondering, general, I'm looking down on I-85. Off to my left in the distance, I can see Athens. To my right, Gainesville isn't far away. This is a heavily populated area."

"So what's your recommendation?" General Warren snapped.

"You probably wanna send up a polka dot flare!"

McFall ignored the slight. "I really don't know," he said. "We can't exactly get inside the plane and disable the IND from up here."

"Why not?" General Warren asked.

"This isn't the movies, sir. I don't have wings and the Mooney is probably booby-trapped."

McFall was watching the horizon. The plane was 500 feet ahead at two o'clock and 500 feet below. "Folks, the Atlanta skyline is getting closer. It is my judgment that boarding the Mooney is not a realistic option."

"So where does that leave us?" Attaway asked, looking up at the EVENT 1 clock that estimated the Mooney's arrival time in Atlanta. "We've got twenty minutes to go. We're running out of time. There must be something we can do!"

"I don't know much about aviation, but something is flying this plane. What's guiding it to Atlanta?" said Preston.

"It's on autopilot," McFall said. "It's either using an inertial navigation system or the Global Positioning System. My bet is GPS because INS isn't as reliable."

"So how is GPS guiding the plane?" Preston asked.

"It uses navigation information from 24 NAVSTAR satellites in orbit over Earth," McFall said. "My guess is when the plane arrives at its preprogrammed destination, it will detonate."

"Can we jam the plane's navigation system?" Preston asked.

"Sure, we can scramble the plane's electronics and avionics," McFall replied, "but the nuclear device is slaved to the GPS system, so if there is any electrical interruption, it will probably blow right then."

There was silence.

"Come on, people! Help me out here," Attaway said, hammering the table.

"Wait," said McFall. "Jamming won't work, but what about deception? Why can't we trick the Mooney?"

"Go on," Attaway said.

"It's what navigators call 'meaconing.' The North Koreans are real pros at it. So were the Vietnamese. They confuse the nav systems on our aircraft, lure us into their airspace, then take their best shot."

"So how would we meacon the Mooney?"

"Why not degrade the GPS navigation data coming down from the satellites?" McFall proposed. "GPS would fool the plane. Its satellites would tell the plane Atlanta is out over the water in the Gulf of Mexico. The Mooney would be tricked into flying to the wrong destination. In other words, we'd whisper a new address into the autopilot's ear. GPS would tell the plane that Atlanta is somewhere off the coast, and the Mooney would fly there instead of smack into the Olympics."

"Is it possible?" Attaway asked. "Can we do it?"

"Hell if I know," McFall said, "but with nineteen minutes to go, does anybody else have a better idea?"

"**T**hey're out of their goddamn minds."

As an opening line the phrase was inflammatory, especially at a place like the Air Force's 50th Space Wing, located at Falcon Air Force Base seventeen miles east of Colorado Springs. The 3,840-acre base, the Air Force's newest facility, was surrounded by wide open plains, cows, and antelope. Inside the razor-wire fences, the 50th Space Wing was responsible for command and control of the Defense Department's communications, navigation, weather, and missile warning satellites.

Wing commander Steven Romick, a tough-talking fifty-three-year-old brigadier general, had been in the middle of his midmorning snack—yogurt and a grapefruit, the same routine every day for thirty years—when he had gotten the call from the 14th Air Force at Vandenburg Air Force Base in California. Romick was the man in charge of milspace, or what he called "the wild black yonder."

"Foam the runways," Romick's boss had said. "We've got a terrorist situation in Atlanta. The White House wants to degrade the GPS system to manage the crisis."

The phrase "They're out of their goddamn minds" had burst forth from Romick's mouth. Degrading the Global Positioning System satellite constellation had never been done before and would create literally millions of spinoff problems.

But orders were orders, especially coming straight from the White House.

Under the command of the 2nd Space Operations Squadron, the GPS Master Control Station was located on the second floor of the Jack Swigert Space Operations Facility, a drab, square, windowless building named after the Apollo 13 command pilot. The MCS "mod" was a large, well-lit, air-conditioned room, its walls bedecked with digital and analog atomic clocks accurate to within one second every 70,000 years. In a side room, a giant wall map showed the twenty-four GPS satellites tracking the Earth.

The seven-person GPS flight crew saluted when Romick entered the room. He marched over to the platform in the middle of the control station and shouted to the airmen. His message was simple and direct: "This is war. Do the right thing. Don't screw up."

The person in the hot seat was the satellite mission analysis officer, First Lieutenant Anita Sutton, twenty-nine years old, tall and trim, wearing a rock-sized cubic zirconium engagement ring on her finger. A week from today, she was marrying her college sweetheart, and they were going to Big Sur, California, for their honeymoon.

As controller of the GPS navigation signal, Sutton had the unenviable assignment of figuring out how to fool the Mooney 201 into flying *away* from Atlanta. Planted in front of an IBM computer station with her nose four inches from the screen, she banged away on the keyboard, frantically reprogramming the software.

Her job was not made easier by Romick's pacing back and forth on the platform. He was flipping a bronze military challenge coin up and down in the air. On one side of the coin—a souvenir handed out by the 50th Space Wing—was the image of the Opinicus, a mythical monster with the combined body of an eagle and a lion. The winged creature was the symbol of the 50th Space Wing, the motto of which was "Master of Space."

On the other side of the coin were two slogans. Across the top ran: "Doubt not our presence in space." And across the bottom: *"logh negh chá qu pung."* The phrase was from the villainous Klingons of "Star Trek." Translated, it meant: "Space warriors show no mercy."

Romick checked the clocks on the wall. "No time!" he screamed at Sutton. "Let's move it! Ain't gonna be no wedding day for you if you don't type faster!"

Sutton gave Romick a long look. He had to be kidding. "This isn't tic-tac-toe," she muttered. "It's gonna take time, sir."

She was game, but she had never before reprogrammed the *entire*

$12 billion network of NAVSTAR satellites tracking in 10,900-mile semisynchronous orbits above Earth.

Designed as a navigation tool for U.S. military forces and for multiple civilian uses, GPS enables anyone with a receiver to identify his latitude, longitude, and altitude with an accuracy between 50 and 330 feet. Using triangulation, a GPS receiver determines its location by timing how long it takes radio signals to reach the Earth from the satellites. The system is so exact that it allows time to be calculated to within a millionth of a second and speed to be determined to within a fraction of a mile per hour. It operates around the clock, in fair weather and foul, and spans the entire globe.

The twenty-four satellites in the system broadcast different positioning signals. The Precision, or P-Code, is encrypted and provides highly accurate positioning signals for U.S. military purposes. The unencrypted Coarse/Acquisition, or C/A, code is intentionally less precise and is available for civilian and commercial uses.

Sutton knew that the first task was to figure out which four satellites were being used by the Mooney 201's GPS system. That was not as elementary as it sounded because there were a dozen satellites tracking in the northern hemisphere.

Working with the satellite systems operators—the GPS pilots— Sutton determined the Mooney was tapping four satellites in four different orbital planes. The satellites were SVN 21, SVN 24, SVN 36, and SVN 16.

Getting the GPS ground antennae up and running and ready to communicate with the four satellites 11,000 miles away was the next step. On a good day, it took ten to twenty minutes to place the call to the sky. Today, they had five minutes, max.

The final challenge was whether they could actually trick the Mooney into flying straight out over the Atlantic Ocean instead of to downtown Atlanta. Sutton thought it was a clever idea, typical of the pie-in-the-sky policy wizards in Washington, but would it really work? Manipulating the navigation signals for four different satellites meant manipulating four sets of complex calculations, and that would take time, too.

Sutton could feel the sweat on the back of her neck. And Romick was pacing faster and faster, cursing to himself as he flipped his coin.

Trying to rewrite the entire GPS software on the fly was a nightmare. If any one of the data points was off, the Mooney's GPS receiver might become confused. And it didn't take a rocket scientist to know what that might trigger.

NBC Sports Update. American swimmer Janet Evans isn't used to being an underdog, but the most successful woman in American Olympic swimming history definitely has her work cut out for her in the pool today. Two German swimmers are heavy favorites in the 400-meter freestyle.

Don't count Evans out. The 24-year-old wants to exit the way she entered—wearing gold.

In 1988 at the Seoul Games, Evans won three gold medals in the 400 and 800 freestyle events and the 400 individual medley. She was 18 years old. In 1992 in Spain, she won again as 800 freestyle champion.

If Evans wins the 800 freestyle today, she would be the second woman swimmer in Olympic history to win her event a third straight time. Dawn Fraser of Australia won the 100 freestyle in 1956, 1960, and 1964.

Kyle Preston sat at her desk, staring at a legal pad.

She felt like that anguished, manic figure engulfed by a swirling orange-red sky in Edvard Munch's *The Scream*. The painting by the Norwegian Expressionist was on loan to the High Museum of Art for the Cultural Olympiad and had stopped her short on opening night. In fact, the masterpiece was already part of Olympic legend: it had been stolen during the 1994 Winter Games in Lillehammer and was later returned mysteriously to Oslo.

Preston focused on the legal pad. There were only four lines penciled in.

> Quinn Lazare.
> Rebecca Deen—ACOG.
> Mooney 201—belongs to Dick Peet, Augusta, Georgia.
> Hartsfield security guard. Killed with ricin.

The UHF military radio hissed on her desk. She turned the volume down and tried to clear her mind.

All around her, it felt like hell was breaking loose.

She had just gotten off the phone with Jared, her boyfriend in New York. Without provocation she had snapped at him, no doubt because of guilt about McFall. The tension from that unhappy conversation had flowed right into the next phone call with her boss at FBI headquarters on Ninth Street and Pennsylvania Avenue in Washington.

Perry Swaggart, chief of the Counter-Terrorism Section, had wanted to call off the rest of the Games. "We just can't guarantee security anymore," he had said.

"Come on, Perry. We've *never* been able to guarantee security," Preston had responded. "The only way we could do that is if no one were allowed to come."

"Kyle, you're losing it," Swaggart said.

"Wrong. It's just that all of you want to control the uncontrollable."

"Kyle, take a walk around the block. You need some time to clear your head." He hung up.

The intercom rang on her phone.

"Dr. Kahng is here," her secretary said.

"Send her in," Preston answered. She leaned back in her chair and relaxed. She and Andrea Kahng went back a long way at the Bureau. They had been roommates at the Academy. Kahng, one of the FBI's top psychologists and investigative profilers, had a reputation that preceded her. In part, it was her own doing. She called herself Queen Kahng and told friends and strangers alike she was nuttier than the serial killers she tracked. Her main preoccupation, however, wasn't stalking mass murderers. Her obsession, bordering on mania, was with a different kind of manhunt—finding an eligible man.

Kahng had just spent all night in the basement offices of the Bureau's Investigative Support Unit in Quantico, putting together a criminal personality profile of Quinn Lazare. Then, without a wink of sleep, she had gone straight to National Airport and caught the first flight to Atlanta.

Kahng appeared in the doorway, her face radiating frantic energy.

"Hiya, Queenie," Preston said.

"Hey, Kyle," Kahng said. They gave each other a quick hug.

"This is really nice," Preston said, touching Kahng's blotchy black-and-white sweater. "Where'd you get it? From Dr. Rorschach?"

"Hardy har har," Kahng said. "So, how's it going?"

"Well, you know—"

"Cut to the chase," Kahng interrupted, pulling out a Marlboro Light. "You got any athletes to introduce me to?"

"Andrea!" Preston said in mock shock. "*You* want to meet Olympic athletes? What on earth has gotten into you, girl?"

"No sleep'll do it to ya," Kahng said.

"No sleep?"

"Yeah, I spent the night profiling your man."

"So who is he?"

Kahng smiled and said, "Who really knows?"

"Come on, Andrea. We don't have a lot of time."

Kahng reached into her briefcase, pulled out a folder, and tossed it onto Preston's desk. "You can read the full report later. I'll give you the Cliffs Notes version. The diagnosis is that Lazare has an extreme paranoid personality disorder. He's been a loner and an oddball ever since he was a boy in North Carolina. He's got a sky-high IQ—in the 200 range. He *does not* have disorganized speech, catatonic behavior, or flat affect. But, to put it clinically, he's totally fucked up."

Preston laughed. "He's a nut, but doesn't act like one?"

"No, he's a nut who hides it pretty well. There's a difference."

"But how did he get past the DOE security clearance checks? Don't they screen for crazies?"

"Yeah, but this guy was tailor-made for the labs. They were probably looking for someone like him. As a paranoid personality, he's suspicious of everyone, has very few friends, and has delusions of grandeur. Those traits would be ideal for an assignment in a secret weapons research program. And by the way, those characteristics probably apply to half the current weapons designers at Los Alamos."

Preston could not help thinking that was a good laugh on McFall.

"When the DOE eliminated the Red Mercury program, the supporting structure around Lazare was stripped away. He had nowhere to hide. And he snapped."

"Snapped?"

"Yeah, he no longer had any protective cover for his psychopathology. He cracked, and his delusions overwhelmed him."

"What are the other signs?"

"Anxiety, anger, aloofness, and argumentativeness. Generally, these people have a superior and patronizing manner and either a stilted, formal quality or extremely intense interpersonal relations."

"What about these delusions?"

"Persecutory or grandiose, or both. He thinks the U.S. government is out to get him, and he probably also believes he's omnipotent."

"Sounds like he definitely deserves his very own private suite at the looney bin in Milledgeville," Preston said. "So what's he going to do?"

"I think he's going to detonate that, uh . . ."

"Red Mercury device."

"Yeah."

"Why?"

"Because he has nothing to lose and everything to gain."

"I don't follow."

"Lazare invested everything in Red Mercury research. It was his entire life. And then the government took the research away from him, paid him a kill fee, and said good-bye."

"The guy was fired. It happens to people all the time."

"Yeah, but Lazare isn't your average guy. For starters, he's got world-class hardware running very screwed-up software. And then there's his work. Nuclear physicists are a different breed. They are dealing with nuclear explosions that come close to approximating the very first chain reaction. We're talking about the origins of the universe. You know, the Big Bang. The power of the sun."

"$E = mc^2$," Preston said, trying to keep up.

"Yeah, exactly. Good old Albert's equation started it all. Some of those scientists understood the dark side of their work and were terrified by it. That's why Einstein, Oppenheimer, and Teller all worried about what they were unleashing."

"So what are you saying?"

"It's in Genesis. 'And God said, Let there be light: and there was light.' Some of these people get off on their mind-boggling power. After all, the nuclear explosions they create are really miniature stars. And if your head isn't screwed on straight, well—"

"So where does this take us?"

"My strong belief is that Lazare will do everything he can to detonate that Red Mercury device."

"No stopping him?"

"Stop him? Maybe. But only with force. He's not going to be reasonable about this."

"Does he care about dying?"

"Not at all. The persecutory themes may predispose him to suicidal behavior, and if you combine that with the anger he feels, it will inevitably lead him to violence."

"Why?"

"Because the means *are* the end. When that Red Mercury device detonates, it will prove he existed. It will prove his life's work wasn't for naught."

"The fireball will mean he's real."

"No, it will mean he's God."

T he city was straight ahead, twelve o'clock.

McFall stared out the window of the DAP.

He wasn't accustomed to feeling utterly powerless, waiting for a signal from the skies.

The Mooney was 300 feet ahead of the DAP and 100 feet below. In one panoramic view, McFall could see the drone and its target.

They were fifteen miles from the city center. South of downtown, a 200-foot-long blimp—the world's largest—circled lazily. It had been loaned to the Atlanta Police Department by the Kroger grocery chain and was being used to monitor traffic. Further north, three brightly colored balloons were tethered to thousand-foot cables over the Olympic Village.

And below the helicopter to the southeast, McFall saw the granite hump of Stone Mountain, where he and Preston had picnicked. He pictured Kyle, sitting in the Joint Command Center. What if the device went off? He would never see her green eyes again. Or touch the wispy hair that laced her neck.

"I'm telling ya. We should have shot it down fifty miles ago with the cannon," Mike Gendler, the pilot, said into the intercom.

"Huh?" McFall said.

"I said, we should have zapped the Mooney way back. But it's too late now. Atlanta approach, Army six-six-five. Request an update from Olympic JCC."

"Army six-six-five. No update. Please stand by."

"The Cape antenna is ready to go," the ground systems operator shouted from across the GPS Master Control Station. "And the

Pike antenna is ready as backup. We can talk to the satellites any-time now."

Anita Sutton was finishing her calculations.

"We're ready whenever you are, Sutton," General Romick hollered.

Sutton checked the numbers as they came off her screen and then handed them to a backup mission analysis officer for triple and quadruple checking. It felt like she was taking *every* final exam of her entire life—high school, college, and Air Force Academy—all rolled into one. She had always been a steady B+ student. This time, how-ever, 85 percent wouldn't make the grade.

"We're ready, sir," she said to Romick.

"Then what's stopping you?"

"If we're wrong, the plane may—"

"Did you do the best you could?"

"Yessir, I did, sir."

"Then send the goddamn signal."

The airburst flattened Atlanta.

The death and destruction were incomprehensible. The scream-ing was deafening. The blood poured.

But of all the horrific images, one endured.

The streets of Atlanta—all the streets—were buried in six feet of melted glass. Literally buried. The blast wave had shattered hundreds of thousands of windows in all the skyscrapers and high-rises. The shards had melted in the extreme heat as they fell to the ground, molten rain for the living and a burning burial for the dead.

There was a loud bang.

Lazare woke up from his sleep. The truck veered off the road. "What the hell?" he said.

"Blowout," Darren Dunn said, eyes bulging, as he slammed on the brakes.

He struggled with the steering wheel. The vehicle swerved into a ditch and came to a blunt stop.

"Get out and fix the fucking tire, you one-handed freak!" Lazare screamed. Then he closed his eyes, trying to find his way back into his delicious dream.

The signal shot from a computer terminal in central Colorado, across the United States to the Cape ground antenna in Florida, then up 11,000 miles into space to four GPS satellites orbiting Earth.

And then it ricocheted back down again from the heavens.

The King KLN-90A GPS in the Mooney 201 received the information.

The plane's autopilot responded instantly to the new navigation information, banking sixty-five degrees to the left.

"There she goes," Mike Gendler said, easing the cyclic to the left and tailing the Mooney.

"Atlanta approach, Army six-six-five. Target is turning sixty-five degrees at angels eight."

"Roger, Army six-six-five. Radar contact. Shadow at eighty-five-hundred."

"Army six-six-five. Shadowing at eight-five-zero-zero."

The Mooney held its left turn for thirty seconds, then leveled off. The plane was flying a half mile east of Atlanta, parallel to the sky-scraping spine of the city. Directly below was the Carter Presidential Center in the rolling green hills of Inman Park.

McFall got on the SATCOM radio, which was patched directly into the Olympic Joint Command Center. "Joint Command Center, Army six-six-five."

"Go ahead, Mack. What have you got?"

"Kyle, the target is flying southeast now." He checked the navigation maps. "We're lined up with Toomsboro, Swainsboro, and Savannah," McFall said.

"That's the shortest distance to the water," Preston said. "The Pentagon debated sending the Mooney down to the Gulf. But it's a longer flight."

"So the idea is for the drone to ditch in the ocean?"

"Yeah, the GPS satellites are telling it that Atlanta is well past the

Bahamas. So it will fly until it runs out of fuel."

"And when will that happen? Over land or water?"

"No way of knowing. We have no idea what's in the tank. But they tell me its range is 1,219 miles at flight idle."

Barry Dogan was utterly confused.

Nathan Weeks was hopelessly lost.

Kathleen Laffer was frantic.

And Carlo and Francesca Barravalle were afraid for their lives.

Barry Dogan was on a John Deere tractor in Garden City, Kansas, working the fields. Suddenly, his Magellan Trailblazer XL GPS receiver flashed a new signal on its LCD screen. If the satellites were to be believed, Dogan was now plowing a field near Knoxville, Tennessee, hundreds of miles to the east.

Nathan Weeks worked his way through the thick forest below Clingman's Dome, elevation 6,643 feet, in the Great Smoky Mountains National Park. He was trying to find his way back to the campsite where his wife and six-year-old daughter were waiting. His Eagle AccuNav Sport GPS receiver, which he wore on his belt, flashed a new message. If it was accurate, his position would have put him somewhere off the coast of North Carolina near Cape Fear.

Kathleen Laffer stared in horror at the computer screen in Chicago's new emergency response command and control center, which handled 14,000 calls a day. Laffer, a 911 dispatcher, pounded her keyboard, trying to get a response from the Trimble GPS-based Automatic Vehicle Location hardware and software. The computer finally answered: Chicago's fifty ambulances, 2,000 police cars, and dozens of fire trucks had vanished and then incredibly turned up again near Pittsburgh, Pennsylvania.

And in downtown Atlanta, Carlo Barravalle and his wife, Francesca, from Milan, Italy, were heading the wrong way down a one-way street. Their Avis rental car was equipped with a GPS navigation system, and its computerized voice had just told them to turn north on Peachtree Street, a jam-packed thoroughfare heading south.

Across Atlanta, Olympic security forces were also lost.

The Pentagon had distributed a thousand AN/PSN-11 Precision Lightweight GPS receivers to key Olympic security personnel. The use of the Rockwell five-channel receivers enabled security to track vehicles, VIPs, and personnel.

When the 2nd Space Operations Squadron degraded the GPS data, it wasn't only the Mooney 201 that flew off on a wild goose chase.

Lazare sat in the musty motel room and cursed at the sputtering air conditioner in the corner. He was sweating profusely, and he wasn't sure if it was the low-grade fever, the heat, or the accommodations.

The Jameson Inn, a mile and a half north of Hartwell, Georgia, on the Anderson Highway, was far from deluxe. The white clapboard, green-shuttered two-story motel wasn't where he had imagined hiding out on the eve of his greatest achievement.

He flipped the remote and watched the local TV news from Greenville, South Carolina. On cable, he found CNN and a few Atlanta channels. On Greenville's NBC affiliate, WYFF, a report called "Countdown to the Closing Ceremonies" caught his attention.

The Games would be over soon, a reporter was saying.

Sooner than anyone thought!

Lazare stretched out on the bed. He was naked except for a stringy white towel wrapped around his waist. He fantasized about watching the press conference on television when Donny Sanders, that arrogant, self-promoting blowhard, would say, *"Basta! The Games must not go on!"*

Poor old Avery Brundage would spin in his grave.

Lazare reached over to the nightstand and checked his watch.

It was about time. He had been generous with the FBI and Olympic security. To stop the lunch box on Sapelo Island, he had given them an hour. To stop the plane, he had allowed them roughly forty-five minutes.

Now he would tighten the noose.

But what about the Mooney? Did they stop the drone?

There was one surefire way to tell.

He reached for the Trimble ScoutMaster GPS receiver in his brief-case and checked the readout.

He smiled.

Just as he expected.

The Atlantic Ocean appeared as a narrow band of blue and white in the distance. McFall had breathed a little easier when the ocean had emerged on the horizon. Slowly, the blue strip grew wider and wider, and little white flecks became visible on the water. The wind was up.

Savannah, population 137,560, was directly below. The two brass spires of Cathedral St. John the Baptist and the gold dome of City Hall glistened in the bright sunshine. Like a green garden hose, the Savannah River gently wound its way fifteen miles to the ocean.

Suddenly, the Mooney's propeller began to sputter. Its nose dipped, and the plane began to lose altitude.

"Army six-six-five, Savannah approach," the tower said. "What's going on up there? Where's triple-seven poppa charlie going?"

"Savannah approach, looks like our target just ran out of gas," Warrant Officer Mike Gendler said. "The engine's stalled, and the plane is gliding."

"Six-six-five, shadow and stand by."

"Roger, Savannah approach."

McFall hit the switch on the comm radio: "Savannah approach, Army six-six-five."

"Go ahead, six-six-five."

"One question for you," McFall said. "What does the pilot's operating handbook say about the Mooney's glide ratio?"

"Army six-six-five, we're checking. Wait one moment."

The question on McFall's mind: how far would the plane go without power?

"Army six-six-five," the tower said, "I've got the Mooney's maximum glide distances graph. From 8,000 feet at the best glide speed of eighty-eight miles per hour, the plane can make it sixteen miles before hitting sea level. That's assuming the usual variables."

"Roger that, Savannah approach," McFall said, feeling some relief. "So we've got sixteen glide miles assuming zero wind, flaps clean, landing gear retracted, and propeller wind-milling."

McFall's mind tackled the critical question: would the plane crash into the city of Tybee Island or make it to the Atlantic? He studied the map; it would definitely be close. Tybee Island was fifteen miles away across an expanse of olive green marshlands and tidal plains. Off to the left, McFall could see Fort Pulaski, the red-brick Civil War installation turned tourist site. Down below, the black strip of U.S.-80 showed the way straight ahead to the ocean.

Gendler hit the intercom switch. "The head wind's definitely picking up as we get closer to the water," he said.

"Army six-six-five, Savannah approach."

"Go ahead, Savannah," Gendler said.

"Shadow to 1,000 feet and then let the Mooney go."

"Roger, Savannah approach. Army six-six-five is at 2,000 descending to 1,000."

On the water ahead, McFall could see that two Coast Guard cutters and a small flotilla of Navy ships had been deployed for the crash. In the light chop, the Mooney was bouncing around, up, then down, like a bucking bronco. The plane dropped lower and lower, through 700 feet. It came in low over Tybee Island, just clearing the low-rise hotels and bungalows, and barely passed over the row of hilly dunes. It was at fifty feet and heading straight for the crowded white-sand beach.

McFall could see the astonished faces of the sunbathers as they looked up and saw the plane, eerily silent without its engine, heading toward them.

Men, women, and children desperately scattered in all directions.

Then an updraft caught the Mooney's wings and lifted it for an instant.

At twenty-five feet, the plane cleared the beach and the breaking surf, and then hit the water, skidding like a skipping stone.

There was spray, a burst of flames, and a cloud of steam. The Mooney floated for a few moments, then sank nose first into the blue water.

"I'm sorry, Mack McFall isn't here right now," Preston said. "He's on assignment."

"I wanna speak with him right now."

"Who's calling, please?"

The voice belonged to a child, a little boy no more than five or six.

"Please lemme talk to Mack," said the high-pitched voice.

Preston waved to one of the tech support people. "Hold on and let me see if I can get him."

Preston hit the hold button. "This could be our guy. He may be using a voice altering machine again. Roll the tape."

She got back on the phone. "Hello? Yes, McFall is away from the office right now. But maybe I can help you. My name is Kyle Preston. I'm Mack's teammate."

"Will you give him a message?" the childish voice said.

"Sure," Preston said.

"There's a nice hotel in downtown Atlanta. Its name is the Marriott Marquis. A man with a big machine is going there. He's wearing a uniform. Inside the machine is a big bad bomb. The man can make it go bang by touching a switch under his shirt."

"Uh, hold on a second," Preston said, stalling for time.

"Bye bye," the little voice said. "Have fun!" Then the phone went dead.

Gus Rybak parked the freshly painted red panel truck in a loading zone on Courtland Street and hopped out of the front seat. He was bare-chested and covered with sweat. The top of his jumpsuit was tied around his waist. It was time to go to work. He pulled on the sleeves and zipped up the outfit. He opened the back door of the truck and let down the ramp. Carefully, he hauled the large machine on the dolly down to the asphalt.

Rybak checked up and down the street, adjusted his baseball cap, and headed into the service entrance of the Marriott Marquis.

A massive gray building, the Marriott had literally been colonized by the Olympics. ACOG had rented the entire hotel—all 1,671 rooms and 70 suites—for the duration of the Games and had turned it into the Olympic Family Hotel, housing members of the International Olympic Committee and the various national federations and committees.

Dressed in a red-and-white jumpsuit and pushing a Coca-Cola vending machine, Rybak felt like he was going to a costume party. Lazare had been absolutely right. He might feel like an idiot in the Coke disguise, but there wasn't a better way to blend into Atlanta. Coca-Cola was spending half a billion dollars worldwide promoting its sponsorship of the Olympics, and it seemed like the lion's share was in Atlanta.

Rybak moved through the service garage and approached the hotel security checkpoint. "Hey, how ya doin' today?" Rybak said, pulling a clipboard out of his jumpsuit.

"All right," said Renato Santos, the Marriott security guard. "How 'bout yourself?"

"Not bad," Rybak said, rubbing his chest. "But this heat is killing me."

"No shit," Santos said. "It must be 115 degrees. I don't know how those Olympic athletes can compete. Here, let me see your papers."

Rybak smiled. "Sorry, no papers. Just got the call a few minutes ago. The machine is out on the forty-seventh floor. The Olympic Committee doesn't want to piss the VIPs off. So they sent me over without any paperwork."

"Well . . ."

"Hey, man, check with your people," Rybak said. "I've got plenty of time. I'm not the one who's screaming on the forty-seventh floor."

Santos took stock of the situation: a Coca-Cola delivery man and his vending machine. No big deal.

"Come on through," the guard said.

"You sure?" Rybak said.

"Yeah," Santos said. Rybak walked through the magnetometer, but the vending machine was too big to fit.

"Let me have a look inside this thing," Santos said.

Rybak swallowed hard.

"No problem," he said. He pulled the keys from his pocket and opened the front panel of the machine.

"Go ahead, help yourself," Rybak said. "Plenty more where that came from."

"Thanks, man," Santos said, reaching for a Classic Coke.

Rybak pretended to make notes on his clipboard while Santos poked around the machine. The stress was extreme. Rybak's chest itched like crazy. He fought the impulse to scratch and swear. He had to stay in control.

"Okay, dude, you're clear," Santos said. "Take your first right, and then—"

"Thanks, I know the way."

"See ya."

Rybak headed down the hallway, made a right, then a left. He had scouted the location months earlier, long before Olympic security was checking every person and package that entered the building.

The freight elevator made no stops. The ride took twenty seconds. Rybak wheeled the vending machine out of the elevator and down the hallway that led to the cavernous forty-seven-story atrium designed by homegrown Atlanta architect John Portman.

Rybak stopped and peered down from the balcony. The atrium was narrow at the top and widened on the lower floors. No doubt about it, the place looked like the belly of a whale. Jonah would definitely have felt at home here. The elevator tower was the spine, and the curved, wavy balconies were the ribs. Rybak thought it was hideous, an architectural abomination.

He headed for the ice room at the end of the hall. A fat man with hair transplant plugs sprouting in neat rows from his shiny skull was locking the door to his suite. Muttering under his breath, he squeezed by the vending machine.

Rybak pulled the machine into the ice room, looked to see that the corridor was clear, fished the keys from his pocket, and opened the front panel again. This time he reached inside behind the change counter. There were twenty-eight tiny electrical switches in a row. He flipped two, watched the yellow lights begin to flash, and slammed the panel shut. He pushed the machine against the wall next to another vending machine, which he then heaved onto the empty dolly.

He was right on schedule. The delivery had proven much easier than he had expected. He pulled the Coke machine backward out of the ice room. By now, he mused, Lazare was probably comatose from the Cobalt-60 in his mattress. And soon, he—Good-for-Nothing-Shakes—would be calling the shots. His father, with whom he had concocted the coup, would be so proud.

"Freeze!" a voice shouted. "Police!"

"You're surrounded. Don't move! Put your hands in the air!"

Rybak was paralyzed. He could not breathe.

"Turn around slowly," the voice said. "Keep your hands visible at all times."

Rybak spun around and saw ten hooded men with semiautomatic rifles trained on his forehead. He felt a wave of panic. His chest was burning. He needed air.

Involuntarily, his face convulsed. His eyes blinked rapidly, and his shoulders jerked. Then he began to reach for his chest to scratch.

"Freeze!" the Javelin Force leader shouted. "Don't move an inch!" The snipers had been briefed about what the young caller had said: the bomb trigger was radio-wired *under* the man's shirt.

But Rybak couldn't stop. He had no control of his movements. His fingers grabbed his chest.

The Javelin Force did not hesitate.

A hail of bullets mowed Rybak down.

Revenge was indeed a dish best served cold.

The AH-60 DAP landed on the rooftop heliport of the Marriott Marquis.

Thirty minutes earlier, after the Mooney 201 had crashed uneventfully into the Atlantic, the special operations helicopter had turned around and backtracked to Atlanta. The DAP had hit an HC-130 aerial refuel tanker sent from the Air Force Special Operations Command at Hurlbert Field, Florida, and then had flown at full tilt to the Marriott.

Preston and three NEST volunteers were waiting, along with Staff Sergeant Milo Rosen of the 52nd EOD.

McFall and Preston shook hands. Both held on for an extra moment, but they knew the rest would have to wait.

"Way to go with the Mooney!" Rosen said.

"Thanks," said McFall. "What's the latest from Savannah?"

"Navy divers are salvaging the plane," Preston said, "and we don't know yet what type of device was on board. A NEST team is on standby."

"And what have we got here?" McFall asked.

"It's *another* IND," Preston said.

"Have you run the diagnostics?"

"Yes," said Rosen. "We've got pictures from the Mark 32 Golden X-ray. And we've also got high-dose radiography images from the Betatron."

"How does it look?"

There was a long pause.

"Come on, people. How does it look?"

"It's elegant as all get out," one of the NEST scientists said.

"Elegant? What the hell does elegant mean?"

"Part of the device is familiar. We've seen it before. And part of it is brand new. The physics package looks pretty fucking incredible. We ran it against the Livermore database. No hits. This thing is one of a kind."

"And it's on a clock," added Preston.

"How much time?"

"Twenty-seven minutes."

"He's turning the screws, eh?" McFall said.

They headed down a dark flight of stairs to the "working point," NEST-speak for the bomb site.

"So tell me about the hotel structure," McFall said to Rosen.

"Just looked at the blueprints. It's a big mother that could withstand a conventional explosion. It's made of 101,300 cubic yards of poured concrete supported by 13,150 tons of rebar."

"Total weight?"

"Four hundred and twenty-three million pounds."

"Where's good old Vasily Alexeyev when you need him?" McFall joked, referring to the Soviet mining engineer who, at the 1976 Montreal Games, shattered the world record by lifting a 562-pound barbell.

"There's another problem."

"Yeah?"

"They've got 40,000 gallons of fuel oil stored for emergency power. That's in the basement. The whole building is sitting on it."

"Great."

Several folding tables had been set up outside the ice room. Portable X-ray equipment was on the floor. Teams of NEST workers and EOD experts were studying images of the device.

"So what's so familiar about this thing?" McFall asked, looking at the X-rays.

"Lake Tahoe, Nevada, 1980."

"Do tell."

"Does the name Harvey's Wagon Wheel Casino ring any bells?"

"Oh shit," McFall said.

"Take a look at these," one of the NEST scientists said, handing McFall several X-rays. The acetate sheets were covered with what looked like knots of spaghetti.

"When we got these, we called the Bomb Reference File in D.C."

"And?"

"It wasn't good news."

"Why?"

"Take a look at the Post Incident Analysis."

Post Incident was the Bureau's euphemism for what happened after a bomb had gone off.

August 27, 1980. Stateline, Nevada. A massive thousand-pound bomb exploded in Harvey's Wagon Wheel Casino, causing $12 million in damage. The blast capped two days of suspense in a $3 million extortion scheme. Disguised as an IBM copying machine, the bomb was left on the second floor of the casino with a letter: "This bomb is so sensitive that the slightest movement either inside or outside will cause it to explode. This bomb can never be dismantled or disarmed without causing an explosion. Not even by the creator."

Turning to the technical analysis, McFall found what he was looking for. The X-rays of the Harvey's device were nearly identical to the images of the improvised nuclear device inside the Coca-Cola machine.

The team laid them side by side and began making comparisons. Both devices had twenty-eight toggle switches and at least eight different triggering mechanisms. With this surfeit of overlapping relays and dummy switches, the intricate wiring looked virtually identical to NASA's blueprints of the space shuttle. And in both bombs, it was impossible to follow a single wire from beginning to end.

Quite noteworthy was the fact that both devices had been put together from everyday materials available in any hardware store. McFall could see the motion detectors were fabricated from tubes lined with tinfoil. Inside were crude pendulums improvised from a length of wire attached to a heavy nut and bolt. If the nut and bolt swung and hit the tinfoil, the circuit would be completed and the device detonated.

The seemingly innocent tinfoil lining the box belied its lethal purpose. Were McFall to cut into the device with a power tool, the metal drill bit would make contact with the inner wrapping, completing the circuit. That meant he could not disable the bomb by injecting it with liquid nitrogen to freeze its components. Both devices also had float balls from a toilet that made it impossible for McFall to flood the bomb container with foam or liquid. The rising fluid level would lift the float, activating the device.

McFall turned to the sixteen-year-old handwritten notes of the Army bomb techs who had vainly attempted to use a seven pound shaped charge of C4 to blow the detonator off the bomb faster than the electrical current could reach the explosive. In theory, since pressure waves burst at right angles, the EOD techs should have been able to aim the shaped charge with precision, but the next set of black-and-white photos showed what happened instead: shattered chandeliers, smashed roulette wheels, and a five-story hole in the side of the casino. The EOD charge had made the bomb collapse on itself, in turn triggering the 1,000-pound dynamite explosion.

A final analysis had demonstrated that the device had been designed by the extortionist so that if just two of the toggle switches had been put in the proper position, the motion detector would have been disabled and the bomb could have been moved to a remote location for demolition. During his criminal trial in March 1985, John Birges, Sr., the bomb maker, had taken great pleasure in revealing this little fact. Then he was hauled off to federal prison.

McFall studied the X-rays of the device in the Coke machine and speculated on which combination of the twenty-eight toggle switches would allow it to be moved. There were 268,435,456 different combinations, he figured. The odds were infinitely better buying a lottery ticket.

In the world of ordnance disposal, there were basically two options when facing a sophisticated improvised explosive device. First, there was "Render Safe," which meant snipping the red wire as the clock counted down, just the way they did in the movies. Second, there was "Emergency Destruct," which meant violently disabling the device.

With Lazare's atomic Coke machine, McFall knew there was only one option.

"We've got eleven minutes," he told the team. "Here's what we're going to do. REECO foams the device. Then the 52nd EOD will take a shot with the Viper."

REECO stood for the Reynolds Electrical Engineering Company of Las Vegas. They were the miners who had drilled shafts at the Nevada Test Site, where the Department of Energy had exploded nuclear weapons.

"I want the tent up and foamed in five minutes. That will leave us six minutes to get the shot lined up," he said.

The team went to work.

Four REECO miners, who always traveled with NEST, unpacked duffel bags and unfurled a large orange geodesic tent made of nylon parachute cloth, which they set up over the Coke machine. Then they filled the containment cone with 30,000 cubic feet of aqueous foam, actually a cloud of dense water droplets, roughly 200 per cubic millimeter, designed to reduce the dispersal of radioactive material. The heat of the explosion would vaporize the water droplets and dissipate. The foam mitigation system reduced by 95 percent the amount of radioactive debris released in detonations involving 1,000 pounds or less of conventional explosive.

McFall strapped on the Scott air pack, a self-contained breathing apparatus. Preston helped him fasten the straps. Feeling like Jacques Cousteau, he dove into the foam.

Whiteness.

Everywhere.

McFall waded through the foam, slowly, arms outstretched. It was like slogging through beer suds. He made a swimming motion with his hands like the breast stroke, moving through the aqueous foam, pushing ahead.

There it is, he thought, as he saw the swirling red-and-white logo on the Coke machine.

McFall had been through this drill a hundred times, but he had never faced the real thing. He could feel his heart pounding, an effect that was especially noticeable with the air pack. He was breathing too fast, and he knew he had to be careful not to hyperventilate.

This job—to blast the nuclear device and pray the shaped charge moved faster than the signal to the physics package—was delicate but straightforward. McFall and Milo Rosen carefully set up the Viper, a 30-millimeter cannon on a tripod that had been specially designed for the violent disablement of improvised nuclear devices.

McFall spoke into his headset mike.

"How're we doing for time? I can't exactly see my watch in here."

"Five minutes," Preston said.

"I'll be home in three," McFall said. "Have my slippers waiting."

Lazare lay on the bed, his throbbing, spinning head warning him that the waves of nausea, fever, and confusion were coming on again. With effort, he focused his eyes to check his watch.

It was almost time.

He reached down to the floor where he had dropped his cellular phone, and clumsily, almost missing the little buttons, punched in the numbers. He didn't have the energy or inclination to bother with the voice alteration box.

"Joint Command Center," a bright Southern voice said. "May I help you?"

"Mack McFall, please," he said.

"I'm sorry. He's unavailable right now."

Understatement of the year, Lazare thought.

"Listen, young lady, I know Dr. McFall wants to speak with me immediately," Lazare snapped.

"Who's calling, please?"

"Never mind who's calling. Just get me McFall."

"Uh, there's really nothing I can do. He's not here, and he's very busy."

"Please tell me your name, young lady." He could feel his ire rising.

"It's Jewel Sutherland."

"Okay, Ms. Sutherland. When Atlanta burns in four minutes, I'll be sure to tell anyone who survives that Jewel Sutherland wasn't able to patch me through to McFall."

He waited for the receptionist to react.

"It's *my* bomb, you idiot," he screamed, the stress all but splitting open his head. "It's my bomb! Get me McFall right away!"

"Yessir, I'll try sir, try my very best sir, sorry sir, so sorry sir."

There was a long silence again. Lazare checked his watch. Even though his digital call was routed across three continents, he knew the FBI's phone tracers were probably closing in on him in Hartwell, Georgia.

There was a click and a hum of activity. "This is Preston," a voice said crisply.

"Who is Preston?"

"We've spoken before, Lazare. I'm with the FBI. Thanks to you we're a little busy right now."

"So, you know my name," Lazare said, chuckling. "Very good. It's only taken two weeks!"

"What do you want?"

"What does the clock say? Three minutes and counting?"

"What do you want?" she said, looking down the corridor toward the ice room.

"What? No chitchat?"

"Come on, Lazare. What do you want?"

"Cancel the Games, Ms. Preston, and I'll tell you which of the twenty-eight switches you need to flip to deactivate the device."

"Call the Games off? Are you serious?"

Preston was stunned. Lazare was a paranoid wacko. But this was beyond insane. There was only one day of competition left to go, and yet he wanted the Games to be canceled.

She repeated his words back to him, stretching out the conversation as the technicians worked to trace the call. "You'll help us deactivate the device if we cancel the Games?"

"It's all very simple," he said. "You hold a big press conference with Donny Sanders. I want to see *him* on CNN saying the Games are over. No substitutes. Only Donny Sanders. I want to hear him say everyone's going home. No more Closing Ceremonies."

"And then what?"

"I go away and leave Atlanta alone."

"But what about the device down the hall? It's ticking."

"One minute and forty-five seconds," Lazare said. "Think fast. Do we have a deal?"

"Wait," she said. It was happening too fast. How could she cut that deal? "You'll take my word?"

"Sure," he said. "After all, you have everything to lose."

"But the Closing Ceremonies are tomorrow. What's the point?"

"Why ask why?" Lazare said. "I'll help you right now, I'll give you what you need, if you promise to call the Games off *before* the Closing Ceremonies."

Suddenly Lazare could hear someone whispering excitedly to Preston.

"Lazare, how do I know this isn't a trick?" Preston said. Her voice was tense. One of the FBI techs motioned with ten fingers that he was seconds away from tracing the call. They had two lines of the triangle; all they needed was the third to pinpoint his position.

Lazare was getting angry. Why was she asking such silly questions? Why was she wasting time? Why was she not treating his generous offer with the respect it deserved?

Lazare sensed something was wrong. Intuitively, he knew the tracers were closing in. It was as if he could feel the triangulation lines strangling him.

In a fury, he hung up.

So much for Mr. Nice Guy, he thought.

And then a wave of nausea crashed down on him.

McFall, dripping aqueous foam on the burgundy carpet of the Marriott Marquis, pulled the breathing mask from his sweat-drenched face.

While he had been inside the mitigation tent inspecting the Coke machine and setting up the Viper, the 52nd EOD had almost completed preparations for the remote-control firing of the shaped charge. Now the weapon was aimed and loaded, and they only had to flip the switch.

"So what did he say?" McFall asked, regretting that he had not been there to deal with Lazare.

"He wants the Games called off," Preston said wearily.

"Called off?"

"And he was willing to disable this device if I agreed."

"So what happened?"

"He hung up."

"Why?"

"I spooked him."

"What do you mean?"

"We almost had a trace on his call. I hesitated for a second. Lazare has a sixth sense or something. He hung up."

"Don't beat yourself up," McFall said, trying to take the burden off of her. "Maybe he was the one doing the stalling. Maybe he was trying to run the clock down. Maybe he wouldn't have helped at all."

"No way," she said. "He was going to give me the toggle combination. And I lost him."

Thirty seconds.

The 52nd EOD shouted they were ready to fire. Hunkered down behind a portable steel blast barrier, McFall and Preston braced for the explosion. If the disablement scheme worked, there would be no explosion at all. Or there would be a limited conventional explosion. But if it failed, there would be a nuclear yield. In the first two cases, the blast walls would make a difference. In the third, the steel, like everything else around it, would liquefy in a nanosecond.

"Fifteen seconds. Say your prayers," Milo Rosen shouted.

Reflexively, McFall reached for Preston's hand.

"Five, four, three—"

Rosen pushed the black guarded switch on the fireset.

There was a muffled noise, like a loud whimpering, down the corridor in the ice room.

Then silence.

And from the lobby below, McFall and Preston heard the sounds of a piano and a violin wafting up through the hotel atrium.

"**C**all off the Closing Ceremonies? What have you been smoking?"

A red-faced Donny Sanders stood behind his desk, madder—as he might say—than a rained-on rooster.

"We've made it through sixteen days," he yelled. "I talked the Russians and Chinese into staying. And I'm not about to pull the plug."

Preston and McFall, on the edges of their dark leather armchairs, had come to brief Sanders on the situation, to ask for help, and if necessary, to negotiate.

But Sanders wasn't playing ball.

"We've spent millions on the Closing Ceremonies. Don Mischer has been working for more than a year on the show. More than four billion people will be watching. The advertisers have already forked out millions. And you expect me to cancel? As my grandson would say, *Not!*"

Preston knew this was Sanders's petty revenge for their encounter at the beginning of the Games when she had stripped him of his authority.

"Don't even think about it," Sanders bellowed. "No way, no deal."

"Donny," Preston said, "why don't you listen to this tape recording before you pour your decision in concrete."

She pulled a microrecorder from her suit pocket, placed it on Sanders's desk, and hit play.

"What do you want?"

"What? No chitchat?"

"Come on, Lazare. What do you want?"

"Cancel the Games, Ms. Preston, and I'll tell you which of the twenty-eight switches you need to flip to deactivate the device."

"Call the Games off? Are you serious? You'll help us deactivate the device if we cancel the Games?"

"It's all very simple. You hold a big press conference with Donny Sanders. I want to see *him* on CNN saying the games are over. No substitutes. Only Donny Sanders. I want to hear him say everyone's going home. No more Closing Ceremonies."

"And then what?"

"I go away and leave Atlanta alone."

"But what about the device down the hall? It's ticking."

"One minute and forty-five seconds. Think fast. Do we have a deal?"

"Wait. You'll take my word?"

"Sure. After all, you have everything to lose."

Preston hit the stop button. Sanders's face was long, his expression grave.

"This guy means business," McFall said. "We've been lucky so far. We've managed to dodge four of his bullets."

Sanders paced back and forth behind his desk. He stopped at the window and looked out on Centennial Park.

"You people are always overreacting," he said finally. "You've got your umpteen scenarios and your gee-whiz gizmos. All you want is an excuse to put them to use!"

"Donny, this isn't an excuse," Preston said. "Please reconsider. You need to go on camera to make this announcement."

Sanders did not respond. He was lost in thought about *his* Olympics.

Shaking their heads, McFall and Preston silently stood up to leave. "We'll get back to you in the morning," she said.

Chuck Flagg was back in the slippery leather chair.

He had a big scoop. Bigger than the first story about Abu Azzam. And he wanted to publish it.

"Look," Flagg said to Claude Guillory, "I'm sorry about how I behaved. I was angry. Real angry. I made a few calls to *The New York Times* and "PrimeTime Live." But then I stumbled onto something *even* bigger. I'm telling you, Claude, it's the story of a lifetime, and I thought you'd want it."

Guillory did not even blink. "I didn't appreciate the way you stormed out of here the other day," he said.

Flagg bit his lip. There would be no Pulitzer Prize if he antagonized Guillory any more. He had to suck it up, to apologize. And then, maybe, they would run his story. "I'm sorry," Flagg said. "I don't know what got into me."

"Quit your lying, boy," Guillory said. "You knew exactly what you were doing. And I know exactly what you're up to now."

He paused, flicking ash from his cigarette. "We're not going with that story about Ahmad Kazzam, or whatever his name is," he said. "And time hasn't changed that decision."

"I understand that, Claude. But I've got a better story. A much bigger story."

"And how's that?"

"When I was finished feeling sorry for myself last week, I got out of bed and made the rounds downtown. Bumped into a few sources, people I know from my days in the Washington bureau. I picked up a few things. And kaboom."

"Okay, Flagg. You can pitch me. But I'm telling you up front, it had better be *really* good 'cause you're starting from minus zero."

Flagg rubbed his hands and grinned.

"Headline: Someone's got a nuclear weapon in Atlanta, and the Feds are going crazy trying to find it."

Flagg studied Guillory's waxen face. The editor blinked slowly, pursed his lips, and pinched the bridge of his nose.

"I've got three independent sources," Flagg said. "They're involved directly in the investigation. They're completely reliable, no axes to grind."

"Why hasn't this leaked yet?" Guillory asked.

"Because there's a total clampdown. Not a soul is allowed to talk. And the clock is ticking."

Most times, Claude Guillory was a hard man to read. This time, he wasn't. His face was expressionless, but his eyes said it all: *stop the presses!*

It was 2 A.M. Sunday.

Preston, swathed in a white cotton robe, sat on the floor of her living room with her face six inches from the air conditioning vent. The machine was at full power, and the cold gusts were soothing. The room was dark, except for a few candles on a low glass coffee table near the pillowy couch. Several white cartons of Hunan Park Chinese takeout lay on the carpet.

She took a sip of Glenfiddich and swirled an ice cube in her mouth.

The Games of the Century would be over in less than twenty hours. A mere twenty hours. And yet she had a sickening sense it wouldn't be a smooth ride to the Closing Ceremonies. Lazare would rear his hideous head again. The only questions: where and when?

McFall emerged from the bathroom, a blue towel wrapped around his waist.

"That felt good," he said, tossing his hair with one hand to dry it.

"I bet," she said, leaning even closer to the air conditioner.

He headed to the small wet bar in the corner of the living room to fix a drink. Then he sat down beside Preston and picked up the carton of Kung Boo Chicken Ding.

"You know, I've been thinking about Lazare and Red Mercury," she said.

"Yeah?"

"Here's a question for you: how do we *really* know he's got it?"

"Honestly," McFall said, "we don't. All we've got are the air samples from Sapelo Island, the connection to Gennady Sobchak and Project Hermes, and his employment files from Los Alamos. And we're still waiting on the lab analysis of the Mooney device."

"It's circumstantial at best," she mused. "I wouldn't want to go to court with this."

"But this isn't a trial," he said. "And Lazare is capable of anything."

They both took sips from their drinks. Preston shook her head. "I just don't know if Lazare's paranoia would get in the way of—"

McFall put his hand up to her mouth.

"Sssh!" he whispered. "Let's give it a rest for a few hours."

"But there isn't—"

"A little sleep will make it all clearer."

He kissed her gently and slipped the robe from her shoulders. There was a spicy blend of scotch, garlic, and ginger on his breath, and she whispered, "It's a good thing we *both* ate Chinese."

They laughed and kissed again. The air conditioner rumbled on the wall as McFall fumbled for an ice cube in his glass.

He smelled her hair, held her closely, and glided the ice along the arching line of her back until she shuddered.

D ay Sixteen. Only eight hours until the Closing Ceremonies and
the end of the XXVI Olympiad.

McFall sat slumped at a desk in the frenzied Joint Command Center in the old Sears Roebuck building. He had the phone to his ear. In
front of him languished a baked kibbi beef sandwich from the Oasis
Café across the street.

"When did it happen?" he said.

Then, "Was he in pain?"

McFall dropped the phone on its cradle and buried his head in his
hands.

Stan Treadwell was dead. Now all McFall wanted was to get on a
plane and go home to Los Alamos. But what was the point? Stan was
gone, and he would never again hear that wise voice. Sadly, he recognized a sense of déjà vu. Jenny had taken a turn for the worse while he
was on a NEST raid in Fez. By the time he made it all the way back to
the hospital in Albuquerque, she had vanished.

Right now he had to pull himself together.

If things weren't already bad enough, there was this smug-faced
shit Chuck Flagg sitting nearby. McFall knew he'd have this hack on his
ass until the Games were over because late last night the Olympic high
command had struck a deal with *The Atlanta Journal-Constitution*.
The paper would hold off printing its story about the Atlanta nuclear
threat in exchange for exclusive access to the final fourteen hours of
the security operation. McFall hoped his gut-level instinct was wrong
that the worst was yet to come. But at minimum, ACOG would be
saved the ordeal of an embarrassing article on Closing Day, and who
cared if Chuck Flagg got a Pulitzer out of it?

McFall had no doubt in his mind that there would be another

threat from Lazare, whose vanity would be flattered to know that more than 25,000 law enforcement officers and security personnel were on his tail.

A needle in a haystack . . . or a hayfield . . . or one of the ten biggest metropolitan areas in the United States.

McFall knew there was little point. The device, if there was one, would be cleverly camouflaged and Lazare invisible. And then they would get the call.

He had not yet made up his mind about what made Lazare tick. The FBI shrinks were certain that Lazare's sole objective was to explode a Red Mercury device. But his latest phone call to Preston before the emergency destruct at the Marriott suggested that his goal was to stop the Games.

There was an important but fine distinction between the two. An explosion would definitely stop the Games. But closing the Games did not require an explosion.

Which was it? And what was the point?

If Lazare really wanted to detonate a device, he never needed to call again. His options were boundless. He could just go to the Atlanta Zoo in Grant Park and leave the device in a trash can next to, say, Willy B., the famed gorilla named after William B. Hartsfield, the long-time mayor of Atlanta who had grown up nearby.

Why bother trying to penetrate the elaborate Olympic defenses? There was no need to sneak the device into one of the many Olympic targets, like the Georgia Dome, Atlanta-Fulton County Stadium, or the Omni Coliseum.

Why bother? Why rob a house where the police were waiting? Wasn't that the cardinal rule of burglary? Rob a house where the police aren't.

McFall was beginning to suspect that Lazare had more to his agenda than just trying to set off his bomb. *But what?*

Unenthusiastically, McFall began reading the FBI report on his desk of last night's raid on an abandoned mining and logging camp in the Uwharrie National Forest near Troy, North Carolina. Unusual chemical and equipment purchases across the United States had alerted investigators, and eventually the trail led to the woods of the Tar Heel state. One hundred feet inside a mining shaft, Bureau agents had found a deserted weapons factory with traces of the heavy chemicals used in making atomic weapons.

"Damn!" McFall muttered, cradling his forehead in his hand. "Close, but no cigar."

"May I take a look?" Flagg said from across the desk.

"Funny," McFall said. "Very funny."

He turned the page and studied the WANTED all-points bulletin that had been sent to every federal, state, and local law enforcement agency in the United States. It featured a grainy ten-year-old Los Alamos ID picture of Quinn Lazare. And there was a series of artist's renditions of how he might look today.

The phone rang on his desk.

"This is McFall," he said.

"Hello, Mack." The voice was familiar.

He motioned to the trace team outside his office. Flagg's attention perked up.

"Who's this?" McFall said.

"You know who," Lazare said. "So let's get to the point before your tracers find me."

"Go ahead."

"I trust you have a pen and paper," Lazare said. "So start taking dictation."

"Hold on a sec," McFall stalled. There was no need for a pen and paper. The phone call was already being recorded and transcribed instantaneously.

"Ready or not, here I come," Lazare said. "I have three demands. Number one: drop all charges against Timothy McVeigh and Terry Nichols for the Oklahoma bombing. I want to see it *live* on CNN. I want President Clinton to announce it on TV. I want McVeigh and Nichols to walk right out the doors of the slammer in Colorado, waving plane tickets to Jamaica or wherever they want to go."

Lazare was certifiable, McFall thought, *but not this crazy*. There was no way charges would be dropped against McVeigh and Nichols.

They would never be set free. Lazare had to know that. He was fucking with them. He was playing mind games.

"Number two," Lazare continued. "I want $100 million deposited into the following Swiss account . . ."

Bingo, McFall thought.

Lazare read the bank account number slowly: "SB13-721-979-21264."

McFall repeated the numbers out loud.

"When the dough arrives in Switzerland, I'll be notified. And finally, number three: *leave me the hell alone!*"

Lazare paused, then continued.

"I want all you people to let me live my life. I want a house and a yard and a laboratory where I can do my research. And so help me God, if anything ever happens to me, if I ever find a scratch on my car, I've arranged for the Red Mercury formula automatically to be sent to ten addresses around the world. Any guesses where?"

"Fuck you, Lazare."

"Naughty, naughty, McFall. If anything ever happens to me, the formula for RM goes straight to the Abu Nidal Organization in Tripoli, Ahmad Jibril in Damascus, the Japanese Red Army in the Bekaa Valley, and the Qassam Brigades in Gaza. Do you get it?"

"You're sick, Lazare."

"Oh, thanks for reminding me, McFall. I forgot to take my medicine. You'd better hurry. Tick tock goes the clock!"

A seat belt was fastened uncomfortably across President Clinton's lap, which had expanded a bit recently from the quadrennial buffeting of the election cycle. "The Red Mercury bomber has finally made his demands," said Chief of Staff Leon Panetta, studying a one-page fax an aide had handed to him before the helicopter doors had closed. "We've just received word from the FBI in Atlanta."

After nearly two weeks of escalating threats, the president and highest levels of government now were in hourly contact with the Joint Command Center in Atlanta. The number 2s on the DC, or

Deputies Committee, did not have the authority to make the necessary decisions.

"So what are we looking at?" the president asked, shifting his weight in the plush leather seats.

No one liked giving the president bad news, not even the chief of staff. Clinton's temper was legendary. Senior White House staffers were well practiced at easing gently into unpleasant topics.

"Good news or bad news first?" Panetta asked, playing an old game that sometimes worked.

"Good news, Leon, gimme the good news."

"He wants $100 million."

"One hundred mill?" the president said, pondering the sum. "So what's the bad news?"

"You're not going to believe this."

"Hit me," the president said.

"He wants charges dropped against Timothy McVeigh and Terry Nichols. And he wants them set free."

Clinton did not know whether to laugh or scream.

When Clinton entered the White House Situation Room, all stood except the first lady. It was certainly not typical for Hillary Rodham Clinton to sit in on a national security action meeting. But nor was it atypical, causing some White House staffers to grumble.

"Let me just say," the president began, sitting down in the black chair next to his wife, "the United States will not give in to terrorists. Period. So let's start from that position. Are you all with me?"

The president's inner circle nodded in agreement.

"Tony," he said, turning to NSA Anthony Lake, "what are our best options?"

"Mr. President, it seems straightforward. Two options: find Lazare and stop him or meet his demands."

"Option one: finding Lazare," the president repeated. "How are we doing?"

"Not well," said Louis Freeh. "We raided his hideout last night. No sign of him. We've got an APB all over the southeast. There isn't a law-man this side of the Mississippi who isn't looking for him."

Attorney General Janet Reno added, "We've just gotten a report from a motel clerk that a man resembling Lazare was in Hartwell, Georgia, last night. That's a couple of hours northeast of Atlanta."

"So he could easily be in Atlanta by now," said Vice President Al Gore, chairman of the White House Task Force on the Olympics, which coordinated all federal assistance to the Games.

"No doubt about it," said Reno.

"So cut to the chase," Hillary Clinton interrupted impatiently. "What is the recommendation of this group? Do we pay the ransom and free these monsters? Or do we follow Golda Meir's rule: absolutely *no* negotiating with terrorists?"

There was a long pause as the president and his senior advisers considered the first lady's question.

"**H**ello, Mack."

"What is it now?" McFall said impatiently.

"What news do you have for me?" Lazare said.

"Nothing," McFall said, watching the tracer team working frantically to track Lazare's call. "I've got nothing for you yet."

"Well, that's too bad," Lazare said.

"We're doing the best we can."

"Well, I guess that just isn't good enough. So just to spice things up a bit, I've got some new lat/longs for you."

McFall braced himself.

"Write this down," Lazare said. "Level 2, Section 4, Row J, Seat 26."

"Level 2, Section 4, Row J, Seat 26," McFall repeated.

Then he heard the receiver click.

The tracer slammed his fist on the table. Another narrow miss.

McFall did not recognize the new coordinates. He ran to the VRS 2000 Center and handed them to Scott Worrell.

"Let's see," Worrell said, punching Level 2, Section 4, Row J, Seat 26 into the computer. "What have we here? Looks like a seat at one of the Olympic venues."

"Which one?" McFall asked.

"Hold on a second," he said, tapping the keyboard. "The computer is working on that. Yes, here we go. It could be any one of seven venues."

"Seven?" McFall said, checking his watch.

"Yup, let's take a closer look."

Worrell punched the keypad controlling the SpeedDome cameras around the Games. On the big monitor in the center of the wall, the Georgia Tech Aquatic Center popped up. It was empty.

McFall hit the intercom button for the EOD Specialized Management Center. "We've got a Threat Level 1 Emergency," he said to Rod Hagerman, director of the center. "We need seven search teams right away. We'll send details in a few minutes."

"Ready when you are, old buddy," Hagerman said.

On the wall monitor, the Omni Coliseum appeared, lights out and empty. Three more venues flashed on the screen, all deserted.

Then Olympic Stadium appeared.

"Oh, no," Worrell said. McFall's stomach dropped.

On the monitor, they could see that the hordes were streaming in for the Closing Ceremonies.

Worrell typed more instructions into the computer. He was searching for Level 2, Section 4, Row J, Seat 26.

A SpeedDome camera panned horizontally across the stadium seats, moving quickly, blurring colors and bodies. Then it stopped and began moving vertically, climbing up the stadium. Again, a flurry of faces and flags.

Finally the camera locked onto its coordinates.

At first, the image was out of focus. Then it became clear.

Level 2, Section 4, Row J, Seat 26.

A little girl sat waving an American flag. She was no older than five, with a little brown pigtail on each side of her head. She was wearing a red dress and a child's backpack.

Vicky Hollister squirmed in her seat. She did not like wearing her party dress, and she especially did not care for her black patent-leather shoes. But her mother and father had insisted she get dressed up for the Closing Ceremonies.

To the west, just over the lip of the stadium, the sun was beginning to drop. The sky was hazy orange, and the banners and flags whipped back and forth in the warm breeze.

The stadium was already three-quarters full, and thousands more were on their way.

Vicky was hungry and uncomfortable. She wanted to take off the

Olympic backpack that the nice man had given her—the same one who spilled soda on her at the Coca-Cola museum and called her "little cherry."

She had bumped into him outside the stadium while her father was waiting in a long line to buy an official Olympic program and her mother had run off to the restroom. Vicky was racing back and forth in a slalom between the flag poles.

Everyone attending the Closing Ceremonies had been given little backpacks stocked with colored plastic squares to be used for the card show during the Closing Ceremonies.

But Vicky's backpack was special. When the man gave it to her, he said there was an Izzy doll inside and other presents. She could not open the pack or take it off, though, until the ceremonies were over. He said the gifts were a secret, and she was not allowed to tell her parents. If she said a word to them about her magic backpack, he would come and take the surprises away.

Vicky was impatient to see her gifts. She tried to unfasten the waist buckle on the pack, but it would not come off. She pulled on it, testing the nylon and plastic. It would not release.

In the Olympic Joint Command Center, McFall and Preston watched the little girl struggle with her backpack.

The SpeedDome Camera zoomed in closer and closer.

Moments before, the computer had spit out all available information on the ticket purchasers for Level 2, Section 4, Row J, Seats 26 through 29:

ACOG SALES	ACCOUNT: 00-050794
Name:	HOLLISTER, HERBERT
Occupation:	CPA
Address:	PO Box 113
	Wilton, Alabama 35187
Telephone:	205-665-0901
CC:	VISA 9731-922-4445-7109 5/97

DOB:	8/1/56
Tickets:	CC/3
DOO:	5/14/95
DOS:	5/19/95
SA:	L2, S4, RJ, 26-29.
FBI:	————-
AL:	————-

The readout was straightforward. On May 14, 1995, Herbert Hollister of Wilton, Alabama, had ordered three tickets to the Closing Ceremonies and paid with a Visa card that expired in May 1997. He had no criminal record with the FBI or police in Alabama.

Herb Hollister had just turned forty years old on August 1, and the tickets to the Games were probably a birthday present from his wife, McFall figured, studying the printout.

"McFall, call for you on line five," someone shouted from the communications center. "It's him!"

He picked up the phone.

Lazare began immediately: "Pretty little girl, isn't she?"

"You're a sick fuck," McFall said.

"Thanks for the diagnosis," he said, laughing. "Now here's a little warning. Do not go near the girl. If you do, the stadium will vaporize. Number two, don't even think about trying to evacuate. If the stadium doesn't fill to capacity, I'll know you're up to something."

"Lazare, if you think you're going to get away—"

"Shut up!" Lazare said. "Just shut up! Now listen, I'm sitting here watching your every movement. I know where the Javelin Force is. I know where your snipers are. I even know where you are. It's a nice system you set up, this Sensor ID. If I see your people moving, I'll detonate the device. I want your snipers and your security people to stay where they are. Not a creature should be stirring. Do you understand?"

McFall was dumbfounded. How could Lazare have hacked into the Olympic security system?

"Just remember," Lazare said, "when the Olympic Flame is passed to Sydney, your time is up."

McFall threw the phone across the room.

Five FBI agents, hunched over, squeezed along the dark, arrow-straight tube. Every hundred feet or so, they halted to study a map with a penlight. Then they plodded on. Tunnel E-5 was definitely the wrong place to be if you were claustrophobic.

A large, thin concrete bowl, Centennial Olympic Stadium had almost no crawlspace or room to maneuver beneath the seats. In certain sections, however, the engineering had mandated small tunnels, searched three times a day by Olympic security, which now offered the potential of unseen access to the grandstand above.

The procession stopped, and an agent pulled out a drill. After putting on a carbonate face shield, he went to work, boring into the gray slab above his head. Another agent sprayed water on the drill bit from a steel canister.

The job would take five minutes.

In the sunlight above, 150 plainclothes ID teams spread out across the stadium. Dressed as tourists, they worked in pairs and carried cameras, hot dogs, flash/bang grenades, and assault weapons. Beneath the smiles and the sunglasses, they were all desperately seeking Lazare.

The likelihood of flushing out McFall's needle in a haystack was next to nil. Lazare was surely in disguise, and their best hope was that one of the police artists had hit it close on the photo contact pages that each agent had been issued. The sheets had images of Lazare in various guises.

The peanut vendor made her way up the steep stairs of the stadium.

"Peanuts, get your Gold Medal peanuts right here. Peanuts, Gold Medal peanuts. Eat 'em now, take 'em home. Gold Medal peanuts . . ."

A man shouted out an order. The hawker spun around, awkwardly fished out two bags, tossed them well wide of the buyer, and moved on, not even waiting to get paid.

"Hey lady, here's your money."

She did not turn back. She was heading toward the girl in Row J, twenty-five feet away. The child was twirling her pigtails and singing to herself.

The vendor worked her way up the steps, bouncing bags of peanuts off spectators' heads and thanking God she did not really sell them for a living.

"Gold Medal peanuts," she shouted. "Right here! Gold Medal peanuts!"

Vicky Hollister saw the vendor coming. "Daddy, pleeeeease! Peanuts!"

Her father shook his head. "No peanuts until you've finished the carrots Mom brought you."

"Daddy! I want some peanuts!"

The vendor heard the girl and knelt down next to her. Kris Aura, NEST volunteer-turned-peanut-hawker, winked and handed over a bag, then moved on.

"Peanuts, get your Gold Medal peanuts . . ."

Aura winced at the shrill noise in her earpiece. The radiation detector, hidden in the bulky peanut sack over her shoulder, was screaming.

"Gamma Alarm One. Gamma Alarm One. Gamma Alarm One."

The little girl in the pretty dress was red hot.

Like an Exxon supertanker, the FBI's ninety-foot mobile command center stolidly plowed toward Centennial Stadium along the route already cleared by its police escort. The trip would take only three minutes.

At a small table in the vehicle's main workspace, McFall and Preston were assessing their options.

"There's no way Lazare is anywhere near the stadium," McFall insisted.

"Worrell is working on that," Preston said. "We should have the answer in a few minutes."

She hit the button at the center of the table. A television monitor glowed. "Ladies and gentlemen, I've got the White House on the bird. The president will be joining us shortly."

There was a pause; then the president appeared on the screen.

"Hey there, Atlanta," Clinton said, munching on something. "Give us an update?"

It was the first time in her career that Preston had spoken directly to the Leader of the Free World. Her mouth was dry as desert, and she could feel butterflies banging around in her stomach.

"Mr. President," she began. "This is Kyle Preston with the Bureau. We've just detected a miniature improvised nuclear device in Olympic Stadium. If we get anywhere near it, the bomber has threatened it will be detonated. Our options are seriously constrained."

"Sweet Jesus," the president said.

"Will you reconsider your decision about the $100 million and dropping charges against McVeigh and Nichols?" McFall asked.

"No way," the president fired back.

"With all due respect, sir," McFall said, "ain't no way there's gonna be an Atlanta if we don't come up with something."

"Who the hell is that?" the president asked.

"Mack McFall, Mr. President. Department of Energy, NEST. I don't know what you all are imagining there in Washington, but don't be fooled into believing this guy will hesitate about pushing the button. We missed our chance on that a while ago. His options are narrowing, too."

"Well, Mr. McFall, my options are pretty slim. And there's no way on God's green earth I'm gonna set McVeigh and Nichols free. No goddamn way. Am I clear?"

"Yessir," Preston replied. "Short of dropping the charges, what about the $100 million? Why not pony up the dough, and then sit on the Swiss banks later to get the money back."

"It's the principle," the president said.

"I hate to say this," Preston said, "but principles aren't going to save Atlanta right now."

"Now what about the Oklahoma bombers?" the president said. "Can we stall?"

"I would advise against that," Preston countered. "We've only got forty-five minutes."

"What about bargaining?" Panetta asked. After a lifetime on Capitol Hill, he was a great negotiator. "You know, a little horse trade to get to yes. We give you the $100 mill, and you leave the Olympics alone."

"He's not going to go for it," Preston said. "This is about shaming the United States. Humiliating America. And $100 million alone won't do it."

"Where does all that shame talk come from?" the president asked.

"We've spent a lot of time profiling this guy," McFall said. "He's a former nuclear scientist who lived for his research. I know the type. The government shut down the whole program and buried his work. In the most basic terms, he wants revenge. Pure and simple."

"Does he really have the capacity to murder hundreds of thousands of innocent people?" the president asked.

"I don't know," Preston replied. "But in the state he's in, I wouldn't want to force him into making that choice."

McFall peered out the window as the mobile command center

headed down Techwood Drive toward Centennial Stadium. Off to the right, he saw CNN Center, a giant cinder block of concrete and glass.

And suddenly, he had an idea. "What about CNN?" he said, thinking out loud.

"What about CNN?" someone at the White House said.

"Why can't CNN help us with this one? That's what Lazare is watching."

"I don't follow," the president said.

"If CNN will play ball, we can stage the whole thing."

"What do you mean?" Panetta asked.

"CNN covers you announcing that federal prosecutors are giving up the case against McVeigh and Nichols. Then they walk out the front door of the federal penitentiary outside Denver."

"No chance."

"No, Mr. President, it's our *only* chance."

"It's out of the question."

"I'm not making myself clear. It wouldn't be *real*! It wouldn't be broadcast. It would be *narrowcast*. It would be staged. You know, faked. CNN would send the phony report straight into Lazare's cable box."

"There's no way," Attorney General Reno said. "Impossible."

"Hold on," the president said, visualizing a way out of the mess for the first time. "It sounds crazy, but I'm following you. How would it work?"

"If we can find where Lazare is, we can beam his cable box with a one-of-a-kind CNN feed. Only CNN and Lazare would ever know about it or see it."

"CNN is never going to play ball," Panetta countered. "There's just no way. This is crazy. It'll never work."

"Respectfully," McFall said, "I have to disagree with all you nattering nabobs of negativism." McFall blanched at the fact that he was so fired up he was quoting from Spiro Agnew.

"Why would Ted Turner ever go along with this?" Panetta asked defiantly.

"Turner loves Atlanta," McFall began. "He helped build this city. He's got too much at stake." McFall knew he was winging it. He had never even met Ted Turner and didn't know the first thing about him except for what he'd read in the newspapers. But Turner was their only hope.

"This is right up Turner's alley," McFall said, feigning supreme confidence. "This will go right to his sense of patriotism."

"Let's get him on the phone right quick," the president said. "Who knows his number? I'll call him myself."

The occupant of the vast office on the top floor of CNN North was indisputably Robert E. Turner III, better known to the world simply as Ted.

Pictures of Ted—sailing, fishing, pitching, hobnobbing, marrying Jane—all but papered the two walls. The third wall was floor-to-ceiling television monitors, dozens of them. And the fourth was all window, overlooking Atlanta.

The call from the White House had produced an instant appointment, and within minutes McFall and Preston had driven there.

Turner had been plucked out of a session with top executives of Time-Warner and was annoyed that the meeting had been interrupted. "I know you're in a hurry, so what do you want?" he began, going to his private refrigerator for a bottle of Evian.

"We need your help fast," Preston began.

"Sit down," he said, pointing to the inviting seating area in one half of his office. "Tell me how."

Turner's attention was total as Preston ran through the scenario.

As she finished, he got up from the couch, walked over to his aircraft-carrier-sized oak desk, reached into a drawer, and pulled out a large legal document.

He threw it on the desk with a loud thud. "You know what this is?" he asked. "This is just one little part of the lawsuit I got dragged into by the U.S. government over broadcasting Manuel Noriega's jailhouse tapes back in 1990. You know how much that case cost me?"

McFall and Preston did not follow.

"No," Preston said. "I don't."

"It cost me an arm and a leg. That's what it cost me! And now you people come here asking for my help. That's a hoot and a half!"

He stepped out from behind the desk and plopped back in one of the couches. "There's a call on my sheet from President Clinton. Is that what this is about?" he asked.

"Yes, it is."

"Well, you can tell the president my answer is no."

"Do you think we—"

"My answer is no," he continued, "because CNN is *not* a broadcasting arm of the United States government. This isn't Russian television. This is CNN, goddammit!"

Turner was working himself into a lather.

"We don't do the government's business. We can't operate as an arm of U.S. law enforcement. That's not our job."

"But this is different," McFall said. "This is very different."

"Do you think I just fell off the turnip truck?" Turner asked. "Of course this is different. But it's a slippery slope. And I don't go for the luge or bobsled."

"But it's been done before," McFall said, looking at some notes written on the back of a paper napkin. An FBI librarian had done a quick search of the databases and turned up a useful example.

"Bear with me for a second," McFall went on, "but this is relevant. In June 1984 in Winston-Salem, a deranged gunman killed a TV station employee and took another hostage. The guy's name was Ronnie Laverne Jackson, and he believed a syndicated religious program was spying on him through his television screen."

Turner fidgeted in his seat and twiddled his thumbs.

"Apparently this guy Jackson surrendered to police after a local cable system broadcast a phony apology to the neighborhood where he was barricaded in his great-aunt's home."

The buzzer rang on Turner's desk.

"Hold on a second," he said, picking up the phone on the table at his side.

"Yes," he said. "Yes, all right, put him through."

Unconsciously, he straightened up, face and body on alert.

"Hello, Mr. President."

He paused.

"Yes, it's good to hear from you."

McFall and Preston watched. What button was Clinton pushing to turn this guy around? Too bad the speakerphone wasn't on.

"Mr. President, you know how strongly I believe in the independence and autonomy of the press," Turner said. "I'm going to have to think this over. Give me ten minutes."

He put the phone down.

"We don't have ten minutes," Preston warned, checking her watch. "You need to decide now."

McFall had been admiring the pictures of Jane Fonda on the wall. All at once, an idea clicked in. He thought for a moment, then decided to gamble. "If you don't mind my asking," he said, "where is your wife right now?"

"Oh, she's over at the stadium for the Closing Ceremonies," Turner answered, and in that nanosecond his eyes widened as he jumped up to look out the window.

"This is a CNN Special Report."

Anchorman Bernard Shaw stared into the camera.

In the television control room, Norm Shapiro, director of CNN special events, counted down into Shaw's earpiece: "Five, four, three, two, one, you're on."

Shaw began the broadcast. "In an unusual development this afternoon, the White House announced that President Clinton would be making a special address to the nation. White House insiders do not know the topic of the speech. With us now at the White House is correspondent Wolf Blitzer. Wolf, what can you tell us?"

"Bernie, the situation is highly unusual, but a few minutes ago White House Press Secretary Michael McCurry handed out a notice that the president would be delivering a special message. His remarks from the Oval Office are scheduled to begin in just thirty seconds. Sources inside the White House tell CNN that the topic of the speech will be the Oklahoma bombing in April of last year."

"Thanks, Wolf. The president has just entered the Oval Office. Let's go to him now."

"Okay, cut!" Norm Shapiro said in the control room. "Nice work, Bernie. Thanks, Wolf. Let's check the tape, and we're done."

A technician rewound the tape and made sure the broadcast had been properly recorded. "Tape checks."

"We're done here, ladies and gentlemen," Shapiro said, pulling off his headset. "Thank you all very much. And remember: forget all about this. It never happened!"

McFall's entire scheme hinged on finding Lazare's hideaway. Without an address and a cable box, the plan would fail.

In his guts, he felt like he was back in the Rung Sat Special Zone on the Mekong Delta. He had carefully planned the SEAL Team 1 insertion and attack on the Soirap River. But then everything had gone to hell.

The plan hadn't worked, and the platoon had been butchered.

In the cramped Mobile Command Center, McFall sat next to Worrell, Preston, and Dr. Andrea Kahng, the zany FBI shrink. The four were hunched over a computer, studying three-dimensional Computer Assisted Design, or CAD, images of Olympic Stadium.

"Lazare must be very distressed," Kahng was saying. "He's been stymied repeatedly, and he's running out of chances. This is his last opportunity. He knows we're closing in on him, and he still has nothing to lose."

"So where do you think he is?" Preston asked. "Do you think he's *in* the stadium?"

"It's definitely possible," Kahng said.

"But being there would be suicidal," Preston said. "It's the old nuclear hand grenade problem. Pull the pin and you blow *yourself* up!"

"Suicidal tendencies aren't inconsistent with his profile," Kahng explained. "He could very well be ready to die for his delusions. On the other hand, since his identity is entirely tied up in this explosion, he probably wants to have a great view. So it's possible that he's watching from someplace else."

"On television?" Worrell asked.

"Possibly," Kahng said. "But more likely, he wants to be present at the creation, if you know what I mean."

"Yeah, it's not the same on TV," Worrell joked.

"Either way," Preston said, "he must be watching the little girl somehow. Otherwise how would he know if we're working on the device?"

"Good point," Worrell agreed. "He's got to be in a position to see the girl."

Worrell manipulated the CAD system, which allowed him to move around the stadium in three dimensions. He put himself into Level 2, Section 4, Row J, Seat 26. On the CAD screen he examined a three-dimensional view of what little Vicky Hollister could see. By reversing the images, he could also see the exact spots from which someone might be watching her.

Worrell examined every angle—north, south, east, and west.

Nothing. No luck.

Then he tried again. To the east, Seat 26 in Row J was partially obscured by the overhang of the broadcasters' booths. To the south and west, it was blocked by light towers.

It had to be the north. But where?

And then he saw it, the one and only possibility, a glistening black skyscraper in the distance. According to the computer, the building was exactly 3,103 feet away from Vicky Hollister's seat in the stadium.

President Clinton tightened the knot of his Hugo Boss tie and finished memorizing the first page of the script on his desk. A makeup artist worked on his ruddy nose and the heavy bags under his eyes. A stylist brushed his hair. The cameraman waited. The TelePrompTer operator fiddled with his controls. A lighting technician checked levels.

"Let's go, folks," Clinton said. "Come on. I don't have all day!"

"I'm ready to roll," said the lighting tech. "Me too," said the audio man. "Then let's do it," said the cameraman.

One of the White House video producers stood behind the camera and cued the president. "All set when you are."

"My fellow Americans," President Clinton began, "good evening."

With all the noise in the stands, Herb Hollister, CPA, did not even hear the thick drill bit punch through the concrete beneath his seat. A hand brandishing an FBI badge and a small speaker-microphone squeezed through the hole and touched his ankle.

"Mr. Herbert Hollister, this is the FBI," a voice hissed. "Do not be alarmed. Repeat, do not be alarmed."

The agent under the grandstand had never trusted that piece of his Quantico training. Flash a badge and tell a person *not* to be alarmed. Dig right under a guy's feet, stick out a badge, and say, "Don't be afraid." *Good luck.*

Herb Hollister heard his name called. He looked around and did not see anyone he knew. Then he felt a tug on his trouser cuff. Irritably, he looked down.

"What the hell?" he shouted when he saw the FBI badge.

"Do not be alarmed, Mr. Hollister," the voice commanded. "Please stay calm. Reach down slowly and pretend to tie your shoelace so that I can have a word with you."

Hollister thought this was a hell of a strange joke, but he did as he was told. He bent down and touched his shoe.

"Mr. Hollister, I'm Anderson George with the FBI. This is an emergency situation, and we need your assistance."

"Jesus, why me?"

"I don't have time to explain. Do not leave your seats. Do not allow your daughter to leave her seat. And do not, I repeat, do not, touch the backpack she is wearing."

Noreen Hollister turned to her husband.

"Are you okay?" she asked.

He shot upright and said, "Yes, dear. Everything's fine."

Feeling like a conspirator in some James Bond movie, he leaned over to kiss her and whispered in her ear.

From the light tower in the stadium, McFall and Preston swept the high-powered binoculars over the shiny black skyscraper. The setting sun glinted off the glass. Just minutes earlier, Scott Worrell had determined Lazare's bird's-eye hiding place had to be on the thirty-sixth floor of the office building at the corner of Marietta, Spring, and Cone streets.

It was the only place in Atlanta outside the stadium that had an unobstructed view of Vicky Hollister and her atomic backpack.

Preston and McFall scanned up and down, floor by floor, but the mirrored surface was visually impenetrable.

McFall flipped the switch on the binoculars to the infrared setting.

Again, he saw nothing. The window panes had been baked all day by the sun. As a result there was no low temperature contrast against which a human being's body-heat signature would stand out. In other words, the heat-sensitive scopes were useless against the hot glass.

Lazare could be anywhere in the huge building, which housed the downtown post office and several federal bureaucracies, including the departments of Agriculture, Commerce, Justice, and State.

Though plainclothes officers had sealed off the area, they had been ordered not to go inside the building. McFall and Preston did not want to startle Lazare, especially if he was holding a detonator in his hand.

Lazare paced back and forth in front of the window, looking south toward the stadium. To his left, he could see the dome of the State Capitol, brilliant in the fading sunlight.

He inspected his watch and continued his restless monitoring from the dark, quiet office. He had rented and set it up months earlier, always paying the rent on time and passing the periodic Olympic-related security checks.

He and his team would disappear when this day was over without leaving a forwarding address.

Lazare was holding a biometric detonation device specially molded and engineered to fit in his right hand and equipped with a palm-reading scanner that precluded its use by any other person.

Impatiently, he knelt in front of the television on the floor and checked CNN. There was no news about Timothy McVeigh and Terry Nichols.

He went to the small telescope and examined the stadium. Now the seats were almost entirely filled, and the tower lights were on, creating a blur in the nighttime haze.

And yes, there was Vicky Hollister.

Lazare had no doubt that by now the NEST pencil-necks had swept past the girl and detected the unique signature of the device in the backpack. But the idiots would only find out what was *really* in the pack when it was already too late.

How thrilling it was to know that McFall and Preston were working frantically against time to meet his demands. Imagining all the frenzy and mania at the Joint Command Center was physically arousing.

He checked the laptop computer screen for the latest bulletin from the Olympic Joint Command Center. Now he had to outwit enemy disinformation concocted to confuse him.

They were afraid of what he knew. They would be afraid that he was watching them. They would be careful, very careful and take very small steps.

Lazare felt untouchable, invulnerable.

He had led them by a leash like dogs in obedience school. He had succeeded in paralyzing the largest security apparatus the world had ever known. And now, he would give them the last lesson: the FBI shrinks were no doubt predicting that he would detonate the bomb *regardless* of whether his demands were met, that exploding the Red Mercury device was his sole purpose, his only cause, his main mission.

They were all such fools.

The sun was gone in the west.

Time was running out.

Relentlessly, McFall moved the infrared binoculars up and down, back and forth, scanning the glass panels.

The shifting of the viewfinder was giving him motion sickness, and his eyes ached. He paused to rest at the corner window.

Suddenly, behind the glass, a blurry reddish shape appeared, disappeared, reappeared, disappeared, then appeared again.

It was definitely a human body, wavy and undefined, moving behind the reflective glass.

"There he is!" McFall shouted excitedly. "The windows must be cooling down."

"Where?"

"At the very top. It must be the thirty-sixth floor. Corner window."

McFall and Preston were standing on one of the stadium light towers. The heat from the mercury-vapor was intense.

"Got him," Preston said.

There he was, moving back and forth in the window. It looked like he was wearing a bulky bulletproof vest and some type of combat helmet.

And he was holding something in his hand.

The CNN technicians were given an address, an office number, and five minutes to solve a problem: how do you send a cable signal to one television out of millions in the greater Atlanta metropolitan area?

It helped that they knew the target: a commercial building on Marietta. There were 287 tenants in the building with cable connections. The technicians had to narrow their focus to one tiny cable wire out of millions. It was like hunting for *one* specific hair in *all* the barbershops in Atlanta.

When they were sure they had it nailed, they dialed the number they had been given. "We've got it," the technician said. "We've got the cable box you wanted."

"Is it ready?" the voice said.

"Yes."

"Then let's go!"

"This is a CNN Special Report."

Lazare spun around and squatted next to the television monitor.

He cranked up the volume. Bernard Shaw introduced Wolf Blitzer at the White House. Then Bill Clinton appeared behind his desk in the Oval Office, addressing the American people.

Lazare felt a rush of power and excitement.

"My fellow Americans," the president began. "Good evening. I come to you tonight with a matter of great national importance. It is a matter that is sure to arouse anger and inflame passions across the land. But it is about justice, fairness, and the American way."

The president paused to look down at his notes.

Lazare could scarcely breathe.

"After carefully examining all the evidence, the federal prosecutors in the Oklahoma bombing case involving Timothy McVeigh and Terry Nichols have reached a momentous decision. They have decided to withdraw charges against both men."

Ha! McFall thought. *The almighty president of the United States capitulating on national television!*

Clinton continued. "The Justice Department has recommended that the case against Mr. McVeigh and his alleged co-conspirator be dropped. The Attorney General has advised me that despite the hard work of thousands of law enforcement officials across the country, the real culprits are still at large."

"Yesssss!" Lazare screamed.

"My fellow Americans, in the days and weeks ahead, you will hear more about these dramatic developments. And I trust you will come to understand what we have done here today."

Lazare listened carefully. The president was creating some wiggle-room.

"In a matter of moments," the president went on, "Mr. McVeigh and Mr. Nichols will be freed from the federal penitentiary in Littleton, Colorado. But let me give you my solemn word that the real perpetrators of this atrocity will be brought to justice."

His jaw clenched, his eyes steely, President Clinton concluded, "Wherever you are, we will find you. We will stop you. And we will make you pay."

Lazare shrieked with glee.

"God bless you," the president said. "And God bless America."

"This is Walter Payne reporting from the Federal Correctional Institution in Littleton, Colorado."

His shaggy brown hair tossed by a Rocky Mountain wind, Payne was standing next to a sixteen-foot razor wire fence with a guard tower behind him. The beige stucco medium-security prison, opened in 1940, housed 1,000 inmates, including two of the most notorious and mysterious in contemporary American history.

Payne continued his report. "In just a minute or two, Timothy McVeigh and Terry Nichols will be released from 15 months in captivity. For security reasons, federal authorities limited media access to the prison for this story. In a special lottery, CNN was awarded pool responsibility for coverage of McVeigh's release."

"Walter, what's the mood of the prison officials?" asked anchorman Bernard Shaw.

"The mood here is about as grim as the weather," Payne said. "Authorities are not talking publicly about the release. But one senior prison staffer told me that it's a dark day for federal law enforcement."

The camera zoomed in on a small metal door. It opened, and a slight, blond man in jeans and a blue shirt strolled down the stairs. He was accompanied by an older man with dark hair. McVeigh looked up at the sky and took a deep breath of air. He and Terry Nichols got into a waiting green station wagon. The vehicle pulled away from the prison, passed through a security checkpoint and two fences, and then drove out onto the perimeter road leading to Kipling Avenue.

The camera followed the car onto Kipling and then watched it disappear heading northeast toward Denver, fifteen miles away.

Lazare's fist stabbed the air with excitement. It was a grim day for federal law enforcement. And this was only the dawn! He hit the mute button on the television set and picked up the phone to dial McFall's number.

"I need to speak with Mack McFall," he said. "It's very urgent."

There was a pause as the operator connected him to McFall, who had moved from the light tower down to the Mobile Command Center parked outside the stadium.

"McFall here."

"Mack, are you watching CNN?"

"Yes, Lazare. You win. Are you happy now?"

"Not yet," Lazare laughed. "One demand down, two to go. How's the money coming?"

"Still working on it."

"Tick tick tick!" Lazare said.

"Give me a fucking break."

It was a round-trip to nowhere.

The green station wagon headed north one mile on Kipling Avenue and then pulled over to the side of the road next to a suburban strip mall. Two black FBI sedans were waiting, engines idling.

Handcuffed, Timothy McVeigh and Terry Nichols were hustled out of the wagon and into one of the cars. The driver put a red flashing light on the roof and then raced back to the Federal Correctional Institution.

The trip took six minutes. It was like rewinding the tape. Thoroughly confused and puzzled, McVeigh and Nichols were escorted right back to their 6 x 10 foot cells in the isolation wing of the penitentiary.

F or a moment McFall allowed himself to watch the Closing Ceremonies on the television screen. More than 10,000 athletes, in
full colors, marched on the field.

Then he returned to the problem.

In chess, there had been glum moments when it was rational to
topple his own king and admit defeat, but he always ordered himself
to study the board again. To look at *all* the pieces. There had to be a
move. There had to be some way to stop Lazare's withering attack.
But what was it?

Think! Deeper! Come on! It's there, somewhere.

He immediately ruled out several alternatives. For starters,
Lazare apparently knew their every move. Using Rebecca Deen's
computer, he had somehow hacked into the Sensor ID system.

The chess analogy filled his thoughts. Both sides played on the
same board, but invariably they saw the pieces differently. McFall
knew he had to find something, some combination of moves, that
Lazare couldn't see or anticipate.

The first option—summarily rejected—had been a Javelin Force
raid on Lazare's hideout. The idea had been discarded because the
moment the troops blew open the door, Lazare would press the detonation button. There just wasn't enough time to disable him.

The second option—also rejected—was a sniper attack at long
distance. The FBI and Javelin Force specialists had balked at the
idea. They did not have the right angle or the exact position. And if
they tried to move into the right spot for the shot, Lazare would probably know because he was watching.

Still, McFall was intrigued by the idea of a sniper attack. The only
question was, who had the best angle to take the shot? Or who could

sneak into position without Lazare noticing?

He stared into space. The television blaring in the background was irritating.

Suddenly, he saw the checkmating combination on the imaginary chessboard in his mind. It was daring. It would take three risky moves. But it was the only chance they had.

The silver medal resplendent on her blue-and-white track suit, Leila Arens sat on the training table in a crowded locker room beneath Centennial Stadium. Anxious Olympic security officials surrounded her.

"Ms. Arens," McFall began, "I'm sorry we had to disturb you at the Closing Ceremonies, but we have a very serious problem, and we need your help."

"What do you want?" Arens had spent enough time with the Israeli Defense Force to decipher the facial expressions of the men and women in the room who had the strained look of being caught between a hammer and a nail.

"We need you to help us stop a terrorist," Preston said.

"What do you mean?"

"We need your skill as a shooter to stop him."

The truth was that McFall would have preferred Ulrike Dassler, the unflappable gold medalist in the 3 x 20 rifle event, for this mission. But the German athlete had skipped the Closing Ceremonies and was already on a plane back to Bonn.

Arens's head was spinning. Was this some cruel joke? Were they serious? Were these Americans asking for her help to shoot a terrorist? Didn't they know who she was? Didn't they know about her father? She felt her hands turn icy cold.

"Ms. Arens," McFall said. "We know this is a very unusual situation. We know how difficult this must be for you. But you have to believe us. The lives of thousands and thousands of people are on the line."

"Tell me more," Arens said.

McFall went to an easel and pointed to a blurry picture.

"The target is in a building at long range," McFall explained. "He appears to be wearing a Kevlar helmet and a sleeveless bulletproof vest. And he is holding a detonator in his right hand."

"So what do you want me to do?"

"We want you to disable the man," Preston said.

"The target is 3,103 feet away," McFall said. "His reaction time is probably in the range of 0.2 to 0.4 seconds. The shot has to be dead on target."

"Point-two seconds," Preston said. "Just a snap of the fingers."

McFall went on. "It looks like a head shot is out of the question. His neck is protected by a flap from his Kevlar vest. Even if you hit him in the neck, he'll still have time to press the button."

"What about blowing his arm off?" Arens asked.

"That's an interesting possibility. Dr. Alpert?"

Dr. Sean Alpert stood up and approached the easel. He quickly sketched a picture of the human arm on the butcher paper.

"The anatomy is straightforward," he said. "A shot to the arm could sever the entire limb. But even so, the impact might cause the thumb to seize involuntarily, triggering the blast."

"What do you mean?"

"You know how chickens with their heads cut off can still run around for a few seconds? It's because the nerve and muscle bundles keep firing after the bird dies. It's the same with humans. Hands blown from bodies can still hold on to a coffee mug or handgun."

"Isn't there any other way to disable Lazare's thumb?" McFall asked. "Why not just blow it off?"

"No way," Preston said. "We're talking about a 3,103-foot shot. Miss by half an inch and the bullet goes right into the detonator."

"You know, there *are* two remote possibilities," Dr. Alpert said.

"Don't hold back," McFall said.

"The thing is, they only try this stuff in the movies," he said, drawing a quick sketch on the butcher paper. "You could try to shoot the flexor pollicis longus. It's the tendon that controls the movement of the thumb. When you use a Zippo lighter, it's the flexor that makes your thumb do the flicking."

"Where is it?" Arens asked. She could feel the adrenaline surging.

"Right here," he said, pointing to his drawing, "on the side of the base of the thumb where it's joined to the wrist."

"So what's the problem?" Preston asked.

"Well, if you hit the flexor in the wrong way, it could cause the thumb to seize."

"In which case Lazare would press the button instead of release it."

"So that's not a good option," Preston said.

"The other possibility is going after the median nerve," Alpert said. He pointed again to the drawing on the easel. "If you destroyed his median nerve, he'd lose all motor control of his hand."

"Where is it, Doc?"

"It's right here," he said, holding his arm up, "between the medial epicondyle and the biceps tendon. It's very thin, about the thickness of a few strands of spaghetti."

"Where's the medial epicondyle?"

"It's the bump on the underside of your elbow. It covers the ulnar nerve, your funny bone."

"Right where the arm bends?" Arens asked.

"Precisely."

"And it's the main nerve to the hand?"

"Yes, it controls all motor function to the thumb."

"How good are the chances of hitting it?"

Alpert laughed nervously. "Let me put it this way. It's hard enough finding the median nerve in surgery with a scalpel. But from 3,000 feet through a glass window, well, it would take a miracle to come close."

Muffled music from the Closing Ceremonies drifted down the dark corridor near the stadium locker rooms. McFall and Preston had paused in the hurry. Around them masses of security personnel were discreetly moving into position.

"I'm glad you were here these past two weeks," Preston said.

"Me too," McFall said.

"Not just for NEST," she continued, "but for me."

McFall nodded.

"You'd better get going," she said. "Knock 'im dead."

"I'll try."

There was an uncomfortable silence. For all McFall knew, this would be his last glimpse of Preston ever, and vice versa.

Finally, he spoke. "I'm not really sure how to say this, but—"

"Then don't say it," Preston interrupted.

"No, I want to say it. I need to say it."

He reached out for her, putting both arms around her waist. He did not care about the swarms of FBI agents and Atlanta police officers around him.

"I love you," he said.

Preston hesitated. She had heard those very words from his mouth once before. And then he had disappeared.

She kissed him softly and turned to leave without saying a word.

Breathing hard, Leila Arens lay on her stomach in the prone position at the top of the 116-foot tower where the Olympic Flame was burning.

It had taken five minutes of tough climbing to get there, up a dark and narrow shaft, and now as she slid over to crouch at the base of the dramatic sixteen-foot caldron designed by international artist Siah Armajani, she could hear the hiss of the gas jets feeding the flame.

The Barrett 82A1 semiautomatic sniper rifle with a Swarovski scope that she held in her hands had been deliberately selected for this mission because of its range and reliability. In fact, the Marine Corps weapon held the record for the longest confirmed sniper kill of the Gulf War: 5,900 feet.

While the .50-caliber 82A1 was a far cry from Arens's .22-caliber Anschütz competition rifle, she had trained with the Barrett during joint exercises at the U.S. Marine Corps Scout Sniper School in Quantico, Virginia, and knew the weapon well. The telescopic sights and the firing power had been a thrill to her when she had done duty on the Golan Heights with a scout and sniper team.

Now she looked through the sights and scanned the black 101 Marietta Tower building in the distance, searching for the thirty-sixth floor corner office. She had been told the building was 3,103 feet away, an eternity from the 100-meter Olympic range where she had won the medal. This shot would not be easy.

Arens knew that a typical sniper bullet, fired at short range, followed a flat trajectory. At long distances, however, a bullet flew in an arc, rising to its highest point at two thirds the distance, then dropping down to the target. The distance-trajectory ratios were geometric. At 1,000 feet the so-called culminating point was 6.7 inches above the line of sight, while at 3,000 feet it was 129 inches, or almost 11 feet.

Arens knew her scope was fitted to account for air resistance and gravity. She double-checked the elevation and windage turrets. And she went through the standard firing sequence in her mind.

Put the reticle on the target. Breathe. Fire. Follow through.

But her immediate problem was that she could not find her target. *Where are you? Come on.*

Arens began to feel the first tinges of panic.

And then suddenly the target appeared, a man in a window 3,103 feet away.

"Elohim zeh kol kach rachock," she whispered to herself. "God, that's so far."

The voice in her headset hissed: "Barak One, Torch Control. Do you copy?"

"Go ahead, Torch Control," she said.

"Are you in position?"

"Affirmative."

"Take aim and stand by for clearance."

"Taking aim and standing by."

The gusts were picking up. Arens sensed it was a half-value, oblique wind blowing from behind her at seven o'clock. She made a minor adjustment in the windage turret.

"Torch Control, this is Barak One. Ready to fire," she said into her mike.

"Barak One, Torch Control. Keep your powder dry until my signal."

"Holding fire," she said.

Lazare watched the Sensor ID screen on the laptop.

He punched in "Mack McFall." And the computer spit back McFall's location. He was at Centennial Stadium.

Then he typed in "Kyle Preston." Same place.

Then he tried "Javelin Force," and he got twelve hits. They were in a truck outside Centennial Stadium.

He snickered. Their fancy high-tech equipment had them all in shackles. Yes, their vaunted fortress had become a prison!

He had not foreseen the knock on the door, and he felt his heart begin to race.

"Who's there?"

"It's Mack McFall," the voice shouted.

Impossible! Lazare thought. *How did they find him?*

"Stay away!" Lazare screamed. "Get away from the door or I'll blow up the stadium!"

"Let me in," McFall demanded. "I've got to talk with you."

There was a long pause. The lock cylinder clicked.

"In fifteen seconds you can come in," Lazare ordered, "but if you make a stupid move, I'll push the button. I will! I really will!"

McFall counted to fifteen, then opened the door slowly.

Wearing a flak jacket and Kevlar helmet, Lazare was standing in the middle of the room, twenty feet from the window.

McFall recognized instantly that Lazare wasn't close enough to the glass for Arens to hit her mark. Trying to keep his eyes averted from the window, he moved cautiously toward Lazare.

"Stay where you are," Lazare whispered. "Don't think you can stop me."

McFall ignored him and crept forward. "I've left the troops outside. It's just you and me."

"What do you want?" Lazare said. "I will *not* negotiate! You know my demands!"

"I just want to talk," McFall said, inching closer.

"You still don't get it, do you?" Lazare said, taking a few steps back. "None of you understands!" He was trembling. "I don't want to talk. I just want to be left alone."

"Left alone?" McFall said.

"Yes, to do my RM research," he said, stepping back farther. "To go beyond where anyone has been before! To push our knowledge to the farthest reaches of the universe."

This madman just wants to be left alone to continue his work? McFall thought. *It doesn't make any sense.*

"Why go on with the RM research?" McFall asked. "You won! You got there first! You did it!"

"Ahhh," Lazare said with a menacing laugh. "How do you know for sure?"

"What do you mean?" McFall was baffled.

"That's my little secret," Lazare said.

He had moved within ten feet of the window. McFall wanted to look at his watch. He knew there was very little time. "Look, we've given you most of what you wanted. McVeigh and Nichols are free. We're working on the $100 million. Just put the detonator down."

Lazare's expression changed dramatically.

"Who do you think I am? A child? Do you think you're dealing with an amateur?"

Lazare's voice rose, and McFall could see tears in his eyes.

"You *will* leave me alone for the rest of my life, or I *will* push this button. No more talking!"

Lazare was decompensating, unraveling fast. There was even less time than McFall had calculated.

"**B**arak One, Torch Control."

"Go ahead, Torch Control."

"Fire when ready!"

Leila Arens trained her rifle on the man more than half a mile away. It was a struggle to keep her mind focused on the mission. Inexorably, her thoughts wandered to a night twenty-four years ago on the Furstenfeldbruck tarmac in Munich when a German sharpshooter had fired too soon.

An errant shot, then disaster. Her father killed by the blast of a hand grenade. His charred body was found in the burnt wreckage of a helicopter, his hands still bound behind his back.

Her concentration was shattered.

"Barak One, Torch Control."

"Yes, Torch Control."

"Fire immediately. Repeat. Fire immediately!"

"Will fire," she said.

Arens visualized her mission: aim, fire, and follow through.

She acquired the target in the scope. The man 3,103 feet away was brandishing something in his hand, no doubt the detonator.

She had a clear line on his elbow.

She put the reticle of the scope on the exact spot between the biceps tendon and medial epicondyle. She took one final deep breath, held it, and squeezed back on the trigger past the first stage.

Something caught her eye.

Behind Lazare was another body, someone moving. It looked like the tall man she had met during the briefing. Mack, the American scientist.

"*Ziyan!*" she cursed. "Fuck!"

When she fired, the bullet would pass through the target's elbow and hit McFall. She'd get the bad guy and the good guy with one bullet.

Arens did *not* have the shot. Her mind raced, examining the options. If she waited, it might be too late. She had to fire. Dr. Alpert had described one other option, the riskier shot to the flexor.

It was her only choice. Her pulse was pounding—not good for sniping.

Instinctively she focused on the new target. Lazare was waving his hand wildly. Each time she lined up her shot, he gesticulated again.

"*Layazel!*" she said. "Dammit!"

The flags rimming the stadium began to flutter in the breeze. Arens made an adjustment for the wind.

She could hear the crowds. She felt the clock ticking, just like in the Olympic shooting competition. Seventy-five seconds for the last shot.

Tick. Tick. Tick.

The fresh and awful memory of her final shot in the gold medal round of the Games returned.

Arens whispered to her father: "*Azor li achshav aba. Har'eh li et HaDerech.*"

Help me now, Dad. Show me the way.

And then she squeezed the trigger past the first stage.

"The United States government should never have killed the RM project," Lazare was saying. "They're just a bunch of Flat Earth Society know-nothings. They don't understand that the march of scientific progress *cannot* be stopped—"

The bullet shattered the windowpane into a thousand fragments.

Lazare first felt a flash of heat, then excruciating pain as his wrist exploded.

His eyes bulged as he stared at his limp, bloody hand. A look of shock spread across his face, followed by a self-satisfied smile.

A moment later, there was a flash from the south. White, blinding light, followed by deafening noise.

McFall dove to the ground.

Lazare dropped to his knees as if to pray and looked out the window toward Olympic Stadium. His face was illuminated by the brilliant light.

The fireworks of the Closing Ceremonies filled the sky in spectacular flashes.

The Javelin Force specialists burst into the room and surrounded Lazare with their semiautomatic assault weapons. He was on his knees, moaning, clutching his mangled hand.

McFall, his heart still pounding from the shock of the fireworks, sprang up and pushed through the troops to pick up the detonation device. It was still sweaty and warm from Lazare's now shredded hand. McFall had thought it was all over. His calculation had been instantaneous: the sniper shot had missed, Lazare had pushed the detonator, and the stadium was gone.

But then he had heard more explosions and had opened his eyes, astonished that he was still alive.

Now over the stadium, the fiery balls of light in the sky burned red, white, and blue through the shattered floor-to-ceiling window. McFall peered through Lazare's telescope. Somewhat miraculously, it was still pointed at Level 2, Section 4, Row J, Seat 26.

Vicky Hollister was waving her flag as she and her parents were escorted away by FBI agents and NEST volunteers.

McFall readjusted the telescope until he zeroed in on the Olympic tower. Leila Arens was standing next to the roiling Olympic flame, looking back at him through her sniper scope. She waved.

Next to her, Kyle Preston was looking through binoculars as well. Her hair was windswept, and her face illuminated from the side by the flame.

McFall had never seen a more beautiful, spectacular sight.

From the stadium, jubilant cheers rose and ebbed from the 85,000 spectators. McFall knew that around the globe more than two billion television viewers were also thrilling to the climax of the Games of the Century.

The world would always remember the gold and glitter of Atlanta, he mused, but they would never know the truth. They would never know that the Olympic Flame, first lit by the sun's rays in ancient Greece, had almost been extinguished forever.

McFall whispered three words into the air. They traveled 3,103 feet, and when they reached Preston, she smiled for a moment. Then her lips moved, too.

At first, McFall wasn't sure, but then he knew, and he was filled with a sense of triumph.

A s soon as the Olympic Flame was handed over to Sydney, security preparations for the XXVII Olympiad began immediately. A special advance team from Australia, inspired by thirteen months in Atlanta at the FBI's Olympic headquarters, flew straight home to New South Wales to begin war-gaming scenarios.

Just days after the lights went out at Olympic Stadium, Donny Sanders held a press conference to announce his candidacy for governor of Georgia in 1998. Marybeth stood graciously at his side, as did Ian Hobbes, his trusty mouthpiece.

Before leaving Atlanta, Buddy Crouse posed for Wheaties photos, then headed straight to Disney World, just as his new TV ads declared. His date for the all-expenses-paid week, as reported in *People* and *Sports Illustrated*, was Leila Arens . . . and her mother.

Vincent Fusco and Vasily Tarazov met in Geneva at a Loose Nukes conference held concurrently with a G-7 Summit. Over a beer, Fusco complimented Tarazov on his fine field reports. The drafts that were intended for interception by the NSA, Tarazov said with a sly smile, always took the longest to write.

Chuck Flagg got even with Claude Guillory and *The Atlanta Journal-Constitution* by keeping his big scoop to himself and instead publishing a book on the events in Atlanta. He pitched the idea to a Hollywood producer, made a small sale, and retired from the news business to brew beer and write fiction.

Mack McFall and Kyle Preston took a richly deserved vacation together in Hawaii, where they spent hours in hand-to-hand contact comparing security techniques. They soon embarked on a long-distance relationship between Washington, D.C., and Los Alamos. The commuting routine did not work. So, after intense negotiations, they married and moved to Memphis, Tennessee, which they figured was *exactly* halfway between New Mexico and Washington.

Quinn Lazare was tried, convicted, and sent to the Marion Federal Penitentiary in southern Illinois. Inmate number 18222-053 was given a 7 x 8 foot cell in K Unit, occasional home to Philadelphia Mob boss Nicodemo "Little Nicky" Scarfo, El Rukn gang leader Jeff Fort, CIA rogue Edwin Wilson, spy Christopher Boyce, and Japanese Red Army terrorist Yu Kikimura. Lazare briefly taught a chemistry class for other inmates, including a brooding fellow named Abu Azzam, but quit in disgust over inadequate laboratory supplies.

And at Los Alamos, NEST scientists analyzed and reanalyzed the contents of the backpack recovered from Vicky Hollister, including a peanut butter and raspberry-jelly sandwich. After elaborate tests, the nuclear experts concluded, to their chagrin, that Quinn Lazare's Red Mercury gel was like all the others.

The mythical substance did not exist . . . yet.